PENGUIN

Bittersweet

Melanie La'Brooy is the author of four previous novels:
Lovestruck, *The Wish List*, *Serendipity* and *The Babymoon*.
Melanie lives in Melbourne with her husband and two sons.

For Charlie, Dashiell & Raleigh
My trio of light, laughter and love

Bittersweet

Melanie La'Brooy

PENGUIN BOOKS

PENGUIN BOOKS

Published by the Penguin Group
Penguin Group (Australia)
250 Camberwell Road, Camberwell, Victoria 3124, Australia
(a division of Pearson Australia Group Pty Ltd)
Penguin Group (USA) Inc.
375 Hudson Street, New York, New York 10014, USA
Penguin Group (Canada)
90 Eglinton Avenue East, Suite 700, Toronto, Canada ON M4P 2Y3
(a division of Pearson Penguin Canada Inc.)
Penguin Books Ltd
80 Strand, London WC2R 0RL, England
Penguin Ireland
25 St Stephen's Green, Dublin 2, Ireland
(a division of Penguin Books Ltd)
Penguin Books India Pvt Ltd
11 Community Centre, Panchsheel Park, New Delhi – 110 017, India
Penguin Group (NZ)
67 Apollo Drive, Rosedale, North Shore 0632, New Zealand
(a division of Pearson New Zealand Ltd)
Penguin Books (South Africa) (Pty) Ltd
24 Sturdee Avenue, Rosebank, Johannesburg 2196, South Africa

Penguin Books Ltd, Registered Offices: 80 Strand, London WC2R 0RL, England

First published by Penguin Group (Australia), 2010

13 5 7 9 10 8 6 4 2

Text copyright © Melanie La'Brooy 2010

The moral right of the author has been asserted

Design by Kirby Armstrong © Penguin Group (Australia)
Cover photograph by Deborah Jaffe/Getty Images
Typeset in Fairfield Light by Post Pre-press Group, Brisbane, Queensland
Printed and bound in Australia by McPherson's Printing Group, Maryborough, Victoria

National Library of Australia
Cataloguing-in-Publication data:

La'Brooy, Melanie, 1973–
Bittersweet / Melanie La'Brooy.
9780143205685 (pbk.)

A823.4

penguin.com.au

Prologue

Six Months Before the Wedding

In Mimi's opinion, it all began with their names. Her older sister got Sabrina. As in Audrey Hepburn in *Sabrina*. Mimi, on the other hand, got stuck with Miriam. During their teenage years, Sabrina liked to point out that 'Miriam' was Hebrew for 'bitter'. Mimi would retaliate by saying that couldn't possibly mean anything because they weren't Jewish. Sabrina would then sadly conclude that either a) Mimi must have been adopted from Jewish parents who hated her or b) their parents hadn't cared enough to spend more than half a minute choosing her (inappropriate) name. Things tended to deteriorate from there.

So it was mainly because of Sabrina that when Mimi first went overseas she shortened her name to Mimi, which she quite liked until she returned home and realised that it was the perfect name for sentences that began, 'Mimi, I need you to pick up some fabric swatches for me. The place closes in ten minutes so you'd better hurry.' Or, 'Mimi, can you please confirm the order of red cymbidium orchids with the florist, drop off the rings for engraving at the jewellers – don't forget we decided we wanted the engraving in upper *and* lower case – and then you'll need to collect my shoes and drop them off at Double Bay so that the designer can hand-dye them to match my dress. Oh, and she needs the shoes by half past seven. *A.M.*'

Mimi was meant to be Miriam's fun new alter-ego. Instead, thanks to Sabrina, she had become Mimi the Bridesmaid Slave.

But Mimi had no choice because she was unemployed and, if she was honest, unemployable. When she first started going for job interviews, following her return to Australia, prospective employers were surprised to discover that she had, at one stage, begun a tertiary degree. This was fair enough really, given that Mimi's sparse employment history gave no hint that she might have either the brains or the inclination for higher education.

'An Arts degree?' they said, a faint note of hope appearing in their voices as they wondered whether she might have studied something that may be useful to their company, like another language or psychology. 'What did you major in?'

'Drama.'

Generally at this point Mimi would be warmly thanked for her time, except at one memorable interview when the bald head of the fifty-something, male interviewer snapped up. He looked at Mimi with respect and said, 'That's acting, isn't it? Did they make you study Bruce Willis in *Die Hard*? Best movie ever made. *Yippee-ki-yay, mother*—. Well, you know how it goes.' He shook his head fondly. 'That guy is a genius.'

The last interview had been the worst. Mimi was dressed in a cast-off hand-woven pashmina of Sabrina's (hats, scarves and jewellery being the only items of fashion that Mimi and Sabrina could share, given their difference in size). The luxurious wrap was so swanky that it fortunately drew attention away from her cheap shirt and pants and the scuffed pair of work shoes she had rescued from the storage boxes filled with her belongings that she had left behind all those years ago.

The interviewer had looked down her nose at Mimi's admittedly short CV. 'You seem to have spent a lot of time travelling overseas, Miriam.'

'It's Mimi. And yes, I have.'

'What were you doing over there?'

'Immersing myself in other cultures. Visiting museums and galleries.' *Sleeping with Scandinavian backpackers,* Mimi added silently. *Getting drunk in hole-in-the-wall bars in Madrid.*

'No, I mean what work did you do overseas?'

'Oh. Um, I didn't really work.'

'But you've been travelling for —' here she briefly consulted Mimi's CV again, 'three years.'

It was actually more like three and a half years but that sounded worse. 'Yes,' Mimi agreed, hoping that would end the matter.

It didn't.

'I don't understand. How did you support yourself all that time?'

This was the bit that Mimi really hated. Because she had learnt from previous interviews that if she answered 'I was a drugs courier until I ended up in prison and paid my debt to society', then they'd probably look at her with compassion and think about hiring her, just to prove that they weren't prejudiced. Instead, she told the truth.

'I inherited a lot of money and that's how I chose to spend it.' Mimi sat back and folded her arms. That was all she was going to say. She could have told the interviewer the entire story and she probably would have got sympathy. But that wasn't what Mimi wanted.

For some prejudices, Mimi had discovered, were socially acceptable. So while not hiring a rehabilitated drug runner would be politically incorrect, sneering at a supposedly spoiled, rich kid with no sense of responsibility – even if the interviewer would have given anything to have spent the last three years of her life in exactly the same manner as Mimi had done, instead of sitting in this shitty fluorescent-lit office – was entirely acceptable.

'Oh. I see. I don't suppose you did any volunteer work while you were over there?'

'No, I didn't. How much volunteer work have you done lately?'

Unsurprisingly this was where the interview was terminated.

So that was how Miriam Falks became Mimi the Bridesmaid Slave. In three and a half years, she had thrown away the sizeable inheritance that her father had left her, and now she was living off Sabrina's share. Only this time, Sabrina was making her earn it.

*

'Mimi, meet me at the studio, would you? There's a lighting problem so I'm stuck in my dressing-room for the next two hours. We may as well use the time to go over the guest list.'

Mimi was already certain that she hated her elder sister's constantly sweet tone veiling commands as requests even more than the degradation of her beloved new moniker. Before Mimi left Australia for the first time, Sabrina never used to speak with the insincerity so endemic in 'showbiz'. She hated all that kind of thing. Sabrina would have preferred to have become a serious actress, or rather, actor (for some reason it was apparently passé to use the gendered form of the word). But she quickly discovered that searing theatrical productions of *King Lear* were thin on the ground, while commercials for yoghurt (Sabrina emerging refreshed from a yoga class holding a mat in one hand and an open tub of Wildberry Delight in the other) or fast food (Sabrina sticking chips up her nose and then snorting them across the room at one of the male models – sadly, the real commercial wasn't quite as interesting) were abundant and paid her outrageous amounts of money.

From commercials it was an easy step to a small, temporary role on a wildly popular television soap named *Sunshine Cove*, which gradually evolved into a permanent, starring role, as audiences in both Australia and the United Kingdom fell in love with Sabrina (or Danielle, as her character was named). Sabrina/Danielle had a beautiful face, a perfect bikini body and a penchant for falling in love with unsuitable men who had a tendency to fall off cliffs and reappear twenty episodes later – generally when she was in her wedding gown about to marry a new bloke, who would then wrestle with the first bloke until one of them fell over a cliff again.

Of course, off-screen, Sabrina would never do anything as stupid as fall in love with someone who couldn't maintain their footing near a treacherous precipice. As much as the tabloids and her adoring public bayed for her to fall in love with her co-star in real life, she fell in love with an investment banker named Edward Forster.

And, thought Mimi resentfully, as she trudged off in search of 250 silver organza bows with which to decorate the reception chairs, it was just Sabrina's luck to become engaged to a handsome, charming, clever and successful man, not because he was a trophy on her arm or because she wanted to marry him for his money or for any stupid, shallow reason. No, the sole reason Sabrina was marrying Edward was because she had genuinely and irrevocably fallen in love with him at first sight.

The only problem was, so had Mimi.

Twelve Months Before the Wedding

- Announce engagement to family & friends
- Choose bridal party
- Hire wedding planner

1

Sabrina

CELEBRITY CONFIDENTIAL RUMOUR ALERT!
Our favourite glamour girl Sabrina Falks was spotted shopping at the Sydney Rocks Market yesterday – and dazzling all bystanders with a brand-new rock of her own! Sabrina's publicist has refused to confirm or deny the rumours, so it looks like we'll have to wait for the official engagement announcement from Sabrina and long-term boyfriend Edward Forster. But, as our exclusive pictures of the gorgeous three-carat diamond ring show, wedding bells can't be too far away . . .

The dress was all wrong. Wrong, wrong, wrong. The ruffles were meant to *cascade*. A gentle, rippling waterfall was the sartorial metaphor for which Sabrina was searching. This dress was not a rainforest waterfall. This dress was a monster water slide at Wet 'N' Wild. It was crass, vulgar and completely the opposite of the brief that she had given the designer. There was no way in the world she was going to wear it to Australia's most important television awards ceremony.

Sabrina looked at herself again in the bank of heavy mirrors. The designer, Corinna, and her three assistants, who had closed the exclusive salon especially for Sabrina, were waiting for her reaction. Sabrina sighed inwardly, knowing that she had to say something soon. What she wanted to do was to tell them they were all hopeless. But there was no way she could express her anger and irritation. If she had an outburst it would probably end up in the hands of the media and a negative story could affect her character's likeability. From there it was but a short slide to Danielle falling off a cliff and into a coma or leaving Sunshine Cove to live in Tasmania. She had seen it happen on countless occasions to other *Sunshine Cove* characters and she would not let it happen to Danielle.

The constant threat of a fatal accident or exile to Tasmania was the reason why Sabrina always put the scriptwriters' birthdays in her iPhone and bought them a cake on the day. One could never be too careful. For such an idyllic setting, there was a surprisingly high number of precarious precipices in Sunshine Cove.

Corinna was still waiting, sensing now that something was wrong. The assistants (whom Sabrina had mentally christened Flora, Fauna and Merryweather, after the three fairies in *Sleeping Beauty* who were forever arguing over their preferred colours for Princess Aurora's gown) continued to flutter around Sabrina, adjusting flounces and making effusive comments about how the colour of the fabric made Sabrina's flawless complexion glow. Meanwhile, the older, more experienced designer was already strategising as to the best way to handle a potentially disastrous situation.

Despite Sabrina's famed 'niceness' ('She was so *nice*', fans would invariably gush after tentatively approaching their idol and being rewarded with an autograph and photographs taken on camera phones), Corinna knew she was no pushover and wouldn't wear a dress that she disliked simply because she was afraid of hurting Corinna's feelings. Besides which, as they both knew but never verbally acknowledged, over the last few years the initial hierarchy of their relationship had inverted and all of the power now lay with Sabrina.

From their first meeting several years ago, Sabrina and Corinna had formed a mutually beneficial professional relationship. In the beginning, when Sabrina had still been synonymous with the borderline derogatory term 'starlet', Corinna had occasionally allowed Sabrina to borrow some of her lesser-value, sample gowns for awards ceremonies or film premieres, due to the simple fact that Sabrina's face and figure set off Corinna's gowns to perfection. A beautiful girl in a stunning dress was always guaranteed to generate a decent-sized photograph in the Sunday paper's social pages, which Corinna had found to be far more influential than a conventional advertisement.

But that had been years ago and it was now, indubitably, Sabrina who was doing Corinna a favour. With the awarding of Sabrina's first trophy for Most Popular Television Personality, the borrowed sample gowns had immediately given way to breathtaking made-to-measure works of art that were stunning achievements of design, construction and embellishment. It was Sabrina's patronage that had been responsible for Corinna's rise from a well-regarded but niche designer to the owner of three opulent salons that catered for an elite clientele, with salons in Melbourne and Perth, as well as the flagship Sydney store where the fitting was taking place, which was in an exclusive, very private residential street in swanky Double Bay.

Dressing Sabrina Falks for the Logie Awards was therefore a rolled-gold guarantee of saturation coverage in all of the women's magazines. Now that it had become de rigueur for the media to ask the stars who had designed their dress or loaned them jewels as they paraded on the red carpet, it was also akin to getting several free advertisements on prime-time television. Last but not least, for the past week, Sabrina had sported a very large, very expensive diamond ring on the fourth finger of her left hand. While media speculation had gone wild, there was yet to be a formal confirmation of the engagement. Corinna had no intention of waiting for the public announcement. She had already, discreetly, launched her bid for the opportunity to create Sabrina's wedding dress, with all the attendant publicity and business that would generate.

It was the thought of the wedding dress and the media circus that would surround it that now made Corinna leap into the breach. The made-to-measure dress that Sabrina was wearing constituted hours and hours of painstaking labour, while designing and making an entirely new gown from scratch, within an impossibly short time frame, was an expense and headache that Corinna could live without. But the thought of Sabrina wearing a dress by a rival designer for the most important televised awards night in Australia was mortifying.

She stepped forward so that she stood directly behind Sabrina and pursed her lips. She would have liked to permit a small, troubled frown to crease her brow, but her regular Botox injections wouldn't allow it.

'Sabrina darling – please don't take this the wrong way, you know that you always look like perfection in my gowns – but do you know, I'm not sure that we've got it *exactly* right.'

One of the assistants (Merryweather; not the sharpest needle in the pincushion) audibly gasped. Only minutes before Sabrina's arrival, Corinna and her assistants had indulged in an orgy of self-congratulation over what they all agreed was one of Corinna's finest creations.

Making a mental note to assign that particular assistant to lace-dying duties for the next three months, Corinna watched Sabrina for her reaction.

Sabrina waited a few moments, as she considered her reflection carefully in the mirror once more. 'I think perhaps you might be right, Corinna,' she finally pronounced. 'The colour is perfect and I like the beading on the bodice —' Flora, who had been responsible for the hand-beading visibly swelled with pride, 'but the skirt is a little . . . over-powering.' Sabrina smiled to take the sting out of her words. 'Why don't I shout us all some cakes and champagne and we can sit down and discuss some ideas and make some new sketches? Providing one of the girls doesn't mind running out to get them for us.' Sabrina watched as her speech mollified Corinna, whose greatest fear was always that she would lose her most valuable client altogether.

Corinna's features relaxed as much as her Botoxed muscles would allow, and Sabrina noted that the assistants' faces had changed from awed to adoring. She could practically see the text messages that they were itching to send to their friends: *OMG! We drank champagne with Sabrina Falks!!*

As Corinna, Flora and Fauna helped her out of the heavy dress and cheerfully discussed the chocolate cannoli that the disgraced Merryweather had been dispatched to procure from a nearby bakery (and which Sabrina had absolutely no intention of eating), none of them had any idea that even as she smiled and thanked them, the picture of graciousness and affability, Sabrina was wearily thinking: *Why, oh why, can't I trust anyone? Why do I always end up having to do everything myself?*

2

Mimi

The first time Mimi met Edward Forster, her soon-to-be brother-in-law and object of desire, was at the party held for his engagement to Sabrina. Mimi had returned home from overseas only weeks before to be greeted by the big news. As she had nowhere to live and no money left, she was staying with their mother's sister, Aunty Bron, in the house in Maroubra where Bron had lived for her entire adult life. Maroubra was a quiet suburb, right on the beach, in the eastern suburbs of Sydney. Although it was only a few suburbs along from the glamorous and popular environs of Bondi and Bronte, Maroubra remained defiantly unfashionable. This had quite a bit to do with the infamous surfing gang 'The Bra Boys', for whom Maroubra Beach was home turf. Personally, Mimi thought that any gang with claims to intimidation should start by changing their name to something less girly and amusing but considering that not once in the thirty-six years that Aunty Bron had lived in Maroubra had she ever encountered a speck of trouble from the gang, maybe they weren't as scary as everyone envisaged – unless perhaps an outsider tried to drop in on one of their waves. Although no-one ever said it, Mimi was also pretty sure that nearly all of the long-term residents of Maroubra, including Aunty Bron, silently blessed the Bra Boys for ruining their beachside suburb's image, thereby saving it from the high-rise development and saturation tourism that dominated Maroubra's neighbouring suburbs.

It had taken Mimi two days to pluck up the courage to telephone her aunt from London to ask whether she could stay with her upon her return to Australia. Aunty Bron was her mother's older sister but the two had never been close, and Mimi had seen her aunt only sporadically over the years. However, since the death of Sabrina and Mimi's mother over a year ago, both of the Falks girls had grown considerably closer to their aunt and contact between them had become much more frequent. To Mimi's great relief, Bronwyn had sounded delighted to hear from her and had immediately said that she would love the company and that Mimi was welcome to stay with her for as long as she wished.

To Mimi's complete lack of surprise, even though her aunt hadn't seen her for ages, it was only about ten minutes after the taxi from the airport had dropped her off at Aunty Bron's neat seaside brick-veneer house that she changed the subject from Mimi's trip home and adventures abroad to the topic of her elder sister.

'How do you feel about being a bridesmaid, Mimsy?' asked Aunty Bron.

Mimi looked at her blankly. 'For whom?'

'For Sabrina, of course! Who else?' Aunty Bron said, exasperated.

'Sabrina's getting married?' This was somehow less of a surprise than the thought that immediately followed. 'And she wants me to be her bridesmaid? Why would she pick me?' To say that Mimi and Sabrina were not close was an understatement. The sisters hadn't spoken since their enormous fight, which had taken place the night before their mother's funeral.

'Who else is there?'

This was true. Sabrina had never had any close girlfriends, and before she died, their mother had expressed her concern in emails to

15

Mimi that Sabrina's new socialite and actor friends all seemed to be of the 'I'm famous, you're famous, let's have our photo taken together on the red carpet' type of acquaintance. Mimi could just imagine that they were not the sort of girls you would want as your bridesmaid. They would undoubtedly all be far too pretty for starters. And, God forbid, some of them might even be skinnier than Sabrina.

Unsure as to whether she was amused or mortified by the idea of being Sabrina's last resort as bridesmaid, Mimi changed the subject instead. 'What's he like? Her fiancé?'

Aunty Bron made a face. 'Charming. Perfect. They look like Ken and Barbie together. Wait till you see. It's hilarious.'

'So you approve?'

'Of course I approve,' Aunty Bron said cheerfully. 'The only thing wrong with him is that he always makes me want to mess up his hair. And it would be nice to see him without a tie just once. I keep thinking that maybe his head falls off if he doesn't wear one. But apart from that, he's what we used to call a good catch. Am I allowed to say that or is it politically incorrect these days?'

'You're an old chauvinist pig,' Mimi reprimanded her sternly. 'Are you sure he's not a closet serial killer or something? The perfect ones always are.'

'That's a bit rich coming from the girl whose English boyfriend looks like a criminal.'

'*Dreadlocks*, Aunty Bron. They're just dreadlocks. It's a hairstyle. Came into fashion a bit after the powdered wig your last boyfriend wore.'

'Very funny. What's happened to Jared anyway? You haven't mentioned him at all.'

Mimi refrained from pointing out that she hadn't had time to mention her personal life before her aunt had steered the topic to Sabrina and instead said briefly, 'We broke up.'

'Is that why you've come home? What happened?'

Under her penetrating gaze, Mimi shifted uncomfortably. 'Let's just say you were right about him, okay? He is a criminal.' She added flippantly, 'He's currently serving a prison sentence for crimes against follicles.'

Aunty Bron laughed. 'I'm glad to see that you haven't lost your sense of humour. And I take it from your reaction that he hasn't broken your heart, which is a good thing. I never thought he was The One for you, I must say.'

'You never even spoke to him! You're just judging him on emailed photographs.' Why Mimi was defending Jared she really had no idea. It was undeniably the third stupidest thing that she had done in the past six weeks, although her first two rash acts were still miles ahead in terms of idiocy.

Aunty Bron looked at her over the top of her glasses. 'Oh come on, Mimi,' she said in a let's-be-reasonable tone. 'Sabrina always says that you never had any taste when it comes to men.' She paused and then added thoughtfully, 'She also says that that must be why you always adored your father.'

*

Mimi had left Australia just as Sabrina's star had started to rapidly ascend. For a while their mother had kept her updated on Sabrina's career via telephone calls and the occasional email but Mimi hadn't realised exactly how famous Sabrina had become until she flew back into Australia and was confronted with her sister's irritatingly perfect face on just about every magazine cover at Sydney Airport.

Mimi had now been home for three weeks, during which time she had grown heartily sick of both job hunting and the sight of her older sister. It was nigh on impossible to escape Sabrina's smiling face; every time Mimi left the house she was confronted with her sister glowing from newsagency racks or in billboard and television advertisements for the network on which *Sunshine Cove* screened. Even when she avoided turning the television on to Sabrina's network, Sabrina kept popping up on the other channels. Mimi's ubiquitous sister had been a contestant on *Dancing With The Stars*, had appeared as a guest on the country's most popular late-night talk show, and had been featured driving a sports car around a racetrack on the Australian version of *Top Gear*. Mimi had been driven to throw the remote control across the room in disgust when she recognised Sabrina's voice in a televised commercial appealing for donations to Taronga Zoo. Apparently even exotic jungle animals weren't safe from Sabrina these days.

Despite this surfeit of Sabrina, Mimi was still yet to catch a glimpse of her sister in the flesh. She knew that Sabrina was aware that she was back because she had overheard the tail end of a telephone conversation between their aunt and her sister. So she couldn't help thinking that Aunty Bron must have been mistaken about Sabrina wanting her to be her bridesmaid as otherwise her elder sister would have surely spoken to her by now.

Their aunt had left the invitation to Sabrina's engagement party on Mimi's bedside table, without saying another word about it. Mimi had thought briefly about calling Sabrina, but launching into small talk or pretending that the past hadn't happened was ridiculous. So, in the end, she just let the elegant square of heavy embossed card sit there and tried not to notice that the date was getting oppressively nearer and nearer.

On the day of the engagement party Mimi was taking comfort in the fact that she hadn't RSVP'd so obviously couldn't go. It would be bad manners. Then Aunty Bron came bustling into her bedroom, dressed to the nines.

'You're coming,' she said firmly, forestalling any argument. 'It's about time this ridiculous stand-off between you and Sabrina ended, and the more I think about it, the better it is that you two meet in public, where you'll both have to behave.'

'I can't go. I didn't RSVP.'

'It's a cocktail party, not a sit-down dinner. There will be room for one more, particularly if that one more is the bride's only sister. Now, what are you going to wear?'

Mimi grimaced as she put aside the book that she hadn't really been reading. 'Not sure. Do you have any spare purple cling-wrap and six-inch stilettos? That's what all of Sabrina's friends will be wearing.'

Aunty Bron ignored this witticism and started to rifle through the bulging backpack that Mimi still hadn't got around to unpacking properly. 'Jeans, T-shirts, more jeans, Birkenstocks – honestly, Mimsy, I thought you spent time in Paris! How could you go to the world's fashion capital and come back with the wardrobe of a German hiker?'

'Hmm, let me see. Oh, that's right. I had an appointment to buy haute couture from Dior but they cancelled it when they saw me. Something about it being bad for their image to let fat girls wear Dior.'

'You're not fat,' said Aunty Bron immediately, not quite meeting Mimi's eyes.

'Of course not. I'm just big-boned,' Mimi said demurely. 'Anyway, that's beside the point. Do you really think I had the money or the inclination to buy designer clothes? I was *backpacking*.'

'You certainly had the money so it must have been a lack of inclination.' Mimi flushed but Aunty Bron didn't notice. 'Didn't you ever go out?' she asked despairingly. 'You don't appear to own a single dress or skirt!'

'I wore my dressy jeans when I went out.'

'Dressy jeans,' Aunty Bron muttered in disgust. 'What a concept. Well, this isn't helping. What are you going to wear?'

Mimi sighed and gave in to the inevitable. Aunty Bron was right. She was going to have to confront Sabrina sooner or later and it was probably better that they met again in a room full of strangers. At least that way they were unlikely to end up screaming at each other and throwing things. And she was kind of curious to meet Sabrina's fiancé.

'My dressy jeans,' Mimi answered cheekily, hauling herself off the bed. She went over to the chest of drawers and pulled out her nicest top – a dark-blue, floaty floral blouse that she'd bought at Camden Market. 'With this top. And there's no point telling me I can't wear jeans because a) it's all I have, b) I'm hardly going to fit into anything of yours, and c) I don't care what anyone thinks of me so if wearing jeans sends Sabrina and her snooty friends and in-laws into conniptions, they can all just bugger off.' She lifted her head and stared at her aunt defiantly.

Aunty Bron heaved a sigh. 'It's an engagement party, Mims, not a showdown at high noon in a Western. Fine. Wear your jeans if you must. That top is lovely and I'll lend you some earrings. Do you have any shoes?'

'I have that old pair that I've been wearing to all my job interviews. They'll do.'

'But they're black and your top is blue,' Aunty Bron said in consternation.

'I don't *care*, Aunty Bron. And it's either those or my Birkenstocks.'

Bronwyn looked at her niece with frustration. 'You've known about this party ever since you got back. You had plenty of time to go out and buy something to wear.'

This was true but Mimi only had a few hundred dollars left to her name and she had to make her money last until she got a job. But she couldn't tell Aunty Bron that.

Her aunt now glared at Mimi with sudden suspicion. 'Dressing down isn't your way of having a cheap shot at Sabrina, is it?'

'No, it's not! Anyway, why would Sabrina care, let alone notice, what I'm wearing?'

'She'll notice all right. And you and I both know that Sabrina loves fashion and always tries to look her best, which is why I can't help thinking that you turning up in jeans is an unsubtle way for you to demonstrate to everyone how unlike your sister you are.'

Mimi hooted as she pulled on her blouse. 'Aunty Bron, they don't need a pair of jeans to tell them that. They just have to stand us side by side. Skinny. Fat. Boring. Fun. Malibu Barbie versus Dora the Explorer. We don't exactly provide the most challenging game of Spot the Difference.'

Aunty Bron sighed. 'The saddest part about this mess between you two is that you're more alike than you know.' She found the pair of old shoes under the bed and threw them to Mimi. 'Now hurry up. We have to leave in fifteen minutes.'

*

To get to the engagement party Mimi talked her aunt into leaving the car at home and catching a ferry from Circular Quay to Rose Bay instead. Bron gave in to what she supposed was her prodigal niece's sentimentalism, unaware that Mimi had chosen the slower mode of transport as a way of deliberately delaying her unwelcome reunion with Sabrina. However, as the ferry moved out of its moorings and made its way slowly across Sydney Harbour, Mimi leaned over the back railing and was surprised to feel tears welling in her eyes. There was just something so *familiar* about it all, and it wasn't merely the postcard-saturated view of the white sails of the Opera House or the looming iron presence of the Harbour Bridge. It was definitely more than that that was causing this belated rush of homesickness. It was triggered by the blue of the sky and the warmth of the breeze. The sound of the seagulls and even the slow chug of the ferry's engine. It was the sight of blossoming jacaranda and of being enveloped by Australian accents. Mimi hadn't realised until this moment just how much she had missed all of these things.

Aunty Bron mistook the expression on her niece's face. She put an arm around Mimi's waist and gave it a squeeze. 'Nervous?'

'Nervous? What have I got to be nervous about?'

She shot Mimi a shrewd look. 'Seeing your estranged sister for the first time in over a year. And you were only back in Australia for a short time the last time anyway. You've been away for well over three years.'

'It's probably done us a world of good not to be around each other for a while after growing up in each other's pockets.'

'See, now that's what I can't understand. Your grandmother always told me how close you two girls were when you were little. Closer than most sisters.'

Mimi shrugged. 'You should understand. You and Mum were never close. Anyway, people change and so do their relationships. Sabrina and I just — We have nothing in common any more.'

'Oh yes you do.'

'Name one thing,' Mimi challenged her.

'Well, for starters, neither one of you will tell me what the ridiculous fight that started all this was actually about.'

Mimi turned away from her aunt and looked back out over the railing at the trail of disruption the ferry was leaving in its wake. Losing herself in the opaque waters of the harbour, she thought back to that day.

She could hear her voice and Sabrina's, shrill with anger, screaming at each other; their uncontrollable display of fury all the more unforgivable because of the funeral parlour in which they were standing. With no difficulty at all, Mimi could still conjure up the sight of Sabrina's face at the worst moment. For the last fourteen months, every time she'd thought of Sabrina it was that look that she had remembered. A lifetime of other memories of Sabrina made no difference at all. It was always her sister's face, contorted with hatred, that Mimi had been unable to erase from her mind.

The hatred that had all been directed at Mimi.

*

To Mimi's judgemental gaze, the engagement party was exactly the sort of stylish, filled-to-the-brim-with-gorgeous-types soirée that you'd expect when Malibu Barbie was marrying Watch-his-head-fall-off Ken. It was a cocktail party at Catalina restaurant in Rose Bay, and while Mimi and Aunty Bron had caught the public ferry, all the other guests seemed to be arriving by private water limousine. Catalina had 180-degree views of the harbour from its floor-to-ceiling glass windows and was renowned as the venue where all of the eastern suburbs princesses of Sydney hosted functions to mark the milestones of their lives. Of course Sabrina and Mimi had grown up in the gritty western suburbs, but judging by this party, Sabrina had well and truly left their dreary childhood origins far behind. With her glamorous career, celebrity status and now her rich, perfect fiancé, Sabrina had morphed into an eastern suburbs princess with the skill of a chameleon. In fact, now that Mimi thought about it, probably the only flaw in her perfect disguise was the appearance of Aunty Bron and Mimi herself.

Pushing their way through the beautiful and fashionable crowd, Aunty Bron and Mimi became separated by a waiter bearing an overflowing tray of full champagne flutes. Within the space of the merest second, hordes of dehydrated Sydney A-listers surrounded them and Mimi completely lost sight of Aunty Bron. She was about to fight her way back through the crush to rescue her aunt when suddenly the throng parted – and there stood her sister.

Coming face to face with Sabrina, Mimi was horrified to feel an all-too-familiar stab of jealousy. The Falks sisters both had tawny-coloured hair and similar features but Sabrina's eyes were the same startling deep blue as their father's. Before she became famous and her eye colour became one of her trademark features, Sabrina had grown used to being asked on a daily basis whether she was wearing coloured contact lenses. Mimi's eyes, however, were standard-issue brown. For Mimi, looking at Sabrina was like looking into a magic mirror that showed her a prettier, slimmer, more successful version of herself. Sabrina was Cameron Diaz, Liv Tyler, Nicole Kidman. Mimi was Chimene Diaz, Mia Tyler, Antonia Kidman. The family resemblance was there but in the younger sibling the heart-stopping beauty was diluted and the sylph-like figure entirely absent. Sabrina was a vision of what Mimi might have been, if only she had had the luck to have been born first.

As one of the guests of honour, Sabrina was being constantly besieged by well-wishers but Mimi knew that she had seen her. She made her way slowly towards Mimi until she was about a foot away and then she stopped. The sisters looked at each other and then, by unspoken agreement, they slipped outside onto the deck, under the pretence of admiring the sunset. Eerily, as soon as they were alone, the little capsule of private space that had surrounded them during their childhood, protecting them but also separating them from the rest of the world, slid silently back into place.

It was obviously up to Mimi to go first. With the exception of their birth order, it had *always* been Mimi who led the way.

'Hi, Breens.'

'It's Sabrina. How are you, Miriam?'

'It's Mimi. And I'm fine.'

'Run out of money, did you?'

'What makes you think that?'

'Because I can't think of any other reason why you would have come home.' There was a note of accusation in her voice. For reasons that had never been clear to Mimi, Sabrina had been immensely critical of Mimi's decision to spend her inheritance on travelling overseas.

Mimi took the strategic option of attacking, rather than confirming or denying. 'What did you do with your share of the inheritance? No – let me guess. It's sitting in a bank account somewhere earning

24

a sensible amount of interest. Have you ever wondered why they call it "interest" when it's hands down the most boring thing you can do with money?'

'And yet, amazingly, I still have money while I bet you have none.'

'Yes, but what's the point if you never spend it?'

'I'm saving it for a little thing called the future. You've probably never heard of it.'

It was inevitable, Mimi decided. It had been less than two minutes and already they were bickering. Then again, this was still an improvement on the screaming match that had constituted their last conversation.

'Sounds like a horrible place to me. Probably best not to think about it.'

'That's a luxury that only people with no responsibilities can afford.'

'What responsibilities do you have apart from making sure you have two facials a week and only eat macrobiotic food? Or have you gone all Brangelina and adopted several orphans while I've been overseas?' Mimi looked around, as though searching for the Jolie-Pitt kids, so she missed the fleeting expression that crossed Sabrina's face. 'Although I just remembered you have acquired a fiancé. Which one is he?'

'He's over there talking to Aunty Bron.' Sabrina paused and then added sarcastically, 'Thank you for your good wishes.'

'Oops, sorry. Congratulations. Based on the back of his head, which is all that I can see, I'm sure you'll be very happy. I can't see any signs of male pattern baldness, which is excellent.'

'I'm sure I will be happy.'

I will be happy, Mimi noted. Not *we* will be happy. Typical.

'So have you got a job?'

'I only just got back!'

'Are you planning on getting one?'

'What do you care? Or would it be embarrassing for you, now that you're famous, if your little sister was on the dole?'

Sabrina flushed.

Bloody hell, Mimi thought. *I got it in one.*

'I was just wondering if all the time you spent overseas had made you grow up. Apparently not.'

'That's weird. I've been wondering whether all the time you've spent playing Danielle has turned you into a shallow, materialistic airhead.' Mimi stopped, and very deliberately looked Sabrina up and down. She *had* changed. She had always been extraordinarily pretty but now her beauty was enhanced by the sort of unreal glow that only celebrities or very rich people can obtain via impossible diet and exercise regimes, designer clothes and the constant ministrations of a professional hairstylist, make-up artist and an array of beauty therapists.

Mimi's blazing gaze met Sabrina's icy stare.

'Edward is coming over to greet you,' Sabrina said quietly, through perfectly made-up lips. 'If it's not too much to ask, I would be grateful if you could manage not to be rude to him.'

Mimi sighed and then turned towards Edward, whom she had already mentally christened 'Deadwood', prepared to meet the last in the long line of Sabrina worshippers, all of whom tended to be handsome, nice and incredibly dull – and all of the platitudes and smart-arse comments that she had rehearsed to deal with this awkward moment died on her lips.

He was *gorgeous*. Outrageously, impossibly handsome. Not like a male model but in an 'I'm a real man' sort of way. Like Daniel Craig as James Bond.

He smiled at Mimi and she actually felt her knees turn to water. 'Aha. The prodigal baby sister has returned.' He held out his hand and it was all that Mimi could do not to fall to her knees and kiss it, pledging her eternal allegiance.

'I'm actually a prodigy. Sabrina never could spell,' Mimi managed weakly, letting her hand rest in his.

He laughed and Sabrina looked annoyed; as far as Mimi was concerned, it was an excellent result all round. To her utter surprise, he didn't shake her hand. Instead, he pulled her into him and kissed her warmly on the cheek, as though they already knew each other. He smelled so delicious that for a moment she seriously considered licking his neck.

'Now what are you doing hiding in a corner? Shouldn't you be inside, regaling us with tales of your exotic life abroad?'

'Nobody puts Baby in the corner,' Mimi said feebly. *Oh crap*, she thought. She had turned into the village idiot. Three and a half years overseas and instead of entertaining him with her best anecdote about the time she got lost in the Medina in Marrakech and unwittingly promised herself in marriage to a carpet seller in exchange for guiding her back out, the best that she could come up with was a quote from *Dirty Dancing*.

'Quite right,' he said, beckoning to a passing waiter to bring her a drink. 'Now if only you had a watermelon.'

He was gorgeous *and* he understood eighties movie references. Despite herself, Mimi was impressed.

For the next four hours, Mimi found herself unable to look away from Edward's handsome face and using the excuse that she hardly knew anyone else there to monopolise his time. By the end of the party her initial attraction to him had morphed into complete infatuation. Mimi was in love.

So that was how the nicknames started. From then on he called Mimi Baby while she christened him Teddy, mainly to annoy Sabrina, who seemed to have contracted an aversion to nicknames now that she was a Star. (Perhaps it was some sort of celebrity thing, Mimi thought. While everyone else was referring to them as Bennifer or TomKat, in privacy they were probably calling each other Mrs Holmes-Cruise and Sir Operating Thetan Level VIII.)

Mimi knew that Baby was really short for Baby Sister, but that night, while she lay in bed, she recalled the timbre of Edward's voice and the look in his eyes when he called out, 'Hey, Baby! Come over here and show us how they mix martinis in Dublin!' And she was powerless to resist the fantasy that he was *her* fiancé and that Baby was really short for sexy baby or baby girl or any of those other nauseating nicknames that people use in public when they're in love and don't care what anyone else thinks.

Sabrina also lay awake that night but the thoughts that were keeping her from slumber were a million miles away from her sister's flights of fantasy. She was facing the inexorable reality that Mimi was back, bringing with her unwelcome memories of a past that Sabrina desperately wanted to remain buried. She punched her pillow into shape and turned over restlessly in bed once more. For Sabrina couldn't shake the disquieting feeling that Mimi's return was a catalyst that had put in motion an unstoppable, unpredictable ride that she had been forcibly strapped into – and from which there was no means of escape.

3

Runaway Bride

'Have you asked Baby to be your bridesmaid yet?' Edward demanded.

It was three days after the engagement party and he and Sabrina were eating breakfast in their luxurious penthouse apartment that overlooked Bondi Beach. That is, Edward was eating toast and bacon. Strictly speaking, Sabrina hadn't *eaten* breakfast for years. Her breakfasts were always liquid, although she did vary them. Today she was having a mix of citrus juices followed by a wheatgrass shot.

'Not yet,' Sabrina replied. 'And why do you insist on calling her that? She's twenty-four. She's hardly a baby.' Halfway through this rejoinder, Sabrina realised that her tone was more snappish than she had intended and she instantly modified it. She was trying to hide the fact that she was still seething over Edward's successful charm attack on Mimi at the engagement party. Being charming came naturally to Edward in the same way that Mimi was inherently gregarious. While Sabrina had dreaded the thought that Mimi might be rude to Edward, she hadn't anticipated how irritable she would feel at the sight of her sister and fiancé getting along famously.

Edward now laughed. 'I don't know. It suits her somehow. There's something a bit childlike or puppyish about her.'

'It's called a lack of maturity and sense of responsibility.' This time Sabrina didn't even try to quell her crotchety tone.

Edward raised one eyebrow. 'I thought you two had made up?'

'We had one conversation at the engagement party. It was a step in the right direction but it wasn't exactly the Paris Peace Accords.'

Edward finished his toast and pushed back his chair from the table. 'I'm sure that asking her to be your bridesmaid will be the olive branch that will set everything back to rights.'

Sabrina disagreed but she couldn't bear to argue with Edward about Mimi at seven o'clock in the morning. Instead she simply smiled as she kissed him goodbye and set off for her morning run.

As she ran along the foreshore towards Bronte, Sabrina couldn't stop thinking about Mimi. She still wasn't sure whether she even wanted her irresponsible younger sister to be her bridesmaid, even though there really wasn't anyone else. And why did *she* have to be the one to extend the olive branch? Why couldn't Mimi say sorry and take some responsibility for a change? As Sabrina's feet pounded the soft sand she already knew the answer: because she was the older sister and that's the way that family dynamics worked. The eldest sibling was expected to shoulder responsibility and to set an example. The youngest was to be cosseted and protected at all costs.

When Edward had proposed three months ago while they were on holiday in Hawaii, the idea of having anyone as her bridesmaid, let alone Mimi, hadn't occurred to her. Thrilled by his romantic proposal, she had wanted to elope.

'Please?' Sabrina begged. 'We could do it straightaway. We could get married on the beach – it would be so simple and beautiful. And then we could go home and throw a huge party and tell everyone.'

Edward had hated the idea. 'I could never do that to my parents, Sabrina. Or my friends. Mum would be devastated if we got married without telling her, let alone not having her there, especially given . . .'

His voice trailed off and she squeezed his hand fiercely to let him know that she understood. Edward gave her a small rueful smile. 'And I want Nate to be my best man.'

Despite a valiant attempt, Sabrina's face expressed her disappointment and trepidation. He watched her for a moment before enfolding her in his arms. 'I know this might sound strange, that I'm the one who wants a big wedding, but my family has done so much for me. This is a way for me to give something back to them. I want to stand up in front of all of our friends and family and tell them how much I love you. And I want them all there as we become husband and wife.' He finished softly, 'Weddings aren't just about celebrating the love between us. They're about the love that all of our family and friends have for us too.'

In retrospect she should have known that Edward would never have gone for her idea of an elopement. He came from the sort of happy, stable family that genuinely enjoyed one another's company and liked spending time together.

Things had finally come to a head at one of the joyful gatherings they'd had with his family following the engagement announcement, when Edward's mother had turned to Sabrina and said, beaming, 'We can't wait to meet your sister when she comes home for the wedding. Is she excited about being a bridesmaid?'

And somehow, the prospect of telling her future mother-in-law that both she and her sister would view the idea of Mimi in the role of bridesmaid with unmitigated horror was just impossible. So Sabrina smiled and nodded and hoped that the issue would quietly go away. If forced, she could always simply answer that Mimi was living overseas and was regrettably unable to make it home for the wedding. But things didn't work out that way.

For starters, from then on every time the wedding was discussed (which was pretty much all of the time now) Chief Bridesmaid Miriam had somehow become a fixture, as unyielding and intrinsic an element as the cake or the bridal waltz. Compounding the problem was the fact that Edward was planning on only having a best man. The bridal party was therefore going to be just the four of them, which elevated Mimi's imaginary role.

But then came the shock announcement from Aunty Bron. In typical Mimi fashion, despite the fact that she had lived overseas for more than three years, she had chosen this year to return home for good. As far as Sabrina knew, Mimi didn't even know that her sister was engaged and was to be married early next year. It was classic Mimi – living her hedonistic lifestyle with no thought for anyone else, unwittingly causing annoyance and frustration simply by being herself.

So it was that with the announcement of Mimi's homecoming, the first of the incontrovertible wedding truths revealed itself to Sabrina. As control over the wedding began to slip through her fingers, she started to realise that weddings weren't really about the bride and groom at all. Weddings were about families: the ones already existing and the one that will come into being from the new union.

Which was why every time she thought about her wedding, her stomach ached from nervous cramps and every morning she ran farther and farther along the beach, simulating the recurring dream that she had started to have of running away.

4

The Proposal

Two weeks after the engagement party, Sabrina decided that she could no longer put off the unpalatable task that awaited her. The wedding was only eleven months away and she was already feeling overwhelmed by the length of her ever-increasing To Do list. So, with a rare gap in her schedule, unwillingly she set off for her aunt's house, in search of her sister.

Despite the fact that it was mid-morning, Mimi opened the front door still wearing her pyjamas.

'Breens! To what do I owe this honour? You might have told me you were coming over,' she added resentfully, as she took in her sister's chic appearance. 'I would have worn my good pyjamas.'

'I would prefer it if you called me Sabrina,' Sabrina replied coldly, already regretting her decision to visit. She pushed past Mimi and made her way into the normally spotless living room, which was scattered with Mimi's breakfast dishes and discarded books lying face-down on the floor and sofa. She turned to face her dishevelled younger sister. 'Where's Aunty Bron?'

'Not sure. What day is it today? On Mondays she volunteers at the Red Cross, Tuesdays is tennis, on Wednesdays she —'

'All right, I get the picture. She's out.'

'Well, you *asked*,' Mimi said, in indignation. 'I don't see why you're getting so huffy.'

'Is this —' Sabrina's sweeping hand gesture took in the messy room and Mimi's unkempt appearance, 'how you spend your days since you got back? Hanging around Aunty Bron's house in your pyjamas?'

Mimi flushed at the naked disdain in her sister's voice. 'What do you care? Would you prefer that I was out getting my nails and hair done, or posing for the front cover of some stupid magazine?'

This time it was Sabrina's cheeks that grew scarlet as the contempt in Mimi's voice mirrored the cutting glance she gave to her sister's stylish but obviously high-maintenance appearance.

Sabrina took a deep breath and remembered the promise she had made to herself during the drive over that she would not let Mimi annoy her. She briefly considered abandoning her plan altogether but then the memory of her terrifying To Do list surfaced. She had no choice. There was no-one else.

'I came to discuss something specific,' she said stiffly. 'I have a proposal.'

Mimi threw herself into an armchair, flung her legs over one arm, and then cocked an eyebrow at her sister. 'Another one? Who from? Does Teddy know that other men are propositioning you?'

Sabrina remained standing. 'Can you please be serious for one minute, Miriam? Aunty Bron told me that you've been looking for a job —'

Mimi immediately cut her off. 'Can you get them to write a part into *Sunshine Cove* for me? I've always wanted to do one of those minute-long stares into the distance that follows some important disclosure – all right, sorry.' Mimi collapsed under the weight of Sabrina's glare. Meekly, she folded her hands in her lap. 'What is it?'

'Like I said, it's just a proposal. Probably a misguided one. But you need a job and I want . . . an assistant. It's only a temporary position,' Sabrina clarified hastily. 'It would be for just under a year. Until the end of next February.'

Mimi sat up. 'You're offering me a job?'

'Yes.'

'You'll pay me?'

'Of course.'

'Fine,' Mimi said cheerfully. 'I'll take it. When do I start?'

'Don't you even want to know what you'll be doing?' Sabrina asked, exasperated by this insouciant approach to decision-making.

'I imagine I'll be fetching your coffee and walking your chihuahua around the studio lot while you're on set.'

'I don't have a chihuahua.'

'Really? That's a grave oversight. It can be my first task to procure one then. I read the trashy mags, you know. Every starlet needs a chihuahua to put in their Birkin. You do have a Birkin, don't you?'

'If you're going to work for me, your first task will be to learn how to shut up and listen instead of making smart-arse comments all the time. And while I might occasionally ask you to get me a coffee if I really can't do it myself, your job won't have anything to do with the show. I need you to do all the running around for my wedding.'

A look of caution came over Mimi's face. 'You want me to be in charge of your wedding arrangements?'

'Don't be ridiculous. I don't want to turn it into a circus sideshow. We'll have a professional wedding planner, of course, but I will need you to liaise with them and with many of the other professionals involved in the wedding. I simply don't have the time. I'll also require you to accompany me to dress fittings and assist with the guest list and invitations and help me get ready on the day. That kind of thing.'

Mimi had a strange look on her face. Finally she said, 'You mean you want me to do all the things that a bridesmaid would.'

Sabrina swallowed and chose her words carefully. 'Yes, I suppose I do. But because of the demands of my career, you'll be doing far more than the average bridesmaid. It's essentially a full-time job for the next twelve months, which is why I wouldn't dream of asking you to do it without paying you for your time.'

'You're *hiring* me to be your bridesmaid?' Mimi didn't know whether she wanted to laugh or to cry.

Sabrina said nothing.

Mimi's thoughts were shooting off in such erratic directions that, more to buy time than anything else, she demanded, 'But we can hardly have a conversation without arguing. What if you decide you want to set fire to me?'

'*What?*'

'Sorry. It's an expression that my friend Amisha, back in London, always used. I meant what happens if you fire me? Who will be your bridesmaid then?'

'You haven't even started working for me yet and you're already envisaging me firing you? God, Miriam, with that attitude it's no wonder you can't find a job.'

There was a long silence.

'There's just one question I need an honest answer to if you're going to take this on.' Sabrina hesitated.

Mimi looked at her curiously.

Sabrina nervously fidgeted with her enormous diamond engagement ring and then looked at her younger sister defiantly. 'Do you have a drug problem?'

Now it was Mimi's turn to yelp, '*What?*'

'You heard me.'

Mimi gazed at her sister open-mouthed for a moment and then made a big production out of pushing up her sleeves. 'No track marks from heroin, see? Clean as a whistle.'

Sabrina looked at Mimi steadily. 'There are other drugs, Miriam.'

'Yes, *Breens*, there are, and I'm not abusing any of them. How about you? Oh, silly me, of course not. Little Miss Perfect is probably the only person working in television who *doesn't* have a coke habit. You know, maybe if you acquired one you'd be more fun.' Mimi paused to draw breath and then said in frustration, 'Jesus, Sabrina, why in the *hell* would you even think that I was a drug addict?'

'Because we both inherited the same amount of money,' Sabrina replied evenly. 'And I haven't the faintest idea how you could have burned through that much money in three and a half years while living in share houses and backpacking hostels unless you have a drug problem or a gambling addiction.' She paused and then added, very deliberately, 'Alcohol just isn't that expensive.'

Mimi flushed scarlet. 'What makes you think I've used up all my inheritance?' she replied, unable to quite meet Sabrina's eyes.

'I *know* you, Miriam. There's no way you would have come home, be living with Aunty Bron or be looking for a job at all unless you had no money left.'

Damn Sabrina. Mimi tried to keep her voice unemotional as she answered. 'Well, that's not really any of your business now, is it?'

'It is if you're going to work for me.'

Mimi took a deep breath and then looked her sister straight in the eyes. 'I do not have a drug problem. I never have and I feel quite safe in saying that I never will. And I'm not a gambler either,' she added, sounding disgusted by the very idea. 'Gambling always makes me think of that Kenny Rogers song and Kenny Rogers is not someone from whom I take my life cues.'

Sabrina held Mimi's gaze and then finally nodded. 'Okay. The job's yours then, if you want it.'

Mimi didn't just want it, she desperately needed it. But she wasn't about to tell Sabrina that.

'What do you think Mum and Dad would have made of this?' Mimi suddenly asked.

Sabrina opened her mouth to reply and then closed it again. There was really nothing she could say.

Mimi stared off into the distance with a furrowed brow for such a long time that Sabrina finally intervened.

'Mimi! You still haven't answered me. Will you do it?'

'Of course I will,' Mimi said, surprised. 'I was just practising for when a part does come up on *Sunshine Cove*.'

She grinned at Sabrina and held out her hand to shake on their deal. As the sisters shook hands, Sabrina couldn't help feeling that this was going to turn out to be a very bad idea, even as Mimi was trying to work out which of them was more to be pitied: Sabrina, for having to pay her own sister to be her bridesmaid, or herself for having to accept.

5

The Luckiest Girl in the World

The first task Sabrina had given Mimi in her new job was, unfortunately, not as easy as purchasing a chihuahua. Sabrina had set her heart on having her wedding planned (or themed or styled – Mimi wasn't exactly sure what the correct terminology was) by a company called FG Weddings and had asked Mimi to set up an appointment with them. Despite the fact that Sabrina was now technically Mimi's boss, Mimi had still managed to argue with her about her very first assignment.

'I don't understand why you need a wedding planner when you've just hired me to do all your wedding stuff.'

'We're inviting 250 people for a sit-down dinner at Strickland House,' Sabrina answered, naming a famous, heritage-listed mansion in the elite suburb of Vaucluse. 'You haven't the first clue what's involved with staging an event of this size and stature.'

'Stature?' Mimi hooted derisively. 'You're not marrying royalty, darl.'

Sabrina flushed. 'And *that* response is exactly why I would never give you that amount of responsibility. You can't take anything seriously. Anyway, the job I've hired you to do is more about doing the running around for me. It will be the wedding planner's role to oversee the smooth running of the ceremony and the reception. But naturally, if she needs help, you'll be expected to assist her.'

Typical, Mimi thought. She had been working for Sabrina for less than twenty minutes and already she was being bumped down the corporate food chain. She was now apparently at the mercy of two bosses, one of whom she hadn't even met.

Two frustrating days later, she was extremely doubtful that she ever would meet her second boss, for trying to find FG Weddings was like trying to track down Jason Bourne or the Abominable Snowman. It was one of those uber-trendy, discreet businesses that only worked for very posh or famous people and deemed advertising vulgar. All of its clients were obtained by word-of-mouth through some sort of Rich People's Morse Code that was either unknown or indecipherable to the rest of the population. FG Weddings wasn't listed in the telephone book. It didn't have a website. It did come up under a Google search (one website detailed a rumour about FG purchasing a first-class aeroplane seat from Paris to Sydney for a *wedding dress*), but all the other links were dead ends to inconsolable social-climbing brides wailing into cyberspace, 'Please, can anyone tell me how to contact FG Weddings? I'm *desperate*!!!'

Mimi was beginning to understand how they felt. She didn't know who was actually behind FG Weddings but she was pretty sure she already hated them.

Sabrina had bought Mimi a BlackBerry that she had absolutely no idea how to use, so she was treating it as a glorified mobile phone, although even that was a bit of an overstatement. A pair of tin cans with a string running between them like the Falks sisters used to communicate when they were kids would probably have done the trick, as the only person who ever called Mimi's BlackBerry was Sabrina. So when the already annoying ringtone trilled, Mimi didn't even bother to look at the caller identification to see who it was.

'You rang?' she answered, in her deepest Lurch from *The Addams Family* voice.

'Have you contacted FG Weddings yet?' Sabrina asked abruptly.

'I've been trying but —'

'Mimi, I want it done *today*! Do you have any idea of how late you've already left it? If they're booked out . . .'

Mimi ignored the fact that *she* hadn't left it late considering that *she* had only been on the job for two days. 'Sabrina, you don't understand. I think FG Weddings might actually be a sub-branch of ASIO. There is no known way of contacting them.'

Sabrina clicked her teeth impatiently. 'Use your brains. Just call one of their other clients and ask for the number.'

'Sure thing. I'll just ring Nicole Kidman and ask her for the secret handshake.'

'Miriam, I have to go.' Mimi knew that Sabrina was pissed off because she had reverted to calling Mimi by her full name again. 'Just find them or else.'

'Or else what?'

'Or else I'll set fire to you,' she said pleasantly. Then she hung up.

*

After three more hours of fruitless research, Mimi decided to follow up the only lead she had, even though it was about as likely to succeed as – actually she couldn't think of anything *less* likely to succeed than what she was about to do.

Finding the number for the firm that handled Nicole Kidman's Australian public relations was surprisingly easy. Mimi suspected that the next stage wouldn't be. Nevertheless, she took a deep breath and called the number.

'Good afternoon, the International Group, this is Candace speaking.'

'Good afternoon, Candace. I'm calling on behalf of Sabrina Falks,' Mimi paused to savour the pleasure that came with the knowledge that dropping Sabrina's name to staff used to representing mega movie stars would make no impression whatsoever. 'I was just wondering —'

Candace's shriek almost punctured Mimi's eardrum. 'OH MY GOD – did you say *Sabrina Falks*? I *looove* her!!'

For fuck's sake, Mimi thought, exasperated. Aloud she said, 'Excuse me but your company does handle Nicole Kidman's affairs in Australia, doesn't it?'

'Uh-huh. Listen, I don't suppose you could get me Sabrina's autograph, could you?'

'If you don't mind me asking, how can you get so excited over Sabrina when you work for Nicole Kidman?'

'Well, it's not like I've ever actually met Ms Kidman,' Candace replied. 'I'm just the receptionist.' She dropped her voice. 'And between you and me, some of her film choices are a little art house for my taste. But I've watched *Sunshine Cove* for, like, forever. And Danielle is my favourite character of all time. Although I did like her evil identical twin Diana who reappeared after the old farmhouse burned down. You remember – when everyone thought she was Danielle because Danielle had been trapped in the cellar during the fire and was still alive, but no-one was looking for her because Diana —'

'Uh-huh.' Mimi had never watched a single episode of *Sunshine Cove*, a fact that she retold with pride in much the same way as other people liked to announce that they had never touched alcohol, cigarettes or a professional rugby player. 'Candace, I wonder if you could help me – I mean Sabrina. I'm trying to track down a contact number for FG Weddings, who I believe Ms Kidman —' (*God, this is a minefield,* Mimi thought. She had only narrowly avoided referring to her as 'Our Nic') 'employed to plan her wedding.'

There was a long pause. 'I'm not meant to give out any of the contact numbers on the database without my boss's approval.'

'It would make Sabrina very happy,' Mimi said wistfully. 'I'm sure she'd be happy to personally autograph a photo for you.'

'A photograph of me with her?' Candace asked cunningly.

'What else?' Mimi laughed merrily. Mimi would promise her a photograph standing between Danielle and her twin sister Diana if that's what it took.

Candace was wavering. In true *Sunshine Cove* style, she was standing right next to the cliff, about to fall into the sea of temptation. Mimi decided to give her a little nudge.

'Naturally you'd have to come to the set of *Sunshine Cove* to have your photo taken with Sabrina.'

She heard Candace's sharp intake of breath. 'Give me your mobile number,' she whispered hoarsely.

Mimi quickly found the page in her notebook where she had written the new number down and then started to thank Candace profusely. But Candace cut her off. 'I want to be like you. I don't want to be a receptionist forever. I want to be a personal assistant to a real star. How did you get the job with Danielle – I mean Sabrina – in the first place?'

'I studied acting for a while and then I went backpacking overseas. From there it was a natural step to holding Sabrina's oversized handbags and making her phone calls.'

'What countries did you go to?' Candace demanded. 'And does it have to be backpacking or could I go on one of those Contiki tours?'

Bloody hell. Mimi could practically hear her taking notes.

'That didn't really have anything to do with it,' Mimi said gently. 'I'm her sister. That's how I got the job.'

'You're her sister *and* you work for her?' Candace said, in a tone of awe. 'Ohmigod. You're, like, the luckiest girl in the world.'

Mimi knew she ought to laugh at this but it was surprisingly hurtful. She had no money, no long-term career prospects, she was single and she was living with her elderly aunt. And now she was getting paid to run around in the shadow of her successful, beautiful older sister. Yep, that was definitely her. The luckiest girl in the world.

'I know,' Mimi finally managed to drawl. 'Sometimes I just sit here pinching myself. Really hard. So, Candace, you'll send through that number?'

'I'll try. Anything for Danielle.'

Mimi hung up and crossed her fingers. For the next five minutes she watched the BlackBerry like it was a votive offering, while she muttered prayers and tried to pull her eyelashes out so that she could blow on them and make wishes for Candace's success.

And then, finally, it beeped.

6

Claudia

Claudia Rosetti had three telephones, all of them mobiles. One was for personal use and one was for her business. The third phone was also used for business but rarely rang. Nevertheless she always kept it recharged and switched on. The third phone was exclusively for the use of VVIP clients. Strictly A-list. The only way to get the number for the third phone was if you were intimately acquainted with someone equally rich or famous or if you slept with James, the concierge at the Four Seasons Hotel in Sydney, whose little black book was more coveted than a date with George Clooney. It was this third phone of Claudia's that was now ringing.

'This is Claudia.'

'Hello? Hello? Is this the number for FG Weddings?'

Claudia's instincts immediately sensed something wrong. This woman did not sound like the polished professional assistants who usually dialled this number. This woman sounded, quite frankly, a bit batty.

'It is.'

'Oh, thank heavens. I was beginning to think you weren't actually real. Like the Abominable Snowman or the Tasmanian Devil.'

'The Tasmanian Devil is real.'

'Oh. Yes, of course it is. And so are you. Luckily for me or my sister would have set fire to me.'

'I beg your pardon?'

'I mean she would have fired me. It's, er – a little joke we have.'

'May I help you?' inquired Claudia politely. By now she was certain that James had got drunk the night before and would soon be ringing her to apologise for his indiscretion. But she wasn't about to hang up. The woman had mentioned a sister, which might explain why she was so unprofessional. Very occasionally celebrities did hire family members, which usually ended in disaster and tell-all memoirs.

'Help me? You can save my life. My sister has just got engaged and she wants you to be her wedding planner.'

Claudia sighed and set about disentangling the incoherent jumble. 'I'm sorry – to whom am I speaking?'

'Mimi. My name's Mimi.'

'And who is your sister, Mimi?'

'Sabrina Falks. She's on *Sunshine Cove*,' Mimi added helpfully, wondering if by any miracle Claudia, like Candace, would be impressed by the dropping of Sabrina's name.

Unfortunately, given that Claudia swiftly changed the subject, it seemed that she wasn't.

'I know who Sabrina is, of course. How did you get this number, Mimi?'

'Sorry. I have to protect my source and all that.'

'I see. Before we go any further, what date has your sister chosen for her wedding?'

'Next February. The sixteenth,' Mimi said eagerly.

'Well, I'm sorry you went to so much trouble to contact me, Mimi, but I can't help you. I already have a wedding booked for that date.'

'No! Wait! There must be something we can do. I mean, it would be good for your business to do Sabrina's wedding, wouldn't it? Given how famous she is?' As soon as the words were out of her mouth, Mimi held the phone away from her ear and silently banged her forehead against the table. Sabrina was famous in Australia and the UK but she wasn't exactly in the same league as a global movie star like Nicole Kidman, who had been one of Claudia's clients. Mimi held the phone to her ear again and tried to think of something to say that would bolster Sabrina's star credentials. 'She has two Gold Logie awards, you know, and she won the inaugural Crystal Soap-On-A-Rope award a few years ago.'

There was a deathly silence.

'That didn't help to change your mind, did it?' Mimi asked in a small voice.

'I'm afraid not. Good luck, Mimi.'

'Wait! Don't hang up. *Please*. We'll pay you double. Sabrina has tons of money and Sabrina's fiancé Teddy – I mean Edward Forster – is loaded and he'll do anything to keep her happy —'

'*Who did you say she's marrying?*'

'Edward Forster. You won't have heard of him. He's not an actor. He's an investment banker.'

There was such a long silence that Mimi began to wonder whether Claudia had hung up. Then, in a strangled tone of voice, Claudia finally said, 'I think we should meet.'

*

'I have to go to Melbourne. It's to do with your wedding.'

Sabrina was sitting in her dressing-room, idly flicking through a magazine as she waited to be called onto set. As her younger sister entered, flushed with exhilaration, she didn't even bother to look up. 'No you don't. I can't think of any reason you would need to go.'

'I *do*. If you want FG Weddings to plan your wedding, you need to buy me a plane ticket. I have a meeting with the woman who runs the company tomorrow.'

Sabrina's head shot up.

'You got in touch with her?'

Mimi nodded, surprised to feel pride sweeping over her.

Sabrina considered her sister for a long moment. 'You wouldn't be trying anything on, would you, Mimi?'

Mimi felt a sense of disappointment replace the pride that she had felt only moments earlier. What an idiot to think that Sabrina might have been impressed or pleased. Sabrina always thought the worst of her.

'Like what?' she demanded angrily. 'Ooh – a free trip to Melbourne for the day. How incredibly exciting for me. For God's sake, Sabrina, you were the one demanding that I do anything to secure this stupid wedding planner. I've set up an appointment for lunch tomorrow. If I don't turn up, she won't do your wedding. It's as simple as that.'

'Why do you have to go to Melbourne? Why won't she come here?'

It was on the tip of Mimi's tongue to tell her sister that Claudia wasn't in the least bit impressed by who she was and that Mimi still had to talk her into doing the wedding. But something stopped her.

'Look, Sabrina, the woman handled Nicole Kidman's wedding to Keith Urban. She did that media billionaire's wedding in France. Quite frankly, we need her more than she needs us. Do you want me to go to Melbourne tomorrow or not?'

They glared at each other.

'Fine,' Sabrina said. She reached into her handbag and pulled out her credit card. 'Book a flight. You can return the same day so no accommodation should be necessary.'

Mimi accepted the card but as she turned to leave Sabrina's voice stopped her.

'Economy class, Miriam.'

Mimi swung back to look at her. 'Do you really think I would book myself a first-class ticket when you're paying?' she said, a look of utter contempt on her face.

Sabrina flushed.

'And for the last time, my name is Mimi.'

*

The wedding planner wasn't at all what Mimi had expected. She had imagined someone tall and elegant, discreetly but expensively dressed, with accessories consisting of a double strand of pearls. Definitely posh, probably blonde and almost certainly middle-aged.

The woman seated at the table by the window of the fashionable city tapas bar had olive skin, brown eyes, unruly dark curls and looked to be only a few years older than Sabrina.

As Mimi crossed the restaurant floor, she had just started to wonder whether perhaps the waiter had waved her in the direction of the wrong table when the woman stood up and held out her hand.

'Mimi Falks?'

Mimi took her hand and shook it, trying to mask her surprise. 'That's me.'

'I'm Claudia Rosetti. Please sit down.'

'I wore black,' Mimi said in a tone of disappointment, taking in Claudia's stylish cherry-red dress. 'Everyone told me that if I was going to Melbourne I had to wear black.'

Claudia simply nodded and then sipped her mineral water. Subdued by this response, Mimi took her seat.

If only Mimi could have known it, Claudia was badly rattled and fighting for composure. Unfortunately for Mimi, her desperate attempt to maintain a veneer of professionalism was transmitting as intimidating coldness.

The waiter appeared and without even consulting Mimi, Claudia ordered a selection of tapas, a bottle of wine and another mineral water for Mimi. With the waiter swiftly dispatched, she met Mimi's look of surprise with a pleasant but firm smile.

'Sorry to rush things along but I have another meeting directly after this one. However, I'm very familiar with this place and, believe me, I ordered the best things on the menu. You don't mind, I'm sure.' It was not a question.

There was nothing to do but nod in acquiescence, however, Mimi was already revising her first impression of Claudia. Despite her youthful and casual appearance, Claudia had an air of capability and authority that suggested she had prepared for her role in life as a wedding planner by undertaking several years in the military, followed by a brief period spent single-handedly quelling a revolutionary uprising in a far-flung Pacific island nation.

The waiter returned with the wine. Once Claudia had approved it, she launched straight in.

'Why are you and your sister so insistent on hiring me as the wedding planner?'

Mimi looked surprised. 'Are you being modest? I'm not sure if you've ever googled yourself but pretty much every bride in Australia wants you to be their wedding planner from what I can tell. To be honest, I'd never heard of you but Sabrina will probably offer you their firstborn child if you agree to do it.'

A strange expression crossed Claudia's face and she took a sip of wine. She tapped the tablecloth with her clipped fingernails and then looked up at Mimi. 'Are you quite sure your sister didn't give you a *specific* reason? Or —' she took refuge in her wine again and then added, 'her fiancé?'

Mimi wondered whether Claudia was trying to put her off by being deliberately strange. 'I think Teddy's sole contribution to the wedding day is to turn up. This is Sabrina's show and it's not part of my job to question any of her commands.' Confused, she added, 'Look, it's not that mysterious, is it? I imagine Sabrina wants you for the same reason that all your clients hire you: you're a status symbol.'

As soon as the words were out of her mouth she wanted to take them back but luckily they didn't seem to have done any harm.

Instead, Claudia gave a short bark of appreciative laughter.

'I grew up in Leichhardt,' she explained, naming the inner-city Sydney suburb that historically had been predominantly inhabited by working-class Italian immigrants. 'Before it became trendy. I find it very funny that people now view a kid from Leichhardt in the same way as a Cartier bracelet or a Mercedes convertible.'

Mimi grinned, starting to like Claudia for the first time since meeting her. 'The suburb that we grew up in still isn't trendy,' she said cheerfully. 'But that's a good sign, I think. It means that you and Sabrina have something in common.'

Mimi instantly regretted her remark as it caused the guarded expression to descend once more upon Claudia's face. Thankfully, however, at that moment their food arrived and as Claudia named and explained the delicious array of small dishes, her glacial demeanour gradually thawed.

They had just started their meal when Claudia abruptly asked, 'What's she like?'

Mimi looked surprised. 'Who – Sabrina?'

'Yes.'

Mimi thought about it and realised that she honestly didn't know the answer to that question any more. 'She's . . . God, I don't know. She's my sister.'

'Shouldn't you know her better than anyone, in that case?'

'I've been living overseas for the past few years.' Realising that this wasn't sufficient, Mimi added, 'She's beautiful. And famous and successful.'

'Must be fun being her sister,' Claudia said unexpectedly.

A flash of humour lit up Mimi's eyes. 'I love it. Reflected glory and all that. You've no idea how glamorous it is. The other day there were paparazzi following us. It was kind of exciting until they yelled at me to stop getting in the way of their shots of Sabrina.' The paparazzi had had no idea that Mimi was Sabrina's sister and neither Sabrina nor Mimi had enlightened them. No-one wanted to take pictures of the hired help unless you happened to be the nanny who had slept with Jude Law.

'Tell me about her fiancé.'

This was easier. 'He's gorgeous. And nice. Their children will undoubtedly be insufferably perfect.'

The words escaped from Claudia's lips before she could stop herself. 'Do they really love each other?'

Mimi looked curious. 'Yes. I think they really do. Look, I don't mean to be rude, but is insisting that your clients are in love another one of your requirements? Did you put Nicole Kidman and Keith Urban through this?'

Mimi was right, Claudia realised. She had to tread more carefully. She fixed a smile on her face. 'It's imperative that I fully understand any situation I walk into. Weddings are incredibly volatile affairs. It's generally one of the biggest events in my clients' lives and the emotions of everyone involved tend to run amok. Ordering the correct number of chairs or finding a harpsichord player who can also sing in Welsh is the easy part of my job. The hard part is making sure that the emotions don't get out of control on the day and ruin all the planning. If I'm to give your sister and her fiancé their dream wedding, I need to understand both of them.'

'Well, in that case, Teddy is perfect.' Claudia cast her a sharp look but said nothing. 'And Sabrina is . . . Sabrina. I really don't know what else to say. When you meet you can come to your own conclusions about her.'

'No,' Claudia said immediately. 'That's one of my conditions. If I take on this job, then all my meetings must be exclusively with you.'

'I hope you don't mind me asking, but are you in witness protection or something? First, you were almost impossible to track down and now this. I feel like I'm hiring the Invisible Woman.'

Claudia laughed. 'How long have you been working for your sister?'

'Almost a week.'

'It shows. Take it from me, Mimi, when you work with celebrities and the really big stars, you soon realise that the most valuable quality you can cultivate is to make yourself invisible. There's only so much attention to go around and they need to have it all.' Claudia hesitated and then asked, 'Will . . . Teddy . . . be involved at all with the wedding preparations?'

'God, no. Like I said, the extent of his involvement with this wedding is to show up on the day. It's probably a good thing you don't want to meet with Sabrina because you'd probably hardly see her anyway. I'll be your main contact person.' Mimi was feeling giddy from the wine she'd drunk and a sense of imminent success. She looked at Claudia, feeling daring. 'So you'll do it?'

Claudia chewed her lip. Every instinct was screaming at her not to be a fool, to walk away. Instead she said sternly, '*If* I agree to take this on, I'm unable to provide what's called full service.'

'Meaning?'

'Meaning I won't be present on the actual wedding day. My assistant will be there in my stead.'

Mimi looked at her curiously.

'You've left it very late,' Claudia said, meeting Mimi's gaze squarely. 'And I've already told you that I have a wedding booked for that same date.' It was a half truth rather than an actual fib, although even if it had been, God knows that wouldn't have made it the first time she'd looked a client in the eyes and told a barefaced lie. She saw Mimi's excitement building and quickly added, 'I also retain the right to walk off the job without notice and receive my fee in its entirety in the event that I'm given any tacky requests to do with thrones, live peacocks or a guest appearance at the reception by an *Australian Idol* contestant.'

'That seems fair.'

Claudia drummed her fingers on the table and then looked directly at Mimi, her mouth set.

'You've got yourself a wedding planner.'

7

Lewis

It was fair to say that Lewis Reynolds loved being a 'pap'. He loved all of it: the long, boring stakeouts and the frenetic, mad chases on foot or in car and occasionally (when the budget allowed) by boat or helicopter. He especially loved his shiny camera, with its array of long and wide lenses that he secretly thought of as his hunting weapons. Lewis had nicknamed his camera 'Magnum' – a double allusion to the famous photographic agency and the handgun that Dirty Harry held when he uttered his famous line: 'Go ahead, make my day.' When the other paparazzi bitched and moaned about having to stand in the cold or rain for five hours in front of restaurants or celebrities' homes or, like now, in the crammed paparazzi holding pen outside Melbourne's Crown Casino, where they were photographing the stars as they arrived for the annual Logie Awards, Lewis never joined in. He didn't believe in biting the hand that fed him, and paparazzi work had been very, very good to Lewis.

In fact, just about the only thing that Lewis didn't like about his job was Sabrina Falks.

When he'd first set eyes on her she had been a pretty nineteen-year-old, but there had been no hint of the fame to come. Back then she had been known as the Wildberry Girl, the recognisable face of a hugely successful advertising campaign for a well-known brand of yoghurt. Although these days the usual sycophants fell over themselves to state publicly how they had known from the start that Sabrina was destined for stardom, Lewis knew that those claims were bullshit. Beautiful, young women were a dime a dozen in Sydney and Sabrina had never stood out from her peers.

Unlike Lewis.

Even in those early days, Lewis had a reputation as the most ruthless of the paps – the one who would go the furthest for the seemingly impossible shot; the one who would always get it. His aggression with both subjects and editors also enabled him to become one of the people who had the power to elevate a pretty girl from a decorative element of the social scene into a 'personality'. Becoming a 'personality' was a much craved-after destiny for a certain portion of Sydney's youth. Personalities had a public profile – a profile that could be parlayed into enticing and glamorous opportunities like a relationship with a well-known football player, or hosting a late-night game show, or becoming an 'ambassador' for the latest brand of underwear or line of hair-styling products.

Lewis no longer shot images for the society pages. Theoretically, he had transcended that type of work on the day that his now-famous pictures of Australian film star Matt Hannaford shoving his wife and newborn child down the hospital steps had run on the front page of just about every tabloid paper in the English-speaking world. Lewis had hired an accomplice to aim a water pistol at Hannaford's wife as she left the hospital holding their newborn babe in her arms. The actor, not knowing that it was only a water pistol, had swiftly pushed his wife and child out of what he believed to be harm's way, but by the time he had realised what was going on it was too late. Lewis had damning pictures of the infamously hot-tempered actor treating his tiny baby and wife with apparent brutality. As extra icing on the cake, when Hannaford's camp issued their version of events in the media storm that followed, Lewis got paid an exorbitant sum for the pictures that he had shot of Hannaford punching Lewis's hapless conspirator. (Lewis's exultant editor-in-chief, Dana, celebrating the magazine's highest ever circulation figures, had happily paid for all hospital, dental and legal bills.)

Despite his success with 'Hannaford-gate', it was true that Lewis had persisted with shooting the social pages for longer than he probably should have, for one simple reason. It had perks. Perky-breasted, female type of perks.

For there was a certain breed of pretty, fashionable girl who believed that the pinnacle of social status was having her picture published in the social pages of the weekend newspapers or weekly magazines. In Lewis's parlance they were known as the stupid, social-climbing tarts.

These girls, who would never have given Lewis a second glance without the magic charm of his Magnum slung around his neck, had actively sought him out at the various make-up launches, fashion parades and the never-ending string of promotional events that made up the more desperate end of the Sydney social scene. They had posed for him and pouted for him. When they cottoned on to the fact that if Lewis ran their picture in the paper on several occasions, then they might make the jump to 'social fixture' and from there, possibly even to 'personality', they sometimes even slept with him. All for a four-by-six-centimetre picture in the newspaper.

With one notable exception.

Right from the start, that snotty, up-herself Sabrina Falks had refused to play the game. Even when she had been a nobody. Just some bloody yoghurt girl.

He had noticed her right away – she was pretty, all right, and knew it. He had managed to wheedle her into a corner where he had started to deliver his usual spiel of insinuations and innuendo, but he had known halfway through that things weren't going well. Fumbling, he had come to a halt. She had raised one eyebrow and stared at him. And then laughed.

'Are you honestly proposing that I sleep with you to get my picture on the back page of the paper?' Her extraordinary sapphire-blue eyes had danced with amusement. 'Do tell – what on earth would I have to do to make it to page three?'

Even now, more than seven years later, as he waited for her red-carpet arrival, Lewis squirmed at the memory of Sabrina's amusement. It was the tone that she had used – the inflection on '*I* sleep with *you*', as though the thought of having sex with him was the most unthinkable – no – the most *absurd* proposition that she had ever heard. Bitch.

From that moment he had wanted to bring her down, to drag her down to the level where she rightfully belonged. But in all those years, she had never let down her guard. Not once.

Sabrina never got drunk in public. (Rumour had it that she had never touched a cigarette or alcohol in her life, but Lewis refused to believe that anyone could be *that* pure.) She never dated unsuitable men who were willing to tell all. In fact, prior to her fiancé, Sabrina didn't appear to have had a serious boyfriend, unless you counted the rumours about her and Ethan Carter, an ex-cast mate from *Sunshine Cove* who had gone to live in Los Angeles. (Editors from both Australia and the UK had tried to bribe every single cast and crew member from *Sunshine Cove* for juicy revelations about Sabrina and her current co-star Chad McGyver, or Sabrina and Ethan, with no success.) At Lewis's instigation, his editor Dana had also hired a private investigator to dig around in the neighbourhood where Sabrina had grown up. He had come up completely empty-handed.

Given that Sabrina had (unbelievably) not had a boyfriend until she was in her twenties, there weren't any youthful indiscretions or embarrassing high-school dance photos to publish. The worst that the investigator had been able to unearth had come from the jealous but nevertheless awe-struck suburban mums who had gone to school with Sabrina. They had all agreed that she had been considered 'stuck-up' and had preferred the company of her sister to making friends. There had been something strange about the father apparently, some garbled story about a kid's birthday party that made no sense, but it was already well known that Sabrina's father had abandoned the family when she was young and that her mother had worked as a cleaner to support her two young daughters. These details had been released early in Sabrina's career by the television station's publicity department, who had gleefully banked on the correct assumption that they would make *Sunshine Cove*'s audience even more sympathetic and receptive to Sabrina. Now her mother was dead and her father was missing, presumed dead, while her sister lived overseas and was untraceable. She was a bloody untouchable Ice Queen.

The thing that most infuriated Lewis was that Sabrina refused to play the game at even its most basic level. Rumours notwithstanding, she had never publicly dated another actor. She had a preference for elegant gowns and never showed too much skin on the red carpet – a crime that, in Lewis's book, was tantamount to identity fraud for a soapie star. She didn't make inane comments in interviews or talk earnestly about her 'craft'. When asked stupid questions by interviewers such as 'Who would you turn gay for?', she would answer evasively but politely, leaving the questioner with the indelible impression that they had behaved in a vulgar manner which had disappointed her.

Sabrina always declined the invitation to the pre-Logie Awards Gifting Suite. Lewis had hung around for the whole of the previous day waiting for her, watching a procession of excited celebrities leave with bags stuffed with free skincare products, designer clothes, the latest electronic gadgets and crates of champagne. It had been like watching a free-for-all at the duty-free. A photograph of Sabrina – wealthy enough now in her own right from all accounts and about to be married to some rich banker – leaving a palatial hotel suite with her arms full of freebies could have been turned into a nice, sly little piece about celebrity greed that might have brought her down a peg or two in the public's estimation. Assuming of course that he could have convinced Dana to run the story in a negative way. That was another problem with Sabrina. All the editors were frightened of getting on the wrong side of her publicist these days. She was firmly ensconced as Australia's sweetheart and her face on a magazine cover was among only a very select few that could push circulation into the stratosphere. She was like Cate Blanchett – polite, gracious, impenetrable, but in Lewis's opinion, too fucking superior for words.

And now, she was here.

The limousine pulled up at the red-carpeted entrance. As a valet sprang to open the car door, some of the assembled crowd of fans caught a glimpse of who was within, and they began to scream and chant her name.

Sabrina emerged gracefully from the car. Her famous mane of hair was pulled back from her face by a jewelled headband and fastened at the nape of her neck in a cluster of glossy curls. Her long, gold silk gown fell to the floor, its soft folds clinging expertly to her flawless figure, making the dress sexy in an understated, tasteful way. Her deep-blue eyes had been expertly made up with liquid eyeliner and golden eye shadow, making them appear even wider and more hypnotic than usual. When Sabrina, laughing and smiling, picked up her skirt and slowly made her way down the red carpet, towards the designated 'posing' spot in front of the sponsors' board, tiny sparkling flashes from her breathtakingly expensive, jewel-encrusted stiletto sandals could be glimpsed.

Lewis had to hand it to her: Sabrina had dressed the part to perfection. She was indisputably Australian television's Golden Girl.

Sabrina faced the phalanx of photographers and assumed 'the position', with the assurance of the model that she had been and the celebrity that she had become. Smoothly and naturally, her left hand went to her hip, while the other arm curved gracefully at her side. She shifted her weight to her back foot, and pulled her shoulders back. Her head was slightly forward and her chin lifted, so as to avoid any suggestion of a double chin from a bad angle.

The blinding barrage of flashes began.

'Going to have a few tonight to celebrate your engagement, Sabrina?' one of the paps called out, hoping to spark a reaction from her.

'Where's your fiancé tonight, Sabrina?' asked another.

'Are you going to win the Gold Logie again?' This last being a reference to the awards' highest accolade for the most popular television personality. Sabrina had won it twice before and was nominated again this year.

Sabrina merely laughed and adjusted her pose as the flashes continued their blinding work. Now her back was turned towards the cameras, in a three-quarter profile pose. Chin down, cheeky look backwards over her shoulder. The photographers loved it and the public would too, when the image was reproduced time and again in newspapers and magazines and on websites the following day.

Lewis saw the massive stone of her engagement ring glitter under the strong lights. Must be worth a hundred grand at least. *Christ, she must be good in bed.* He took several close-ups of the ring – *Celebrity Confidential* readers loved that kind of stuff – and then focused on getting a bad shot of Sabrina. A bad shot was oddly worth more than a good shot these days. Squinting eyes, ugly knees, an awkward angle that could be construed as evidence of weight gain: these could all be cruelly blown up within the pages of a glossy magazine to provide entertainment for readers who had an insatiable desire for images of perfection, but were also, perversely, sick to death of them.

After several attempts he was about to give up; Sabrina was too much of an old pro to fall into those traps. Then he thought, *Bugger it*. It was worth one last shot.

'Why don't you cut loose for a change tonight, Sabrina baby, and show us your tits?' he called out, hoping to shock her into a demonstration of anger or disgust.

Sabrina ignored him, as she had done for years now. Not by the merest flicker of an eyelid did she betray that she had even heard him. Lewis gritted his teeth and, for now, abandoned his long-cherished dream of taking a truly terrible, humiliating picture of her. Instead, he did what he was there to do: he took shot after shot of Sabrina – exquisite, shimmering, adored Sabrina. The photographs gradually filled up the memory card of his beloved Magnum, like a necklace of tiny jewels, turning his pride and joy, his sleek weapon, into a treasure chest, filled with glowing images of her beauty and perfection.

He fucking hated her.

8

Seat-Warming

Like most Australians, Mimi had a love/hate relationship with the Logie Awards. The Logies, as it was universally known, had been around since 1959 but still seemed to sit uneasily within an Australian culture that disdained any overt display of self-congratulation. In common with most television and film awards ceremonies, which feted overpaid actors while ignoring underpaid writers, the Logies was a three-hour endurance marathon of awkward attempts at humour by the host, nauseating acceptance speeches, mediocre song-and-dance routines, and an invited guest list of hundreds who, thanks to the recent tsunami of reality-television shows, tended to be less of the Who's Who variety and more of the Who's That? crowd.

Dressed in requisite Logies-watching attire of pyjamas and Ugg boots, Mimi was comfortably ensconced in one of Aunty Bron's armchairs. She was watching the delayed and edited broadcast of the red-carpet arrivals, which both preceded and outrated the actual awards ceremony, with a mixture of avidness and disdain. It hadn't had to be this way.

'I can't believe you could have been there and you turned it down,' Aunty Bron said reprovingly, entering from the kitchen and bringing with her two bowls of ice-cream with chocolate topping.

Mimi accepted her bowl with her face screwed up. 'Sabrina offered to get me a job as a *seat-warmer*, Aunty Bron. I do have some dignity left, you know.'

Aunty Bron settled herself comfortably into a corner of the couch and began to eat her ice-cream. 'I don't know what you're talking about. You could have gone to Melbourne and you would have been able to get all dressed up and have your hair and make-up done. And you would have met all of the stars – it would have been exciting.'

'Why does everyone in this family think a trip to Melbourne is the pinnacle of excitement? And do you even know what seat-warmers do? They have to quickly sit in an empty place whenever anyone goes to the loo or to the bar so that if the camera pans over the ballroom there are no empty seats. As soon as the famous person comes back you have to get up and go back to the sidelines until another seat becomes vacant. It's like some humiliating, warped version of musical chairs. No-one at the table would have bothered to talk to me because they'd have known I wasn't going to be there for very long, and anyway, I'm a "nobody". I wouldn't have been allowed to eat or drink or attend the after-parties. I've had some crappy jobs in my time but I do draw the line at being a human appliance. I mean, honestly. Asking me if I'd like to be a *seat-warmer*! Next thing you know she'll be setting me up on a blind date with an electric blanket or a toaster.'

Aunty Bron looked at her niece sternly. 'She meant it kindly and you know it.'

Mimi merely grunted and then brandished her spoon at the television as a recognisable face caught her eye. 'Don't think you're hot just because you're Bert Newton's daughter!' she yelled.

'I don't think she does,' Aunty Bron said mildly. 'Although I must say, her hair looks lovely. You should get something done with yours, Mims.'

Mimi made a face. 'Who *are* all these people?' she asked despairingly, as the endless parade on the red carpet continued.

Aunty Bron peered closer. 'Ooh – it's the cast from *Sunshine Cove*. Sabrina will be arriving any minute, then. She comes in a separate limousine because she's nominated for the Gold Logie.' She added in a reproving tone, 'I can't believe you don't recognise them. The one with blonde tips in his hair is Chad McGyver, Sabrina's on-screen love interest.'

'What's his real name?'

'Chad McGyver *is* his real name. His character's name is Antonio Vincenzi. Everyone desperately wants Antonio and Danielle to get married.'

'Chad McGyver,' Mimi repeated, shaking her head. 'Good grief, with a name like that he didn't really ever have a chance to be anything but a soap star.' She surveyed the tall, muscled, blonde, blue-eyed, bronzed Aussie surfer-looking dude who was cheerfully answering every question put to him with a combination of the words 'awesome' and 'stoked'. 'But couldn't they have at least given him a more realistic name on the show? I mean, Antonio Vincenzi! He looks about as Italian as Skippy the Kangaroo.'

Aunty Bron nodded. 'It used to be Tony Wilson but he found out last season that he was adopted from a Sicilian family. Mafia. They came to Sunshine Cove to reclaim him and take him back to Italy so that he could take his rightful place as head of the family crime syndicate. He refused, though, because he would never leave Danielle, so in the final episode of the year, the Mob opened fire with machine guns and there was a massacre in the Sunshine Cove fish-and-chip shop. We didn't know who had survived until this year.' Aunty Bron sighed with satisfaction at the memory.

Mimi blinked as she tried to digest this narrative. 'I don't mean to be rude, but the idea of *that guy* —' Mimi nodded towards the television, which was screening footage of Chad opening his tuxedo jacket to reveal a T-shirt bearing the legend 'Life is a Soap Opera/Soap Opera is Life', 'as a criminal mastermind is irresponsible screenwriting. Fettucine probably has a higher IQ.'

'IQ?' Aunty Bron said in a lascivious tone. 'Who cares about his IQ? Ninety per cent of his scenes are shot on the beach and he wears nothing but a pair of Speedos. I almost didn't recognise him with his shirt and trousers on tonight.'

Mimi squealed and let her spoon clatter into her dish as she put her hands over her ears. 'Eeew! Stop it! You're grossing me out completely!'

Aunty Bron grinned but then they both fell silent as Sabrina appeared. Mimi turned the volume up louder. There wasn't much point to this as Sabrina had just emerged from the limousine and was nowhere near a microphone so only the gushing voice-over of the red-carpet host, announcing her arrival, could be heard. Sabrina slowly made her way up the red carpet and then paused, as was required, in front of the sponsors' board, where she began to expertly pose for the cameras.

Mimi hated the envy that was eating her up inside. She could almost say honestly that she didn't care about Sabrina's beauty – okay, so it would be nice to look glamorous but Mimi was well aware that looking glamorous involved serious commitments of time and effort that she would never have the inclination to make. The thought of having to diet or blow-dry her hair or apply make-up every morning was appalling. Too much like hard work.

It just didn't seem fair that Sabrina had it all. Mimi would settle for just a sliver of Sabrina's life. Like having Teddy. And maybe Sabrina's career. Not the *Sunshine Cove* part obviously, that was cringe-worthy. But acting for a living would be amazing. And the free clothes would also be gratefully received. And the personal stylist and on-call hairdresser and make-up artist. Okay, so maybe she didn't want just a sliver of Sabrina's life. A wedge was probably more accurate.

Right now, the only silver lining for Mimi was that Teddy obviously hadn't accompanied Sabrina to the awards ceremony. If he'd been on her arm, looking devastatingly handsome all over the place, Mimi really didn't think she could have borne it. She wondered briefly why he wasn't there, but when she started to ask, Aunty Bron frantically hushed her so she subsided and turned her attention once more to the television.

Sabrina had finished posing for the paparazzi now and was making her way up the red carpet towards the broadcast's host, pausing to smile and wave to her fans as she did so. The camera panned over the crowd, who had been whipped into a frenzy by her arrival. They were screaming Sabrina's name, yelling that they loved her, brandishing cameras and waving bits of paper and photographs for her to autograph.

Who on earth were these people? Mimi wondered. Why would anyone brave a miserable Melbourne night and stand in the rain holding an umbrella for hours in order to catch a glimpse of her sister? It was bizarre. Mainly because most of those professing their undying love for Sabrina were women. And they didn't look like a brigade of lesbian pride either. There were middle-aged, professional-looking women accompanied by their teenage daughters. Tweens dressed up in fashions that mimicked what Lily Allen had worn to a recent rock festival. Older women, serious soap addicts, who had no doubt watched *Sunshine Cove* since its first episode almost twenty-five years ago. They didn't even know Sabrina; they only knew Danielle.

Mimi watched as Sabrina paused for photos with some of the luckier fans. Her sister playfully took their cameras away from them and instructed a PR flunkey, who was toting a bulging satchel, to take the photo. The fans loved her for it. Mimi watched their faces closely. Love wasn't quite the right word. It was something other than love, something that mixed worship with longing and awe. It was adulation. Her sister looked different too. Warmer. Friendlier. Sabrina had always been more reserved than Mimi, but the reserve had inexplicably turned to coldness when Mimi had first announced her intention of using her inheritance to travel overseas. Mimi still had no idea why this decision had angered Sabrina so much. Two years later, their still-unresolved fight in the funeral parlour had taken place, and now, whenever Mimi thought of her sister, she imagined her on the other side of a sheet of impenetrable, glistening ice. Mimi realised that she had not yet really observed her sister with Teddy. She wondered whether the ice disappeared when she was with him, or whether it was just with adoring strangers that her formidable sister could relax.

The publicist, who was clearly playing the bad-cop role, now gently nudged Sabrina on her way. The red-carpet host pounced and immediately began to besiege the star with the obligatory questions about who had made her dress and supplied her jewels. Why all the actors didn't just wear sponsor logos like athletes was beyond Mimi. The host then proceeded to ask questions about Edward and the plans for the wedding, all of which Sabrina artfully dodged. Finally the host wished her luck for the evening, and as Sabrina made her way inside the venue, he proceeded to gush about her for a further two minutes, commenting on her hair, her dress, those jewels, that engagement ring! He was so enthusiastically inane that Mimi wanted to slap him.

Two hours later Sabrina was presented with her third Gold Logie Award, cementing her place in popular culture as Australian television's quintessential golden girl. She made a gracious and unfaltering speech, free of gushing platitudes, in which she thanked the writers, her fellow cast members, the crew and the voting public. She saved her final thank you for her fiancé Edward, which induced whistles and catcalls of approval from the public balconies.

Aunty Bron went to bed soon after Sabrina's moment of glory but Mimi stayed up and watched the telecast to the end. And Mimi was perhaps the only person who noticed that, unlike all the other winners who made an acceptance speech that night, Sabrina did not mention her family.

9

Sabrina's Diary

CELEBRITY CONFIDENTIAL EXCLUSIVE!
We asked Sunshine Cove's Sabrina Falks, who this year won her third Gold Logie, to keep an exclusive Logies diary, just for our readers! Take a peek inside the exciting and glamorous award-winning day of Australian Television's Golden Girl!

6 a.m. Wake up in South Yarra hotel room. Why is Melbourne always grey and rainy? It's infinitely depressing. Have breakfast (goji berry juice) sent to my room. Listen to the four messages already on my iPhone. They're all from my publicist. Edward must have taken advantage of my absence to go into work early.

6.30 a.m. Decide to go for a run around the Tan. The concierge has already warned me that there are paparazzi everywhere. I put on two sports bras so that they can't take any embarrassing visible nipple or jiggling breast shots. Bloody uncomfortable. Make it out the door and am instantly ambushed by cameras and a journalist from a current-affairs show that screens on a rival station to *Sunshine Cove*. I'm under exclusive contract to the current-affairs show that screens on my network so I retreat hastily to the hotel. Run on the treadmill in the hotel gym for forty-five minutes instead. Even though I'm inside, I still wear both bras. There are windows in the gym and some of those lenses are very long and powerful. Also, I know that Lewis Reynolds is in Melbourne to shoot the Logies and, as much as I hate to admit it, I'm slightly scared of him. He can't stand me and he's capable of anything.

9 a.m. Once I'm showered and dressed, the limousine (all Gold Logie nominees are provided with a limousine for their personal use on the day of the awards) takes me to the ballroom where the awards will be held this evening. It's madness – there are staff running around everywhere still setting up the stage and the tables. As part of my contractual obligations I have to take part in a truly awful 'comedy' sketch during the awards that features all of the Gold Logie nominees. It's a mock news show and the supposedly funny part is that all of the traditional roles have been reversed. So the sports reporter is played by the elderly matriarch from a long-running comedy series, while Bob 'Tackle' Bailey, a former football player and now the host of a sports show, is dressed in a glamorous gown and presents the weather. I'm the political commentator, which is obviously hilarious because in real life I am considered an airhead soapie star who presumably thinks that 'Politix' is solely a clothing brand. But the absolute worst part is that the main news anchor is played by a respected actor from an award-winning drama, who also happens to be middle-aged, not that attractive and from an Australian-Lebanese background. Her dialogue isn't funny but it's not because the jokes are bad; it's because they haven't bothered to give her any jokes. The idea of an older, unattractive, ethnic woman being a prime-time news anchor *is* the joke and the depressing part is that everyone watching will probably get it.

12 p.m. Back at the hotel. Hair and make-up team have arrived. Spend the next three hours being fussed over by Delta, my rock-chick hairdresser and Eamon, my make-up artist. An enormous bouquet of roses arrives from Edward. We've been calling but missing each other – he's forever in meetings and I'm now unable to answer my phone as every time I move Delta and Eamon shriek that I'm ruining all their hard work. I am constantly told that I'm beautiful, and yet three hours in hair and make-up is only barely enough to make me ready to face the public.

I try to ignore the sniping between Eamon and Delta. Eamon is jealous of Delta because up until seven months ago my eyes were always my signature feature, which meant that Eamon's job was deemed slightly more important than Delta's. But then Delta persuaded me to try a different cut and within a week it seemed that half of the women and teenage girls in Sydney had the same style. The magazines even started calling the haircut 'the Sabrina'. I've gone back to wearing it how I used to, much to Delta's disappointment, and I don't ever want to change my hair like that again. The last thing I need is even more close attention being paid to my head.

Skip lunch. No time.

3 p.m. Corinna has arrived to help me into my dress. It's not necessary but she always insists on being present for the big occasions to do the final press of the dress herself, and in case last-minute alterations are needed. Corinna's worst nightmare is the story of Sharon Stone putting her high heels through her haute-couture gown before the Oscars and having to wear a Gap T-shirt and a skirt to the ceremony instead. So I'm not allowed to put on my shoes first. I have to be helped into the gown and then I balance on Delta and Eamon's arms while Corinna kneels at my feet and does up my shoes.

By the age of eight, my morning weekday routine was to dress myself and Miriam, get breakfast for both of us, brush our teeth and make sure we both got to school on time. Almost two decades later, I'm not even trusted to dress myself any more.

3.30 p.m. The limo arrives to take me to Crown Casino. It usually takes the Gold Logie nominees about an hour and a half to walk the red carpet, by the time we sign autographs and pose for photographs and do interviews with all of the different television networks covering the event. They stagger our entrances so that we don't clog up the red carpet, and the most popular star (which this year is me) always goes last. Tackle Bailey, who has been nominated for the first time, has deliberately arrived late so I have to sit in the limo for another half an hour with my publicist, aimlessly circling the streets, while we wait for him to finish hogging the spotlight. My publicist's name is Laura. She uses the extra time to ring Tackle's publicist and blast her for 'unprofessionalism' and 'amateurism' and several other sorts of 'isms'.

I spend the time surreptitiously watching Laura, who is the same age as me. Laura is wearing a cheapish sort of cocktail dress, sensible shoes, hastily applied make-up and looks harassed. She hasn't had time to get her hair done. She is carrying a satchel that is roughly the size of a mountaineering backpack. It holds a BlackBerry, a laptop, two mobile phones and chargers, two press releases detailing my feelings and opinions (one for if I win, the other for if I miss out – no-one ever loses, you understand, they simply 'miss out'), bottles of water, a low-calorie energy bar, and the network's standard-issue Logies medical kit that Laura has never had to open but that is rumoured to contain an emergency line of coke and a fifty-dollar note. (Legend has it that during the eighties it was a hundred-dollar bill but that drugs paraphernalia was a victim of recent cost-cutting measures.) The satchel also contains a number of other things that I might conceivably need or that will contribute to my comfort.

I am carrying a diamond-encrusted clutch that has been loaned to me from Chanel. My very posh paternal grandmother would have approved as it contains the only items that she deemed essential for a lady to have with her on an evening out – a lipstick and a handkerchief. I try not to mull on the differences between Laura and myself. They make me feel simultaneously guilty and relieved.

4 p.m. Finally get the go-ahead to emerge from the limo and I start walking the red carpet. There are fans everywhere, screaming my name. A pregnant woman tells me that she's having a little girl and she's going to call the baby Danielle Sabrina. I can't help wondering why Danielle gets top billing when she's not even real. Stop to have photos taken and that prick of a photographer, Lewis Reynolds, is disgusting, as usual. It takes me almost two hours to make it down the red carpet and into the ballroom. I haven't eaten since breakfast and I won't be able to eat during the night in case the camera pans over me. I feel dizzy and tired and wish that it was all over.

11 p.m. I've won again. Feel nothing but say all the right things about being overjoyed and delighted. I'd like to fly straight home but I have to put in an appearance at one after-party at the very least. I always wish desperately that I could have Edward by my side at these functions – it would make them bearable – but, of course, that's out of the question. Wild, drunken parties are a form of torture for him and I would never ask him to endure them for my sake. I hate them too – I've never mastered Mimi's trick of walking into a room full of strangers and knowing exactly what to say and how to make them laugh.

My network's after-party distinguishes itself by having even lower standards than usual. In the first hour, the drunk host of an afternoon children's television show invites me back to his hotel room for a threesome. I'm tempted to ask whether the third party will be his sidekick from the show, a puppet named Barnaby that looks uncannily like a cross between a Muppet and our current Prime Minister. Instead I just smile and say no thank you. Spend the next half-hour wondering why I felt the need to smile and be polite to him.

Then the sleazy CEO of my network, Nigel Thompson, calls me over to help him demonstrate his one party trick. In front of a crowd of people, he says that he'll bet anyone any amount of money that he can touch me without using his hands or any other part of his body. After several people place their bets, he immediately puts both of his meaty hands on my breasts, squeezes them hard and says, 'I lied.' He then starts laughing uproariously and so does everyone else because he can fire or promote any of us at will. Naturally no-one will expect him to pay up on the bets.

As the Gold Logie winner, I have to be up by four a.m. tomorrow to do all of the breakfast radio and television interviews, so for once I have an excuse for being the only sober person in the room. I look around the party and wonder who all these overdressed, drunken, drug-taking, insincere people are. I despise all of them.

*

The following evening, on the flight back to Sydney, Sabrina looked at the screen of her notebook computer and sighed. It was completely unprintable and she knew it. She'd written it just to relieve her feelings. She'd give Laura a few quotes and get her to write the piece for *Celebrity Confidential*. She deleted the file and closed down her computer. Leaning back in her first-class seat, she felt a wave of exhaustion wash over her. All that she wanted to do was to figure out how she was going to hide the bruises on her breasts from Edward and then go to sleep. Savouring this glorious, rare moment of solitude, she closed her tired eyes.

'Excuse me?' a voice nearby made her struggle back to consciousness. 'You're Sabrina Falks, aren't you? You must be *so* excited to have won another Gold Logie! Would you mind signing an autograph for my niece?'

Wearily, Sabrina opened her eyes and forced a smile to her face. Yes, she was overjoyed. And of course she wouldn't mind signing an autograph. She would be delighted.

10

The Moment of Insight

'I think it only fair that I get to call the next meeting, not you,' Mimi said in a dark tone, as she struggled through the door of Claudia's harbourside hotel room, bearing an enormous stack of magazines. 'This is the second work meeting you've made me attend in a fortnight. It also happens to be the second work meeting I've ever had to attend in my *life*. And I'm warning you, at *my* meeting we're going to discuss what the sensible number of meetings for a single wedding should be.'

Claudia grinned. After the first dubious impression, Mimi had grown on her, via phone calls and emails. Claudia definitely preferred Mimi to her sister, although she still hadn't met Sabrina and had no desire to change this state of affairs. Even though she had known who Sabrina was, Claudia had googled the elder Falks sibling after meeting with Mimi, in order to bring herself up to date with her newest client. The image of polished perfection with the riveting blue eyes that had popped up on her computer screen had been enough to form an unfavourable impression in Claudia's admittedly biased mind. Women like Sabrina were annoying enough when they appeared as unreachable fantasy figures in the pages of glossy magazines. While Claudia dealt with beautiful, famous and pampered women on a daily basis, she had discovered that it could be utterly demoralising to have them pervade your real life and then to realise that they were *nice* as well. For reasons of her own, the last thing that Claudia wanted was to feel sympathy for Sabrina Falks.

'What on earth is all of this?' she asked, relieving Mimi of some of her load.

'Bridal magazines,' Mimi gasped, letting the rest of her burden slide onto the pristine white leather couch and then dramatically throwing herself down on the remaining seat. 'Do you have any idea how much these things *weigh*? Sabrina must have ordered every single title available. *Australian Bride*, *Sydney Bride*, *Bride To Be* . . . I swear there's even one in there called *One Perfect Day*. I almost threw up right then and there in the newsagency.'

'I take it you're not a fan of traditional weddings?' Claudia asked, amused.

'They're ridiculous,' Mimi stated with conviction. 'And I've only had a few weeks' experience of *this* wedding. How do you bear it?' she demanded of Claudia. 'Why would you want to do this every day for strangers? *Why?*'

'I love weddings,' Claudia answered simply.

'Then you're pathological! If you ask me, anyone who gets married these days can't be in their right mind —' Mimi stopped abruptly.

Claudia grinned. 'Lots of people find it hard to understand, I know.' She thought for a moment. 'Have you seen the film *Muriel's Wedding*?'

'Of course.'

'Do you remember the scene where Muriel goes into the bridal shop and tries on the dresses even though she's not engaged?'

Mimi nodded.

'Well, I understand that. It's such a powerful fantasy. The thing that captivates people about weddings isn't just the realisation of the dream of finding true love – it's about the pull of transformation.'

Mimi made a face. 'That's exactly what I hate about it. The whole 'Princess for a day' crap. Grown women ought to know better.'

'So you're completely happy with everything about yourself, are you, Mimi?'

'Of course not. But that doesn't mean I'm going to run around spending tens of thousands of dollars for the sake of looking different for *one* day. Anyway, surely you ought to want to look like yourself on your wedding day?'

Claudia laughed and gave up. 'Have it your way. You can remain a spinster like —' She caught herself just in time. Rattled, she twisted the wedding ring that she wore around and around her finger. She had to be more careful. She was so used to her regular spiels to newly engaged couples that dealing with Mimi had thrown her completely off balance.

'You can't even think of a single spinster,' Mimi said gloomily, but it didn't sound as though her heart was in the riposte. In fact she was looking utterly woebegone. Claudia wondered what her relationship status was but didn't think now was the right time to ask. In fact, never was probably the best time. She was already occupying treacherous ground in her role as wedding planner for Sabrina and Edward; the more professional she kept things, the better.

'We should get down to business. I have another meeting in under an hour. My assistant always packs my schedules full when I'm in Sydney.'

'How long are you here for?'

'Just the day,' Claudia said briskly. 'Unless I have a wedding to oversee I prefer to keep my trips short and go home as soon as possible.'

Mimi groaned. 'I hate Melbourne/Sydney rivalry. It's such a waste of time. Everyone knows that Sydney is the better city by far. You grew up in Leichhardt so you must know it too.'

Claudia smiled but refused to rise to the bait. It was precisely because Sydney used to be her home town that she always stayed within the confines of the same hotel and left the city as soon as she could. The possibility of running into someone she knew from her previous life still had the power to send a chill right through to her bones.

Luckily Mimi showed no desire to continue with that topic of conversation. Instead, she made a great show of dragging herself up to a sitting position. Then she opened her notebook and uncapped her pen. 'Okay. Let's get this over with. Shoot.'

Claudia tried not to laugh again. Mimi's laconic manner was the antithesis of the overwrought brides she was used to dealing with. It made a refreshing change.

'Very well. For starters, it's a little unusual for me to be dealing solely with the Matron of Honour so —'

'Your Honour,' Mimi interrupted her.

'I beg your pardon?'

'I prefer my title to be "Your Honour",' she explained. '"Matron" sounds like some ghastly character in a hospital drama with the body shape of a refrigerator and chin whiskers. And "Chief Bridesmaid" sounds like my Apache Indian name. So I'd rather be known as Your Honour. It has a nice judge-like quality to it. It sounds both serious and respectful.'

'Two qualities that everyone would naturally associate with you,' Claudia said, nodding thoughtfully.

Mimi grinned. 'Besides which, I don't think I want to be the brides-maid. There's an article in one of those magazines about all of the different wedding superstitions and traditions. Apparently during the medieval period, the bridesmaid's role was to ward off evil spirits, allowing the wedding to come to pass, which meant that she had to act as a decoy for possible kidnappers. Here was I thinking that wearing a hideous dress was the worst thing that could happen to me.' Mimi paused and then declared dramatically, 'No-one mentioned that *I might actually die.*'

'We'll do our best to avoid your kidnapping and death while dressed in a taffeta ballgown,' Claudia said unemotionally. 'Now, Your Honour, if we could return to the point, I think we need to run through a list of the tasks involved so that we have a clear demarcation of duties. First and foremost, is it just the two of us who will be in charge of this wedding? Mothers-of-the-bride tend to hate wedding planners,' she finished with a wry smile.

Mimi didn't smile back. 'It will just be us. Mum died a bit over a year ago and Dad left when I was eight years old. We never heard from him again so I'm sure he's dead too. He was actually declared legally dead years ago.'

'Mimi, I'm sorry.'

'Don't be. You couldn't possibly have known.'

There was a silence during which Claudia tried not to think of her own parents.

'Would you like to see a photo of them?' Mimi asked suddenly.

Claudia nodded.

Mimi pulled her purse from her bag and extracted a creased, dog-eared photo that, judging by the fashions, must have been taken during the 1970s. Margaret Falks had been extremely pretty with the sort of bone structure that perfectly suited her very short Mia Farrow-style haircut. Judging by her timid smile and shyly dipped head, however, she'd had none of Mimi's natural vivacity and bravado. Both of the Falks sisters looked a great deal like their handsome father, who'd had the same startling blue eyes as Sabrina, although Claudia could only see the colour of one of his eyes as he had been snapped winking impudently at the photographer. That would be where Mimi's cheekiness came from then.

Silently, Claudia handed the photo back to Mimi, unsure of what to say.

'God, sorry,' Mimi said, accepting the photo and tucking it back into her purse. 'I don't know why I'm boring you with a family photo. It's just – we never talk about them. Ever.' Mimi stopped and then, with a clear effort, she returned to her normal flippant tone. 'So, anyway, you only have to deal with me. How do you want to divide things up?'

Claudia cleared her throat, which had developed an inconvenient lump. 'Well, the way I understand it, I'm in charge of all of the preparations for the wedding ceremony and reception.'

'How is that a demarcation?' Mimi asked indignantly. 'It sounds more like a complete conquest. What is there left for me to do?'

'You really are a wedding novice, aren't you? I thought your role was to take over the bride's tasks.'

'So? Sabrina just has to choose a wedding dress and that's pretty much it.'

Claudia grinned wickedly. 'Pretty much. Except she'll need shoes, of course. And underwear. And jewellery. Perhaps a headpiece. Which might be jewels, fresh flowers or something made by a milliner. Speaking of flowers, she'll need a bouquet. The type of flowers will have to be decided upon and their seasonal availability assessed. Some brides who have their hearts set on a certain type of flower have them flown in from interstate or overseas, so do be sure to have that discussion with Sabrina soon to allow enough time to place an international order if it's required. Let's see, what else? She'll need a make-up artist, which will mean scheduling a make-up trial and a hairstylist, which, for a wedding like this, usually entails a minimum of three hair trials. Will she be wearing a veil or a going-away outfit? There will be pre-wedding beauty treatments to book in for, and we mustn't forget that you're in the wedding party too.

You'll need to find time for dress fittings for yourself. And then, of course, you'll need shoes. And underwear. And jewellery. Perhaps a headpiece and certainly a bouquet . . .'

Mimi had gone pale. *'Ten months?'* she said in a faint voice. 'I'll need *ten years* to get all that organised.'

Claudia hadn't finished. 'That's just the start of it. I can do as much or as little as you want, and although I can easily give you a short list of well-regarded professionals and make as many suggestions as you like, ultimately it's still up to the bride and groom to choose the photographer and celebrant, and the style of wedding cake, and the reception music, and the flowers, and the ceremony readings and — Mimi, are you okay? Do you need a glass of water?'

For Mimi had let her notebook and pen drop to the floor and had buried herself face down in the couch. A muffled moaning emanated from the depths of the cushions. Claudia thought she could make out the words 'Should have tried harder for telemarketing job'.

Claudia relented and spoke in a louder than normal tone that penetrated through Mimi's moans. 'You do have one thing working to your advantage when it comes to the tight time frame – Sabrina herself. All of the designers and suppliers will be falling over themselves to be chosen for your sister's wedding. So the problem that most engaged couples face in actually securing their suppliers of choice won't be an issue.'

Mimi lifted her head from the cushions and regarded Claudia suspiciously through a tangle of hair. 'Providing they're not invisible and impossible to contact like you,' she said, heaving an enormous sigh. 'Are there any other bright spots to this hideous situation?'

Claudia thought hard. 'You'll probably get to try lots of delicious cake samples when it comes to choosing the wedding cake.'

Mimi sniffed and sat up. 'That's a point,' she said begrudgingly. 'I should probably taste the champagne and wine that's going to be served at dinner too. Just to make sure they're all right. Okay, I've recovered. Tell me the worst. What else is there to do?'

'I'll make a professional out of you yet.' Claudia looked down at her list and then back up at Mimi. 'The ceremony and reception venues are one and the same, and Strickland House in Vaucluse has already been booked, so my next priority is to secure a celebrant. I need you to finalise the theme of the wedding and the budget with Sabrina so that I can pull together a list of the best suppliers for you both to choose from. I'd be happy if within the next fortnight we locked in the photographers – still and video – the musicians for the ceremony and reception, an invitation design and, ideally, the florist.'

'I think I need to take a horse tranquiliser and have a lie-down,' Mimi said faintly. 'Give me that list.'

Claudia handed it over and watched as Mimi read aloud in disbelief. 'Guest list, gift registry, bridal party suits and dresses, reception MC, reception equipment: marquee, tables, chairs, dance floor, swimming pool – *swimming pool*?'

'That list is from a wedding I did a few months ago.' Claudia met Mimi's disbelieving gaze and shrugged. 'It was on a beach in the Maldives and the couple decided that they'd rather have their guests swim in a pool than in the sea. So we had a temporary one constructed.'

'There are people in the world who are *homeless and starving*, you know,' Mimi said reprovingly. She turned her attention back to the list. 'Wedding cake, accommodation for out-of-town guests, transport for wedding day, wedding night accommodation, menu, name change documents, Notice of Intended Marriage – what's that?'

'It's a legal requirement in Australia. It's the celebrant's responsibility really, but I like to double-check all the paperwork. It's a simple form that has to be lodged at least one month prior to the wedding.' She added, 'It's a safeguard against spur-of-the-moment elopements and "Marry in haste, repent at leisure" weddings.'

A haunted look came over Mimi's face and in silence she handed the list back to Claudia.

Claudia looked at Mimi and thought smugly that she knew exactly the feeling that was overwhelming her protégé. Mimi now had some conception of the number of things that had to be planned, and could envisage, with awful clarity, how so many of them could go wrong. Of course, to be strictly accurate, Claudia didn't really *know* how it felt, as she had never personally experienced a crisis of confidence when planning a wedding. However, she could imagine it and she had even come up with a name to describe what Mimi was currently experiencing.

Claudia liked to call it 'The Moment of Insight', and generally she preferred it to take place early on in her dealings with new clients. The sooner a bride became semi-hysterical with the realisation of exactly how much work was involved in pulling off a successful wedding, the easier Claudia's job became. She had learnt early on in her career that the 'Shock and Awe' approach she had just used on Mimi was the perfect catalyst to spark the Moment of Insight. When Claudia was able to successfully shock a bride and groom into an understanding of the immense effort required to turn their dream wedding into a reality, they were invariably even more in awe of her when she pulled it off successfully. Which, with a bit of luck, resulted in less of a shock when her awe-inspiring invoice arrived.

So, despite the look on Mimi's face, now was not the time to tread lightly. 'Of course, these are all just the broad brushstrokes. I have another five or six lists of minor decisions that we're yet to contend with,' Claudia added airily.

The troubled expression faded from Mimi's eyes and she made a clear effort to pay attention to Claudia. 'Such as?'

'Such as the colour, width and length of the ribbon that will be used to bind the bouquets. The table settings at the reception incorporate an infinite number of decisions, as do the wedding invitations. Apart from the design, there's the weight of the stationery, the font and the wording to choose, and we'll also need to ascertain whether Sabrina wants personalised stamps affixed to the envelopes.'

'Personalised stamps?' Mimi asked in bewilderment. 'I thought only *very* famous people were put on stamps.'

Claudia shook her head. 'It's a new service offered by Australia Post, especially for weddings. They can turn a photo of the bride and groom into a stamp. It's very popular.'

Slowly, Mimi put her notebook and pen to one side and stood up. She then walked over to the wall and methodically started to bang her head against it.

At this point, Claudia's assistant, Olivia, tapped on the door and was bidden to enter. Although Olivia immediately registered the sight of Mimi headbutting the wall, Claudia noted with approval that she didn't accord it the slightest bit of interest. Olivia's level of discretion was almost on a par with Claudia's these days. She must remember to give her a raise sometime soon.

'What is it, Olivia?'

'Mrs Priscilla Tennyson-Banks-Worthington-Fitzroy's chauffeur just telephoned. They're about two minutes away. She understands that she's half an hour early,' Olivia finished, in an expressionless tone that somehow still managed to convey disapproval.

Claudia grinned. Olivia was really coming along very well indeed. 'The concierge can send her up when she arrives but she'll need to wait,' Claudia said firmly. 'Mimi and I haven't quite finished yet.'

'Oh yes we have,' Mimi said, pausing in her act of self-flagellation. 'I'm going home to study those lists. Once I've made my own list with *my* jobs on it, we can have another meeting, which will no doubt make you happy. Can we have meetings on the phone or do we have to keep flying back and forth between Melbourne and Sydney?'

'You have my number,' Claudia said drily, remembering that she still hadn't discovered how Mimi had got the number for her VIP-exclusive phone. 'You can call or email me any time. Olivia, I want you to give Mimi the folder we prepared for her. It will help you get organised, Mimi, and it also contains brochures from a number of the suppliers that we recommend. I need you to show them to Sabrina and get a feel for the theme that she wants for her wedding. I also think that in the coming week you should sit down with the bridal party and other close family members and have a discussion about some of the points we've raised today. Then you and Sabrina can make some choices and you and I can start locking suppliers into place.'

Claudia heard her voice, calm and authoritative. It felt as though it was coming from someone else's body. It was best that she didn't stop and think about what she was doing. If she thought about it too much she might lose her nerve.

Mimi nodded and started to gather up her bridal magazines, moving mechanically, as though her body didn't really belong to her. What was she *doing* here, pretending to be the same sort of competent assistant as the scarily professional Olivia? And she was helping to plan Sabrina's wedding to the man that she had developed an unhealthy habit of fantasising about. Bizarre didn't even begin to describe it.

A minute after Mimi's exit, Claudia closed her eyes, allowing, for the briefest instant, an image from the past to appear behind her lowered lids. At that exact same moment, Mimi watched the elevator doors close. She leant back against the wall of the lift, clutching her heavy bundle to her chest, as she shut her eyes and thought back to the last time she had seen Teddy. He and Sabrina had dropped in to Aunty Bron's three nights ago, in order to give Mimi a blank cheque book that Sabrina had instructed her to use for all necessary wedding expenses. They had set up a special account for the wedding and authorised their bank to add Mimi as a signatory to the cheque account. Sabrina had rattled on about Mimi needing to go into the bank to perform an identity check before she could begin using the cheque book but Mimi had barely heard a word. She had been so unsettled by the sight of all those blank cheques that the schoolgirl thrill of seeing Teddy had almost come second. Almost. She had managed to make him laugh again – several times – in the few minutes that he was there before Sabrina, clearly irritated, had whisked him away.

Mimi opened her eyes as the lift doors parted and she made her way through the lobby and out into the busy street. She knew that she really ought to stop daydreaming about Teddy but she couldn't help imagining how elated she would feel right now to be organising this wedding, if only the groom was still Teddy – but she was the bride.

11

The Best Man

Following Claudia's instructions, Mimi had called a meeting. The email that she sent to Sabrina and Teddy, which she had requested them to forward on to immediate family and the bridal party, had been titled 'Summit of Key Stakeholders in Forthcoming Falks–Forster Nuptials' and signed 'Your Honour'. Mimi had secretly hoped that her supposed familiarity with corporate language would impress Teddy. Unfortunately, Sabrina had responded by asking again whether she was on drugs, while Teddy emailed Mimi back to say that he had laughed so hard his secretary had come into his office to check that he was okay. While falling about laughing wasn't exactly the reaction that Mimi had been hoping for, she didn't really mind as her disappointment was far outweighed by the thrill of seeing his name in her inbox and the delicious pleasure that came from knowing that he thought she was funny.

It was decided that the meeting would be held on Thursday evening at Teddy's family home. At which point, Aunty Bron refused to attend for reasons that were still unclear to Mimi, but that involved muttered repetitions of the dire but oblique warning, 'You'll see.'

'But why won't you come?' Mimi protested. 'I met Teddy's parents and his sister at the engagement party. They seemed nice.'

'They are. Very,' Aunty Bron said shortly. Mimi wasn't sure but she thought she saw her aunt shudder. 'They're a charming family. Lovely home.' Under her breath she muttered, 'It's all just perfect until you undo his tie and his head rolls off.'

'Aunty Bron, what on earth are you going on about? Stop being so ridiculous. You made me go to the engagement party; now I'm insisting that you come with me to this meeting.'

'Insist away all you like, Mimsy. I'm fifty-eight and I refuse to be ordered around by either of my nieces. Tell Sabrina that I'm very much looking forward to her wedding but I haven't the slightest intention of sticking my nose into any of the arrangements. Now, I'm going to see a film with the Markovs from next door so feel free to borrow my car to get to the meeting.'

And with that Aunty Bron pulled on her coat, kissed her youngest niece goodbye and exited through the back door.

*

Forty minutes later, as Mimi pulled into the driveway of Teddy's family home in Watson's Bay, she rather thought that she had an inkling of what Aunty Bron had been hinting at.

The house looked *exactly* like the sort of residence that would spawn a successful young man. The imposing stone façade was complemented by impeccably maintained grounds. In the middle of a long and sustained drought, the Forster's substantial front lawn was emerald green – the ultimate contemporary Australian signifier of wealth.

Mimi suddenly wondered how her mother would have felt, arriving at this grand house to meet her future in-laws. She also couldn't help thinking that Sabrina must be immeasurably relieved that she was spared having to invite the Forsters to what had been their (rented) family home.

'Miriam!' Edward's mother smiled as she opened the front door. She looked exactly how most people would want their mother to look.

She had a warm smile and was elegantly dressed. Her accessories were neat pearl earrings and a discreet silver necklace. Not a remote control or antidepressant in sight. Mum perfection.

'Hi – er . . .' *Bugger,* thought Mimi. They had been introduced at the engagement party but Mimi had promptly forgotten her name. It wasn't exactly Mimi's fault, as two seconds after meeting her she had been besieged by various other relatives of Teddy, all of whom seemed to have difficult-to-remember double-barrelled surnames. They were that sort of family.

'Blanche,' she reminded Mimi, ushering her into the entrance hall. There was an enormous arrangement of fresh Oriental lilies on the hall table. Mimi and Sabrina's mother always used to sigh that fresh flowers were an indulgence that only rich people could afford. *She ought to have known,* Mimi thought. *She cleaned enough of their houses.* Occasionally an employer would let their mother bring home a bouquet that was past its prime. Sabrina maintained that it was a lovely gesture. It used to make Mimi impotent with rage. Fancy giving someone a bunch of second-hand flowers that you were about to throw out. How scummy could you get?

'Sorry,' Mimi now said. 'I'm hopeless with names.' She proffered a bottle of wine. 'I brought you this.'

Blanche accepted it gracefully, even though it was clearly of a vintage that, in this house, would be used for cooking rather than drinking. She helped Mimi off with her coat. 'Let me hang this up for you. Go through to the drawing room, Mimi. Sabrina will be pleased to see you. She's anxious to start.'

Mimi made her way alone towards the open door Blanche had indicated. Standing at the threshold, the reason why Aunty Bron had so steadfastly refused to come hit her with full force.

Arranged like an artful tableau, Sabrina and her in-laws-to-be presented a picture of perfection. It was like a scene from an English drawing-room play. Everyone was well dressed, speaking in muted, polite tones of cultural or social matters, and had had their hair professionally cut at some stage during the last six weeks.

Suddenly self-conscious, Mimi raised a hand to smooth her own messy hair, which was more frizz than curl as usual. The movement caught everyone's attention. As all eyes turned towards her, she tried to change the smoothing gesture into a wave and promptly dropped her carefully prepared accordion file and notebook onto the polished parquetry.

'I guess I'm not the only Falks girl who knows how to make an entrance,' Sabrina drawled, and everyone laughed.

Normally, Mimi didn't get embarrassed when she dropped or spilled things or tripped over, which happened to her more frequently than she would have liked. But acting like a klutz in front of Teddy's perfect family was humiliating. It seemed to show up, in stark relief, why someone like Teddy would always end up with someone like Sabrina, rather than with someone like Mimi. Her cheeks flushed scarlet and she dropped to her hands and knees to gather up her scattered belongings.

From somewhere behind her, Blanche called out to Sabrina that Teddy was on the phone. Sabrina's silken skirt brushed past Mimi's face on her way to take the phone call. *I feel like Cinderella*, thought Mimi glumly, although even that wasn't accurate as there was no way Sabrina could ever be classified as an Ugly Sister. A wave of self-pity and resentment washed over Mimi. Great. So now someone would have to invent a new hybrid fairytale just for her. Like Ugly Sisterella. Cursed at birth and doomed forever to crawl in the shadow of her radiant sister, who was the lucky one who got to marry Prince Charming. There would be no happy ever after for Ugly Sisterella. She would be lucky to get a date with a troll.

Someone joined Mimi on the floor and started to help her gather up her various pieces of paper. She looked up in surprise, hoping that it was the man of her dreams, until she belatedly remembered that Teddy was on the telephone to Sabrina.

'Hi, Mimi.'

'Er, hi.' Mimi had absolutely no idea who he was. He didn't look like a member of Teddy's family. She had a vague feeling that she might have seen him at the engagement party but, her terrible memory notwithstanding, she was quite sure they hadn't spoken.

'Nate,' he said helpfully. 'We met when you came home a year ago for . . .' his voice trailed off.

'Mum's funeral,' Mimi said briskly. 'I'm sorry, I don't remember meeting you.' He looked so utterly mortified by his blundering opening that Mimi felt sorry for him. 'To be honest it probably wouldn't have mattered where we met,' she added kindly. 'I'm generally hopeless with names. And faces.'

He looked thoughtful, then rolled up one trouser leg, stuck his leg out and looked at her expectantly.

'What *are* you doing?'

'Showing you my scar so that next time you'll remember me.' He pointed to a long-healed but still noticeable scar that ran from his knee almost all the way down to his ankle, on the outside of an impressively strong-looking calf muscle. 'I got that rockclimbing Mount Arapiles in Victoria. I fell almost twenty feet down a cliff face. My fall was broken by a rocky ledge where I had to spend the night in sub-zero temperatures before a helicopter winched me to safety the next day.'

'Really?' Mimi asked, impressed.

'Of course not,' he said cheerfully, rolling his trouser leg back down. He handed her the last of her errant pieces of paper and then helped her up. 'It's an old skateboarding injury from when I was thirteen. But I'm pretty sure you'll remember me next time. Which is just as well, seeing as we're going to be partnered up.'

'For what?'

'The wedding. You're the maid of honour, right?'

'The maid of dishonour is probably more appropriate, except that even the maid bit is wildly inaccurate. I'm sorry but who *exactly* are you?'

He smiled. 'Nate Jamieson. I'm Ed's best man.'

'You're Teddy's friend?' This was promising. The best friend was always a valuable source of information and influence. If Mimi could win Nate over, maybe he would give Teddy some positive feedback about her that would negate all of the horrible things that Sabrina was undoubtedly saying. Plastering a brilliant smile on her face, Mimi let Nate relieve her of her file. 'If you're the best man, we definitely need to get to know one another. I've never been a bridesmaid before so I'll have to rely on you to make sure that I don't fall flat on my face when I walk down the aisle.'

He laughed. 'Sadly, you're on your own for that one. I'll be waiting at the altar next to Ed, remember? I can help you back up the aisle, though.'

'Oh,' Mimi said, crestfallen. 'I forgot. Oh well, if I trip up on my high heels, I suppose I'll just have to try to break my fall on a flower girl or something.'

'Do you know, I find myself looking forward to this wedding even more now?'

'You enjoy watching small children get squashed by taffeta-wearing elephants? I wouldn't tell too many other people that, if I were you.'

Mimi would have liked to prolong the conversation but at that point Sabrina re-entered the room, followed by Blanche. They sat down, side by side on the sofa. Mimi looked at them, trying to visu-alise her mum on the other side of Sabrina, but it was impossible to imagine her mum sitting upright on a sofa. In pretty much every memory Mimi had of her mum on their old couch, she was slumped over: either tired to the bone in Mimi's early memories, or, in the last years of her life, vacantly staring at the television, the remote control slipping from one hand.

'If you're ready now, Mimi, we can make a start.' Sabrina's voice cut in. Although the words were impatient, her tone was sweet, presumably for the sake of Teddy's family.

Mimi sat down in the empty chair that Nate had fetched for her and smiled and nodded hello to Teddy's father and older sister Phoebe and her husband, whose name she couldn't remember but which was something like Giles or Miles. Sabrina had asked Phoebe to be a bridesmaid but Phoebe had politely declined, with the full approval of Teddy and his family, as she was hoping to be pregnant with her third child by the time of the wedding. Why you couldn't have a pregnant bridesmaid was a complete mystery to Mimi but apparently in certain circles it just wasn't done. Teddy's other sibling, Harry, was a merchant banker who lived in Hong Kong. His job was so frightfully important/ Master of the Universe-ish that Mimi had gathered everyone would be prostrate with gratitude if he managed to make it back to Sydney for twenty-four hours to attend the wedding. It was clearly out of the question to ask Harry to be a groomsman, which was why the bridal party was to consist of only Teddy, Sabrina, Nate and Mimi.

'But where's Teddy?' Mimi asked, trying not to let her disappointment show. 'Shouldn't we wait for him?'

'He's been delayed in a . . . meeting,' Sabrina answered shortly. 'He'll make it if he can.'

Mimi looked at her sister in surprise, wondering what she had done to deserve being spoken to in such a sharp tone. She glanced around the room but something peculiar was happening. Every single member of Teddy's family was avoiding her gaze. She turned her head just in time to see Nate and Sabrina sharing a fleeting, loaded look. What was going on? Sabrina didn't give her the chance to find out.

'Before we start, what *are* those ridiculous things that you're carrying? I bought you a BlackBerry and a laptop!' Sabrina's tone was back to normal.

Teddy's family smiled and Mimi silently conceded Sabrina a well-scored hit. It was obvious what they were all thinking. Generous Sabrina. Eccentric Mimi.

'It's an accordion file and a notebook. I prefer to use a pen and paper,' Mimi said stubbornly.

'Excuse my sister,' Sabrina said lightly. 'She's stuck in the nineteenth century.'

Everyone laughed except for Nate.

'Twentieth century,' he corrected Sabrina.

'I beg your pardon?'

'There were no ballpoint pens in the nineteenth century,' he said. 'I'm pretty sure they were still using inkpots. So Mimi's not *that* old-fashioned, really.'

Mimi smiled gratefully at him and he winked. Sabrina moved the conversation swiftly on to the first item on the list that Claudia had provided, but as Mimi started to take notes in her out-of date longhand, the warm feeling towards Nate remained. Not since their dad had a man ever taken Mimi's side against Sabrina.

12

The Theme

Three days later, as Mimi entered Sabrina's favourite beachside café, she spotted her sister immediately. Sabrina was seated at one of the coveted window tables, signing autographs for two teenage girls who Mimi correctly surmised were neither locals nor regular patrons of this café. She could deduce this by the fact that every other customer was studiously ignoring both Sabrina and the commotion that the autograph hunters were creating. The café was the sort of hip hangout where failure to be impressed by famous people was a measure both of its coolness and of the people who regularly went there.

Still gushing, the autograph hunters took their leave of Sabrina. As they exited, speaking in the shrill higher octaves that only excited teenage girls can reach in normal conversation, a too-cool-for-school Bondi couple at a nearby table (Him: muscular, too-tight T-shirt, probably a celebrity chef; Her: professionally tousled hair, an expensive-looking sequinned beach caftan, probably a fashion designer) exchanged a look of utter contempt.

Snobs, Mimi thought. *You might be groovy now but I bet when you were fourteen you had Jason Donovan posters on your bedroom walls. Both of you.*

Mimi hated all forms of pretension. She couldn't resist.

'Ohmigod! Sabrina Falks!' she shrieked, as she passed the cool couple's table. To her satisfaction, her voice had been loud enough to make the too-tight T-shirt man jump. He spilled his Fairtrade coffee all over his partner's brand-new issue of *frankie* and they instantly started bickering. As at least three other people also looked up from their newspapers, Mimi was able to walk in triumph to Sabrina's table.

'Very funny,' Sabrina said drily, indicating for her to sit down in the vacant chair.

Mimi grinned and plonked her belongings onto the small table.

'Oh God, that folder,' Sabrina groaned, as the offensive item immediately swamped all of the available table surface. 'I mean, *really*, Mimi. An accordion folder? If you absolutely refuse to enter the electronic age, couldn't you at least buy something stylish and leather-bound?'

Mimi ignored her. 'It's practical. I can find things instantly without having to flick through pages. See?' She undid the clasp on the file and it instantly sprang open, displaying compartments that were neatly labelled with headings such as 'Ceremony', 'Reception', 'Bride' and 'Financial'. 'Before you ask, we didn't forget the 'Groom' compartment. I asked Clau— FG, I mean, about it,' Claudia had been weirdly insistent that Mimi refer to the company by its name rather than hers, 'and the wedding planner just laughed and said that apart from showing up, the groom has virtually nothing to do with the wedding. She did say that if you felt strongly about including him we could give him his own Post-it note,' Mimi added magnanimously.

Despite herself, Sabrina was impressed. She had never known Mimi to be organised in her life. 'It looks very orderly, I must say. I can't believe you did this.'

'Well, I didn't really,' Mimi confessed. 'The wedding planner put it together for me.'

'Oh,' Sabrina said, mollified. 'I suppose it's quite cool in a retro way.'

Mimi looked at her in disgust. 'You style slaves are all the same. If

I'm carrying an accordion file around, it's daggy. If a wedding planner to the stars starts doing it, it's all of a sudden retro and hip. It's sad, that's what it is.'

Sabrina looked up, all charm, as the handsome young waiter came towards them. Despite the fact that neither of them had ordered, he placed a glass of ice, an open bottle of mineral water and a concoction of mixed juices in front of Sabrina.

Sabrina thanked him and he flashed a smile that Mimi would have given anything to have had directed at her.

The waiter turned to leave and Mimi felt the old frustration creep over her. What was it about being in Sabrina's presence that made her invisible?

'Oi,' she said, annoyed. 'I'd like to order too.'

He spun back around, an apologetic look on his face. 'I'm so sorry. It's just that Sabrina often comes in here alone and I know what she always has.'

'Fair point,' Mimi said kindly. 'But it might further your career if you realise that the number of human beings sitting at a table can change. Just a friendly tip.'

'*Mimi*,' Sabrina said, scandalised, as the waiter flushed a deep red. 'Excuse my sister,' she apologised. 'She's only joking.'

The waiter looked from Sabrina to Mimi and back again. 'I didn't even know you had a sister!' he said, in a tone that was almost verging on the accusatory.

'Why would he know your family tree?' Mimi asked, irritated, once she had ordered an iced chocolate and a toasted focaccia and the waiter had departed. 'He's a waiter in your local café, not your friend.'

Sabrina refrained from reminding her sister that most of the Australian and English public felt that they did have a right to know everything about her and instead said, '*Must* you be rude to everyone?'

'*Must* you be sickeningly sweet to everyone?' Mimi retaliated.

'Besides which, I wasn't rude – he was. Walking off without taking my order. And then looking at me like I had two heads when I said that I wanted to order some food too. Do people in Bondi no longer eat? What's the point in opening a café?'

'I can't stay while you eat lunch,' Sabrina answered, wisely deciding to ignore this diatribe. She daintily sipped her non-alcoholic fruit cocktail through a straw. 'I have to be back at the studio in half an hour, so let's get on with it.'

Mimi pulled out her pen and notepad. 'We got through a bit the other night but the one thing we really have to decide on is the theme for your wedding. The wedding planner can't do a thing until that's fixed.'

'Did she suggest anything?'

Mimi consulted her notes and dutifully reeled off, 'The hot themes at the moment are Bollywood, Vintage, strong jewel-like colours, and destination weddings. That's where you fly yourselves and your guests to a tropical beach or a mountain top and get hitched. But considering that you've already booked Strickland House, I suppose that's out,' Mimi concluded wistfully.

Sabrina thought back to her original wish of wanting to get married on the Hawaiian beach where Edward had proposed. 'Yes, that's out,' she said in a cool tone, refusing to allow a trace of regret to colour her response. 'I don't particularly like any of those ideas. What else is there?'

'Well, it doesn't have to be an obvious theme. The unifying idea could be a colour or a single motif. For example, FG did one wedding where the theme was lace. The invitations had lace on them, the bride's dress was made from hand-crafted lace flown in from Barcelona and the same lace pattern was piped onto the wedding cake.' Claudia had neglected to tell Mimi that the wedding had almost been called off over the groom's refusal to wear a specially ordered lace cravat and cuffs. Both the wedding and the marriage had been saved by Claudia's suggestion that the groom's lacy attire be limited to a discreet pocket handkerchief.

Sabrina was looking unconvinced.

'Or you could choose an historical period,' Mimi said helpfully. 'Like a medieval wedding where you'd arrive on horseback and your hair would be all loose and flowing and you'd wear a thin golden circlet on your head and your gown would have huge batwing sleeves and —'

'We'd all drink mead from goblets and throw half-chewed pheasant bones over our shoulders onto the floor at the reception,' Sabrina finished acerbically. 'No thank you.'

Mimi sighed. 'I think we're coming at this the wrong way, Sabrina. Instead of imposing a theme on your wedding just for the sake of it, maybe we should be thinking about who you and Teddy are.' Mimi's brow creased. 'Let's see, you're a successful actor and celebrity and Teddy is —' she wanted to say 'perfect' but managed to restrain herself just in time, 'a successful banker. They're both very modern careers.' She thought for a few more moments and then snapped her fingers. 'Got it! Modern Glamour.'

'Which means . . . ?'

'Absolutely no idea. But I bet if we flick that suggestion to FG, they'll match it to place settings and stationery and mood lighting in three minutes flat. What do you think?'

'I think I want to know how she intends to interpret it. But as a general concept it's not bad.'

'Not bad?' Mimi asked indignantly. 'Two minutes ago your guests were in the Dark Ages throwing pheasant bones around. It's *fantastic*.'

Sabrina looked at her sister's animated face and, for the first time in a long time, felt an unaccustomed twinge of affection for Mimi. She supposed that she ought not to be surprised that her sister was throwing herself into her new bridesmaid role with gusto. Mimi had always gone full throttle into every latest enthusiasm. How long it would last, however, was another matter entirely.

'I have to get back to the studio,' Sabrina said, standing up and throwing some money down on the table.

'That's too much,' Mimi said immediately.

'This was a work lunch, Mimi. I ought to pay for it.'

'Yes, but I'm the only one who's actually *eating* lunch.'

'Forget it,' Sabrina said edgily. 'Anyway, speaking of payment, have you set up a bank account yet? It's inconvenient for me to keep paying you in cash. It would be much easier if I could just make regular transfers online. There's a very good high-interest account with my bank that I could send you information about —'

Mimi felt the usual impatience creep over her that she always experienced whenever dull matters like banking or bills were brought up. 'I'll look into it,' she said shortly. Knowing that she had sounded ungrateful, she made an effort. 'Thanks.'

At that moment Mimi's sandwich arrived. She pushed aside the accordion file and all of the wedding paraphernalia in order to make room for it and then, as Sabrina prepared to leave, she suddenly said, 'It's funny, isn't it?'

'What is?'

'The whole wedding thing. I mean —' Mimi paused and then said with difficulty, 'Weddings are really all about happy endings, aren't they?'

Sabrina said nothing. Mimi looked up at her to try to read her expression, but Sabrina's face was impassive as she swiftly extracted her designer sunglasses from their monogrammed case and pushed them into place over her eyes.

Sabrina left without saying another word. Through the window, Mimi watched her glamorous sister stride down the street, admiring heads turning in her wake. She should have known that it was futile to try to provoke a display of emotion from Sabrina. Mimi shrugged and turned her attention to her lunch, her belief in her sister's Ice-Princess personality reinforced.

It didn't occur to Mimi to wonder why Sabrina had felt the need for an added layer of concealment via the sunglasses, when her feelings were already hidden beneath her mask-like expression.

*

The Falks family tradition of realistic endings to stories had begun with a fight.

Arguing over a single copy of *Sleeping Beauty*, Mimi and Sabrina had torn the final pages. Sabrina had promptly started to howl, while Mimi protested her innocence. Their mother had come into the room to arbitrate but, to everyone's surprise, their father had put down his drink and intervened.

'Stop that noise,' he said to Sabrina. She did. She knew what would happen if she didn't. 'Right. Now, what's the problem?'

Sabrina pointed at Mimi. 'She tore the book.'

Mimi opened her mouth to defend herself but their father spoke first. 'Aren't you too old for that book anyway?'

Sabrina's cheeks flushed scarlet. She was ten years old and she knew that loving *Sleeping Beauty* so much was slightly shameful. But she couldn't help it. It had always been her favourite book.

'The ending is all ruined,' Mimi said, belatedly realising the consequences of her actions.

'Is that all? That doesn't matter in the slightest. We can make up our own ending.' Intrigued they came closer to him. He pulled Mimi onto his lap and she snuggled in, breathing in the familiar, warm smell of scotch. 'All right, what do you think happens?'

'I think the prince kills the dragon and wakes up Sleeping Beauty with a kiss,' Sabrina said eagerly, knowing that she was right. She had read the book hundreds of times.

Their father pulled a face. 'I thought we were making up our own ending, not reciting the one that we already know.'

Sabrina's face fell. She was conscious of having disappointed her father. She felt stupid and dull.

'I think the dragon flies away with the prince in her mouth and she drops him into the sea and Sleeping Beauty wakes up when she's hungry and then she eats a sandwich and goes back to sleep,' Mimi reeled off, without pausing for breath.

Their father kissed her soundly on the cheek. 'Much better!' he said approvingly.

Mimi beamed.

'But I can think of an even better ending,' he said thoughtfully. 'How about the dragon breathes fire during her battle with the prince and the castle catches on fire?'

Sabrina stared at him aghast. 'I don't want Sleeping Beauty to die!'

'Who said she has to die?' their father asked impatiently. 'She could escape.'

'But she's asleep. And she can't wake up unless the Prince kisses her and —'

'For God's sake, Sabrina, don't you have *any* imagination at all? That's what happens in the story. We're making up our own version, remember?'

Sabrina nodded, trying hard to choke back a sob. She loved Sleeping Beauty. The thought of her being asleep during a fire was terrible. In the background, their mother, who had been silently watching, slipped away.

'Anyway, the castle *would* catch on fire if you were fighting a fire-breathing dragon. It's much more realistic.'

'What does that mean?' asked Mimi.

'It's the opposite of the silly happy endings that all your books have. I think from now on we should make up realistic endings for all of our books. Okay? No more happy endings!' He bounced Mimi on his knee and she giggled with joy and joined in the chant. 'No more happy endings! No more happy endings!'

Sabrina tried to join in, knowing that that was what was expected of her. But her heart wasn't in it. She couldn't look away from the lovely cover picture that showed the Prince about to kiss Sleeping Beauty.

The new game of realistic endings lasted precisely seven months, which was all the time that remained until their father left for good. During that time the Three Bears made Goldilocks work as their housekeeper to make up for stealing from them, the troll defeated the Three Billy Goats Gruff, and Cinderella decided that glass slippers were stupid and impractical so opted for sneakers instead. This meant that she made a clean getaway from the ball, never saw the Prince again and spent the rest of her life as a housemaid.

Sabrina hated the game and even Mimi started to have doubts when her beloved Winnie-the-Pooh was made to eat grass and fruit instead of honey.

When their father abandoned them, Sabrina knew that she was as wicked as Maleficent in *Sleeping Beauty*. Because she couldn't help being glad that now he was gone, there was no longer any need to continue to make up the realistic endings that she so hated. She could retreat once again to her beloved fairytales and dream endlessly of a wonderful future, where her handsome prince and a perfect life, complete with a happy ending, awaited her.

Nine Months Before the Wedding

- Discuss and finalise guest list
- Order bridesmaid's dress
- Begin exercise program if so desired
- Choose wedding dress

13

The Guest List

CELEBRITY CONFIDENTIAL: MAY ISSUE

Forget rock concerts and the opening night of the new James Cameron blockbuster! Pretty soon the hottest ticket around town will be an invitation to Sabrina Falks' ultra-chic wedding to Edward Forster, scheduled to take place on the 16th of February next year. Rumour has it that Edward and Sabrina (or as we like to call them – Edina – cute, huh?) have hired wedding planner to the stars FG Weddings, so it's bound to be a showstopper. Hey, Edina – if you're reading this, when you put together the guest list, don't forget your mates at Celebrity Confidential!

Mimi paused in her task of transcribing Sabrina and Blanche's handwritten guest lists onto her laptop computer and frowned. According to Sabrina's rough tally there should be a total of 311 names, which would hopefully be whittled down to 250 guests on the actual day. But who on earth *were* all these people? It wasn't Blanche's list that was bothering her – it was to be expected that she had no idea who any of Teddy's friends and relatives were. No, the thing that was puzzling Mimi was Sabrina's list.

Thus far Mimi had typed 118 names into the 'Bride's side' column. Apart from Aunty Bron, Mimi and Sabrina didn't have any family.

Their father had been an only child and their mother's only sibling, Bronwyn, had never married or had children. Their grandparents, on both sides, were long dead. So Sabrina's list must be predominantly comprised of friends and work colleagues.

She quickly scrolled through the names again. She recognised some of the names as belonging to Sabrina's cast mates from *Sunshine Cove*. It looked like Chad McGyver would be dusting off his tuxedo, T-shirt and two-word vocabulary for the occasion. But who on earth was Nigel Thompson? Or Lewis Reynolds?

With Mimi, to think was to act. She dialled Sabrina's number.

'It's me,' Mimi said. 'Can you talk?'

'Yes. I'm waiting to be called on set.'

'Do you ever actually go on set, or do you just sit in that dressing-room for eight hours a day?' Mimi demanded.

'There is a lot of waiting around in television and film work,' Sabrina agreed, in that reasonable tone of voice that made Mimi want to pinch her. 'What do we need to talk about?'

It occurred to Mimi that a very long time ago she and Sabrina used to have conversations in which both of their lives played an equal role. Although they were on speaking terms once more, their conversations remained purely professional and were all about Sabrina's wedding.

I'm fine, Mimi thought silently. *Thanks for asking*. Aloud, she said, 'I'm doing the guest list. Who's Lewis Reynolds?'

'Hmm? What? Oh, *him*. He's a pap.'

The bewilderment that Mimi was feeling sounded in her voice. 'Why on earth are you inviting paparazzi to the wedding? I thought the whole idea was to keep them *out*.'

'We've giving Lewis and *Celebrity Confidential,* the magazine that he works for, exclusive access to the wedding. We'll donate the fee to charity. It's just easier that way. If we don't invite him, I'll spend the entire day with knots in my stomach wondering how he's going to crash the wedding. Not *if,* but *how.* And he'd probably do something awful just to get back at us for not inviting him.'

'Let me get this straight. You're inviting some horrible photographer to your wedding simply because if he wasn't invited, he'd ruin your wedding?'

'Exactly.'

'Well, why can't you stick him in a corner to take his pictures and let him beg for a Vegemite sandwich? Why is he being invited as a proper *guest*?'

Sabrina sounded amused. 'Lewis isn't just any pap. He knows everyone and he has a lot of editorial power. So he really has to be invited as a guest or he'll make sure every picture of me is horrible.'

Mimi opened her mouth to argue against this twisted logic, then shut it again and simply shook her head. 'Okay then, who's Nigel Thompson?'

'The CEO of my network. If you're nice to me I'll make sure that you're seated next to him.'

'The only person I have to be nice to is *me,* considering that I'm in charge of the seating plan,' Mimi replied snootily. She then relaxed her demeanour to ask eagerly, 'Would I like him? Is he cute?'

'You know that awful ex-footy player, Tackle Bailey, who hosts the sports show on Friday nights?'

Mimi sounded revolted. 'Of course.'

'Well, Nigel makes Tackle look like Germaine Greer.'

'Then why on earth would I want to sit next to him?'

'You wouldn't. But I'd give anything to eavesdrop on your conversation.'

Unable to think of an adequate response, Mimi blew a raspberry into the phone. Sabrina laughed, and for the briefest flicker of a moment, there was a return to their childhood camaraderie. As soon as they both recognised it, however, the uncomfortable, strained feeling returned. To overcome it, Mimi brought her attention back to the puzzling guest list. 'All right, well, there are other names I don't know. Who are Jodi and George Liakos?'

Sabrina's voice instantly changed, sounded colder. 'Are we really going to go through every name on the list?'

'We'll have to at some stage. I need to know how the guests know you and Teddy and each other to make sure that the seating arrangements work.'

Sabrina hesitated and then said, 'She used to be Jodi Morrison. She married a Greek guy.' She waited for the explosion and it came.

'*Jodi Morrison?* As in Jodi Morrison from high school who hated your guts? The same Jodi Morrison who used to get all her horrible mates to trash your locker and who spread rumours that you were sleeping with Mr Gardener, the geography teacher?'

The reasonable tone that Mimi hated was back. 'That's her. We were in the same year at school.'

'Yes, Sabrina, I remember,' Mimi's voice was heavy with sarcasm. 'I also remember how much you hated school, mainly because of the things that bitch and her gang did to you. Why the *hell* are you inviting her to your *wedding*?'

'I have my reasons. Mimi, I have to go now. I'll speak to you later.' Sabrina hung up.

Mimi put down the phone and looked once more at the list. Viewed through the prism of history, more names now became recognisable. There were names of girls and boys who had been at school with them, none of whom had been Sabrina's friends. There were neighbours who had never been neighbourly. Sabrina's first modelling agent was on the list, despite the fact that she had thrown Sabrina to the wolves when she was only fifteen and inexperienced. When Sabrina, visibly distraught at being manhandled by a lecherous photographer, had complained, the agent had told her, in a bored voice, that if she wanted to be a successful model she would need to get a boob job and toughen up, in that order.

As far as Mimi could tell, none of these people were friends or family. Sabrina *hated* most of these people. But if Sabrina was planning some sort of revenge, Mimi couldn't think for the life of her what form it was going to take. As far as she could see, the only person who would be hurt by these people attending the wedding would be Sabrina herself. For on what ought to be the happiest day of her life, Sabrina would be surrounded by a mass of people who had bullied, ignored or humiliated her, even while they had envied and used her.

*

When they were young, Sabrina and Miriam were closer than most sisters. Everyone commented on it. 'Best friends *and* sisters,' the old ducks in the local shops would say, beaming at the two little girls who were always seen in one another's company. 'Now, isn't that lovely?'

And it was — even if it was a bond that was born out of pure necessity. For both of the Falks girls realised very early on that their family was different from those of their schoolfriends. In the beginning, Sabrina attended birthday parties and sleepovers and accepted invitations to play at her friends' houses after school. But by the time she was eight, those invitations had started to dry up, and so had her friendships with the girls in her class. Because it became apparent that Sabrina would never reciprocate. No-one was ever invited to play at her house. She never hosted a birthday or slumber party. The conviction soon spread through Grade Three at Grovedale Primary School that Sabrina Falks was up herself. She thought she was too good for anyone else. If she wanted to be left alone, then that's exactly what she would get.

At night, Sabrina wept bitterly into her pillow but during the day she never said a word, least of all to her mother. She was old enough to have noticed the difference between her family and house and those of the girls and boys at school. While the suburb that they lived in was far from wealthy, the homes of her classmates were all uncannily similar. They lived in neat brick veneers, with lawns that were mowed on the weekends and interiors that embodied the word 'houseproud'. None of the other mothers worked as a cleaner. None of the kids in her class had the responsibility of getting dinner on. They could play outside until dusk.

Most importantly, no-one else seemed to have a dad like Sabrina and Miriam's. The other dads were kind but serious; Sabrina could never imagine them playing the sort of wild games that their dad did. She doubted that they ever burst through the front door, late at night, singing at the tops of their voices. She often wondered whether they did the other things that her dad did – the things that made her hide under her blankets when her mother cried out.

Back when Sabrina used to get invited over to play at other kids' houses, she had always tried to make herself invisible when her classmates' fathers came home from work, just to be on the safe side. She would tense, alert for the warning signals that heralded a swift change of mood. It was safest to stand in a corner and watch, as her classmate flung herself at her father, clambering over him along with her siblings, all of them trying at once to tell him about their days. When he eventually disentangled himself and said a kindly hello to Sabrina, she would be so overawed that she could only look at him, wondering what the right thing to say was, fearing retribution if she got it wrong. Feeling himself summed up and judged harshly, the father would later remark to his wife, often within earshot of their offspring, that there was 'something funny' about that Falks girl. All of these things combined meant that Sabrina had no chance.

It was the start of Sabrina's social ostracism, and as everyone gradually moved up from primary school to the local high school, the ban remained in place. There was a slight thaw around the time she turned fifteen, when her extreme prettiness and fledgling modelling career made her an acceptable friend and a desirable girlfriend, but by that time Sabrina's heart had hardened and she was merely biding her time until she could get the hell out of that god-awful suburb and leave them all behind. Things hadn't changed that much anyway – she still couldn't bring people back to their house, only now it was because of her mum, not her dad. The thought of bringing one of the local boys (who she was convinced only wanted to have sex with her because she was considered pretty) back to their house, only to have him say vile things about her mum the next day at school, was more than enough to enable her to withstand the enticements of a normal teenage social life, such as going to the movies or attending her high-school dance. It was too high a price to pay for the humiliation that would inevitably follow. So, growing up, the only friend that Sabrina had was her sister.

Miriam was different. She constantly raged to be allowed to invite friends home, seemingly unaware or uncaring of the differences that Sabrina found so painfully embarrassing. On Miriam's eighth birthday she finally won the right to invite home half a dozen girls from her class for a party. The birthday party was to be held straight after school, which seemed reasonably safe as their father rarely returned home from wherever it was that he went during the day until well after dinnertime. Miriam was far too excited by the prospect of a birthday party to consider that the timing meant her beloved father would not be able to attend. *From three-thirty until five*, the invitations read, making the finishing time clear and a good three hours before he usually returned. It seemed safe enough.

It wasn't.

The next day the whispers had spread all over the school. The Falks family was 'weird'. Their dad had acted funny, coming home early and insisting on joining in the game that they were playing. He had swung Andrea up on to his shoulders, and when she had started to cry because he was frightening her, he had told her that she was 'a little sook' and had dropped her down quite roughly. Lisa swore that after the birthday-cake disaster, she had seen Miriam's mum crying in the kitchen, although this wasn't universally believed. *No-one* at Grovedale Primary had ever seen their mum cry unless someone old had died. And Lisa had a reputation as a not entirely credible source.

But it was true that Mr Falks had entered the small back garden while Miriam and her friends were playing Pin the Tail on the Donkey. Sabrina, carefully holding the birthday cake on its special plate, had just stepped out onto the tiled back verandah from the kitchen. She froze when she saw – and smelled – her father.

He had just dropped the whimpering Andrea down and joined in the game. It was the birthday girl's turn. Miriam was already blindfolded and she was holding the tail that had been fashioned out of a pair of old pantyhose. A large, sharp needle, which Miriam's mother had sternly warned the girls to be careful of, was stuck through the sheer fabric.

Their father grabbed hold of his youngest daughter and began to spin her around forcefully, again and again and again. Sabrina knew that such treatment would have made her sick, but Miriam simply squealed with joy. When he finally released her, Miriam giddily reeled away, hopelessly out of control, looking for all the world as though she were drunk.

What happened next only Sabrina was old enough to understand. Their mother, Margaret, came out from the kitchen, smiling and wiping her hands on her apron. Like Sabrina had done, she stood immobile when she saw her husband. Sabrina saw her look at the garden full of Miriam's friends and watched an anguished expression come over her face. Sabrina knew that if it had been just the four of them at home their mother would have been more careful. It was why, in the days to come, she would be so furious with her sister for insisting on inviting those girls over in the first place.

Sabrina clutched the birthday-cake plate even tighter as her mother approached her father. She saw her speak softly to him and lay a cajoling hand on his arm, a hand that tried to draw him away towards the house. Sabrina held her breath as she saw the expression on her father's face change, saw her mother shrink away as she realised her mistake. But it was too late.

Their father's hand shot out and grabbed Margaret around the upper arm. Sabrina gripped the plate harder, suppressing a scream, trying not to let the panic within show on her face. Miriam was still lurching around blindfolded, staggering across the garden with her hands outstretched as she searched for the tree with the picture of the donkey tacked to it. The tail swung in her hands, the sharp point of the needle turned out, ready to stab unerringly into its target.

'Over here, Mirri,' their father called out. Miriam turned, faithfully obedient as always to her father. She blundered her way across the lawn as their father held their white-faced mother in front of him like a shield. 'That's it. A little closer,' he encouraged Miriam, laughing now, finding delight in the perversity of it.

With the exception of the still-distressed Andrea, the other girls were also laughing, not understanding, thinking that it was all part of the game. Sabrina knew that somehow she had to stop it but she was paralysed with terror.

'That's it,' their father coaxed, digging his fingers further into the soft flesh of their mother's upper arms. 'Almost there, Mirri. On the count of three, I want you to jam it in straight in front of you, as hard as you can.'

A hush fell over the back garden as some of the little girls began to look from Miriam's hand holding the needle to her mother and back again. Their faces were still uncomprehending but Sabrina knew that within seconds everyone, including Miriam, would know the shameful secret that she and her mother had so carefully kept.

'Ready, Mirri?

'One.

'Two . . .'

In one rapid movement, Sabrina brought the birthday cake up high over her head with both hands and then smashed it down onto the tiled patio floor as hard as she could. The sudden crash of the breaking plate shocked their father into loosening his grip. Swiftly and silently, Margaret escaped back into the house.

Miriam tore her blindfold off, saw the destruction of her birthday cake and promptly burst into tears. The other girls stared at Sabrina in bewilderment, as she stood amidst the wreckage of the broken plate and cake.

'It was an accident,' she whispered, her hands hanging limply by her sides.

She knew better than to look directly at her father. He knew. And he hated her for taking her mother's side.

When the lively, efficient mothers of the girls who had attended the party came to collect their daughters, they were confronted with a scene of confusion and chaos. They saw no sign of Mr Falks, who by that stage had passed out in the bedroom, but they took the measure of hopeless, incompetent Margaret Falks ('I mean, really, the woman can barely string a sentence together') and found her severely lacking. The pinched and disapproving looks on their faces conveyed to their daughters, without a single word, the correct attitude to take towards the Falks family.

Left alone on the back verandah, Miriam sat next to the remains of her birthday cake, tears streaming down her face. She dipped one finger in a gob of icing and lifted it to her mouth.

The sugary icing mixed with the saltiness of her tears created a curious flavour that somehow managed to be both bitter and sweet at the same time. To eight-year-old Miriam, it tasted exactly like a ruined birthday party should.

*

The day after Miriam's disastrous birthday party was the first time that the Falks sisters had a proper fight.

Raging mad, Sabrina confronted Miriam on the walk home from school. She had spent the entire intolerable day feeling furious with her younger sister and she had now reached boiling point.

'This is *your* fault! You and your stupid birthday party! Why did you have to invite those girls over? Do you know what everyone's saying about us?'

'*You're* the klutz who dropped my cake! And what do you care what everyone thinks of us?' Miriam paused and added pitilessly, 'It's not like you have any friends, anyway.'

And somehow, Sabrina, who had carefully rehearsed what she was going to say to Miriam so that she could vent her anger without revealing what had taken place between their parents, was stopped in her tracks by this one cruel observation. This was one of the first times that Miriam would wield her uncanny ability to render Sabrina helpless with a vicious, stinging remark, the truth or logic of which simply couldn't be denied. It was far from being the last.

Miriam had lunchtime detention for the next two weeks as a consequence of fighting with some of the girls who had attended her party and spread the gossip. Sabrina consoled herself with the knowledge that at least now Miriam would understand what it was like to be ostracised at school. They would be outcasts together.

Only of course that wasn't what happened. To Sabrina's complete incomprehension, somehow the fuss over the birthday party died down and was forgotten. Against all the odds, Miriam did not become the social pariah that Sabrina was. For starters, Miriam was funny, and being the class clown was always good for popularity. She learnt how to make fun of their situation and when, six months later, it became known throughout the school that their dad had left for good, Miriam played the situation to her advantage, accepting sympathy and making up increasingly inventive stories for her wide-eyed friends that explained why their dad had left. ('He's a spy for ASIO, we're not meant to tell anyone. He's a treasure hunter and he's digging up a king's tomb in Egypt. It might take *years*.') Sabrina simply retreated further.

Somehow Miriam managed to have friends who didn't mind that they never played at her house or used her toys. As she grew into a teenager, Miriam went to the movies, went shopping for clothes and attended slumber parties. At the dinner table, fifteen-year-old Miriam would talk at a million miles an hour about Karen and Sarah and Lara and a horde of other girls whose names her mum knew but whom she had never met because Miriam was still wary enough not to bring friends home. She even had boyfriends, who rang the home phone and tooted their car horns in the driveway, although, on strict instructions from Miriam, they never once came inside.

For years Sabrina watched all of this from the sidelines, with a mixture of awe and agonising envy. How Miriam did it she didn't know. But somehow, the mud attached to the Falks name clung only to Sabrina, leaving her younger sister untouched.

14

The Bridesmaid's Dress

'Where are we going?' asked Mimi, throwing her accordion file into the back of Sabrina's BMW convertible and swinging herself into the front passenger seat. Mimi hated the fact that she was secretly impressed by Sabrina's car and tried to compensate by treating the car with casual disdain – kicking her shoes off and putting her feet on the dashboard, throwing her belongings into the back seat or slamming the car door with her hip or foot. Sabrina ignored all of these provocations, correctly identifying them as remnants of Mimi's backpacker ethos, which disdained luxuries such as hotel rooms and airconditioned modes of transport while celebrating the 'authenticity' of a fleapit hostel and a twenty-hour bus journey through the Himalayas while racked with dysentery.

'To see Corinna. My dressmaker,' Sabrina elaborated, as she saw the uncomprehending look on Mimi's face. It seemed strange that Mimi didn't know who Corinna was. Corinna was such a huge part of Sabrina's life these days.

'Oh, thank God. I was starting to get worried. The wedding planner said that if you didn't order your dress in the next week even you would have problems getting exactly what you wanted made on time,' Mimi said in a relieved tone.

'Don't worry about my dress. I know exactly what I want. Today is about you.'

'*Me?* Isn't that a gross breach of Bridezilla etiquette?' Then it dawned on her. 'Are we going shopping for my *bridesmaid's* dress?'

Sabrina nodded as she swung expertly into Anzac Parade.

Mimi rubbed her hands in glee. 'Yippee! Can I choose it? Please? I want the most bridesmaid-y dress in the history of weddings.'

'What does that mean?'

'Well, to begin with, it has to be a god-awful colour. Something that *sounds* horrible. Like puce. Or melon. And it needs *trimmings*. Flounces and bows made out of enormous velvet ribbons and rosettes, and leg-of-mutton sleeves, and —'

'Stop being so ridiculous. There's no way you're wearing something horrible. You can look as revolting as you choose when you're paying, but this is *my* wedding, remember.'

'But you can't put me in something nice,' Mimi protested. 'It's against tradition. It will bring you bad luck.'

Sabrina bit her lip so as not to let Mimi see her smile. 'Can you *please* – for *once* – try to behave like a normal person? Just once?'

'I know how to behave like a normal person,' Mimi said, affronted. 'You watch. I'll be so posh and proper your dressmaker will think that I'm a star too.'

*

'We're looking for a bridesmaid's dress for me,' Mimi grandly announced, the instant they stepped over the threshold into the salon. Flora, who had opened the front door for them, gazed at her in bewilderment. 'Please bring forth all of your purple taffeta gowns. Anything in peach with puffed sleeves will also be looked upon favourably.'

Sabrina sighed. 'Ignore my sister. She often mistakes inanities for humour.'

'You're sisters? But you don't —'

'Look anything alike,' Mimi finished for her. 'I know. We used to, but then Sabrina had all that work done so —'

Sabrina cut her off. She turned to Flora and said smoothly, 'Could you tell Corinna that Sabrina is here with her sister, to try on the bridesmaid's dress that we discussed some weeks ago? Thank you so much.'

No need for a surname for Sabrina, Mimi noticed. And no need for a first name for *her*.

Flora bolted off as though entrusted with a mission that would bring about world peace. Sabrina promptly grabbed Mimi's arm and dragged her into the adjoining dressing-room that had been modelled on Marie Antoinette's boudoir at Versailles. She pulled the heavy brocade curtains closed and turned on her sister.

'Stop it. Now. Do you really think that comment was funny? Do you have any idea what it could do to my career if people thought I'd had plastic surgery?'

'Ow!' Mimi rubbed her arm and looked aggrievedly at Sabrina. 'That hurt!'

'I don't care! Say something like that in front of strangers again and I'll do worse.'

'For God's sake, Sabrina, it was a joke. You remember jokes, don't you? In the olden days people used to laugh at them.'

'And I'm telling you that it wasn't funny and that if you do anything to hurt my career I will make you extremely sorry. Understood?'

'The funny part is that for an actress – sorry, I mean ac-*tor* – you really know how to overreact.'

'You think I'm overreacting? Let me tell you how your very funny joke will probably play out. There are two, maybe three paparazzi over the road, hoping to get a photograph of the wedding dress that they think I'm here to try on. At least one of them will probably offer that assistant some money or a freebie of some kind for any juicy information. For a revelation along the lines of "Sister tells all about Sabrina Falks' plastic surgery", she'll probably get an all-expenses-paid trip to the Whitsundays. Next I'll get hauled into our CEO Nigel's office to explain how I could be so stupid as to let something like that go public. Because he'll assume it's true, naturally. Then the *Sunshine Cove* PR team will have to work 24-hour days in order to spin the story, which will make them hate me.

'Knowing my luck, one of the PR team will be sleeping with one of the producers, who will decide to teach me a lesson for turning their lover into a PR slave, and before I know it Danielle will be shooting her final scene on the *Spirit of Tasmania*, and my agent will be telling me that the only work I'm being offered is a rhinoplasty endorsement on a late-night infomercial.'

Mimi's mouth had dropped open. 'But you haven't had any plastic surgery!' She added uncertainly, 'Have you?'

'Of course I haven't!' Sabrina snapped. 'But do you honestly think anyone cares about the truth? God knows the readers of those magazines don't care, seeing as they buy the same crap every week and must know that all of it is whipped up from an ambiguous photo and a quote from a supposedly close source, who is really the work-experience girl. Nigel and the PR team couldn't care less – it's not the truth that matters to them; it's the public's reaction to the story and how that affects ratings. So keep your mouth shut, because in case you'd forgotten, if I'm out of a job, you're out of a job.' She glared at Mimi to ensure that her words had sunk in, then turned to exit.

'At least you'd have Teddy to support you,' Mimi said, trying to mount some sort of defence.

Sabrina spun around. 'Stop calling him that! And maybe that's what you would do, but I could *never* rely on my partner financially.'

Mimi gave a sudden laugh. 'I've never relied on any of my boyfriends financially either. Quite the opposite, in fact.' She held up her hands in surrender. 'Okay, okay. If you're that sensitive, I promise I'll try to be more careful in future.'

'Good.' Sabrina took a deep breath. 'Now you'd better get undressed because I can hear them coming back. I'll be waiting outside.'

*

'What do you think?'

Mimi stood on the dais and eyed her multiple reflections in the bank of mirrors. 'I think I've had myself cloned.'

'The *dress,* Miriam. What do you think of the dress?'

Mimi looked down at the swirling cream confection as she fingered the shoulder straps, which were made out of delicate lace flowers. 'I dunno. It's a bit . . . tasteful, isn't it? And what's with the colour? I thought the bride was meant to be the one wearing white.'

'It's not white, it's alabaster,' Corinna retorted haughtily.

'What's the difference?'

'There are five main types of white,' Merryweather chimed in earnestly. 'Stark White, Ice White, Creamy White, Champagne White and Ivory. After that come the stone whites.' Seeing Mimi's incomprehension, she began to reel off, 'Marble, Porcelain, Alabaster, China . . .'

'You're not an Eskimo by any chance, are you?' Mimi interrupted.

Merryweather looked confused. 'No. Why?'

'Something that I read once about Eskimos having over 100 words for snow.' She caught Sabrina's warning glare and held up her palms. 'What? I'm just trying to make the point that it's unusual for the bridesmaid to be the one wearing whi— alabaster.'

Corinna's eyes had turned dreamy. 'That's the whole point of the design. We'll be inverting traditional expectations – transfiguring the clichés of European wedding narratives into their Antipodean counterpart.'

'It's brilliant,' chimed in Fauna, looking like she was about to cry.

'All right, steady on,' Mimi protested. 'It's not like you invented the internet. Does that mean Sabrina will be wearing puce?'

'Don't you like it?' asked Flora in disbelief.

Sabrina glared at her younger sister. 'It doesn't matter if she likes it or not. I love it. She's wearing it.'

'It's okay, I suppose,' Mimi sighed, doing a twirl and watching admiringly as the skirt swirled around her legs. 'I can't say that I'm not a *leetle* disappointed, though. You're positive we can't add a hoop to it?'

'Was that another one of your very funny jokes, Miriam?' Sabrina asked, in a sweet voice with an underlying threat that only Mimi could hear.

Mimi gulped. 'Nope. Serious suggestion. I thought perhaps the hoop could symbolise, um, the wedding ring. The eternal, unbroken circle of love.'

Corinna's eyes lit up. 'You know, she has a point —'

'No hoops,' snapped Sabrina. 'Okay, take her measurements and we'll have one exactly the same made to fit.'

Mimi looked down at the dress. 'Why can't we buy this one? It only needs to be taken up a bit.'

The designer smiled indulgently. 'That's just one of our standard rough-cut samples.'

'It's not *exactly* one of our standard samples,' Merryweather interjected helpfully. 'We had to make it especially because our samples are usually a size eigh—' She yelped in pain as the quick-thinking Fauna trod heavily on her foot.

Corinna nodded approvingly at Fauna and then cast a threatening look at Merryweather, who quailed miserably. There was hem-stitching by hand in her future, she just knew it. Thousands and thousands of tiny stitches that Corinna would make her unpick and start again if they weren't all exactly the same length. Merryweather had lately started to wonder whether she should go and work for a cheap-end fashion chain store. She was beginning to suspect that she wasn't suited to working for a demanding couturière like Corinna.

Mimi felt a flash of humiliation but, being Mimi, she was about to do what she always did and cover up her real feelings by making a joke. Before she could do so however, Corinna attempted to make amends.

'All of my gowns are made to measure, Mimi. I couldn't possibly let you wear something that wasn't fitted properly from the initial calico to the finished product. Besides which, this sample won't fit once you've lost weight in the lead-up to the wedding.' Corinna smiled as she spoke, utterly oblivious to the fact that this comment might be construed as an insult. She had worked with far too many brides and bridesmaids over the years to view weight loss before a wedding as anything but an inevitability.

'Lost weight? The last time I lost weight was when I had dysentery in India.' Corinna winced at the mention of dysentery in her gilded salon. 'Come to think of it, that might have been the *only* time I've ever lost weight,' Mimi added thoughtfully.

Sabrina was standing very still. *Screw Mimi*, she suddenly thought, still furious over her sister's tactless plastic-surgery comment. *Let her know what it feels like for a change.*

Sabrina turned to Corinna and her assistants. 'Would you give us a moment, please?' She waited until they had departed but even then she lowered her voice, so that there wasn't the remotest possibility that she could be overheard. 'Now that this topic has come up, I would appreciate it if you could lose some weight before the wedding.'

'Bugger off,' Mimi answered flatly. 'If you want to exist on almonds and grapefruit juice, that's your business. Leave my body alone. I'm perfectly happy with myself, exactly the way I am.'

'Oh really?' A not very nice smile curved Sabrina's lips. 'In that case, take the dress off.' As Mimi made to climb down from the dais and move back towards the dressing-room, Sabrina restrained her with one hand. 'No. Out here.'

Their gazes locked. Softly, Sabrina said, 'I dare you.'

Colour rose in Mimi's cheeks but she stepped back and then let the dress drop to her ankles. Her reflection was still multiplied in all of the mirrors. There were endless Mimis, dressed only in a worn, cheap cotton bra and knickers. But it was not at Mimi's underwear that they both looked. It was at her wobbly thighs and heavy breasts that spilled out over the cups. They saw the ripple of flesh squeezing out from under the band of her bra, her flabby upper arms and the unsightly bulge of her stomach.

Sabrina stepped lightly up onto the podium, so that for a moment there was an infinity of perfectly toned, size-six Sabrinas standing next to heavy, unfit Mimi. Then Sabrina shrugged and let out a tinkling laugh. 'Suit yourself, Mimi,' she said lightly. 'If you're happy with the way you look, that's fine by me.'

As Mimi furiously pulled on her clothes in the safety of the dressing-room, it occurred to her that Sabrina, always conscious of her audience, had made sure that her final words had been loud enough to be overheard.

15

Let's Get Physical

Mimi paused in front of the ice-cream parlour. The owners of the parlour were clearly sadists, as they kept a pot of melted chocolate on a low simmer throughout the entire day so that passers-by would be enticed in by the aroma of warm fudge. Breathing in the deliciously rich smell, Mimi closed her eyes for one brief moment as she envisaged the house special: chocolate-brownie ice-cream smothered in hot fudge with a dollop of rich cream on the side.

Opening her eyes she was confronted by her image in the glass of the entrance doors. The unwelcome memory of her reflection in the mirrors of Corinna's salon stabbed her unpleasantly. That had been the first time in a very long time that Mimi had looked properly at her semi-naked body in a full-length mirror, and she had been utterly horrified to see exactly how much weight she had gained. While Mimi had never been as slender as Sabrina, until now she could never have been considered overweight either. But while overseas she had unwittingly slipped into an unhealthy, sedentary lifestyle that, when coupled with her habit of eating and drinking injudiciously, had led to her buying larger-sized, looser-fitting clothes. Somehow the kilos had just piled on. Her only defence was that before she had returned to Australia, she had had other, much greater, issues than her figure to worry about.

But now she could no longer avoid the unpalatable truth. She was not just 'heavy' or 'out of shape'; she was well on her way to being seriously overweight. With a sigh, Mimi turned away from the ice-cream parlour and headed deeper into the over-lit shopping centre, towards the unfamiliar environs of a large sporting-goods store.

As she picked her way past the racks of lycra clothes and the aisles of sporting equipment in search of the diet drinks, she wondered briefly whether she ought to try some form of exercise but then pushed the thought away. Sabrina had always been the sporty one. Mimi was the bookish one. And if you were bookish you didn't play tennis, and if you played tennis you didn't join the debating team. That's just how it was, and although childhood labels could be limiting, there was no denying that they were also bestowed for very good reasons.

She was trying to decipher the byzantine label information on a product that seemed too good to be true – a tin of chocolate-flavoured milkshake powder that promised to help her lose ten kilos in ten weeks – when she was startled to hear someone say her name.

'Mimi?'

'Huh? Oh, hi, um . . .' He helpfully stuck out one leg. 'Nate!'

He beamed. 'I knew it would work. What are you doing here?'

She held up the tin of milkshake powder for his inspection. 'Trying to understand what the term "liquid food" means,' she said ruefully. 'It sounds like the sort of thing Sabrina would have for lunch.'

'Are you planning on losing all of your teeth in the near future?'

'Very funny. I have to go on a diet. For Teddy and Sabrina's wedding. And please don't tell me that I don't need to lose weight. It would be very irritating coming from someone who looks like they do 100 daily push-ups before dawn.'

He grinned but merely said, 'I thought it was usually the bride who went on a diet.'

'For Sabrina to go on a diet she'd have to ingest food first. I'm reasonably certain she hasn't eaten since the late twentieth century. I'm the one who loves pasta and ice-cream and —'

A dreamy look entered Nate's eyes. 'I wish you hadn't mentioned ice-cream. Do you know that ice-cream parlour on the next level down?'

'Nope,' Mimi said grimly, clutching the tin and breathing deeper in the hope that she could catch a comforting whiff of chocolate from its contents. 'Never been there.'

'You're really missing out. They do these amazing sundaes with hot fudge sauce and —'

'Chocolate-brownie ice-cream,' she finished for him. 'Of course I know the place! Everyone who comes here knows it. I was trying not to think about it. Why would you even mention those sundaes? Did I not just tell you that I'm going on a diet?'

He grinned. 'That sounds to me like you haven't started it yet. Have you got time for one of those sundaes now? My treat. If we share one you won't feel so guilty.'

Realising that she was a feckless creature, Mimi sighed and nodded.

'Excellent. I'll just buy these sneakers.' He brandished the box that he was holding. 'Are you going to buy that?' He nodded at the tin of chocolate powder.

Mimi glared at him and put it back on the shelf. 'Do you think I'm a *complete* pig? I'm hardly going to eat a chocolate sundae and then go home and make myself a chocolate milkshake.'

'Good point,' he said meekly. 'Okay, let's go.'

*

Ten minutes later Mimi and Nate were ensconced in a booth at the ice-cream parlour, savouring their first bites of the house special.

'These are sooo good,' Mimi sighed with pleasure.

'I know. It's the little ripples of chocolate in the ice-cream with the melted fudge on top that gets me every time.'

'Stop it or you'll make me order another one.' Mimi paused and considered him as she licked some fudge off her spoon. 'How come you're so fit-looking if you eat these all the time?'

He shrugged. 'I don't eat them all the time. And I look fit because that's what I do for a living. I'm a personal trainer. I run and exercise a lot, which means I can also have an occasional guilt-free treat.'

'Ugh. People like you ought to be given their own island to live on so the rest of us aren't put to shame.'

'You do know that diet drinks aren't a sensible way to lose weight?'

Mimi nodded. 'In the event that using a straw instead of cutlery for the next eight months doesn't work, I have a foolproof back-up plan.'

'Which is?'

'It involves a sauna and several rolls of cling wrap. Beyond that it's none of your business.'

Nate started to laugh. 'I have a much better idea. Why don't I train you?'

'Train me to do what? I've been house-broken for years, I'll have you know.'

'Train you to run and do sit-ups. I could even teach you how to box if you like. It would mean you don't have to live on stupid diet drinks, which, quite frankly, aren't going to help you anyway.'

'You mean *exercise*?' Mimi said, in a tone of deepest horror.

Nate nodded.

'I don't think you understand,' Mimi explained patiently, in the same tone that she would use with a toddler. 'I was the girl who spent every Physical-Education class pretending that I had period cramps so that I wouldn't get hit in the head with a volleyball or end up head-butting the pole-vault. I menstruated every week for three months until the P.E. teacher told me to stop it before I bled to death and let me inflate balls for the rest of the year instead. I'm hopelessly unco-ordinated, completely out of shape, and I hate all games and sport.

I'm completely un-Australian in that respect. When I first arrived in England, I felt at home for the first time among all those pale, unfit people eating chip butties.'

'What's a chip buttie?'

Mimi looked wistful. 'It's a white-bread sandwich with lots of butter and the filling is hot chips fried in lard with sauce on top.'

Nate looked repulsed. 'That reminds me – diet is important too if you want to lose weight. You can still eat properly but absolutely no chip butties and not too many of these, okay?' He tapped the side of the sundae dish with his finger.

'*You* bought this for me!' Mimi said indignantly.

He grinned and moved the sundae away from her. Taking her spoon he polished it off. 'I know. I had to use some incentive to get you to come and talk to me. I didn't think my charming personality on its own would do it. So what do you think? Are you in?'

'I really liked the idea of the cling wrap in the sauna,' Mimi said longingly.

'Excellent. That's settled then. Starting tomorrow, it's Operation Get Fit Mimi.'

'I don't want to get fit. I want to lose weight. Actually I'm not sure I even want to do that.' She knew that this last sentence wasn't true. She was definitely uncomfortable with the way she now looked. She just wasn't sure about the effort that she knew it would require to get back to her former shape.

Nate looked at her oddly. 'If you're happy with yourself the way you are, then why were you thinking of going on a diet?'

Because I'm going to have to stand next to Sabrina while she marries Teddy and everyone will compare us. Like they always have.

'Because you don't know Sabrina! She's hell-bent on everything being perfect for this wedding, and while she'd prefer me to morph into Jessica Alba for the day, the best that can realistically be achieved is to make me lose weight. The rest is up to hair, make-up and a dress with revolutionary leanings.'

'Huh?'

'Never mind. All that matters to Sabrina is that I look nothing like this,' Mimi swept a hand down herself, 'on her big day.'

Nate looked unconvinced. 'I've got to know Sabrina pretty well over the years. I know she works in television and that she likes looking glamorous, but I would never have thought she'd be that shallow. Are you sure you haven't got the wrong end of the stick?'

Mimi bit down her annoyance. Typical. Even when Sabrina wasn't physically present, men leapt to her defence.

'No. I haven't,' she said shortly. She wondered, not for the first time, what it would be like to have the power over men that went hand in hand with Sabrina's physical attractiveness. She looked at the swirls of leftover melted ice-cream in the glass dish and suddenly felt sickened. Abruptly, she changed her mind.

'Maybe I will take you up on your offer. How much do you charge?'

Nate smiled. 'I'll do it for free. You can tell Sabrina it's my wedding gift to her. Okay then. Here's my mobile number.' He pulled out a pen and scribbled his number down on the back of a napkin. 'You're staying at Maroubra, right? So I'll meet you at seven tomorrow morning in front of the Bondi Pavilion. We'll run from Bondi to Bronte. It was nice seeing you, Mimi. I'm really glad we ran into each other.'

'Wait a minute,' Mimi called out in alarm, as he got up and made his way out of the ice-cream parlour. 'Seven *a.m.*? *Run*?'

16

Bridesmaid Boot Camp

Mimi was lying on her back on the soft grassy hill overlooking the rock pool at Maroubra Beach. Teddy's handsome face was only centimetres away from her own. She was aware of passers-by looking at them, smiling, thinking what a picture-perfect couple they were. She knew it was wrong. But she never wanted it to end.

Somehow she mustered the strength to give voice to her conscience. 'But what about Sabrina?'

'Sabrina? I'm not in love with her. Baby, I'm in love with you.'

At the exact moment that Teddy leaned in to kiss her, Mimi's alarm clock sounded, shattering her delicious dream and making her sit bolt upright, her heart pounding, as she wondered wildly what was going on. It was a very long time since Mimi had had to set a morning alarm.

She looked at the bedside clock and groaned. Six-thirty a.m. She had to meet Nate in half an hour. God, she was going to have to *run* in half an hour. Something made her look down at her generous chest and she suddenly went cold. She didn't own a sports bra. That clinched it. She couldn't do it. She would die of embarrassment, trying to keep up with Nate, while her breasts flopped every which way. Heaving herself out of bed, she scrambled in her bag for her BlackBerry and the napkin with Nate's number written on it.

He answered on the first ring, as though he'd been expecting her call.

'I'm really sorry, Nate, but we'll have to do this another time. I can't come.'

'Why not?'

'I don't have the proper . . . equipment.'

'We're going for a run. I assume you have sneakers?'

'Of course I do. That's not what I'm talking about.'

'You need sneakers, a T-shirt and tracksuit pants or shorts. That's it. Stop making excuses.'

'No, that is not it!' Mimi snapped, no longer caring if she embarrassed herself or him. She took a deep breath. 'The point that I'm trying to make is I'm a girl.'

'I had noticed.'

'So I'm a girl with breasts and I don't have a proper sports bra.' If he started laughing, she was going to hang up on him and never speak to him again. Not even at the wedding.

He didn't laugh. Without missing a beat he simply said, 'Fair enough. But it's still not a problem. We don't have to run, we can just do some low-impact stuff today. I'm planning on training you three times a week though, so you'd better get some proper exercise clothes as soon as possible.'

'Nate, you're not listening to me. I'm not coming.'

His tone changed, became sterner. 'Mimi, I know how confronting it can be to start a new exercise program when you're not used to it. But the important thing is to make a start. Now look, it's cool this morning and we're only going to do a short stint as I don't want you to overdo it. So wear a windcheater and you don't have to take it off. We won't do any running or jumping or anything that will make you uncomfortable, I promise.'

'It's too late now. I won't make it to Bondi by seven. I don't want to put out your schedule for the whole day,' answered Mimi, still finding excuses.

'You won't. We can exercise on Maroubra Beach instead. Which is even more convenient, considering that I've just pulled into your driveway.'

Disbelieving, Mimi ran to the living room. She pulled open the curtain and gasped as she saw Nate spring from his car and cheerfully wave to her, the other hand holding his mobile phone to his ear.

'How did you know where I live?' she demanded.

'I already knew the suburb and I texted Sabrina last night and got the full address. I had a feeling you were going to try to wriggle out of it. Most new clients do, which is why the first training session usually ends up being a house call. Do you want to keep talking on the mobile or shall we hang up and yell through the front door instead?'

Mimi looked at him, knowing when she was cornered.

'No running?' she asked.

He crossed his heart. 'Get dressed. We need to get started if we're going to make Jessica Alba jealous.'

*

At the start of the session Mimi felt quite good. Being on the beach, early in the morning, with the only other people around being surfers or fishermen or sportily dressed people running and doing tai chi, made her feel like one of those healthy, outdoorsy Sydney-ites who exercised in the morning, ate muesli with fresh fruit and yoghurt for breakfast and started work at half past eight, glowing with vitality, while their unfit colleagues struggled in looking bleary-eyed and clutching coffees and doughnuts. Admittedly, she was the only person wearing hot-pink Converse Hi Tops instead of proper, sporty, space-age sneakers (Nate had looked at her Hi Tops and said sternly, 'You call *those* sneakers?'), and there wasn't a speck of mesh or lycra anywhere on her body, but apart from that she almost felt like one of them.

Fifteen minutes later, Mimi felt like a coffee and a doughnut. Not like drinking a coffee and eating a doughnut – she actually physically resembled a coffee and a doughnut. Her muscles had gone all hot and watery like coffee. And she was undeniably the shape of a doughnut, and always would be, so WHY THE HELL WAS SHE BOTHERING TO LEARN HOW TO DO A STOMACH CRUNCH CORRECTLY? Everyone knew that doughnuts did not crunch. They gently crumbled.

Half an hour after that, Mimi felt quite good once more. Because the exercise session had just ended and she was never, ever going to do it again. Of that she was utterly certain.

She closed her eyes and lay on her back on the grassy slope that overlooked the rock pool, her face bright red, still breathing heavily despite the fact that they had been doing warming-down stretches for the last ten minutes.

As she opened her eyes, Nate's face came into focus. He wasn't as close as Teddy had been in her dream but it still gave her a weird feeling of déjà vu, even though it was déjà vu with a serious mix-up with the leading man.

'You okay?' he asked. 'Don't forget that you will feel sore tomorrow and probably sorer still in two days' time.'

'Oh good. Something else to look forward to apart from eating celery for dinner,' Mimi said sourly.

Nate laughed. 'I already told you that a diet is a stupid idea. Just cut out junk food and sugary things and eat proper, healthy meals. When you combine it with four sessions a week with me, you'll be feeling amazing in no time.'

'*Four* sessions a week? I thought you said three.'

'Damn. I thought you might not have been paying attention. I was trying to sneak in some extra time with you.'

Mimi looked into his twinkling eyes and realised with a shock that

Nate was *flirting* with her. No-one had flirted with her since Jared back in London. The memory of Jared and what he had done to her made Mimi tense up, as all of her defences sprang into place. She wondered what it was that Nate wanted from her. She should have guessed from the start that he had an ulterior motive. In hindsight, the way that he had been so nice to her, corralling her into these exercise sessions and then turning up at her door, *was* suspicious.

And then, with ice-cold clarity, she knew. He was using her to get to Sabrina. It had happened throughout her life, and now it was happening again. The irony of the fact that she had been extra nice to Nate in the hope that he would say good things about her to Teddy didn't immediately dawn on Mimi.

Without answering him, she sat up and started to brush off the grass that was stuck to the back of her windcheater.

'Mimi?' Nate was looking at her oddly. 'Are you okay?'

She refused to meet his gaze. 'I'm fine.'

'Okay, then.' She could tell that he was embarrassed but was trying to keep his voice normal. 'So I'll see you here again on Thursday morning at the same time. Make sure you get some proper sneakers and whatever else you need in the meantime.'

She fully intended to tell him thanks very much but no thanks. She didn't want to be used, either as some sort of fitness experiment or as a means to get to her sister. But then something inside Mimi wavered. Perhaps it was the constant focus on the wedding, and all of the plans and arrangements that were designed to bring a fantasy to life. The dream of transformation seemed to have finally got to her too. From the moment she had looked properly at her body in the salon mirror, the idea of change had started to tug insistently at her and she realised, to her surprise, that she didn't want to resist its siren call. And Nate was the means by which she could be transformed. She knew that she couldn't do it alone.

'Great,' she said crisply, getting to her feet. She tried to make her voice sound pleasant. 'See you then.'

Still annoyed with him and distrustful, she got up and began to make her way up the hill, heading towards Aunty Bron's house. She was infuriated to realise that he had jogged up next to her, ruining her perfect exit.

He looked at her apologetically. 'I left my car in your aunt's driveway.'

17

The Wedding Dress

As she waited for Sabrina to emerge from her bedroom in the wedding gown she had chosen, Mimi was meant to be choosing a font for the invitations. But she had grown distracted and was instead idly flicking through one of the bridal magazines. A double-spread advertisement caught her eye, and she paused to consider the image of a model wearing a ball-gown-style hooped taffeta frock with feather trim, standing on a tree branch above flood waters in the moonlight. As you would. She was about to call out to Sabrina to see if she could explain the high design concept behind the advertisement, when Sabrina materialised in front of her, wearing the wedding dress. All other thoughts fled from Mimi's head as one, anguished word burst from her lips.

'*No!*'

*

'You're not wearing Mum's wedding dress. I won't let you.' Mimi's face had drained of colour as she stood, confronting her sister, her arms tightly folded across her chest so as to stop herself tearing the dress from Sabrina's body.

'You won't *let* me?' Two spots of colour rose in Sabrina's cheeks.

'She didn't leave it to you. It's not yours.'

'It's not yours either.'

'Why do you even want to wear it? I thought you'd be wearing some hundred-thousand-dollar dress from a famous designer.'

Sabrina had a stubborn look on her face. 'I want to wear Mum's dress. I'm going to wear Mum's dress.'

'It doesn't even fit you. It's miles too big.'

'I'll have it taken in.'

'*No! No, no, no!* Sabrina, if you start cutting into Mum's wedding dress, I'll . . .'

'You'll what, Miriam? For God's sake, Mum would have loved one of us to wear it, you know she would. And apart from the fact that you're about as close to getting married as a nun, I hate to point out that the dress can't be made *bigger*.'

Sabrina had no idea how well chosen her words were. Her comments hit Mimi directly on the two fronts where she was most sensitive. Mimi stared at her for a long moment in silence. 'I don't know when you turned into such a complete bitch, Sabrina, but I do know this – one day Teddy will see you for what you are. And you'll lose him.'

'But then who would you make puppy dog eyes at?' Sabrina laughed at Mimi's startled expression. 'Of course I've noticed. It's impossible not to. Poor *Teddy* has tried to be nice to you but you really are too embarrassing for words.'

Mimi fought down the tidal wave of humiliation that was sweeping over her. 'I haven't the faintest idea what you're talking about. I've tried to be nice to Ted— Edward, for your sake, but I think it's pretty clear that I find him about as mind-numbingly boring as an afternoon at the polo,' she finished, with a reasonable imitation of Edward's plummy accent. *Sorry, Teddy*, she thought. *I don't want to be mean to you but I have to.* Sabrina flushed so it had obviously worked. The thought of Teddy and every other flawless element in Sabrina's perfect life only strengthened Mimi's resolve. Her voice hardened. 'I'm giving you a choice, Sabrina. You can either wear Mum's dress or have me as your bridesmaid. You can't have both. So choose.'

'What does it even matter to you? You haven't told me *why* you don't want me to wear it.'

Because you have everything. Everything. And then you'll have this with Mum too and I'll be left out. Again.

'I just think we should treat it with respect. It's one of the few special things of Mum's that we have left. I don't want it getting stepped on or having red wine spilled on it and ruined.'

As Sabrina stared at her resolute younger sister, she experienced an unfamiliar and unpleasant sensation that she suddenly recognised as frustration. Sabrina was not used to frustration. Frustration occurred when you were prevented from doing as you wished, and, for a very long time now, Sabrina had been constantly indulged and fawned over and had done precisely as she wished. The frustration was compounded by the realisation that she couldn't give in to her initial impulse and tell Mimi to leave if that was the way that she felt; that she neither wanted nor needed her as her bridesmaid. Sabrina did need her. And knowing that she had come to need and rely upon Mimi made her feel humiliated and weak.

Sabrina waited until she was sure that her fury was tightly leashed and then gave her sister a small, hard smile. When she replied, it was in a conversational tone, but her words belied her voice. 'That was a charming comment that you made about not knowing when I turned into such a complete bitch. The funny thing is I was just wondering the same thing about you.'

*

Neither of the Falks girls could have said for sure when the alliances first began. But gradually and imperceptibly the labels were affixed: Miriam became 'Daddy's girl', while Sabrina was 'Mummy's little helper'. Both of them liked their roles and they suited them.

Being 'Daddy's girl' in the Falks family didn't simply mean that Miriam was her father's favourite, although that seemed fairly obvious to everyone. Being 'Daddy's girl' meant being *like* him, a reflection of his personality and mercurial temperament. Fortunately for Miriam, this was something that came naturally to her, although throughout her early childhood she learned to exaggerate the traits that brought her attention and applause from her father. Miriam had inherited his sense of humour and love of acting outrageously, and she quickly learnt, from her father and her schoolfriends, that making people laugh was her key to popularity. Seriousness was dull and to be avoided at all costs.

She delighted in performing, in both scandalising and amusing an audience. Recognising his own traits and impulses, their father encouraged her rebelliousness, laughing with relish the cheekier she became. Miriam's naughtiness and occasional defiance amused him, and she proceeded to push even harder at boundaries, becoming ever more disrespectful and defiant, even when she found herself in trouble. Both her mother and her father invariably found themselves unwillingly giving into smiles or laughter, the need to discipline swiftly unravelling thanks to something mischievous that Miriam said or did. Sabrina, who tried this tactic once and was unceremoniously smacked and sent to her room, realised early on that she lacked the escape-artist gene with which Miriam seemed to have been born.

Sabrina's maturity and highly developed sense of responsibility was both a godsend and a source of guilt for their mother. She was acutely aware that from an early age she had asked Sabrina to shoulder responsibilities beyond her years. When the depression first took hold of her, she often felt guilty at the expectations that were put upon Sabrina. That *she* put upon Sabrina. Later, the guilt faded away, to be replaced by a sense of immense relief that she no longer needed to struggle or to try. Sabrina would look after them. She was better at it and, indeed, seemed to pride herself on her ability to shoulder burdens that were too much for the other members of her family. Sabrina became 'the strong one', a title that was said so often it became her new appellation, replacing her former juvenile nickname, 'Mummy's little helper'. No-one remarked on the fact that Miriam remained 'Daddy's girl', even after he'd left. No-one took the time to consider that if Sabrina was the strong one of the family, the corollary was that the others must be weak.

That Sabrina and Miriam each aligned themselves with one parent wasn't a problem at first. Indeed, it seemed to create a perfect harmony. It was only when the shadowy cracks in their parents' marriage opened up into a gaping fissure that the formerly inseparable Falks sisters found themselves stranded on opposing sides of an abyss. Because arguments meant taking sides. And taking sides meant seeing family history, family truths in different, opposing ways.

When their father left, all of the Falks women felt abandoned. It wasn't until much later they realised that, for all intents and purposes, the day that he had left, he had taken Mimi away with him.

Six Months
Before the Wedding

- Choose bonbonnière
- Book honeymoon
- Order groom's and groomsman's suits

18

Seal-Klum Syndrome

CELEBRITY CONFIDENTIAL: WEDDINGS ISSUE!
If your big day is coming up, then this is the magazine for you! We've searched our archives to bring you the best – and worst – of celebrity weddings. The dresses, the rings, the hair, the flowers – if you're looking for inspiration for your perfect day, then we've got it all right here. And if your budget doesn't stretch to an Armani gown and a wedding in an Italian castle, like Katie Holmes, or a $2.5 million engagement ring (we wanna be you, Mariah Carey!), then maybe wearing a bikini and a sailor's hat to your wedding, like Pamela Anderson, will float your boat . . . then again, maybe not! So take your cue from the stars and remember that you're only limited by your imagination . . .

It had been three months since Claudia and Mimi had met in person, although they emailed each other almost every day. (Mimi had moaned to Nate during one of their training sessions, 'Today I received an email from the wedding planner with the subject heading "Napkin rings" and I was *excited*. Kill me now.')

Once again, however, Claudia was in Sydney, this time for a week, and she beckoned for her assistant Olivia to usher Mimi in as she finished a mobile call.

'Creature of habit, aren't you?' Mimi commented, as she looked approvingly around the exact same hotel suite that Claudia had stayed in the last time she was in Sydney. 'Mind you, if I had the money, I'd stay here every chance I could get.' She stopped, thought about what she'd just said and then almost laughed aloud. She had had the money once and had chosen instead to stay in places that were *nothing* like this.

'You're looking well, Your Honour,' Claudia commented.

As much as Mimi hated being seen to care about her appearance, she couldn't help feeling a flush of pride. All her gruelling exercise sessions with Nate were finally starting to pay off.

'You mean I'm looking skinny,' she said reprovingly. 'Or skinni*er*, at least. *Well* could mean happy or cheerful. I haven't spent hours of my life skipping rope and learning how to do a horrible exercise called a frog squat in order to have people comment on my state of mind.'

'You're practically Kate Moss,' Claudia said soothingly. 'Now sit down and we'll get started.' Claudia gestured for Mimi to take a seat on the white couch. She put on her glasses, clicked open Sabrina's file on her laptop and started to scroll through various spreadsheets.

'Right. I'm reasonably happy with where we're at for six months out. All of the major suppliers have been briefed and the florist has confirmed the supply of red cymbidium orchids.'

'How on earth are you getting cymbidium orchids in February?'

'Flying them in from Indonesia,' Claudia said, without looking up.

Mimi was silent. 'Do you ever feel we should be – I don't know – teaching underprivileged children to read or serving soup to the homeless?'

'Often,' Claudia said briskly. 'The sort of weddings I handle are outrageously expensive and extravagant and they promote trivialities to a level of importance that is unquestionably out of all proportion. On the other hand, I only do weddings. I don't do corporate events or parties. I like to think that weddings have a cultural meaning and a social purpose that is incredibly important. And weddings like your sister's provide employment for hundreds of people. Someone has to grow and pick those orchids in Indonesia, you know. Someone who probably has a family and children to feed and —'

'I get it, I get it,' Mimi groaned. 'We're all one global village and Sabrina's inexplicable desire to have out-of-season tropical flowers is indirectly putting food in the mouth of a needy child. I'll tell her to resign as an ambassador for World Vision before she overdoes it and people start mistaking her for Mother Teresa.'

'Good. Now if you've squared things with your social conscience and we can proceed, we really need to discuss the bonbonnière.'

'Angelina Jolie would be proud,' Mimi murmured. 'Remind me again what exactly is bonbon— whatever you said?'

'Bonbonnière. It's a French word that translates as a small, decorative dish for bonbons. With regard to contemporary weddings, it's come to mean the gifts that the bridal couple give to their wedding guests.'

'Sabrina and Teddy have to give their guests gifts? Isn't it enough that they're paying about one thousand dollars a head for their dinner and entertainment?'

'It's *tradition*,' Claudia said severely.

Mimi sighed and opened her notebook. 'What sort of gifts do people give their guests?' she asked in a resigned tone.

'At a wedding I did last month in Perth, the female guests received a love-heart charm and the male guests received cufflinks. I purchased them in bulk from Tiffany's.'

Mimi raised her eyebrows. 'And that ancient wedding tradition would date back to when? Donald Trump's first marriage?' Without waiting for an answer, she asked in a stern tone, 'What do the people *without* too much money and *with* commonsense give their guests?'

'Sugared almonds,' Claudia said meekly. 'Or candles or handmade chocolates or a bottle of wine with a customised label printed with the bride and groom's names and the date of the wedding.'

'Okay. I'll speak to Sabrina but I feel reasonably certain that their bonbonnière will be somewhere above sugared almonds but below jewellery from Tiffany's.'

'The theme is Modern Glamour,' Claudia said thoughtfully. 'Do you know what might be fun? Perhaps we could give all the women a signature red lipstick by Chanel. And for the men . . .' Her brow creased as she thought hard. She clicked her fingers and looked at Mimi triumphantly. 'Got it!'

'What?'

'Cufflinks from Tiffany's,' Claudia said apologetically. 'I've been doing weddings for years and choosing bonbonnière for male guests is a nightmare. I grew up with four older brothers,' she added. 'Pretty much every Christmas and birthday, my parents and I used to give them either cufflinks or a tie or a shirt. I used to spend a lot of time thinking about appropriate gifts for my brothers and, believe me, the choices for men are limited.' A sudden shadow crossed Claudia's face but Mimi didn't notice. She was lost in her own thoughts.

The idea of four older brothers seemed wonderfully exotic to Mimi. The only male relative she had ever given a gift to was her father. Mimi thought back to her childhood, to before her father left. She could clearly remember giving him a Christmas pine cone that she had decorated with paint and glitter in her art class at primary school. He had sat her on his knee and together they had solemnly regarded the pine cone, treating it as a thing of wonder. Her father had turned it around in his hands, commenting on her brilliant use of colour, pointing out the way that the glitter caught the light. He had hugged and kissed her and told her that it was the most beautiful pine cone that he had ever seen in his life. Mimi had been swollen with pride and love.

'I like the lipstick idea,' Mimi said, snapping back to the present. 'I'm pretty sure Sabrina will agree to it. I'll sound her out about the cufflinks, and if she doesn't have a better idea, then we'll go ahead with both of those.'

'Okay, then. Now, what about the honeymoon?'

'I'm pretty sure we're not invited.'

'Very funny. I mean, who's organising it?'

'It's bloody well not going to be me,' Mimi answered indignantly. 'If I have to organise honeymoon suites and spa baths for my newlywed sister, I'll end up in therapy for the rest of my life.' An image of Teddy smiling at her from a bubble bath in a plush hotel suite sprang to mind. He was holding a glass of champagne. While she was lingering in the land of Romantic Clichés, she added a soundtrack by Barry White, and herself wearing nothing but a silk dressing-gown and a pair of high-heeled fluffy bedroom mules. She dwelled longingly on this delightful scenario before Claudia's voice saying 'Er – Mimi?' returned her to the matter at hand.

'Sorry. I was away with the fairies for a minute. I'll check with Sabrina about the honeymoon. If Teddy's secretary isn't onto it, it's all yours. I don't want anything to do with it. What else is there to do?'

Before Claudia could respond, Olivia knocked on the door. With an impassive face she informed Claudia that Mrs Priscilla Tennyson-Banks-Worthington-Fitzroy had arrived. Without an appointment.

Claudia bit her lip in frustration. Prissy, as Claudia and Olivia secretly called Mrs Tennyson-Banks-Worthington-Fitzroy (for the simple sake of expediency), was always demanding of Claudia's time, and constantly brimming over with enthusiasm and eagerness to share whatever bright new idea had popped into her head. She *knew* that she shouldn't have let it slip to Prissy that she would be in Sydney this week.

Claudia was actually genuinely fond of Prissy, who, despite her appearance of frivolous self-interest, was also very kind-hearted and gave unstintingly of her time and enormous wealth to various charitable causes. The wedding that Claudia was planning for Prissy was to be her fifth marriage and Claudia had organised the last two. She knew her client well. Certainly well enough to give her a gentle reprimand this time.

Claudia turned to Mimi. 'Mimi, I'm so sorry about this, but I think it would be better if I quickly dealt with this bride and then we can continue. Is that okay?'

'Of course,' Mimi said cheerfully. 'Do you want me to wait outside?'

'No, I doubt that she'll mind,' Claudia said, knowing full well that Prissy loved an audience. 'All right, show her in, Olivia.'

Olivia withdrew through the partially opened door. Moments later she opened it fully and ushered Mrs Priscilla Tennyson-Banks-Worthington-Fitzroy to the doorway.

Mimi took one look at Prissy where she stood, dramatically posed on the threshold, and it was all that she could do not to let her mouth drop open.

The bride-to-be had platinum-blonde hair that was impeccably styled in waves that fell to her shoulders. She wore a long double strand of pearls around her neck, and was dressed in a *gorgeous* 1940s-style tailored tweed suit, comprised of a fitted jacket with a peplum and a figure-hugging skirt that flared out just below the knees. An enormous ruby brooch was pinned to her lapel, while the diamond of her engagement ring was about twice the size of Sabrina's not-inconsiderable jewel. The shade of her lipstick perfectly matched the scarlet of her high-heeled shoes.

She was the most utterly stylish woman that Mimi had ever seen. She was also, at least, seventy-five years old.

'Priscilla,' Claudia said, standing up. 'I'd like you to meet Mimi Falks. Mimi, this is Mrs Priscilla Tennyson-Banks-Worthington-Fitzroy.'

Prissy swept into the room. 'Soon to be Mrs Priscilla Tennyson-Banks-Worthington-Fitzroy-*Sheridan*,' she reminded Claudia, with a dazzling smile. 'How do you do, Ms Falks. Are you a Ms? I find so many girls today are. I much prefer the term Miss myself but no doubt I'm old-fashioned.'

Mimi shook her hand dazedly, but before she could reply, Prissy had already continued on. '*Do* forgive me for arriving uninvited,' she said, with a coaxing smile in Claudia's direction. 'Terribly rude of me but I knew you'd be here and I just had to tell you face to face – I've thought of a simply marvellous crowning touch for my wedding to darling Alexander!' She waited a beat and then disclosed. 'I want you to find a father of the bride!'

Even Claudia, who was used to outrageous demands, was taken aback. 'I beg your pardon? You want me to find your father?'

'No, no,' Prissy's girlish laughter tinkled forth. 'My beloved Papa died many years ago. I want you to hire an actor to play my father. So that he can walk me down the aisle, you see.'

It wasn't often that a client request left Claudia lost for words but this was one of those rare occasions. Both she and Mimi stood in stunned silence.

'Think about it!' Prissy said excitedly. 'It's an element that hasn't been in any of my weddings since the very first one. Papa was alive for my second marriage, of course, but he utterly *refused* to walk me down the aisle. I was a divorcée for starters, and then he did hate poor Willy so. Called him a flibbertigibbet homosexual. Papa was right, of course, but still. We had a wonderful three months together before Willy ran off with the gardener.' She broke out of her fond reminiscing with a nostalgic smile. 'But the stroke of genius is that having a pretend father walk me down the aisle will make me look so *young*. Really, Claudia,' she finished reprovingly. 'I'm quite surprised you haven't thought of it before.' She looked kindly at Mimi. 'Don't let me tarnish your opinion of Claudia though, dear. She's very good and will do a wonderful job with your wedding. I'm just a tad more experienced than she is.'

Mimi managed to gather her wits. 'I'm not getting married. My sister Sabrina is.'

Priscilla's beautifully shaped eyebrows drew together. 'Sabrina? Sabrina *Falks*?'

Mimi waited for the inevitable gush that followed recognition of Sabrina's name. It was odd though. She wouldn't have picked Priscilla for a *Sunshine Cove* aficionado. It turned out that she wasn't.

An expression of annoyance descended upon Priscilla's face. 'That wouldn't happen to be the same Sabrina Falks who has booked Strickland House for the sixteenth of February?'

Mimi nodded, wondering what was going on. Claudia intervened quickly to smooth things over between her two clients.

'Priscilla's wedding is on the same day,' she explained, thanking her lucky stars, not for the first time, that Priscilla had chosen the exact same date as Sabrina. It had given her the perfect cover to explain why she couldn't personally oversee Sabrina's wedding, without having to lie to Mimi. 'She was hoping to book Strickland House for her own wedding but Sabrina had already booked it. Fortunately we were able to secure Vaucluse House for her instead.'

'Oh. Well, that's just down the road,' Mimi said, trying to sound hearty and wondering why she felt guilty.

'Mmm. It's not *quite* the same, however,' Priscilla retorted, still obviously put out. A calculating glint appeared in her eyes. 'You're quite sure your sister's wedding is . . . inevitable? Perhaps it would help if I had a chat to her. This will be my fifth marriage, you know. I could give her the benefit of my experience. I'm very good at spotting a bad match. One wouldn't want one so young to proceed with an ill-fated union.'

Mimi was rendered speechless by this blatant attempt by Priscilla to derail Sabrina's wedding in order to obtain Strickland House for herself. Knowing Prissy, Claudia was merely amused, but she decided it was high time to put a stop to any further plotting. For a few minutes she politely enthused over Priscilla's idea for a substitute father of the bride, and then, after making some desultory notes, she summoned Olivia to show Priscilla out.

'She's fabulous,' Mimi breathed, as soon as the door had closed behind Priscilla and Olivia. 'I want to be *exactly* like her when I'm old.' Claudia grinned as Mimi eagerly continued, 'Is she *completely* bonkers?'

'Some of the time. But it's not entirely her fault. She has a severe case of Seal-Klum Syndrome.'

'Of what?'

'I coined the phrase to label a phenomenon that I come across quite a bit in my work. It's named after the singer Seal and his supermodel wife, Heidi Klum. It afflicts people who just can't let go of the wedding fantasy. Some, like Priscilla, indulge themselves by getting married over and over again. Others, like Seal and Heidi, keep the same spouse but renew their vows every year in wedding-style ceremonies.'

Mimi was looking horrified. 'They get married *every year*?'

'Technically speaking it's a renewal-of-vows ceremony, but they seem to put as much effort into it as most people do their weddings.'

Mimi was shaking her head violently. 'It's not possible. It's *inhumane*. They couldn't possibly put their bridal party through that again and again.'

'They can and they do, believe me.'

'Then someday they'll be murdered by their flower girl, who will be deranged after being forced into a rosebud-embroidered dress for twenty-two consecutive years. She'll kill them both and no jury in the land will convict her,' Mimi said decisively.

Claudia laughed. 'Heidi and Seal aren't alone in this, you know. Lots of people do it nowadays. Not every year, admittedly, but I've done the planning for a number of vow-renewal ceremonies for five- or ten-year anniversaries. And Priscilla isn't alone in her preference for marriage. There are loads of divorced people who hate the idea of a de facto partnership and would rather try marriage again than simply live with their new partner. I have a surprisingly high proportion of repeat clients, given the nature of my business. Take Priscilla, for example. It's her fifth marriage and yet she stubbornly refuses to let go of any of the traditions. This will be the fifth time that her family and friends have had to attend her engagement party, kitchen tea, hen's night and the wedding. Now what's wrong?' For Mimi had screwed her face up with disapproval.

'It's sexist, that's what's wrong. Listen to the language. Women have hen's nights and kitchen teas. Men have buck's nights.' Mimi paused for a moment and then demanded, 'What the hell is a kitchen tea? Should I organise one for Sabrina?'

Claudia shrugged. 'It's entirely up to you. Kitchen teas are some-times called bridal showers. They're a bit old-fashioned. The trend these days is for most women to just have a hen's night. Kitchen teas are more about giving household gifts, which isn't so relevant any more, now that most couples live together before they get married and have already set up their house.'

Mimi groaned. 'I'd forgotten about the hen's night. I'd better ask Sabrina about it, I suppose. Bloody hell! *Another* thing to organise. Does it ever end?'

'You've had it easy with Sabrina. The guests for Priscilla's wed-ding will receive six separate pieces of documentation,' Claudia said mischievously. She began ticking them off on her fingers. 'Save-the-date notice, kitchen-tea invitation, hens'-night invitation, separate invitations to the wedding and ceremony and the gift registry card.'

'Don't you think it's a bit *off* for her to ask her friends and family to keep giving wedding presents?'

'They're having a charity gift registry. She did it for her last two weddings too. She's the patron of an overseas adoption agency and her wedding registries have raised hundreds of thousands of dollars for the orphanage that houses and educates the children until they're adopted.'

'I knew that it would get back to this. Between Priscilla's wedding fundraisers and Sabrina's support of Indonesian flower-pickers, I'm surprised you haven't been given the Order of Australia for your outstanding charity work, building temporary swimming pools on the beach for rich people and purchasing first-class aeroplane seats from Paris to Sydney for a *dress*.'

Claudia raised her eyebrows, acknowledging the hit. 'It's sarcasm, is it, Your Honour? In that case, I think it's time we discussed the butter dishes that are to be used at the reception. I'm not *entirely* happy with the crystal ones that they normally use, so I thought perhaps you could do some research into current trends for butter dishes and —'

Mimi didn't disappoint. Within seconds, Mimi had put her hands over her ears, shut her eyes tightly and emitted a scream.

'*Butter dishes*,' she said bitterly, when she had finished. 'This is what my life has come to.'

'Never mind, Mimi,' Claudia said consolingly. 'It might seem meaningless but just think – in the scheme of things, you're practically working for the Red Cross.'

Mimi looked at her suspiciously. 'I still don't understand why you do this, you know. If I didn't know better I would never have picked you for a hopeless romantic.'

'What makes you think I'm a hopeless romantic?'

'All – *this*.' Mimi flung her arms out to encompass the spreadsheets, bridal magazines, fabric samples and a stray tiara that were spread out across the room. 'Look at it. You *choose* to live in Wedding World. *Why?*'

'See, now that's where you're getting confused. Don't forget this is all business, not pleasure, as far as I'm concerned. For me, it's about the reality of earning a living, not romance.'

'Yes, but you obviously love it. And given that you're married,' Mimi glanced down at Claudia's wedding band, 'on a personal level, you must believe in the whole Happily Ever After crap. I don't mean to be rude,' Mimi scrambled hastily. 'I hope you and your husband are very happy. And I've nothing against people getting married. I just can't get over my problems with the fantasy land that weddings try to create.'

Claudia managed a stiff smile. 'I'm not sure that I know what I believe, Mimi. You might be surprised by what I really think.'

Mimi snorted. 'I doubt it. You talk tough but you're just a little romance-loving, sugar-coated icing rose on the inside. I bet you fifty bucks you married your childhood sweetheart and you're still living happily ever after.'

Mimi bent her head to her notebook once again so she didn't see the very strange expression that had fallen on Claudia's face. Claudia took a deep breath and then, very, very softly, so that it was only barely audible to herself, she whispered two words.

'You'd lose.'

19

Atonement

In the aftermath of the worst day of Claudia's life, there was an entire Greek chorus of family, friends and acquaintances, who all felt personally aggrieved, humiliated and hurt by what Claudia had done. This made it even more remarkable that the one person who had a greater claim than most to having been placed in a difficult situation by her drastic actions didn't join in the unanimous condemnation of Claudia.

That person was her childhood sweetheart.

Nate.

They had grown up together, the proverbial girl and boy next door. While from the age of about ten, Claudia had dispensed with her childhood plans to marry Nate, he continued to not-so-secretly love her well into their twenties. Her actions on that fateful day had placed Nate in an impossible position: torn between conflicting loyalties, even though the rights and wrongs of the situation were clearly defined. For Claudia was, without a doubt, the guilty party. Despite this, Nate couldn't help feeling sorry for her. It was obviously an unpopular response, as was his interpretation of her actions as courageous rather than cowardly.

So it was that Nate was the only person who did not leave an hysterical message on Claudia's mobile phone or email, berating her, demanding that she explain herself or sending her helpful links to psychiatric hospitals and mental-health websites, as the only conclusion that could logically be reached was that she had gone completely stark raving mad.

Instead, Nate sent her a two-word text message.

When Claudia read it, she burst into tears. Those two words: *Call me*, said all that she needed to know. Nate's first response was not to judge her or advise her, as everyone else was doing. He was prepared to listen to her, to hear her side of the story.

And he did. He drove for five and a half hours to the horrible motel where she was holed up, bringing with him a suitcase of clothes that her mother had packed for her. When she falteringly asked after her parents, he told her the truth: that her mother was spending most of her time at the church, praying and crying. Her father was very angry. Yes, Nate thought he would come around. No, he didn't think it would be any time soon. Her brothers were bewildered and didn't know what to say to her. No-one did. She hadn't spoken to her closest girlfriends. They didn't understand either. While there was genuine concern and love in the messages that they left for her, Claudia couldn't help thinking that there was also an underlying current of exasperation, as though she had behaved with immense ingratitude. How could Claudia be so *stupid*? What more could she have possibly wanted?

One week later, Claudia's father had a fatal heart attack.

It was Nate who gently broke the news to her. No-one from her family, not her mother nor her brothers, contacted her. The meaning of their silence was clear.

They blamed the shock caused by her scandalous behaviour for his death.

It was Nate who came up with the idea of her moving to Melbourne, and Nate who stood by her in those following difficult months. With the exception of their first two emotional meetings after The Disaster, as she had come to think of it, and her father's death, he didn't act as her shoulder to cry on and she didn't ask it of him. It would have been too much to expect. But he stood by her, in a quiet, solid way that she found immensely comforting.

For a while after she moved to Melbourne, they had almost no contact, as Claudia buried her grief and guilt in work and set about establishing her business. But then she sent him a Christmas card and he rang her soon afterwards. After that they kept in touch sporadically via email and telephone. Neither of them ever mentioned her father or The Disaster. While even now, almost eight years later, Claudia longed to ask after her mother, she also dreaded hearing the answer. Because what could Nate possibly say? 'Your mum is still devastated and doesn't want to speak to you.' It was better that she simply disappeared.

*

For some time now, Claudia had been on Nate's mind. He knew he ought to ring her; he just didn't know how to tell her what he had to say. He thought about it for a week, during which he tossed up whether to write out a speech or just wing it. In the end, he decided both to wing it and to call her right this second, mainly so that he could stop thinking about it.

'Claude, it's Nate.'

Olivia looked up curiously as Claudia dropped her professional tone. It must be that guy again. She knew that he wasn't Claudia's workaholic husband (whom Olivia had never met), because Claudia's husband never rang her at work. But there was only one person who Claudia spoke to like that. Her voice changed; it became warm and she always walked off to take the call in private, like she was doing now. Olivia's head drooped in disappointment. She might have been a master of discretion but she still liked to eavesdrop as much as the next person. Especially if her boss was having an affair, which Olivia rather suspected she was.

'Hello, Nit,' said Claudia, using his teenage nickname. 'How are you?'

'I'm fine. Have I caught you at a bad time?'

'Not at all. I'm in Sydney actually. I've just finished up a very busy afternoon. Do you remember my best client, Prissy?'

'Good grief. Is she getting married *again*? What happened to the last one? No, wait – let me guess —' There was a moment's silence while Nate thought hard. 'D3?' he eventually chose.

D3 stood for Desertion. The other major reasons for a marriage breaking down were D1, which was Death, and D2, which was Divorce.

'Nope. D4.'

'There is no D4.'

'There is now. It stands for Dog. Fitzroy couldn't stand Prissy's beloved schnauzer. Thought it was insanitary that he ate at the dining table with them. I believe that in the divorce papers Periwinkle was actually cited as the other party.'

'So who's the new lucky man?'

'Alexander Sheridan. I think she might actually have got it right this time. He seems perfect for her. He was a friend of one of her other husbands – I think it might have been her first husband – and he's terribly rich in his own right, so he's not after her money, unlike her second husband. He seems to genuinely adore her. And, more to the point, Periwinkle likes him. The only problem, from my point of view, is that he's seventy-eight years old, and I just spent the afternoon interviewing octogenarian actors to play the role of father of the bride to Priscilla. I'm thinking for the sake of realism, I might have to up the ante to nonagerian actors. Do you think a motorised scooter will spoil the photographs?'

'And to think that I spent the afternoon forcing a group of business consultants to run up flights of stairs,' Nate said in a regretful tone. 'If you ever want to swap jobs for a day, let me know.'

'Corporate boot camp?' asked Claudia.

'Yep. The pay is much better than individual training sessions so I can't knock the work back, but, my God, you should hear the way they *whine*. It's all voluntary too – the company doesn't make them do it. You'd think they'd be grateful for getting an all-expenses paid workout but instead they always spend the entire session moaning.'

'Have they not yet worked out that the more they whine, the more you torture them?' Claudia demanded.

Nate chuckled. 'Nup. So when they'd finished complaining about running up the biggest hill I could find, I made them do it again. Backwards.'

Claudia grimaced. 'Ugh. I remember when you made me do that one time. My thigh muscles actually *trembled* afterwards.'

As they chatted, Nate was still wondering how he was going to broach the sensitive subject. He was now heartily wishing that he hadn't chosen the 'wing it' approach. The 'write out a prepared speech' option seemed extremely enticing right now. Thankfully Claudia was still talking, which gave him the opportunity to think of an opening.

'If it makes you feel any better, I'm certainly not immune to complaining clients. I spent my morning defending my business against charges of First-World profligacy. I did it, but only just. I must say, Mimi put up a persuasive case.' As soon as the words were out of her mouth, Claudia wanted to kick herself. Careless. She had got so careless. She had spent years covering her tracks, carefully lying while in her professional capacity. But talking to Nate and, if she was honest, to Mimi, was like being given the freedom to be herself again. She had spent so long being lonely, having professional dealings with only couples, that she had grown sloppy. She was unused to talking to friends.

'Mimi?' Nate asked sharply. 'Mimi who?'

Claudia bit her lip, hard enough to draw blood. She desperately wanted to lie but she couldn't. Not to Nate, anyway. She took a deep breath and rushed the words out. 'Mimi Falks. Sabrina's sister. But, Nate, you can't say anything.'

'What the *hell* are you doing, Claudia?'

Hearing the suspicion in his voice, her temper flared – a quick-fire response from years of being judged and blamed. 'What the hell is that supposed to mean? What do you think I'm doing other than my job?'

'*You're* the wedding planner for Sabrina and Ed's wedding?'

'Yes,' she said shortly. 'And I didn't want the job at first, believe me. But Sabrina's little sister Mimi can be surprisingly persuasive.'

'Mimi hired you?' There was a pause and then, to Claudia's surprise, he laughed. 'I bet you she has no idea who you are, does she?'

'No. She doesn't.'

'That sounds like Mimi, all right.' Nate's tone of voice was affectionate and Claudia was surprised to feel a stab of jealousy. It made no difference that she had never wanted Nate for herself. It was still possible to feel possessive about him.

'Listen, Nate, promise me you won't say anything.'

'You promise me first that you're not up to anything.'

'What would I be up to?'

'I really don't know,' he admitted. 'It's just so bizarre that I feel like there should be a sinister motive.'

'Well, there's not. So please, whatever you do, don't tell anyone. If anyone other than Mimi finds out I'm involved, I'll be fired, and that would set everything back weeks, possibly months, and I'd be responsible for ruining the wedding day.' She let the ramifications of this scenario sink in and then added, 'So promise.'

Nate hesitated. Claudia's heart beat faster. If he agreed, it meant that he trusted her. And it had been such a long time since anyone she cared about had trusted Claudia.

'Okay,' he finally said, and her heart lifted. 'I promise. But this just seems so crazy! Come on, Claude – tell me what this is really all about.'

There was a short pause and then Claudia answered softly, 'Atonement.'

20

The Groom's Suit

Mimi's mobile phone beeped with two voicemail messages from Sabrina. Usually the notification of a new wedding-related task filled Mimi with a mixture of hilarity and despair – e.g. 'Mimi, can you please call Planet Cake and tell them that we've definitely decided on the bittersweet chocolate ganache but we're still uncertain about the rectangular four-tier design with sugar roses. So perhaps you could have a conversation with them about a circular design using fresh flowers. Thanks.'

But what sort of design, Sabrina? Mimi would scream silently, as the message ended. *What type of fresh flowers? What colour? Do you still want four tiers?* Acting as Sabrina's go-between was exhausting; every new errand threw up another barrage of questions, to which Mimi then had to find answers. But this message was different. This message was both welcome and – well – exciting.

'Mimi, it's Sabrina. I need you to write an appointment in that ridiculous notebook of yours so take out your quill. Right. Tomorrow at two. You're meeting Edward at the Armani store in Martin Place. I need you to help him choose his suit for the wedding. Edward has very good taste, but his mother has probably put the idea into his head that he ought to wear a morning suit with tails, which is obviously out of the question. Nothing grey, no garish waistcoats and definitely no top hats, okay? Call me if you need to, although I'd rather his final choice remains a surprise for me.'

There was a beep and then the second message from Sabrina, recorded only a minute later and in the same matter-of-fact tone, came through. 'I forgot to mention that if Edward turns up wearing a paisley cravat, a ruffled shirt or a suit that even faintly resembles the one that Jamie Oliver wore to his wedding, I'll have you killed. And not in a nice way.'

The message clicked off and Mimi grinned. She couldn't remember the last time her sister had tried to be funny. Things had been especially cold between them for several weeks after the fight over their mother's wedding dress. Without mentioning their argument again, they had somehow managed to make it back to a level of professional politeness, which was about as much as could be expected. Nevertheless, it was quite nice to hear Sabrina attempting a joke, even if the best that she could do was a crack about murdering Mimi. But, if she were honest, Sabrina was really only a fleeting thought through Mimi's mind. She couldn't stop thinking about Teddy, and how tomorrow afternoon, for the first time ever, she would have him all to herself.

*

Because she was meeting Teddy, for once Mimi actually made an effort with her appearance. She was wearing the nice dark-blue floaty top that she had worn to the engagement party, her new I've-lost-weight celebratory dressy jeans and a brand-new pair of ballet slipper-style shoes. Even so, the beautiful, snooty salesgirl who watched Mimi walk through the hallowed Armani doors instantly managed to make her feel like she was suffering from one of the more insanitary diseases of the 21st century.

The sales assistant glided forward and smoothly asked, 'May I help you?' in a tone that clearly indicated she would prefer to have Mimi thrown out.

Luckily for Mimi, her ten months at drama school hadn't been entirely wasted. She instantly adopted the poshest of the accents that she had in her repertoire.

'I'm meeting Edward Forster. Where is he?' Mimi looked around the shop as she spoke, deliberately avoiding the assistant's gaze and dispensing with any pleasantries. In her experience, rude sales staff and waiters responded with more respect when she treated them with utter contempt. If she tried to be nice to them, they simply despised her even more. Go figure.

Unsurprisingly it worked, although it might have been the combination of Teddy's name with Mimi's rudeness which convinced the assistant that if Mimi was not herself Somebody, then she was, at the very least, closely connected to Somebody.

She indicated towards the adjoining room. 'Mr Forster is trying on a suit in there. I'll show you through.'

Mimi gave her the sort of look that she had thrown at Mimi when she walked through the door. 'I'm fairly certain I can find my way.'

The assistant flushed red and fell back. Feeling rather pleased with herself, Mimi sauntered into the antechamber, where all of her superiority and haughtiness suddenly washed away in a tidal wave of longing.

The door to Teddy's fitting room was slightly ajar, and as he reached up for a shirt and began to put it on, Mimi caught a glimpse of muscled male back. She knew that she should look away but she really, really didn't want to. She wanted to look some more. And then she wanted to touch. Lost in an erotic dream, the sudden sound of a voice behind her made her jump out of her skin.

'Hello, Baby.'

Mimi spun around and found herself face to face with Teddy.

'Huh? What?' She looked at him in shock. The object of her fantasies was standing right in front of her and was definitely fully clothed. 'But I thought you were —' She turned back in confusion to the fitting room and her shock increased when she saw Nate emerge, still doing up the buttons on a white evening shirt.

'Hello, Mimi,' Nate greeted her, smiling. He looked at Teddy. 'It's about time you got here. You always have to choose the most pretentious places in Sydney to buy your clothes, don't you? You should have seen the way that girl out there looked at me when I walked in wearing my work clothes. I told them I was you by the way,' he added casually. 'I wasn't sure that they would even let me try on the clothes otherwise. Dropping your name often makes things easier, I find.'

Teddy grinned. 'Glad to see you went ahead without me.' He looked at Nate approvingly. 'God, I'd almost forgotten what you look like in a suit. I haven't seen you in a suit since . . .' Teddy's voice trailed away and Mimi looked at him curiously.

Nate hastily intervened. 'Yeah, well, I don't think Armani make running shorts, unfortunately. So, what do you think? Will this do or do you want me to try on another five white shirts that all look the same to me anyway?'

'Why don't we ask Mimi?' Teddy said, in an innocent tone. 'She had the chance to, er, study you more closely.'

Mimi blushed. Damn. Now Teddy would think that she had a thing for Nate. Whether this was better or worse than him suspecting that she had a crush on him, she wasn't entirely sure.

'Sabrina asked me to come,' Mimi said lamely, as though she had been accused of following them around like a lovesick puppy dog. 'But I'm not like Sabrina – I really don't know anything about clothes. You look . . . fine to me.' She said this while gazing somewhere in the vicinity of an overstuffed couch and ornate lampshade. She just couldn't look at Nate. She was still far too mortified that she had unintentionally been having lustful thoughts about him. And probably would again in the future unless there was some way that she could erase the memory of Nate's lovely, strong body.

Clearly enjoying himself, Teddy spoke in a teasing voice. 'But how can we give you our opinion when we haven't even seen the full effect yet? Get back in there and put on the suit jacket, Nate. Mimi and I will sit down over here and you can come out and give us a fashion parade.' He grabbed Mimi's hand and dragged her over to the couch. Numbly, she allowed herself to be pulled down next to him. By this stage, Mimi was a morass of physical desire and confusion. The confusion was because she wasn't entirely certain whether the desire she was feeling was the remnants of her inadvertent lustful thoughts about Nate or because she was now sitting disturbingly close to Teddy.

When Nate spoke, he sounded as embarrassed as Mimi felt. 'Get stuffed,' he managed to mumble, which wasn't the wittiest repartee that she had ever heard from him but understandable, given the circumstances.

'Oh, come on, mate. You can do it. Just pretend you're David Beckham. He's a sporting legend and a fashion icon. Nothing to be ashamed of these days. Would it help if Mimi braided your hair?'

This time, Nate and Mimi responded simultaneously.

'Get stuffed,' they chorused.

Teddy's eyebrows went up. 'Great minds think alike.' He continued thoughtfully, 'I read somewhere once that thinking alike is one of the foremost prerequisites for a successful relationship.'

Neither Nate nor Mimi could think of a suitable response to this blatant attempt at matchmaking that didn't involve the words 'get' and 'stuffed', so instead Nate fled into the fitting room and Mimi squished up into the far corner of the couch, as far away from Teddy as possible, so that the chance of her losing control, giving into temptation and snuggling up to her future brother-in-law was as remote as Armani making running shorts.

*

Thanks to Teddy's newfound conviction that Nate and Mimi were destined to be together, the hour and a half that Mimi spent with Teddy and Nate as they tried on suits turned out to be not as much fun as she had envisaged. Being in Teddy's presence usually made Mimi feel on edge, as she was always trying so hard to impress him, but it was excessively strange to feel uncomfortable around Nate as well. This had the effect of making Mimi almost cross with Teddy for making her feel this way. She had come to enjoy her exercise sessions with Nate and didn't give two hoots that he invariably saw her looking her worst: red-faced and panting, sweaty and wearing horrible baggy T-shirts and tracky dacks. She was also still convinced that the only reason Nate actively sought her company and occasionally flirted with her was because he had a thing for Sabrina. Mimi would have held this against him if she hadn't belatedly realised that, upon meeting Nate, her first inclination had been to use him to get to Teddy. So Mimi had forgiven him and they had formed a friendship based on their attraction to other people. Or so Mimi thought. For the idea of there being a genuine attraction between them and having to care about what she looked like in front of him was appalling.

All in all, it was a considerable relief for Mimi when the men finally chose their suits and all three of them exited the store – leaving Ms Armani still hyperventilating from her close encounter with Teddy's inside-leg measurement. Teddy bid Mimi and Nate farewell and set off for his office. Mimi was relieved to find that as soon as Teddy vanished around the corner, everything slipped back into normality again.

Nate rolled his eyes. 'Don't you hate happily-in-love people?' he asked. 'They always have to try to pair everyone else up.'

'There oughta be a law against it,' Mimi agreed.

Without the need for discussion, they fell into step and started to walk through the city, against the tide of people wearing business suits, towards Hyde Park. Although it was spring, the day was unseasonably cold. Mimi tucked her hands deep into the pockets of her coat.

'You know, even though I'll be out of a job, I'll be glad when this wedding is over. I can't believe how long that took just to choose two tuxedos. It's absolutely ridiculous how much time and energy is involved, every single step along the way, just to get two people to say "I do".'

'What do you mean – you'll be out of a job? I was under the impression that you were so busy being a bridesmaid that you didn't have time for anything else.'

'Um, nothing really. It's just . . . Sabrina's sort of paying me to help organise the wedding.'

'But I thought she had a wedding planner?'

'She does. But there are still stupid amounts of things to do. You wouldn't believe the amount of detail that goes into planning a wedding. So because Sabrina is busy all the time and I had just got back from overseas and didn't have a job . . .' Mimi's voice trailed off. It sounded weird that Sabrina was paying her own sister to be her bridesmaid and she knew it. And she still wasn't sure which one of them came off looking worse.

Luckily Nate knew how to be tactful. 'Sounds like the perfect arrangement,' he said. 'If you need a hand with anything, let me know. I haven't been asked to do anything yet.'

'The best man only has three official duties,' Mimi informed him authoritatively. She ticked them off on her fingers as she spoke. 'You have to make sure Teddy gets through his buck's night with both eyebrows intact and nothing but a professional relationship with any strippers named Bambi. You have to look after the rings on the day, of course, and then you need to make a tasteful but funny speech at the reception that doesn't refer to Teddy's dark past.'

Nate shot Mimi a searching look. 'So you know then?'

'Know? Know what?'

Nate started to flounder. 'Nothing. It's just, when you said about his dark past, I . . .'

'It was a joke!' Mimi had stopped dead, thoroughly intrigued by now. 'What *are* you talking about?' The idea of Teddy having a dark past was both exciting and implausible. Men like Teddy didn't have dark pasts. They stepped from the pages of magazines, perfect and complete.

Nate's mind raced through various lies, evasions and denials. He finally settled on telling Mimi something less than the whole truth. 'I thought you knew. Although obviously you don't because I would hardly make a wedding speech in which I mentioned his previous engagement —'

'His *what*?'

'Ed was engaged to be married. Years ago. It's no big, dark secret. I can't believe Sabrina hasn't told you about it.'

He was assuming that Sabrina and Mimi had normal, sisterly conversations in which they confided in one another, Mimi realised. She had read *Little Women* so she knew the kind of cosy tete-a-tetes to which he was referring. They generally involved nightgowns, reciprocal hair-brushing and the topic was always love. To the best of Mimi's knowledge, no-one had yet written a heart-warming bestseller about sisters whose chief mode of communication was an accordion file stuffed with spreadsheets.

'So what happened? Why did he call the engagement off?'

'He didn't. She did.' Nate sounded wary and Mimi wondered why. 'Look, it's really no big deal, after all these years, but I just think maybe, if you didn't know, Sabrina should be the one to tell you about it, not me.'

Mimi nodded, still grappling with the idea of some other lucky woman who had been engaged to Teddy but had been insane enough not to go through with it. Perhaps she'd had a terrible disease.

'Was Teddy's other wedding going to be like this one?' Mimi asked, deciding to come at the subject from a different angle. She wasn't sure if Sabrina would discuss it with her and she really didn't want to change the topic. She needed to know more.

'Kind of. The girl he was marrying was from an Italian family so it was going to be a big wedding. But more family oriented. Not as – I don't know – I guess the word is . . . swish, as Sabrina and Ed's wedding will be. But it still would have been pretty over the top.'

'What is it about perfectly rational women that the minute they get engaged they turn into frustrated Cinderellas?' Mimi demanded, only just managing to hold herself back from demanding the ex-fiancée's name, age, occupation, details of her physical appearance and her star sign.

To Mimi's surprise, Nate didn't immediately concur. Instead he said mildly, 'Think about it this way. Have you ever wondered why countries spend so much money and effort on the Olympic opening and closing ceremonies?'

'To show off?' Mimi suggested.

He grinned. 'Precisely. But my point is that human beings in general love the spectacle of ceremonies. It's not confined to weddings and I don't think it's necessarily a "girl thing".'

They stopped as they reached Hyde Park's famous giant chess set and watched for a moment, as a player moved the black rook. Adjacent to the chessboard were some shallow steps. Mimi sat down on the top stair and Nate promptly sat down beside her.

'Have you heard of a singer named Seal and his wife Heidi Klum?' Mimi asked, determined to show Nate the error of his thinking when it came to his calm acceptance of lavish weddings and would-be princesses for a day.

Nate looked blank. 'The names ring a bell – let me think.' He looked off into the distance and his expression became thoughtful. Then he snapped his fingers. 'I think I know who you're talking about. Do you mean the same Heidi Klum who had a major breakthrough in 1998 when she appeared on the cover of *Sports Illustrated*? The Heidi Klum who models for Victoria's Secret and hosts *Project Runway* and —'

'Okay, okay. Very funny.' Mimi stuck her tongue out at Nate as he grinned unrepentantly. 'So it was stupid to ask a straight guy if he's ever heard of a supermodel.'

'She's kind of hot,' he answered apologetically. 'I might have accidentally logged onto her website a couple of hundred times.'

'Hot she might be but she's also seriously high-maintenance. Stick to admiring her online – believe me, you wouldn't last a week with her in the real world.'

Nate looked wounded. 'Putting aside the fact that she'd never look twice at an Average Joe like me, why wouldn't Heidi and I ever work out?'

'She'd be lucky to get a date with you,' Mimi said briskly, trying not to notice how pleased Nate looked. 'But that's not the point. *You'd* end up dumping her.'

'Yeah right.'

'Do you know anything about her relationship with Seal?'

'I know they've been married for a while and they have kids.'

'Technically they've been married several times but I'll get to that later. I've looked her up on the web too and what I found was *terrifying*.'

He looked at Mimi doubtfully. 'I think you must have been looking at the wrong websites. "Terrifying" isn't exactly the word I'd use to describe the one I've got saved into favourites. Do you want me to send you the screensaver?'

Mimi ignored him. 'You'll be terrified by the time I've finished educating you. Let's start with the initial proposal. Seal flew Heidi by helicopter to a glacier in the Canadian Rockies where he'd had a custom-made igloo built.'

'Why an igloo?'

'What?'

'I just think a teepee would have been more geographically appropriate. Was it actually made of ice?'

'I have no idea. Shut up and listen. So the igloo had a proper bed with sheets in it and rose petals had been scattered everywhere and there were lit candles too.'

'Can't really have been made of ice then. Not very romantic to have the ceiling and walls dripping on the supermodel's face while you propose.'

'Can you please stop bounding off on tangents? What I'm trying to tell you is that they then got married on a beach in Mexico, but the scary thing about Heidi and Seal is that they didn't stop there. Ever since then, they've renewed their vows *every single year*. They basically get married all over again, once a year, only they keep changing the style of wedding. They've had an Indian-style wedding, and a white-trash celebration in Malibu.'

'So what? They're a romantic couple with resources.'

Mimi looked at him in disgust. He was missing the point entirely. 'You're exactly like Claudia,' she said, frustrated. 'She thinks everyone ought to go all out on their weddings too. The fact that it's a bizarre waste of money and completely disregards reality seems to be lost on you two.'

'Well, Claudia would be all for people going overboard on their weddings, wouldn't she? Considering that she gets paid to organise lavish weddings.' He stopped, arrested by the expression of confusion on Mimi's face. 'What is it?'

'I'm pretty sure I've never mentioned Claudia by name to you before,' Mimi said slowly. 'So how did you know she's the wedding planner?'

He tried to laugh it off. 'If it wasn't you it must have been Ed.'

Mimi shook her head and looked at him curiously, still trying to ascertain what this revelation meant. 'It definitely wasn't Teddy. He hasn't even met Claudia and I'm sure he doesn't even know her name.'

Now he was definitely looking uneasy. 'Must have been Sabrina then.'

Mimi shot him a look that he didn't like at all. 'Must have been,' she said thoughtfully. She didn't mention that Sabrina didn't know Claudia's name either.

In what Mimi thought was a hilariously unconvincing performance, Nate then looked at his watch and realised that he was running late for a client. (He did just about everything but clap his palm to his forehead and exclaim, 'Goodness gracious! Is that the time?') They said goodbye and he disappeared through the park.

Despite the cold, Mimi sat on the step for at least another twenty minutes after Nate left. In front of her, the chess players continued to play out their game.

Mimi couldn't help thinking that if they were all chess pieces on an enormous wedding chess set, Sabrina and Teddy would be the White Queen and King. She thought of Nate and involuntarily smiled. Nate would be a knight – the only one with the energy and ability to charge around on a horse, jumping all over the place. She'd be a lowly pawn, naturally. And Claudia? All of a sudden she wasn't at all sure what Claudia would be. Half an hour ago she would have said, without a moment's hesitation, that Claudia was a rook: an immensely useful and strategically important background piece. But now Mimi wasn't so sure.

So she sat there as the game slowly unfolded, brooding over Nate's disclosures, wondering what it could all mean; unable for some reason, to take her eyes off the Black Queen.

21

The Ex-Fiancée

It had been so long since Sabrina and Mimi had discussed anything apart from the wedding that broaching a personal topic with Sabrina felt to Mimi like she was asking her boss an inappropriate question. But she couldn't hold out any longer. Her curiosity about Teddy's former fiancée was eating her up from the inside.

Sabrina and Mimi were sitting side by side at Sabrina's dining table. Neat stacks of wedding invitations, gift-registry cards and pre-addressed envelopes were piled in front of them. Using a master guest list, Sabrina was ensuring that the right invitation was matched with its correct envelope before handing it to Mimi to double-check the spelling and address against a separate copy of the list. Mimi then stuffed the envelope with the invitation and the charity gift-registry card and sealed it. The final step involved Mimi reading aloud the names on the envelope. Sabrina then ruled a neat line through the recipients' name on her master guest list and they began the next one. Mimi had no idea whether this system of double-checking was normal organised bride behaviour or whether her sister was a psychotic control freak. Her third (and strongest) suspicion was that Sabrina simply didn't trust her to complete the task alone and not stuff it up.

Apart from Mimi's recitation of the names (she had initially tried to liven up proceedings by pretending to be a royal servant announcing the arrival of guests to a castle ball, but this had quickly palled as Sabrina had refused to be amused), the sisters had been working in total silence for almost forty minutes.

'Sabrina?' Mimi tried to sound casual.

'Yes?'

'I didn't know that Teddy had been engaged before.'

Sabrina raised her head and looked at Mimi with a cool expression for a long moment. 'Well, obviously, now you do.'

Then she lowered her head again and silently handed Mimi another invitation and envelope.

Strike One.

*

'Nate?' Mimi was finding it very difficult to talk between gasps as they ran around the Centennial Park running track. To compensate for the fact that he wasn't making her run up hills today, Nate had set an utterly unsustainable pace. Mimi was already completely out of breath and they were only halfway around the six-kilometre track, having run from the Woollahra gates to the duck pond. 'You know . . . how the other day . . . we were talking . . .' she took a deep gasp of air, 'about Teddy being engaged . . .'

Nate looked down at Mimi kindly. When he spoke, his breathing was so normal that he might as well have been sitting down. 'Tell you what, Mimi. If you can catch me, I'll answer honestly any question you like. Let's see how strong your curiosity really is.'

And with that he lengthened his stride. Within about five seconds he had disappeared into the distance. Mimi stopped, doubled over and drew in deep lungfuls of air, wisely deciding to curse Nate silently, instead of wasting more valuable oxygen.

Damn.

Strike Two.

*

That left Mimi with her third and final option.

She was eating dinner with Aunty Bron. Mimi had cooked spaghetti carbonara, which was one of the few dishes she could make without needing a recipe. She often had cravings for it after an exercise session with Nate. She still had no idea how she had been able to lose weight, when exercise just seemed to make her hungrier and eat more, but she was comforted by the fact that Nate kept impressing upon her that there was absolutely no need to diet. She had cut out junk food and rarely drank alcohol these days, thanks mainly to the fact that she was living with Aunty Bron, who was a teetotaller.

Although she had lost several kilos, Mimi still had a way to go before she reached a healthy weight for her height and the wedding was less than five months away. Still sceptical that Nate's approach would be a complete success, she had purchased a tin of the diet milkshake powder and was keeping it in the pantry, just in case. If she was still overweight a week before the wedding, she had promised herself that she would have nothing but liquid food and go to the sauna every day for a week, wearing cling wrap. Until then, she would try things Nate's way.

'Aunty Bron?'

'Yes, Mimsy?'

Mimi took a deep breath. 'Did you know that Teddy was engaged to be married to someone before Sabrina?'

Aunty Bron twisted another forkful of spaghetti and didn't look remotely surprised. 'Of course.'

'Why didn't anyone tell me?' Mimi didn't mean to but she sounded aggrieved. Even Aunty Bron had known!

'Well, clearly someone has. But I didn't realise that Edward's relationship history was of such interest to you.' Aunty Bron shot her a sudden, sharp look that made Mimi frantically wonder for a second whether she had guessed at the starring role played by Teddy in Mimi's inner fantasy life. Then Mimi relaxed. She couldn't possibly know or suspect. She'd hardly ever seen them in the same room.

'He's going to be my brother-in-law. I just think it's a bit weird that I had no idea.' Mimi's hypocrisy was utterly shocking but Aunty Bron couldn't know that. And Mimi certainly wasn't about to tell her. Teddy's past was one thing. Her own secrets were entirely another.

She looked at Mimi and sighed. 'I'm not sure Sabrina will like us discussing it but I suppose he is going to be family.'

'Bloody hell. I hope that doesn't mean he has the right to know all of *our* family history,' Mimi said, horrified by the thought of opening the Falks' family history crypt that contained skeletons more numerous than the catacombs of Rome.

Aunty Bron grinned. 'I think an "Ask, don't tell" policy can apply to the retelling of family history. Unless he asks, I see no reason to tell. But now that *you've* asked, tell me what you know and then I can fill in the rest.'

'All I know is Teddy was engaged to be married years ago and the girl called it off. What happened? What was *wrong* with her?'

Aunty Bron gave her another one of those looks that Mimi didn't at all like but merely said, 'There's not a whole lot more to it, I'm afraid. Although it did happen in a very dramatic fashion. She ran away on their wedding day. Left him standing at the altar.'

'No!'

'Yes.' Aunty Bron seemed to be enjoying Mimi's reaction to her sensational tale. 'Then she disappeared off the face of the earth.'

'Did anyone call the police? Maybe something terrible happened to her?' This was finally starting to make sense. Being abducted or falling down a mine shaft were plausible reasons for not showing up to marry Teddy. Mimi almost felt sorry for the unknown fiancée.

Aunty Bron looked shamefaced. 'Well, perhaps saying that she disappeared off the face of the earth was a bit over the top. She definitely moved away from Sydney though, which is practically the same thing.'

'Oh.' Mimi tried not to be disappointed that the ex-fiancée hadn't been in mortal danger.

'I believe that nice young sporty man of yours was friends with her. He was the only person she contacted after she ran away, which did make some people wonder . . . But, anyway, I'm sure that was only gossip.'

'*Nate?*' Mimi was back to gasping mode again. For the first time in her life she understood why some people found *Sunshine Cove* gripping viewing. 'Nate was the person she turned to?'

'Yes, but I find it very difficult to believe that Nate would ever have done anything to hurt Edward. Besides, if he had, I doubt they'd still be such good friends that Edward would ask him to be his best man. Again.' She watched Mimi for a moment and then concluded, 'That's about it. Well, that's as much as I know anyway.'

Mimi looked down into her bowl, her thoughts as tangled as her spaghetti. She didn't know what to make of any of this. Then she realised that she hadn't asked the most basic question of all.

'What was the ex-fiancée's name?'

Aunty Bron looked up at the ceiling and squinted, the way she always did when she was racking her brains. 'Oh dear – what *was* her name? It was something nice, I know.'

'I know that her family was Italian,' Mimi said helpfully, hoping that this would prompt a recollection.

Aunty Bron thought for another minute and then her expression cleared.

'Claudia,' she finally announced, looking pleased with herself. 'That's right. Her name was Claudia.'

22

Fairy Godmother

'Why did you not tell me that you used to be engaged to Teddy?'

It was five past eight in the morning and Mimi hadn't so much stormed into Claudia's hotel suite as she had hurricaned in. She had actually pushed past the formidable Olivia, who now stood uncertainly in the doorway, wondering what to do.

Claudia sat frozen for a moment, as she called upon every ounce of experience that she'd attained over the years in maintaining her composure when dealing with hysterical clients. She should have known from the moment she agreed to do Sabrina and Ned's wedding that she would be found out. Now Mimi had arrived, looking like her own personal avenging Fury.

With a carefully concealed unsteadiness, Claudia stood up and calmly informed Olivia that she would handle this. Olivia regretfully withdrew, closing the door behind her. Claudia's husband's name was Peter, Olivia thought to herself, which meant that she must have been previously engaged to this Teddy. Curiouser and curiouser. Olivia looked thoughtfully at her water glass and wondered if that thing you often saw in the movies where someone held a glass against a closed door to hear what was going on inside a room really worked.

On the other side of the door, Claudia was gesturing for Mimi to sit down. Mimi refused, of course, and remained standing, her arms crossed in front of her chest.

Claudia did her best to assume a nonchalance that she was far from feeling. 'It was a long time ago. I saw no reason to bring it up.'

Even though she had spent the previous night tossing and turning in bed, knowing what the truth must be, Mimi's expression collapsed. 'So it's *true*? Fuck. *FUCK!* Sabrina is going to *kill* me, do you understand?'

Claudia tried to stay calm. 'I'm sure she'll do no such thing, especially considering that she was the one who forced you to hire me at all costs.'

'Yes, but she didn't know – she still doesn't know – that you're Teddy's ex-fiancée!'

Forgetting that moments ago she had haughtily refused Claudia's offer of a seat, Mimi now slumped on the white sofa. She looked up at Claudia, intrigued, as though seeing an entirely different person. Claudia had been engaged to *Teddy*. It was so bizarre. Mimi's curiosity fought with her anger and her curiosity won. 'What happened?' she asked, in a far less hysterical tone.

Claudia sat down in an armchair but still looked uncomfortable. 'We were engaged. I called it off.'

'You didn't call it off – you jilted him! You left him standing at the altar on your wedding day. How could you do that to him?' The outrage Mimi felt on Teddy's behalf was evident.

'Oh my God,' Claudia said softly. 'You too.'

'Me too what?'

'You . . . like him.' Her meaning was unmistakable.

Mimi fought hard to subdue the waves of scarlet that she could feel rising on her cheeks. First Aunty Bron and now Claudia. Had someone tattooed her feelings on her forehead? 'Don't be ridiculous. He's going to be my brother-in-law. I'm very . . . fond of him.'

'I know what it's like to have feelings for Ned, Mimi.'

'*Ned?* Ugh. No wonder you couldn't go through with it. What an awful thing to call him. Anyway, I'm not here to talk about what you imagine about *me*. I want to talk about what I know about *you*.'

Even though it was now quite clear to Claudia that Mimi had a crush on Ned and was here out of loyalty to him rather than to Sabrina, Claudia decided to leave the topic alone. The last thing she wanted was to reignite Mimi's anger. 'I don't know what to tell you, Mimi. All I know is that when it came to the crunch, I realised that I wasn't cut out to be Cinderella. I much prefer being the Fairy Godmother. That's why I set up this business.' She smiled faintly. 'FG Weddings. The initials stand for Fairy Godmother.'

'You *jilted* Teddy and then your next logical step was to set up a wedding-planning business? You're unbelievable.'

Claudia's smile faded as Mimi's thoughts swung in another direction. 'What about Nate? What does he have to do with all this? Did you cheat on Teddy with him?'

'Nate had nothing to do with it! I'd known him for most of my life and we'd always been friends. I knew that he wanted more but I was never in love with him. I wish I could have fallen in love with him – it would have made my life much easier.' She stopped to gather her thoughts. It was so long since she'd had to find the words to tell this story. She had hoped she'd never have to explain herself again. 'Mimi, I didn't marry Ned because I just couldn't go through with it. Afterwards, everyone kept looking for some deep, dark reason and there wasn't one. I was minutes away from leaving for the church and suddenly I felt like I was suffocating or drowning. I just remember *knowing*, without a doubt, that marrying him was the wrong thing to do. For both of us.'

'But you can't have felt like that only five minutes before the wedding! You *must* have had doubts beforehand. Why didn't you say something to Teddy? How could you just let him go on thinking that everything was fine and that it was going to be the happiest day of his life?'

'Because you don't know what it was like! Afterwards that was the one thing everyone kept saying to me. How could I have let it go on that long? How could I have stood there, throughout all those endless preparations and dress fittings and conversations about the cake and seating charts and reception song lists and all the rest of it? And the answer is – I don't know. Of course I had doubts prior to the wedding day. But I thought that it was just cold feet. I kept thinking that if I could make it through the wedding, then being married would be the easy bit. But when it came to it, I couldn't do it.'

Mimi was silent for a moment. Then she looked at Claudia with a very hard expression. 'Why did you agree to do Sabrina and Teddy's wedding? Are you planning on sabotaging it?'

Claudia looked horrified. '*No!* Why would you even think that?'

Mimi looked shamefaced. 'Possibly because I've been spending too much time around Sabrina and *Sunshine Cove*. That's the sort of thing that goes on there. Based on the scripts that Sabrina has left lying around, no-one ever seems to go to the supermarket but they're forever finding time to plot against one another.'

'It's the exact opposite. I wasn't going to do Sabrina's wedding – I wouldn't have done it if you hadn't mentioned Ned. But then I thought – if I could do it, without him knowing that I was involved, maybe I could make up a bit for the hurt that I caused him. I ruined our wedding eight years ago and now I was being given the opportunity to make sure that he had the perfect wedding day. It seemed like fate. Like a chance to put things right.' There was a short silence and then Claudia looked at Mimi. 'Are you going to tell Sabrina and Ned?'

Mimi chewed her lip. 'No. Maybe. I don't know. How can I be sure that I can trust you? What if you get cold feet and freak out again?'

'I'm the wedding planner, Mimi. It's only the bride or bridegroom who gets cold feet.'

There was another silence and then Mimi heaved an enormous sigh. 'Who am I kidding? If I tell Sabrina and Teddy who you are, Sabrina will kill me and everything else will turn into chaos. You win. You know, I can't help thinking that you'd make a great evil mastermind. Have you ever thought about moving to *Sunshine Cove*? Their resident villain is a property developer called Barry Huggins but you could run rings around him.'

Claudia stood up, trying to suppress a smile. 'I really am sorry that I didn't tell you, Mimi. Do you forgive me?'

Mimi clambered to her feet. 'I suppose so. Providing that you're not planning to spike the horses' water trough so that Sabrina's wedding carriage bolts.'

'Sabrina isn't having a horsedrawn carriage.'

'I know. But slashing the limo's tyres didn't sound stylish enough for you.'

'Well, I'm not going to do anything like that. Cross my heart.' Claudia performed the action and then held out her hand. After a brief moment, Mimi shook it.

'Okay, fine. But if Sabrina is running even *one* minute late on the day, I'm going to break into your car to make sure you haven't got her bound and gagged in the boot.'

Now Claudia did smile. 'Good*bye*, Mimi.'

Mimi picked up her bag and walked across the room. With her hand on the door handle, she paused and then turned back. 'I still don't understand how you could have done that to him, you know.'

Claudia shrugged helplessly. 'I don't know how else to explain it. Except to say that there's a reason why everyone knows words and phrases like "jilted" or "runaway bride" or "cold feet" or "left at the altar". It's because people do it. It happens.'

23

Claudia's Almost-Wedding Day

The first wedding dress that Claudia ever wore was made of white taffeta and had puffed sleeves. She was eight and, given that she was dressed like a bride in that white dress and a veil, she quite understandably thought that she was marrying Jesus. Claudia could still remember that dress. She was so in love with it at the time that it was hard to concentrate on what Father Giordano was saying during the first communion ceremony, so unfortunately the religious significance was somewhat wasted on her. But the thrill of dressing up to get married remained.

Her parents took about three rolls of film of Claudia wearing that dress and put the pictures up all over the house, next to the photos of her four elder brothers playing soccer and standing in front of famous European landmarks. In retrospect, the message couldn't have been clearer. Good Italian boys played sport and went places. As the only daughter it was Claudia's duty to stay home and get married.

It was almost impossible for Claudia to imagine now, twenty-one years later, that that younger Claudia never once questioned the role of wife that had been laid out for her. Despite growing up in Australia in the late twentieth century, not once did she ever think that she might have a future in which marriage played no part. In the

Italian–Australian households of relations and friends, in which she ran amok as a child and teenager, the importance of marriage was always on display – through framed wedding photos that hung on walls and sat proudly on mantelpieces, and through the strong bonds of family.

It wasn't as though it was a choice between a career and marriage either. Her parents weren't that old-fashioned. They believed in the importance of education and supported her entrepreneurial flair, which was evident from her early teenage years. Throughout high school, Claudia was forever starting businesses. Some of them even made money, which impressed her father. But a consistent refrain ran through family conversations from the time that she was small:

'When you are married, Claudia . . .'

'Ah, wait until you have bambini of your own, Bella . . .'

'You must make sure you choose a husband who is a good provider like your father . . .'

Such comments were always directed at Claudia. Never at her brothers. That they would one day get married was probably also taken for granted. But for Claudia, the sole daughter of the family, marriage was not just one element of the wonderful life that her parents wanted for her. It was the foremost element, the one that would ensure her happiness forever after, that would mean her mother and father could sit back and know that their job as good parents was complete, once their daughter was a wife and a mother.

*

Claudia had met Ned a decade ago, through Nate. She was nineteen. Nate had been hired by one of the big investment banks in the city to conduct lunchtime training sessions for some of its staff. Ed was one of his clients and they had gradually become mates.

'You'll fall in love with him,' Nate had warned her glumly, as they drove towards a bar one night. 'Everyone does.'

'Everyone?' she teased. 'What about your mum?'

'She'd leave Dad in a second if Ed said the word.'

'What's so great about him anyway?'

'Oh, you know. Just the usual. Good-looking, well educated, sporty, articulate, dresses well, has a social conscience and befriends home-less puppies.'

'I think I'm starting to dislike him already. He sounds annoyingly perfect.'

'He is. But unfortunately he's not annoying. And he has a way of making you like him. I wanted to *hate* him when he first began train-ing with me but it didn't work. He's a great guy,' Nate finished, in a tone of resignation. But then he brightened up. 'The only good thing is I don't think you're his type.'

'If he has a type, then I'm definitely not his type,' Claudia said waspishly.

'That means you have a type,' Nate pointed out. 'Your type is the sort of man who doesn't have a type. Have I mentioned that I really will date anyone? That includes close relations, women with dubious political views or criminal records, and anyone who has ever owned a Matchbox Twenty CD. Which should be a criminal offence in my opinion.'

She laughed, and leaning over she planted a kiss on his cheek.

He took his eyes off the road for a moment to look at her earnestly. 'Just promise me you'll get a crush on him and then get over it, okay? No falling in love for real?'

She looked at him and felt her heart turn over. He was in love with her and made no attempt to conceal it. 'I promise,' she said solemnly.

Three hours later Claudia was holding true to her word. She had a crush on Ned.

One month later they were seriously dating.

Six weeks after that first meeting she had broken her promise and with it, Nate's heart, by falling head over heels in love with Ned. Then, eight months later, Ned proposed.

*

Claudia knew that her parents would have preferred a son-in-law of Italian origin. They could be racist like that. But she had faith in Ned. Before she brought him home to meet them for the first time, she bet him twenty dollars that her parents and brothers wouldn't hold out half an hour against him.

They lasted ten minutes.

Ned's saving grace was that he liked soccer, which was almost unheard of for a 'skip'. Claudia's brothers declared him passable, and her father was impressed by his job and obvious breeding. Her mum was female so she simply fell for him like every other woman on the planet.

When they announced their engagement, her parents both cried. Ned had done the 'right' thing and formally asked her father for her hand in marriage beforehand. Claudia could remember feeling both pleased that he had adhered to tradition, which gratified her parents, and slightly miffed that her father had known that she would be getting married before she did.

Regardless, her parents' joy was palpable. Their only daughter was getting married. They could look forward to more grandchildren. As parents, they were a success.

Claudia looked at the pride and pleasure brimming from their faces and felt a surge of supreme happiness.

She was getting married. Her destiny would soon be fulfilled.

*

For the next year, Claudia was in heaven. The only (small) cloud on her horizon was that Ned's parents were not as thrilled about the wedding as her own parents had been. Harold and Blanche Forster would have infinitely preferred the young couple's engagement to be longer as they were worried about Claudia's youth and concerned that their son was rushing into marriage primarily because of his fiancée's family's strong religious beliefs. Claudia ended up wishing that they could have had a longer engagement too but for different reasons. Chief of these was the dawning realisation that, at the risk of mixing her Mediterranean metaphors, organising a wedding of Italian proportions was a Herculean task.

Despite the time pressures and logistical nightmares, there was no denying that she *loved* it. She adored every moment and every minute detail. For a girl who had grown up in a male-dominated household it was bliss – like plunging into a delicious cloud of tulle, all sweetness and light, where female concerns of dress and hairstyle and shoes assumed monumental significance. Claudia loved being immersed in the tiny details of sugar roses and corsages and invitation design. She had always had formidable organisational skills and an eye for detail, and she now discovered that she could use this proficiency to plan the most perfect day of her life.

And then the perfect day dawned and on that day, that terrible, awful day she still couldn't bear to think about, everything suddenly went wrong.

*

It was almost time to leave for the church. Claudia had been surrounded by her bridesmaids and family for the entire day, but oddly, now, she found herself alone, in her parents' bedroom. Her mother's dressing-table mirror was the only decent-sized mirror in the house. One of her bridesmaids had had an emergency with a popped button on her dress and the other bridesmaids had whisked her away to fix it, terrified that a disaster of this scale would ruin the day. Claudia's mother was in the downstairs bathroom, finishing her make-up. (She had refused to put her make-up on until Claudia was safely ensconced in her wedding dress, in case she somehow stained Claudia's gown with lipstick or foundation. How exactly this might happen Claudia had no idea but it had been wiser not to argue.)

Now Claudia could hear the noise and bustle up and down the stairs of her brothers and their wives and girlfriends and children as they assembled all of the children in the back garden for a group photograph. She could hear the high-pitched excitement and nervous giggles of her bridesmaids as they hastily fixed the errant button in what, she realised with a shock, would henceforth be her former bedroom. Above all else she could hear her father's voice singing 'That's Amore' (out of tune). Why he was singing so loudly she had no idea. He hardly ever sang, mainly because he couldn't. Claudia would never know that the morning of her wedding, her father wandered around the house, singing at the top of his voice so that he wouldn't give way to tears too early in the day. Her mother, who was carefully applying her lipstick, knew exactly why he was doing it. Claudia's mother paused for a moment as she listened. The sound of all those terrible wrong notes filled her heart with such love that she wanted to both smile and weep. She did neither, of course. An Italian mother, especially on a wedding day, and especially when she is the mother of the bride, is made of exceptionally strong stuff. But she did permit herself a moment of quiet gratitude to God. Her marriage had been a blessedly happy one for almost thirty years.

Claudia looked at herself in the dressing-table mirror. And, thirteen years after she had worn her first wedding dress, she was still thinking about how much she loved her dress, as well as how beautiful the flowers in her bouquet were and how she was dying to see the reception venue decorated exactly as she had carefully planned it.

Claudia was thinking about every aspect of the wedding, in fact, except one.

The groom.

Ned's face flashed into her mind and that's when it all began to unravel. Because it suddenly occurred to her that she was going to be married to him *forever*. Claudia had been brought up Roman Catholic. No-one in her large extended family had ever gotten divorced. That wasn't to say that there weren't unhappy marriages amongst them but that was a different story.

Trembling, she sat down and forced herself to think about Ned. She loved him. Of course she loved him. *Everyone* loved him. He was one of those people who moved through life with the gifts and blessings bestowed by the fairy godmothers at birth, without the threat of a curse to come hanging over him.

But, if she was honest, should her love for Ned more properly be called *pride*? Hadn't she been the teensiest bit thrilled that *he* had singled *her* out? The curly-headed brunette in a sea of glamorous Aussie blondes?

He was very proper. A bit stiff. He was always immersed in his work, which meant that he often couldn't come to her family gatherings, disappointing her mother tremendously.

He was charming, but next to the template of masculinity that her brothers had set for her growing up, he could also be a bit – Claudia could hardly believe that she was about to even *think* this – weak. When they argued she always won – primarily through default because Ned never argued back. She had started to suspect that he didn't actually know how. The vociferous family arguments that had taught Claudia to attack and feint and strategically withdraw before lunging in for the kill were unknown to Ned. She had only ever once witnessed his family having a 'disagreement'. (They were too well bred to have 'fights'.) Ned's mother Blanche had said something that everyone had obviously opposed. Claudia had been about to launch a spirited challenge when she glanced around the table. Ned's father was faintly smiling, as though Blanche had been joking. His sister Phoebe looked disapproving. Harry had coughed uncomfortably and Ned had simply looked away. And that was it. The subject was dropped.

At the time Claudia had felt faint discomfort, as though she had sat silently by or pretended to be amused by a racist joke, even though Blanche's opinion hadn't been anywhere near that awful. But now, the recollection made her feel positively ill. It wasn't just that she was going to marry Ned; she was about to become a part of his *family*. His well-bred, polite, utterly *passionless* family.

She couldn't do it. She wasn't one of them and she didn't *want* to be one of them.

The truth was finally right in front of her. It was the wedding that she was in love with, not the idea of marriage. Claudia had said yes to Ned because it would never occur to a girl who had been brought up as she had to say no to a man on bended knee.

But it had all been an illusion. A wonderful, glorious roller-coaster of planning and preparation, only now, abruptly, it was time to get off.

So she did.

In spectacularly dramatic style.

As Ned stood at the altar in the crowded church with Nate by his side, ten kilometres away Claudia was ripping off her wedding dress, tearing the delicate lace and sending the small pearl buttons flying. She stripped off the dress, pulled on her jeans and T-shirt and ran barefoot to her car. The last thing she saw in the rear-view mirror as she drove away was her father, his face ashen as he waved his arms and pleaded with her to stop. She drove non-stop for five hours until she finally pulled over. Sitting in her car on the side of the desolate freeway she finally started to sob, as her heart splintered inside her and the consequences of what she had just done began to sink in.

*

A few months after moving to Melbourne (although escaping to Melbourne was more accurate), Claudia finally picked up the pieces of herself that remained after her disastrous wedding day that never was and faced the fact she had been living in wedding fantasy land. This was immediately followed by the realisation that this land was still the only place that she truly wanted to be. From this awakening was born her business idea, but she knew that it was doomed to fail for one reason and one reason only: superstition.

No bride (and it was always the bride who made the big decisions) would hire a wedding planner who had run away from her own wedding. That sort of karma was not just bad; it had been left to rot in a haunted house. So before Claudia could even think about practicalities like a work space or a name for her company, she had to overcome the problem of herself.

She decided to lie.

She never felt particularly good about this decision and she never, not once, told the story of her fake wedding and imaginary husband to any client who hadn't directly asked about her marital status. The problem, as she had known from the start, was that every single client asked.

Radiant with happiness and bursting with enthusiasm for all things wedding-related, the newly engaged couples who came to see Claudia wanted to be reassured that not only were they in the hands of a consummate professional, but that the service provided would also be personal. Weddings were deeply emotional affairs and no prospective bride or groom ever purchased a wedding-related product or a service from anyone who treated them like anything other than a trusted confidant. So Claudia confided.

'When did you get married?' they would ask, glancing at the reassuring wedding band that Claudia had purchased for herself.

Claudia would smile. 'Three years ago.' Three years was long enough for her pretend marriage to seem comfortably solid and short enough for her clients to relate to her as a newlywed.

'What does your husband do? What's his name?'

Claudia's imaginary husband's name was Peter and he was a mid-level manager at a large multinational. His job had to sound both vague and dull so that it wouldn't precipitate more questions. It never did. Besides which, her husband wasn't that interesting to her clients. It was the wedding they wanted to hear about.

'Your wedding must have been *amazing*,' they would coo, eyes round with imagined wonders like specially trained flocks of doves spelling out entwined initials in the sky and a reception that was so painfully chic, bridal magazines had been clamouring for the exclusive rights with blank cheques in hand.

'We liked it,' Claudia would say modestly. When pressed for details she would tell of an enchanting mid-winter ceremony conducted at dusk, near a spectacular waterfall deep in the ash-mountain forests of the Dandenong Ranges. Two hundred of their closest friends and relatives had attended. Claudia had carried a bridal bouquet of tuberoses and worn a floaty, wisp of a dress, made of chiffon, with beaded spaghetti straps. A note of whimsy was added by the attendance of their beloved hound, Bruno.

No-one ever remarked on the fact that it would be virtually impossible to have a bouquet of tuberoses, which only bloom in summer, in July. Not once did anyone query Claudia's professional judgement in scheduling her wedding to take place outdoors, near nightfall, next to freezing cold water in the middle of winter. Nor did they express concern about the appropriateness of her outfit for the sub-zero temperatures that occur in the mountains at that time of year. Not a single client ever wondered whether, after the ceremony, her guests had been provided with individual torches to aid their stumbling progress back through the now pitch-black forest to the reception. And as for her long-gone childhood companion, Bruno, dogs were forbidden under all circumstances in national parks and the only exception ever made was for guide or assistance dogs.

In short, no-one ever wanted to be bothered by prosaic details when it came to their ideal of a perfect, romantic wedding.

Which was exactly why they hired Claudia.

Haunted by guilt over her abandoned wedding and her father's death, Claudia sought refuge in the most improbable place of all. By immersing herself in the organisation of other people's dream weddings she found a way to live in her fantasy land for good – but this time without hurting anyone else.

Four Months
Before the Wedding

- Renew contact with old friends whom you
  wish to invite to the wedding

- Arrange first consultation with hairdresser
  and make-up artist

24

Ethan

'Just one kiss,' Chad was teasing her.

Just one kiss. It couldn't hurt . . .

Sabrina leaned in to him, feeling his strong arms enfolding her. Bending her head back, his lips met hers and she gave in to the familiar feeling of his muscular body pressed against hers.

'And – cut! Good work, both of you. If Sabrina wasn't about to become a respectable married woman, I'd be starting rumours about you two.' The director winked at Sabrina as she disentangled herself from Chad's sweaty embrace. Chad was perennially sweaty under the hot studio lights. Given that it was always meant to be sunny blue skies in *Sunshine Cove*, Sabrina was never entirely sure whether he was a brilliant method actor or just had a disturbing gland problem.

Danielle was about to get married. Again. Sabrina had lost track of the number of times her alter-ego had either tied the knot or else attempted to. She did have fond memories of Danielle's first marriage attempt, which had been to a mysterious stranger who had come to *Sunshine Cove*. Thankfully the relationship had never been consummated given that the mysterious stranger had turned out to be Danielle's half-brother. There had also been chaotic scenes at Danielle's wedding to heart-throb Ethan Carter. Ethan's character, Mickey Donaldson, had been bitten by a snake on his way to the wedding, leaving Danielle thinking that she had been jilted at the altar. Luckily all had been resolved and tear-jerking nuptials had taken place at Mickey's hospital bedside. (Resulting in the second highest ratings *Sunshine Cove* had ever recorded. First place belonged to the birth of Danielle and Mickey's daughter, who had promptly aged seven years overnight so that she could become an interesting character.)

Looking at Chad, who was now towelling himself dry, Sabrina thought longingly of the old days with Ethan, who had not only been a professional through and through, but had also been great fun to work with. And only normally moist. But Ethan had quit *Sunshine Cove* and left Australia to seek his fortune in Los Angeles. They occasionally spoke on the phone but Sabrina still missed him terribly. Ethan had been more than just a cast mate to Sabrina; he had been a rare friend.

As Sabrina made her way down the hall to her dressing-room, someone stepped out from a side corridor behind her and placed their hands over her eyes.

'Guess who?' boomed a deep male voice.

'*Ethan?*' she gasped, whirling around and thrusting his hands away from her face. 'What *on earth* are you doing here?'

'Now is that any way to greet your former husband? And the father of your child? What *was* our daughter's name again? It was horrible, I remember.' His green eyes twinkled at her and she thought, not for the first time, that Ethan really was the most devastatingly handsome man she had ever met in her life, even including Edward.

She flung herself into his open arms and kissed him resoundingly on the cheek, causing more than one passing crew member to raise an eyebrow. Sabrina was not renowned for being the demonstrative type.

'Dorothy,' Sabrina said, laughing up at him. 'Our daughter's name was Dorothy.'

'God, that's right. Dorothy. I always had the overwhelming urge to click my heels three times whenever she entered a scene. Let's see, I've been away for almost three years, so how old is dear Dorothy nowadays? She must be close to a double century, surely.'

Sabrina laughed and linked her arm through his, pulling him in the direction of her dressing-room. 'I've been a dreadful mother. Dorothy got socked.'

'*No,*' Ethan gasped, in mock horror. 'Why?'

'Socked' was a term that Ethan had coined years ago. It was a play on the word 'sacked', of course, but was used only to refer to those specific cases where not only was an actor fired from *Sunshine Cove*, but their (usually minor) character suffered the indignity of not even having their story-line concluded. Like a misplaced sock, they simply disappeared without a trace, leaving the audience with utterly no explanation whatsoever as to what had happened to them.

'The girl who played Dorothy hit adolescence and they already had the teenage-girl side of the story wrapped up with Tiffany – do you remember her? The girl who played Tiffany had two hit singles in the UK and then quietly disappeared down the gurgler. Anyway, poor old Dorothy wasn't really needed any more so she got socked.'

'What a terrible shame. She was such a promising child too. I seem to remember she walked and talked before her first birthday.'

'That was because she was being played by a seven-year-old,' Sabrina reminded him. She pushed open the door to her dressing-room and led him in. 'Now forget about Dorothy and tell me about you. What are you doing back in Australia?'

He grinned lopsidedly as he took a seat. 'I've come home with my tail between my legs.' He paused for extra drama and then announced, 'I'm a failure!'

Knowing Ethan's preferences, Sabrina opened a bottle of champagne from the bar fridge in the corner and poured him a flute. As he accepted it, she looked at him in disbelief. 'I don't believe it. You were doing so well. I kept seeing your name on all those films —'

'Spend a lot of time in the straight-to-DVD section of the video library, do you?' he grinned. 'Oh, don't look like that. It's not like I don't *know*. I went to Hollywood like a million actors before me and the million that will come after me. I tried my luck and had the worst of all possible outcomes. I was a modest success. I became a perfectly respectable, jobbing actor who was never going to hit the big time and would never die young and handsome and broken by the City of Dreams in a seedy hotel room either.'

'But if you were getting steady work, why have you come home?' she asked, sitting in the chair facing him, her own drink a bottle of water.

'Ego. Pure and simple. I was a star here – not as big as you've become, from all I hear, but a star nonetheless. Over there I was nothing – I was just one more begging actor whom no-one, not even my agent, recognised. No invitations to the cool parties, no freebies, no fans – God, Sabrina, it got so bad that I even missed the *fans*. Spotty teenage girls howling my name and begging me to sign their posters used to drive me out of my mind. In L.A. I even started to miss that weird stalker girl who used to wait outside the studio every day.'

'She transferred her obsession to Chad after you left,' Sabrina informed him.

'To *Chad?*' he repeated in disgust. 'Bloody hell, even stalkers don't have loyalty any more. Anyway, I just got sick of it all. So here I am, begging for work.'

Sabrina sat upright. 'Is Mickey coming back to *Sunshine Cove?*' she asked, breathless with excitement. She'd give anything to work with Ethan again and to escape Chad's sweaty embraces.

Ethan raised an eyebrow. 'How exactly could Mickey reappear given that he was eaten by a shark?'

'Damn, I'd forgotten about that. That scriptwriter was completely in love with you and she was *so* pissed off when she heard you'd quit. She must have really had it in for you to end Mickey that way.'

'Well, she might have written it but she did it with Nigel's blessing. I believe the last thing dear old Nige said to me was, 'Don't even think about coming back here and licking my arse to get your old job back, you cock-sucking Hollywood sell-out.' Ethan paused and took a sip of his champagne. 'Actually maybe he didn't say that to me. That might have been what he wrote on my farewell card. Either way, he was more accurate than he knew.' He raised one eyebrow at Sabrina and she laughed.

'Have you seen Nigel yet?'

'But of course. I'm exceptionally talented, as we both know, but even I haven't conquered the art of arse-licking from a distance. The good news is it was successful arse-licking.'

Sabrina clasped her hands together. 'But if Mickey was eaten by a shark how can you be coming back to the show?'

Ethan tut-tutted and shook his head gently. 'You disappoint me, beautiful one. After all these years on *Sunshine Cove,* and especially given Danielle's personal history, I would have thought you'd get it straightaway.'

'*No,*' Sabrina looked at him and then collapsed into laughter. 'They couldn't. They wouldn't.'

'They can and they will.' He stood up and gave a deep bow. 'Allow me to introduce myself. Ricky – cute, huh? – Donaldson. The long-lost, identical twin brother of the late Mickey Donaldson.'

'But it's such *crap*,' Sabrina protested, through gales of laughter. 'It was bad enough when I had to play Danielle's evil twin Diana but if Mickey, I mean Ricky, is an identical twin too . . . How can people watch this *shite*?'

'No idea,' Ethan said, pleased with her reception to his news. He sat down again. 'But watch it they do, and it pays us very well. And for your information, I believe that we will very soon discover that about three decades ago the inhabitants of Sunshine Cove were unwittingly used as participants in experimental IVF technology that resulted in a mass outbreak of twin births. Naturally it had to be hushed up, so one child from each pair of siblings was spirited away by the government.'

Sabrina's laughter subsided and she was silent for a moment. 'That's actually quite brilliant,' she said in awe. 'That means they can bring in an identical twin for pretty much any character between the ages of twenty and thirty whenever they want, without having to find a new explanation.'

'Exactly. And you call it shite. Shame on you. It's practically Shake-speare. Now, are you going to offer to buy me dinner or do I have to drop delicate hints?'

A rueful expression crossed Sabrina's face as she moved across to her dressing table and began to take off her make-up. 'Oh, Ethan, I'd love to but I'm having dinner with Edward tonight.'

'Aha! The fiancé. I was reading about you two in a trashy mag at reception while I was waiting to see Nige. Is he really as perfect as he sounds?'

She grinned. 'Yep. And he's all mine.'

'Gloating is a very unattractive quality, Ms Falks. But I can't see why this affects our dinner plans. Why don't you just take me home to meet him?'

Sabrina shook her head. 'Sorry, Ethan. We're having dinner with his family tonight and I really can't take you along to that.' She avoided his gaze as she lied to him, instead busying herself by searching in her bag for her iPhone. 'Here, put your number into my phone and we'll have dinner together one night next week. Edward's work schedule is impossible so it will probably just be the two of us. But that will be even better! It'll be just like the old days.'

'Oh, fine,' he said sulkily. 'But don't think you can brush me off just because you're more famous than me these days. And as I love you to pieces, the sooner I meet this Edward, the better. I won't have my best girl marrying someone I haven't personally approved.'

*

That evening Sabrina lay on the sofa, a script that she was having immense difficulty concentrating upon held in one hand.

'Are you okay, darling?' Edward looked at her with concern as he emerged from the kitchen. 'Anything the matter?'

Sabrina forced a smile to her lips. 'I'm fine. What's for dinner? It smells delicious.'

Edward gave her a wry smile. 'Does that mean you might actually eat some of it? It's not much fun cooking for you, you know.' He saw the defensive look on her face and instantly changed his tone. 'It's grilled fish and salad. Virtually no calories, I promise.'

Sabrina did manage to eat a few forkfuls of the fish that Edward had prepared, but every mouthful was an effort, as her churning stomach and mind rebelled against the food. As a result, conversation over the dinner table was desultory and soon afterwards, Sabrina went to bed, pleading a headache.

Edward watched her go, a worried expression on his face, as he wondered whether she was anxious about the wedding or if Mimi or one of the paparazzi had done something to upset her once again. But there was no point asking. He had learnt, long ago, that Sabrina almost never confided in anyone. She preferred to keep her troubles to herself, a trait that Edward admired and tacitly encouraged by rarely probing her further for details or explanations. In his opinion, it was another example of her inherent classiness. Edward deplored the *Oprah* mentality that dictated it was beneficial to discuss one's every thought, feeling, problem or (that revolting word) *issue* with family, friends, work colleagues or, God forbid, complete strangers. Although he loved Sabrina and was genuinely concerned about her strange mood, he didn't for a moment therefore contemplate coaxing her to reveal what was wrong.

So Sabrina went to bed alone, where she curled up tightly against her pillow and tried not to think about the fact that Ethan was back.

The one person who knew her secret.

The one person who could ruin everything.

25

The Trial

Sabrina sat docilely in the salon chair while her hairdresser, Delta, and make-up artist, Eamon, buzzed excitedly around her.

Sabrina and Mimi were ensconced in the private parlour of Delta's plush Woollahra salon, as all four of them workshopped Sabrina's 'look' for her wedding day.

'The trend is still for "barely there" make-up,' Eamon nodded. 'Light foundation, subtle eye make-up and a simple, glossy lip. But it's not as though you're having a beach wedding. And, of course, with your face, darling, we can break all the rules. I'm tempted to do a really glamorous, smoky eye with lots of kohl and a beautiful dark-red lip. What do you think, Delts?'

'I'm thinking a classic bridal look. You know – an up-do of ringlets, tons of hairspray, strategically placed baby's breath and a tiara,' Delta said solemnly, before collapsing into helpless laughter.

Eamon screeched with horror at the thought of it and Sabrina gave a faint smile before returning to flicking through a bridal magazine.

Mimi looked at her sister curiously. She seemed so passive, so uninterested. Didn't Sabrina *want* to marry Teddy? Most brides would kill to have their own hair and make-up artists fussing over them. Yet here was Sabrina, acting as though this hair and make-up trial was, well, a trial.

She wasn't the only one watching Sabrina. Noting Sabrina's lack of interest in the conversation, Delta and Eamon had hurriedly snapped back into professional mode, which discomfited Mimi even further. It was as though no-one could act naturally around Sabrina for more than a few minutes. Her every expression and mood was constantly scrutinised, setting the tone for everyone present.

'Sorry,' Delta said. 'But if you'd seen some of the horror weddings I worked on when I was straight out of my apprenticeship . . .' Her voice trailed off. Sabrina hadn't even glanced up from her magazine. Mimi wanted to slap her. What was Delta apologising for? Laughing? And Delta was *talking* to Sabrina. Couldn't Sabrina even acknowledge her?

Eamon busied himself with his brushes as Delta tried again. 'What are your thoughts, Sabrina? Hair up or down?'

Sabrina, who had been lost in thought, heard her name and realised that Delta was addressing her. She spent so many hours of her life sitting in make-up chairs, being worked on, that she had developed the habit of drifting off into her own world the instant that the smock was wrapped around her. She liked Delta and Eamon and their work was always of an impeccably high standard, but she had long ago abandoned the effort of talking to them constantly for the hours it took to prepare her for major events. Sabrina was always polite to them but she never engaged in social chitchat as she found their constant flow of industry gossip tiring and not especially interesting. It was easier just to sit there quietly unless she was directly addressed.

Sabrina opened her mouth to ask what the question had been but Delta spoke over the top of her. 'A lot will depend on the dress and jewellery that you've chosen, of course.'

Now it was Mimi's turn to squirm. They hadn't discussed Sabrina's choice of wedding dress since their argument, months ago, over Sabrina wearing their mother's gown. Since then, Mimi had felt ashamed of her outburst and ultimatum but her feelings remained unchanged.

However, the thought of Sabrina looking for an alternative wedding dress made her feel unpleasantly small, so she had done her best to avoid the topic altogether.

'My dress is strapless except for three thin strands of crystals over one shoulder,' Sabrina answered, as though discussing the weather. 'And I'm wearing some diamond drop earrings from Bulgari. No necklace.'

'Corinna's making your dress?' asked Eamon.

'Of course,' replied Sabrina. She and Mimi did not look at one another.

'If you're wearing diamond earrings from Bulgari, then we'd better show them off,' Delta said decisively. 'So I think hair up. Nothing too scraped back or hard though. Let's see. We could do a soft look – a bit like how Scarlett Johansson wore her hair to that awards ceremony last month. I have a picture somewhere . . .' Delta pulled a magazine from an overloaded table nearby and started to search through it, while Eamon chimed in with suggestions for eyeshadow.

Mimi looked at Sabrina's reflection in the mirror. For a brief moment, their eyes met and then Sabrina dropped her gaze back down to the magazine that lay in her lap.

Where are you? Mimi wanted to yell at her sister. *What's happened to you? Where have you gone?*

*

After the trial, which, as far as Mimi could tell, had taken two and a half hours to establish that Sabrina would be wearing her hair up, Sabrina dropped Mimi home. (They had all agreed that they would need to schedule a separate make-up trial, as it would take at least another two hours for Eamon to create Sabrina's face for the day.)

As they pulled into Aunty Bron's driveway, Mimi's stomach started to rumble at the thought of the home-cooked dinner that Aunty Bron would have waiting.

'I'm starving,' she announced. 'Thank God Aunty Bron is cooking tonight. We do take turns,' she added hastily, not wanting Sabrina to think she was taking advantage of their aunt. 'I hope it's lasagne. Aunty Bron's lasagne is to die for.'

Gathering up her accordion file, bridal magazines and bag, Mimi straightened up and turned to say goodnight to her sister. She was brought up short by the sight of Sabrina gazing at the warm yellow light that was spilling from the front windows of the small brick-veneer home. There was a look on her sister's face that she couldn't quite name.

'Sabrina? Are you okay?'

Sabrina immediately snapped out of her reverie and the unfathomable look was replaced by one of clear embarrassment. 'Of course.'

There was a moment's silence and then Sabrina cleared her throat as she appeared to make up her mind about something. In a tone of deliberate casualness, she asked, 'What are you doing for Christmas?'

'Christmas? Not sure yet. It's still a month away.'

'I just thought I'd mention that you're welcome to join Edward and me. Aunty Bron too, of course. We'll be having Christmas lunch at his family's house.'

Mimi looked at her curiously but Sabrina had her head down as she fiddled with her iPod. Mimi hesitated. The odd thing was that it wasn't the thought of spending a part of Christmas Day with Teddy that was tempting her to accept. It was the idea of spending Christmas with Sabrina. She thought back to the first Christmas that she had spent in England and then looked at Sabrina. She willed her sister to look up and meet her gaze, to give her a sign of some sort that Sabrina wanted to spend Christmas with her too, that she hadn't asked out of mere politeness.

Sabrina's head stayed down.

'Oh. Well, thanks. But I just had an email from some friends of mine who live in London to say that they're coming to Australia over Christmas and New Year's. They were very good to me when I was over there and I want to look after them while they're here. So I'll probably spend the day with them. We wouldn't want to intrude on a family gathering and I think asking Teddy's parents to host an extra four people on Christmas Day would be a bit much.'

'It probably would,' Sabrina agreed, her face inscrutable. 'Okay then, I'll speak to you later.'

'Yep. Okay. Bye.' Unable to shake the feeling that something strange had just taken place, Mimi alighted from the car and made her way up the drive where she unlocked the aluminium screen door.

It was only much later that night that she was finally able to name the expression that she had glimpsed on Sabrina's face as she had gazed at Aunty Bron's small, welcoming home. But even then Mimi was no closer to solving the puzzle.

The expression had been wistfulness – a combination of sadness and longing. But what on earth could Sabrina, who had been heading back to her gorgeous fiancé and beautiful, luxury penthouse, possibly want from an undistinguished suburban house, her maiden aunt and her irritating sister?

26

Sabrina's Perfect Christmas

Two years previously, the only bright spot for Sabrina, on that first Christmas Day after their mother's death, had been the morning that she'd spent with Aunty Bron. Sabrina had tried desperately for weeks to convince Bron to accompany her to Christmas lunch with Edward's family but she was still refusing point blank.

'Thank you, Sabrina, it's very kind of you but I really can't.'

'Why not?' Sabrina demanded. It was Christmas morning and she was visiting her aunt before she set off for Edward's family home. 'You can still change your mind. They wouldn't mind in the least. His mother has constantly said that they can always make room for one more on Christmas Day.'

Sabrina couldn't be entirely sure but she thought that at this point Aunty Bron shuddered. 'Ah well, I wouldn't want to inconvenience any wandering hobos who might knock upon the door then. No, I'm sorry, Sabrina, but in truth, the reason I can't come is that I'm fairly certain the one time I visited Edward's parents' house I spied a piano.'

'They have one in the drawing room,' Sabrina said, puzzled. 'So what?'

'So they're the sort of family who are entirely likely to gather around that piano and sing Christmas carols. In tune. I couldn't bear it.'

She shook her head firmly. 'I'm sorry, my darling, I really am, but to be around Edward's family in all their perfect harmony and . . . and *tastefulness* just isn't my cup of tea. After Mum and Dad died I just got used to spending Christmas alone. It doesn't bother me in the slightest and I'm too set in my ways now to change.'

Sabrina bit her lip. She could hardly bear it either, which was why she desperately wanted her aunt to be there. Her memories of childhood Christmases were of her father getting roaring drunk and arguing violently with her mother. Under strict instructions from their mother, Sabrina would drag Mimi off for a bike ride in order to protect her. Sabrina often felt resentful towards Mimi on those long, hot, Christmas Days as she couldn't help thinking that, of all of them, Mimi was the one who least needed protecting from their father. Nonetheless, Sabrina had had it drummed into her that it was her duty to look after Mimi, to hide the shameful truth from her, so they would play aimlessly for hours in the local park, which was always deserted on Christmas Day because all of the other kids were at home with their families. Sabrina longed to be by her mother's side, to help and protect her, but she was conscious also of feeling shamefully relieved that looking after Mimi gave her an excuse to escape from the father that she so feared.

Eventually, their father would either storm out of the house or pass out somewhere, leaving their mother in tears, while Mimi and Sabrina, tired and hot after spending the day roaming the neighbourhood, argued over their invariably burnt dinner. It was unsurprising therefore, that Sabrina hated Christmas. What she *really* wanted now was to stay right here with Aunty Bron and watch action movies on DVD and eat takeaway food that wasn't remotely Christmas-themed. But she couldn't. She had to put on a brave face for Edward's sake.

'Fine,' Sabrina said, getting up to leave. 'Here's your Christmas present then, Aunty Scrooge. Open it when I'm gone. Merry

Christmas.' She kissed her aunt on the cheek and without a backwards look, she left.

*

Dear Aunty Bron,
I know you two weren't close but I thought you might like this
anyway.
For what it's worth, she did love you.
Merry Christmas,
Love, Sabrina

Bron put aside the card and tore the wrapping to show a white box. Opening it, she lifted away layers of tissue paper to reveal an exquisite photo frame. Behind the glass surface was a faded Kodachrome photograph of two laughing little girls with messy plaits. They were wearing striped swimsuits and digging in the sand with buckets and spades. On the reverse, in Sabrina's neat handwriting, was written *Bronwyn & Margaret, Botany Bay, 1961.*

She knew now why Sabrina hadn't stayed to watch her open it. Sabrina and Mimi hadn't spoken to one another since their vicious fight in the funeral parlour three weeks ago. So Sabrina probably thought it would have given her aunt the perfect opportunity to deliver a homily on the importance of sisters and not leaving it too long to resolve arguments. Bron gazed at the photograph for a long moment and then, moving slowly, like the old woman that she had become, she got up and went into her bedroom. She opened a dresser drawer and gently placed the photograph, face down, under a pile of clothes. Then she quietly closed the drawer and returned to the living room. She sat down in front of the television and switched it on, gazing unseeingly at the flickering screen. As she prepared to spend another Christmas Day alone, her eyes were hard and bright with unshed tears.

*

Pulling up before Edward's parents' house, Sabrina turned off the engine and took a deep breath.

It's going to be fine, she told herself. *It's just one day. Not even a whole day. You can get through this.*

What she wanted, she realised with a shock, was to walk in and see Mimi there. Mimi had always been the companion who had made Sabrina's childhood Christmases bearable. Despite the fact that those long ago Christmases had been filled with arguments and their father getting drunk and their mother keeping a desperately cheerful mask on that Sabrina had gradually learnt to see through as she had grown older, they had nevertheless been the only Christmases that they'd known. And, if she was honest, they hadn't all been bad.

One year their grandmother had given Sabrina and Mimi a cubby-house and they had played in it all day – all summer it had felt like, escaping from the adult tensions inside the house to their back-garden refuge. Another year, she and Mimi had written and put on their own Christmas show. They had forced their parents to sit down and watch. She was hazy on the plot details but she seemed to remember that Mimi had insisted on playing Rudolph the Red-Nosed Reindeer as a dog, while she had played the part of Miss Claus, the much mis-understood daughter of Santa and Mrs Claus. Miss Claus, who was fed up with snow and the cold, had delivered a long and poignant soliloquy in which she expressed her desire to have a holiday at a sunshine-filled beach for Christmas, rather than receiving any toys. Nine-year-old Sabrina had thought it a sombre and moving speech and had been somewhat puzzled by the fact that her parents had laughed uncontrollably.

Nevertheless, she could still remember the way her parents had clapped and cheered as she and Mimi made their bows. She could also recall the pride that she had felt at making both of her parents laugh – and the anxiety she had been unable to quell that their laughter and unified happiness wouldn't last. A pop psychologist would probably trace the germination of her career as an actor to that Christmas play, ascribing her subsequent professional success to her need for parental approval or to a deep-seated desire to find an escape from reality. Sabrina shrugged off this thought. The truth was that she had followed Mimi into acting, in the same way that she had followed Mimi's lead in all of their childhood games.

Mimi had always been acclaimed as the actor of the family. Mimi was the natural entertainer, the exuberant one who could improvise and act out a story, turning an account of a trip to the shops to buy groceries into a wildly improbable tale that would have her audience transfixed and in stitches. It was Mimi who had been accepted, straight out of high school, into the National Institute of Dramatic Arts, the prestigious Australian performing arts school that had trained the likes of Cate Blanchett, Toni Collette and Mel Gibson. And it was Mimi, Sabrina recalled, as she continued to sit staring at Edward's parents' house, unwilling to get out of the car, who had quit NIDA after only ten months, carelessly giving up an opportunity that hundreds of others would have begged for. Including Sabrina.

She thrust away the memories from the past. There was no point dwelling on thoughts of her sister. She couldn't call Mimi even if she wanted to. She knew from Aunty Bron that Mimi was living in London but she had no idea where. And she certainly wasn't going to ring Aunty Bron now to see if she had a number for Mimi. She was just feeling stupidly sentimental because it was Christmas. God, she could just imagine the conversation that would ensue if she *did* telephone Mimi. Mimi would no doubt laugh, humiliate her with one of her bitingly acidic comments that always contained just enough truth to draw blood, and by the time Sabrina hung up she would undoubtedly be left feeling worse than she already did.

She shook herself free from the ghosts of Christmases past and alighted from the car. Carrying her basket of gift-wrapped presents, she pressed the doorbell, willing herself into playing the part of the happy girlfriend.

The door opened and Edward's mother stood there, a picture of refined elegance, a spotless apron over her expensive clothes. With a pang, Sabrina pictured her mother's sole 'good' dress that she had worn every Christmas Sabrina could remember, until Sabrina had scored her first modelling job and bought her mother a new dress with the money that she earned.

'Sabrina! Merry Christmas, darling. Come in, come in. Edward's already here. We're just about to taste Harold's eggnog. Homemade, of course.'

Edward's father had made eggnog. As Sabrina followed Blanche into the house, she silently thanked her stars that Aunty Bron hadn't come. Things were only bound to get worse.

*

And they did. Edward's niece and nephew, Anthea and Maximilian, were boisterous and over-excited but also sweet and reasonably well behaved. Stylishly wrapped and thoughtfully chosen gifts were exchanged beside the beautifully decorated Christmas tree. The Christmas lunch was traditional: turkey and ham with all the trimmings, but with a contemporary edge, courtesy of Blanche's slavish devotion to Nigella, Jamie and Gordon. The meal was served on white bone china and they ate with heavy sterling-silver cutlery. Then, after lunch, Aunty Bron's worst nightmare was realised. Edward's sister, Phoebe, was encouraged to sit at the piano.

Within two minutes everyone had drifted over to surround her and was enthusiastically joining in the chorus of 'The First Noel'.

Sabrina watched them from her armchair, clutching her glass of mineral water tightly and desperately fighting the urge to burst into hysterical laughter.

They can't be this perfect, she told herself. *They simply can't be. Phoebe must be having an affair with the plumber. Anthea is secretly on medication for Attention Deficit Disorder. Blanche is* — she paused as she tried to come up with a suitable flaw for Edward's mother. She couldn't. *Blanche is really a Stepford Wife fembot, which means her perfection doesn't count.* She tried to take comfort in the fact that at least she knew Edward wasn't perfect, but she couldn't help thinking that his transgressions were all in the past. He was annoyingly close to perfect these days.

'No-o-el, No-o-el, No-o-el, No-el!'

Edward turned around and smiled at her. 'Sabrina! Come and join us!'

Oh dear God. Sabrina, who had never touched alcohol in her life, found herself longing for a strong drink to numb the rage and the pain that she felt as she watched this scene of domestic bliss. She was an actor but she had no idea how to play this scene. She had never learned the script for happy families. She didn't know how to stand or join in or sing, without in some way feeling that she was betraying her own fractured tribe, to whom she still felt a fierce, albeit incomprehensible loyalty.

Summoning every ounce of composure, Sabrina went to stand with her carolling future in-laws. As she dutifully began to sing the third verse, she couldn't help thinking wistfully that, even though she had absolutely no idea how Mimi was spending this Christmas, she would bet her life that she was having a better time than Sabrina.

27

Mimi's Perfect Christmas

The first Christmas after their mother's death was so utterly awful that Mimi could still hardly bear to think about it.

The funniest part, Mimi often thought (meaning funny peculiar not funny ha-ha), was that ever since she was a child, she had longed to experience a traditional English Christmas. Growing up in Australia, you couldn't help but yearn for the Mother Country at yuletide. It was the only explanation as to why most Australian families still cooked and ate a traditional turkey dinner with all the trimmings, even when it was forty degrees in the shade. It also had to be the reason why Australians gave each other inappropriate Christmas cards featuring snowy landscapes and ice-skaters. And if, like Mimi, you had grown up reading *A Christmas Carol* and *'Twas the Night Before Christmas,* then quite frankly, you were done for. The conviction took hold that a real Christmas – a *proper* Christmas – required winter, snow and some orphaned Victorian-era children to befriend.

So, ever since heading off overseas, Mimi had been determined to experience a Proper English Christmas. Only the first year she had somehow ended up in Thailand for Christmas, which had been fun, but given that about ninety-five per cent of the population was Buddhist, Christmas understandably wasn't really their thing. She had been determined that the following year would be the year of her Proper English Christmas and so it was. She had her location and the season perfectly aligned. The only thing that had gone AWOL was her Christmas spirit.

Because the thing Mimi discovered that year about Christmas was that if you have a happy, loving family, you're free to bitch and moan about the crass commercialism and the shopping and the crowds and all of the other petty annoyances. On the other hand, if your family is grieving or damaged in any way, the sentimentality of the season has the opposite effect. You can't laugh at it. It just makes you want to cry. So she did.

Mimi burst into tears in Tesco's when they played carols over the loudspeakers. She sobbed the first time that it snowed. She wept when she saw the lights of Christmas trees through the windows of houses, and she positively bawled when she went to see the local Christmas pantomime. (It was a performance of *Snow White and the Seven Dwarfs*. For some reason, she found Sneezy particularly poignant.)

Making the situation worse was the fact that she didn't have a job or anything to structure her days, which enabled her to wallow. So, on Christmas Eve, she spent the afternoon getting blind drunk at one of those quintessentially English named pubs (The Moon and Sixpence near Oxford Circus) with a whole lot of other homesick Aussies.

She wanted her mum so badly it hurt. And her dad. Or Aunty Bron. She even wanted Sabrina, despite the awful things that she'd said to Mimi the last time Mimi had seen her. She wanted . . . she wanted someone who had known her when she was a kid. Which, given her drunken state and geographical location, left only one logical option.

Mimi reeled out of the pub, into the freezing evening air and made her way down Oxford Street. When she reached her destination, she pressed her nose to the glass. As she looked through the window of the famous Hamleys Toy Shop, she felt like the Little Match Girl: standing cold and alone, peering in at an enticing vision of warmth and happiness. Tears started to stream down her face, blurring her view of the teddy bears, dolls, train sets and jigsaw puzzles. She had never felt more miserable or forlorn in her life. She paused at the entrance and then, buffeted again by a blast of icy wind and another harried shopper, she made up her mind and went in.

The lights, decorations and crowds were completely disorienting in her drunken state, but somehow she allowed herself to be carried along by the mass towards the elevator. The hot, close press of wet woollen coats inside the elevator made her want to throw up, but thankfully, just as she was thinking she might, the doors slid open.

'Santa's Grotto!' a cheerful voice announced.

Mimi staggered out, attracting some concerned looks from a few parents. Luckily for Mimi, it was almost dinnertime so there were only a few kids waiting in the queue to see Santa. She joined the line and held onto a bollard for support as she waited her turn.

Finally, the lumpish seven-year-old boy in front of her finished cataloguing his wish list of every medieval-war-themed computer game that had ever been released and then finished with a modest 'Oh – and maybe a flat-screen TV too.' He jumped off Santa's knee and ran into the arms of his adoring parents, while Mimi heroically suppressed the urge to holler, 'A bike! Buy the kid a bike! Or he'll end up an obese forty-three-year-old virgin nerd!'

'Next!' said a harassed-looking elf. He glanced at Mimi and then looked around. 'Where's your kid, missus?'

'I don't have a kid. I want to see Santa.'

'You're kind of . . . big, aren't you?'

Mimi shot him a death stare. 'Old,' she said, as icily as she could in her tipsy state. 'I believe you meant old. Not big.'

He looked Mimi up and down. 'I reckon I meant both.'

223

'I'm getting personal remarks from a six-foot *elf*?'

'Oh yeah. Like that's really going to hurt me. I'm too tall. Ouch.'

'You're not very nice for a Christmas elf, you know.'

He leant in closer. 'Let's see. Maybe that's because I'm not really an elf but a repeat offender with over thirty road-safety and traffic violations who is serving out a court order to undertake 100 hours of community service. Maybe that's why I'm dressed like a frigging freak and having to put up with even bigger freaks like you.' His face had gone red and not in a merry, apple-cheeked way. He paused to take a deep breath and Mimi tried to intervene diplomatically.

'It *is* a bit insensitive that they dressed you in traffic-light colours,' she said, noting his red-and-green-striped outfit, embroidered with yellow stars, and stumbling slightly over the pronunciation of 'insensitive', which was quite a hard word to say after imbibing numerous large tumblers of vodka.

'Tell me about it.' He softened a bit. 'Are you really here to see Santa?'

'No. I came for your sparkling conversation,' Mimi retorted, exasperated. 'Yes. I. Would. Like. To. See. Santa. So if you're finished with your little door-bitch act, can you please let me through? Sorry,' she said, immediately swinging around to face an outraged Sloane Ranger mother, who had let out an audible gasp prior to clapping her hands over her darling daughter's ears.

The elf reluctantly let her pass and Mimi clambered up the stairs to Santa's throne. Santa looked at her doubtfully and kept his hands in his lap.

For God's sake, Mimi thought. *It's not that hard, is it?* She pointed to his lap. 'I want to sit down.'

Santa and the elf looked at each other with worried expressions and Mimi saw the elf mouth the word 'Security?'

'You want to sit on my knee?' Santa asked tentatively.

'Of course I want to sit on your knee,' Mimi said crossly. 'Things can't have changed *that* much since I was five. Or do kids these days talk to you via Skype or something?'

The elf and Santa had a hasty, muttered confabulation, during which Mimi caught phrases such as 'has to be eleven stone minimum' and 'makes a nice change though' and 'sexual harassment policy'. Finally, Santa looked up, and judging by the resentful look on the elf's face, Mimi had clearly won.

'Right then,' Santa said with a return to his jolly voice. 'Up you come. What's your name, young lady?'

'Mimi,' she said, making herself comfortable on his lap and ignoring his muffled 'Ergh!' as her full weight descended.

'You're Australian,' he said, a note of resignation creeping into his voice as he smelt the booze on her breath.

'Yes, I am. Have you been there? Oops. Silly question,' Mimi giggled. 'Sorry, Santa. I forgot that you've been everywhere.'

'Well, Mimi, what do you want for Christmas then?'

'I want to know how my mum is,' Mimi promptly answered.

There was a pause. 'And why do you think I would know the answer to that?' asked Santa, feeling his way forward carefully.

'Because she lives in the North Pole, of course.'

'Ah. I see. So, er, you think your mum is Mrs Claus?'

Mimi looked at him, horrified. 'Of course not. What's wrong with you? You'd better not have laid a hand on my mum.'

'I haven't touched your mum,' Santa protested, belatedly lowering his voice as he registered the shocked expressions of the Sloane Ranger mother and her little girl who were next in line.

With an outraged 'Come, Felicity! This is only one of Santa's helpers. We'll go and see the *real* Santa at Harrods!', Felicity's mother bundled her daughter off towards the elevator.

Santa sighed and then turned his attention back to Mimi. 'Why do you think your mum is living at the North Pole, Mimi?'

'Because she can't be in heaven,' Mimi explained patiently. 'Mum didn't believe in heaven. So I thought about it and I realised that Mum is probably at the North Pole. It's the perfect place for her because before she got . . . sick, she always liked to keep busy too.'

Mimi saw Santa flap his hand to gesture that the elf, who, acting on a complaint from the Sloane Ranger mother, had reappeared with a security guard, should step back.

'Now, can you just remind me – my memory is terrible these days – when did your mum come to join me at the North Pole?'

Mimi swallowed hard. 'Three weeks ago.'

Santa's expression changed and he patted Mimi gently on the shoulder. 'Of course. I remember. We got her straight to work with some sewing.'

'Mum can't sew.'

'She can now,' Santa said, a touch defiantly.

'Really?' Mimi asked in wonder. 'Mum always wanted to be able to sew.'

'She's in charge of making all the doll's clothes,' Santa said firmly. 'She makes the most beautiful dresses that you've ever seen. We're very glad that she came to live with us, Mimi. And she's very happy, you know.'

'Is she really? Really and truly happy? Or is she just pretending? Because she's very good at pretending, Santa. I thought she was happy and I never knew about any of it – about Dad or —' Mimi stopped and then looked at him pleadingly. 'Please, when you see her again, can you just tell her how much I miss her and that I'm sorry – I'm so sorry – that I didn't get to say goodbye?'

And then, because she was drunk and alone and far away from home at Christmas, and both her parents were dead and her only sister hated her, Mimi burst into tears.

So that was Mimi's abiding memory of her long looked-forward-to first ever Proper English Christmas. Not gently falling snowflakes or ruddy-cheeked carol singers or ice-skating in front of the Tower of London, but of being twenty-three years old and sitting on the knee of a toy store Santa, crying like a lost little girl, until finally Santa put his arms around her in a comforting hug and stroked her hair while he said the only thing that he reasonably could, even if they both knew that it was a lie.

'There, there. It's going to be all right. I promise you, Mimi, everything is going to be all right.'

Two Months Before the Wedding

- Ensure out-of-town guests have booked accommodation
- Organise hen's night
- Discuss details of the service with ceremony official
- Determine amount of alcohol required

28

The Bridesmaid Commandments

'Mimi!'

In a whirl of long, flying black hair, Amisha burst through the international arrivals door of Sydney Airport. Mimi only just had time to register the white teeth of Raj, grinning as he brought up the rear with their luggage piled onto a trolley, before Amisha launched herself at Mimi and flung her arms around her neck.

It was six days before Christmas and Mimi's friends had come to spend five weeks in Australia. Mimi had met Amisha and her husband, Raj, in London. They were both Indian-born and bred lawyers who had studied and now worked in London. As a teenager Amisha had spent an exchange year in Sydney. After hearing Mimi's accent as she ordered a drink at the Globe Theatre bar during an interval in *Macbeth*, Amisha had barrelled up to her and said in her gorgeous Anglo-Indian accent, 'G'day, mate! How's it hanging?'

'I beg your pardon?'

Amisha laughed, introduced herself, explained her love for Australia and all things Australian, and when the bell chimed for the recommencement of the performance, they were still chatting. They organised to meet in the foyer after the play ended, and following an enthusiastic dissection of the performance and staging of the play in a nearby tea shop, their friendship was sealed. When Amisha discovered that Mimi knew only a handful of people in London, she promptly made her exchange telephone numbers. From that point on Mimi became Amisha's theatre companion, to the great relief of Raj, who considered the task of accompanying his wife to plays to be filed under the 'For Worse' category of their marriage vows.

'I'm so glad you're finally here!' Mimi let go of Amisha and turned to hug Raj. 'How was your flight?'

'It went on for so long I feel like we must be on a different planet at the very least.'

'Ignore him,' Amisha instructed her, tucking her arm through Mimi's as they made their way through the terminal towards the car park. 'He's just a whining Pom.'

'Whingeing Pom,' Mimi corrected her. Amisha loved Australian slang and colloquialisms but had a tendency to get them wrong.

'Two minutes I've been in this country and already I'm getting abused,' Raj complained.

'That's a *good* thing,' Mimi said earnestly, swinging round to face him. 'If we're mean to you and insult you, it means that we like you.'

'Oh. In that case I suppose that instead of telling you that you look amazingly well, I'd better say bollocks to you too.'

Mimi stopped dead. 'I don't look *well*, I look SKINNY! Skinny for me, anyway,' she amended honestly. 'Why can't anyone just come out and say it?'

'Because it's more than weight loss. You look . . . happy.' Amisha paused as she wondered where to begin. She decided that Sabrina was the less raw of Mimi's two great issues. 'So, how are things going with Sabrina and the wedding? I must say, I'm glad for *my* sake that you two have made up. I'm under strict instructions from Mum not to return home without an autograph and some photos. Mum's completely mad about *Sunshine Cove*.'

Mimi wondered wryly whether everyone she saw for the first time in ages would always instantly skewer the conversation towards Sabrina. But she wasn't cross with her friend. It was just about impossible to get mad with Amisha.

'It's fine. It's actually kind of . . . fun being a bridesmaid.' Mimi surprised herself with this last statement. She hadn't stopped to consider her job in ages. It had just become a part of her life. But it was fun, she realised. Somewhere along the line she had started to enjoy herself.

'Have you got your bridesmaid's dress yet? What's it like?'

From behind them, Raj groaned loudly but they both ignored him.

'It's beautiful,' Mimi said morosely. 'It also encapsulates the entire Australian post-modernist experience in chiffon. Or something like that. You'll have to ask the designer.'

Amisha squeezed her arm sympathetically. 'Are you disappointed?'

'Horribly. This is the first time that I've ever been a bridesmaid. I wanted to experience it in all its gory glory. Instead I'm getting a beautiful dress and shoes so expensive – Sabrina's paying for everything – that I think it only right that they should walk on me instead of the other way around.'

'Oh well. Maybe all's not lost. You could always ruin it with accessories.'

'That's true,' said Mimi, cheering up. 'Like a pair of elbow-length satin gloves.'

'Perfect. What about some novelty earrings? I'm sure we could get some wedding-cake ones at Paddington Market. Or maybe some flashing red love hearts.'

'Now you're talking. Considering that the dress is white, maybe I should be the one to wear a tiara too.'

'You're wearing white?'

Mimi clapped a hand to her mouth. 'Oh crap. Please don't tell

Sabrina I told you that. I just broke one of the Bridesmaid's Commandments: Thou shalt not reveal the colour of thy frock.'

'Oh well, as long as you don't break the first commandment, you should be fine,' Amisha said, as they reached Aunty Bron's car and started to haul their luggage off the trolley and into the boot.

'Which is?'

'Thou shalt not sleep with the bridegroom.'

Mimi laughed unconvincingly and then turned swiftly away, before Amisha could see the bright-red blush that had spread all over her face.

*

'So is there anything in particular you want to do while you're here?' Mimi asked, as she bounced on the bed in Amisha and Raj's hotel room. 'I'm all yours as soon as I finish up with work for the Christmas break. I thought we could go down Oxford Street, of course, for the shopping, and there's a fantastic exhibition of Aboriginal art on at the Art Gallery of New South Wales at the moment. I know you know Sydney, Mish, but Raj hasn't been here before, have you?'

'Nope,' panted Raj, as he heaved one of their suitcases onto the luggage stand. 'But you know me, Mimi – can't think of anything I'd rather be doing than shopping for hours or visiting art galleries.'

Mimi stuck her tongue out at him. 'Luckily for you, my one sporty friend in the world has offered to take you to the Test match at the Sydney Cricket Ground in the new year. So Mish and I can go shopping that day, which is perfect as all of the big sales will be on. And I thought we could go to watch the start of the Sydney to Hobart yacht race on Boxing Day. It's great fun – we can take a picnic up to the Heads.'

Raj came over to her and planted a big kiss on her cheek. 'Bless you, my child,' he said fondly.

Mimi pushed him away. 'Mmm. Thought you'd like those plans.'

'Who's this sporty friend?' asked Amisha, sensing intrigue. 'Is it a male friend?'

'Yup. But you can stop looking like that. He's my personal trainer.'

'Is that how you lost weight? I'd love to have a personal trainer but with our mortgage I can't afford it.'

'Neither can I. He's doing it for free.'

As Amisha raised one eyebrow, Mimi quickly set her straight. 'He's Sabrina's fiancé's best friend. He's doing it as a favour to Sabrina so that she doesn't have to suffer the humiliation of having an obese bridesmaid.'

'You were never that overweight,' Amisha scolded. 'You just ate badly and drank too much beer and never went outside or did any exercise, like everyone who has to live through an English winter.'

'And went up two dress sizes as a consequence,' Mimi sighed. She cheered up. 'But I've dropped one size already. If I can just drop another five or six sizes, I'll be able to borrow Sabrina's clothes.'

'So when do we get to meet the famous Sabrina?' asked Raj. Mimi grinned. He had tried to sound casual but the nonchalance was too studied. It still freaked her out that people got a buzz out of simply meeting her sister.

'Whenever you like. She and Teddy – that's her fiancé – are doing their own thing on Christmas Day, but apart from that they're around. They're not going away this year as they both have too much on with the wedding only a couple of months away. Speaking of Christmas, I know it's not really your holiday –' Amisha and Raj were nominally Hindu, although neither was particularly religious to the best of Mimi's knowledge. 'So I've kept our options simple. We can have lunch at Aunty Bron's house – just the four of us – or we can go to a restaurant. The only thing is if you'd rather do that, we'll have to book somewhere as soon as possible because all of the nicest places with water views are almost booked out.'

Amisha looked at her curiously. 'You're not spending Christmas Day with your sister?'

Mimi shook her head. 'No. Things have improved between us but I think we're better off doing our own thing on Christmas Day.'

'But your aunt will be with you,' Amisha persisted gently.

Mimi looked blank. 'Yes, of course. So?'

'Nothing,' Amisha said, succumbing to a warning look from Raj that plainly said she was interfering. But she couldn't help thinking that if she were Sabrina, with only two living relatives in the world, the one thing that she would want, more than anything, would be to share Christmas with them and to know that they wanted to share it with her too.

29

Hen's Night Fight

'Before we call it quits for Christmas, we need to discuss what you want to do for your hen's night,' Mimi said, tossing a bundle of glossy brochures onto Sabrina's bed. Of course it was Teddy's bed too but it was better that Mimi didn't dwell on that. As it was, she was trying not to stare at his bedside table. She had already noted what he was reading (*The Road* by Cormac McCarthy: impressive but depressing), and it was requiring a considerable effort of willpower not to throw herself casually onto the bed so that she could discreetly sniff his pillow. Sad but true.

It was the twenty-second of December and Sabrina was getting ready to attend her network's Christmas party. Mimi might have been jealous that she didn't have an office party to go to if she hadn't had plans to meet up with Amisha and Raj at the Slip Inn at Darling Harbour. The Slip Inn had gained fame as the bar where Crown Prince Frederik of Denmark had met his future Australian princess, Mary Donaldson. Despite Mimi's vehement protestations that the patrons of the Slip Inn were far more likely to be drunken stockbrokers wearing their ties around their foreheads than visiting royalty, Amisha (who had a weakness for royal romances) had insisted on meeting there.

Sabrina picked up one of the brochures and looked, aghast, at the image of a beaming blonde model, wearing a fetching straw hat in the shape of a large hen on her head.

'So we need to decide whether you're a naughty hen, which will entail a male-stripper harbour cruise, semi-naked waiters and games along the lines of dick-tac-toe. You'll probably also be dressed like a sexy nurse and you'll be wearing a lot of plastic penises,' Mimi added, as though she had committed a frightful oversight by almost leaving this important detail out. 'Penis earrings, penis bracelet, that sort of thing.'

'Why?'

'Not entirely sure. I think it might symbolise all the penises that you're renouncing for the sake of Teddy's. When you think about it, it's actually quite a lovely statement about fidelity,' Mimi said thoughtfully, looking up at her sister from the armchair in which she had sprawled in lieu of the bed.

'Maybe Edward and I should exchange penis-themed rings during the ceremony instead of traditional wedding bands,' Sabrina said acidly.

'I can probably source those for you. I can definitely get you penis slippers and a rather terrifying penis-shaped mug. The handles on either side are the — well, you get the picture.'

'What are my other options?' Sabrina asked in a resigned tone.

Mimi grinned. 'A girls' weekend away. Very classy. Lots of spa and beauty treatments. Everyone will be lounging around in fluffy white dressing-gowns all weekend, sipping on chamomile tea. Or you can have a dinner somewhere nice and we can play 'clean' games, which would be more appropriate if Aunty Bron and Teddy's mum are going to be there. By the way, you have to give me a list of who you want to invite.'

Sabrina suddenly felt sickened. Who did she want to invite? Old classmates who she hadn't seen or talked to since she'd left school and who had never liked her anyway? Her make-up artist and her hairdresser? The other female cast members who sucked up to her even while they not-so-secretly resented her success? Corinna and her assistants? That only left Edward's female relatives, Ethan, Aunty Bron and Mimi.

'So what's it to be?' Mimi prompted. 'I'm assuming that you probably don't want to parade around town sucking on a penis-shaped dummy.'

'Why would someone even invent something like that?' Sabrina asked in horror.

'Oh, believe me, there's worse out there. Much, much worse. My internet filter actually blocked me from getting onto some of the hen's party websites. They're utterly filthy. For some reason, marrying the love of their life turns certain women into wannabe porn stars with a vulgarity threshold that Jordan would deem objectionably low.' Mimi looked at Sabrina with her pen poised expectantly over her open, hard-backed notebook. 'So what do you want to do?'

Sabrina shifted uncomfortably. 'Why don't you choose?'

Mimi's mouth dropped open. 'Huh?'

'I said, why don't you choose?' Sabrina snapped, her embarrassment causing her to become abrupt. 'I think I'd like a surprise.'

'But . . . but . . . that means I'd be in charge of organising the whole thing.' *Like a real sister and bridesmaid*, Mimi thought, but didn't say.

'I'll pay you extra,' Sabrina said stiffly.

Disappointment, closely followed by a wave of fury, broke over Mimi. 'You'll pay me extra?' she demanded, standing up. 'Did I *ask* you for anything?'

'Sit down, Miriam, and stop being so dramatic. God, I wouldn't have offered to help you out in the first place if I'd known that taking this job would end up making you touchy about being paid.'

Mimi ignored Sabrina's command and stayed standing. 'You think *you've* been helping *me* out?' She stared at Sabrina in disbelief. 'That's really how you see it?'

239

'Why wouldn't I?' asked Sabrina defensively. 'You were unemployed, you couldn't get a job if you tried, and I hired you as my assistant.'

'And I've been working my arse off for you! You're completely impossible, did you know that? You're selfish and demanding and you're rude to people, and you don't even have the excuse that it's because you're a Bridezilla because it's just your normal personality.'

'*I'm* rude to people? You're the one who goes around saying whatever you think without bothering about the consequences!'

'A few weeks ago Delta was talking to you and you didn't even look at her! Jesus, Sabrina, who do you think you are? Angelina Jolie? You're a *soapie actress.*' The scorn in Mimi's voice was unmistakable.

There was a silence and then Sabrina spoke with calculating intent. '*You're* treating *me* with contempt? Let me ask you this – I might be just *a soapie actress* but what exactly are you?'

Mimi tried to respond but Sabrina didn't let her. She was already continuing in a strange, cold voice. 'You're nothing, Miriam. Nothing. You've done nothing with your life and you never will. I actually feel sorry for you, do you know that?' She paused and then added, 'But glad and grateful too.'

Mimi looked at her with incomprehension.

'Glad because I'm not you. And grateful because I take after Mum. You're exactly like Dad and you always will be.'

Her final words were chosen deliberately. Mimi stared at her sister for a long moment, remembering the last time that she had heard Sabrina liken her to their father. She felt now, as she had then, that Sabrina wasn't just attacking her; she was savaging the memory of their father, the father who Mimi had adored.

'You always have to prove that you're perfect, don't you?' Mimi said hoarsely, slipping unconsciously into her lifelong role as their father's defender. 'Well, you're not. *I'll* always be grateful that I'm not like you and Mum – sour and thinking that I'm better than everyone.'

Sabrina laughed. 'By what measure could you ever prove that you were better than anyone? You're a failure on just about every level there is. Like Dad.'

In blind fury, Mimi slammed her heavy notebook shut and then hurled it at Sabrina's face. Sabrina ducked and the missile flew past her to land with a heavy thump on the floor. The sisters stared at one another, as the old, impenetrable hatred flared up between them once more.

'Organise your own hen's night,' Mimi finally managed to say. 'In fact, you can organise your whole wedding. I quit.'

Mimi grabbed her bag and stormed out of the apartment, slamming the door behind her. Her rage at Sabrina was only surpassed by her fury with herself when she made it outside and realised that she was sobbing. Blinded by tears, she unthinkingly stepped off the kerb without looking.

Mimi looked up, too late. There was a blinding glare of headlights, a squeal of brakes and a last-minute desperate swerve by the driver. A moment of surprise at being airborne and then the sharp shock of physical pain.

And then, darkness.

30

The Funeral

The procession of people seemed endless.

'Hello. Thank you very much. Yes, it's a terrible loss. Far too young.'

Mimi felt desperately sorry for all of the people, most of whom seemed to be strangers, who had come to the funeral home to pay their last respects to her mother. What else was there to say but platitudes, when the truth was so indecent? *I'm so dreadfully sorry your mother died from heart disease at the age of fifty-two.* Mimi could sense the undercurrent of the unvoiced thoughts: *Then again, perhaps it was for the best. She spent the last few years cocooned in that flat Sabrina bought for her, only moving from her bed to the couch and back again. Depression. It was all her husband's fault, of course. He abandoned them years ago. Ruined her life and broke her heart. She never really recovered. Fitting, in a way, that she died from heart disease.*

Mimi wanted to defend her father from the silent accusations but she didn't know how. And the situation was made worse by Sabrina's very odd decision to display their parents' wedding photo on the same table as the condolences book. Why she had chosen this photograph of their mother, above all others, was utterly beyond Mimi's comprehension, but as she had only just flown in from London the day before, all of the funeral arrangements had been left to Sabrina.

The whole concept of the 'viewing' was repulsive, as far as Mimi was concerned. Their mother's casket lay open on a raised platform at the far end of the room. Benches were positioned in front of it, giving the impression of pews in a church to what was supposedly an atheistic send-off to — well, nowhere, now that Mimi thought about it. Her mother hadn't believed in heaven. She didn't know where her mum was any more. She certainly wasn't that – *thing* – lying in the coffin. Mimi had shuddered at the glimpse she'd caught before she turned away, wishing with all her heart that she could erase the memory. The styled hair and carefully applied make-up, the chemicals that the mortician must have used to puff up her skin and smooth away the signs of suffering and disease, had all contributed to create an unnatural stranger, seemingly neither dead nor alive but simply inanimate – as though she had never breathed or laughed or really lived.

'You must be Miriam, Sabrina's sister.'

Mimi tried hard to focus as another stranger materialised before her. Young this time. Around her age. Male. No idea who he was.

'I'm Nate,' he said, extending his hand. 'I'm a good friend of Sabrina's boyfriend, Ed.'

Sabrina had a boyfriend? This was news to Mimi. She and Sabrina had barely exchanged twenty words since she'd arrived home. Mimi had collapsed into tears as soon as she saw her sister, but while Sabrina had put her arms around her, there had been no warmth in her embrace, only a kind of weary duty, and Mimi had soon withdrawn to the comfort offered by Aunty Bron. Since then, Sabrina had barely seemed to be in the room at times; she was physically present but so detached that Mimi had felt as though she was talking to an automaton.

'Thank you for coming,' Mimi forced the words out. 'It's very kind of you.' She mustered up a vestige of interest from somewhere and added, 'Is, um, Ed here with you?'

Nate shook his head. 'I'm here in his place. He had a meeting that he couldn't miss. He'll be at the funeral tomorrow, of course.'

'Of course.' Over the last hour, Mimi had discovered that repeating the end of what the person she was talking to had just said was a satisfactory way of seeming to be engaged in the conversation. Thankfully, Nate seemed to realise she wasn't in the mood to talk further and he moved off towards Sabrina, who was standing, graceful and at ease as ever, skilfully remembering names and accepting condolences and comforting other people's tears, even as she shed none of her own.

How did she do it? Mimi wondered. Was she that good an actor? Or, Mimi shied away from the nasty thought, was Sabrina really as unfeeling as she seemed?

*

An hour later, only the sisters and Aunty Bron were left in the funeral parlour.

Aunty Bron, who to Mimi's eyes seemed much older than her mother had been, gestured to Mimi to help her up out of her seat.

'I've said my goodbyes. I'm not coming to the funeral tomorrow,' Bron said, in an unsteady voice.

'What? Why not?' asked Mimi, startled.

Bron started to sob – terrible, heaving old lady sobs. 'I can't, girls.' She looked at them pleadingly. 'Please don't ask it of me. You don't understand . . .'

Mimi moved instinctively to put an arm around her aunt. 'It's okay, Aunty Bron,' she said quietly. 'We understand.' Concentrating on her distressed aunt, she didn't notice the look on Sabrina's face.

Sabrina gazed dispassionately at her aunt for a long moment and then looked away.

'Do you want to wait in the next room for us?' Mimi asked, once Bron had got her emotions under control once more.

Bron shook her head. 'I'd rather wait in the car. I'll give you girls some time alone with your mother.' Without another glance at the coffin, she turned away. Mimi gently led her out of the room, returning a few minutes later with the funeral director following behind.

Sabrina roused herself to appear engaged. She knew that she had to keep making an effort. It wasn't as though she even wanted to cry. She just wanted to sit on the floor in a quiet room, all by herself, with the door closed. It didn't seem too much to ask. And yet, somehow, it was.

'Is she okay?' Sabrina asked.

Mimi shrugged.

The funeral director glided forward. 'Would you like me to close the casket now or would you prefer it to remain open?' he asked, in his peculiarly hushed and solicitous voice. Mimi wondered whether he spoke like that all the time and, if so, whether he ever managed to get served in a busy pub.

'Closed.'

'Open.'

Mimi and Sabrina spoke simultaneously. The funeral director looked from one to the other. Sabrina shook her head. 'It doesn't matter. Close it then.'

She took one last look at her mother's face and then turned away towards the window. She stood with her back to the room, looking out over the manicured rose gardens. The funeral director looked at Mimi to see if she wanted to say a last goodbye. Mimi shook her head.

He closed the lid of the coffin and then picked up the framed wedding photograph and placed it on top of the casket. He stood back to survey the effect, adjusted the photograph slightly and then nodded with satisfaction. Mimi repressed a hysterical urge to giggle. *He's styling her coffin*, she thought incredulously. Satisfied with his handiwork, the funeral director turned towards them.

'Take as long as you need,' he said sympathetically. Then he slipped away, noiselessly closing the door behind him. Mimi and Sabrina were left alone.

'I don't know why you wanted it open,' Mimi finally said. 'It doesn't even look like her.'

I'm glad it doesn't look like her. It helped to take away the memories of what she looked like with all those tubes and machines attached, Sabrina thought.

There was a silence.

'Why did you choose *that* photograph?' Mimi nodded towards the framed wedding photograph. 'I couldn't believe it when I saw it. I can't imagine what everyone thought.'

'I don't care what everyone thought.' It was a struggle to pay attention to Mimi. Sabrina felt as though she was drifting far away from her body and this room. She knew that she should be explaining things to Mimi, rather than cutting her off like this. She should tell her about their mother's incoherent ramblings, the thoughts and the memories that she had voiced aloud during her last confused weeks as she lay dying in hospital. She should explain about their mother's constant unconscious return to her wedding day and the first bright, happy years of marriage with their father, for that was why Sabrina had chosen the photograph. But she couldn't. Explaining things to Mimi would mean reliving the past few weeks in that claustrophobic hospital room, when it was just Sabrina, their mother and the ever-present ghost of their father. She was too exhausted, too close to the edge. She just wanted to forget.

'Was she —' Mimi swallowed and tried again. 'Was she in pain?'

She was being eaten alive by heart disease, Miriam. What do you think? A sudden sharp surge of anger brought Sabrina back to the present. She bit down her fury and spoke in a precise tone. 'Yes. She was. It was a relief when she died.'

'For you or for her?' Mimi couldn't stop herself. Sabrina had been so horrible ever since she arrived home. So cold.

Sabrina stared at her sister for a long moment and then turned away. 'For both of us, I imagine,' she said coolly. She stared out the window as she dug her nails into her palms, hard enough to leave deep crescents in the flesh. She would not allow Miriam to upset her.

'Jesus, Sabrina, you're talking about Mum! How can you sound so unfeeling?'

Sabrina turned to consider her younger sister and the ice in her gaze made Mimi flinch. 'Unfeeling? I suppose it's the height of consideration to make it back for Mum's funeral? Shame you couldn't make it back when she was still alive. But I suppose sitting in a hospital room watching your mother die can't compare with travelling through Europe and having a good time.'

'She begged me *not* to come home,' Mimi said, through gritted teeth. 'You know she did. She said she liked hearing about my adventures. I wrote her a postcard or a letter every single day. And you knew that I was coming home for Christmas. None of us knew that she —'

'Would die so quickly? No, I don't suppose we did. I do know that she didn't want to interrupt your good time. That Mum could be unselfish doesn't surprise me. That you could be *that* selfish does.'

Mimi waited until she had choked back the lump in her throat and could speak again. 'I didn't think she needed me.'

'You're her *daughter*, Miriam.'

'She had you.'

'So that absolves you of responsibility?'

'Mum never needs me the way that she needs you. You two always stick together and leave me out! Always!'

Sabrina stared at her sister. She felt nothing any more. Nothing. 'Needed,' she finally said. 'Stuck.'

'What?'

'You should have used the past tense. Mum *needed* me. Mum and I always *stuck* together. Because she's dead, Miriam. She's dead and you didn't even bother to make it home to say goodbye.' Sabrina allowed this to sink in and then added, 'Anyway, that's complete rubbish about us leaving you out. Mum always favoured you and you know it.'

'*Me?* What in the hell are you talking about? Mum and I didn't have anything in common!'

'She loved you because you're exactly like Dad,' Sabrina said bitterly. 'You could always make her laugh. It didn't matter how irresponsible or careless you were, you got away with everything because you reminded her of him.'

Do you think I don't know that? Mimi wanted to scream. *I wanted her to love me for me! Not because I reminded her of Dad.* Instead, she took a deep breath and tried again. 'This doesn't have to be about taking sides.'

'I agree. We shouldn't take sides. No-one should ever be on Dad's side.'

Mimi felt her anger start to rise. 'Why are you always so set on proving Mum right and Dad wrong? What if the truth is that they were both right and both wrong? I always hated how you made Mum out to be a saint and Dad some sort of criminal.' She stopped as she registered the look on her sister's face.

Sabrina had gone very still. 'You are unbelievable, do you know that? You're irresponsible and aimless and drift through life expecting other people to look after you.' She waited a beat and then said deliberately, 'Just like Dad.'

To her surprise, Mimi laughed. 'That's it? That's your big gun? Is likening me to Dad really the absolute worst thing you can think of? I have bad news for you, Breens. I loved Dad – he was funny and fun and I cried myself to sleep every night after he left because no-one ever laughed in our house or played games any more.'

'You expected Mum and me to make you *laugh*? You selfish little brat. Dad walked out, Mum was working to pay the bills and I was trying to run the house. And you were feeling sorry for yourself because your playmate had gone? Well, *I* have news for *you* – Dad was a bundle of laughs because most of the time he was drunk.'

Mimi stared at her sister. 'What are you talking about?'

'You were eight years old when he left, Miriam. You don't remember. He was a drunk and he used to hit Mum and if I tried to stop it he . . . hurt me too.'

'I don't believe you. I know that you did something to make him leave —'

It was as though Sabrina had turned to stone. Then, slowly, almost in a dreamlike state, she lifted her hands and parted her luxuriant mane of hair, just above her right temple. Mimi stared, aghast, at a raised line of puckered flesh.

'He smashed a beer bottle and then threw it at my head,' Sabrina said, in an expressionless voice. 'I was eleven years old. And he didn't stop there. So Mum finally called the police. That's why he left.'

Mimi had gone white. 'You're lying,' she said hoarsely. 'He would never have done that to you.'

'No, Miriam – he would never have done that to *you*. But he did do that and much worse to me and to Mum. Do you want to hear how he held a lit cigarette to my arm? Or about the time he kicked Mum so badly she couldn't get out of bed for a week?'

A memory suddenly reared up in Mimi's mind, of her mother, ill in bed, unable to move, vomiting into a bucket by the side of the bed.

'She had the flu —'

'No, she had internal bleeding of some kind, I think. We never knew exactly what injuries she had because she always refused to go to the hospital or see a doctor in case she got Dad into trouble.'

'I don't believe it. It's not true,' Mimi managed to rasp out, although, sick to her stomach, she already knew that Sabrina must be telling the truth. Mimi had always been secretly exasperated by her mother's helplessness and hopelessness in the last years of her life. Her mother's increasing dependency had also been one of the reasons why Mimi, always keen to evade responsibilities, had been so anxious to escape overseas. And now, all of a sudden, her mother's prematurely haggard face and withdrawal from life made sense. Long-forgotten memories of shouting, of her father drinking, always drinking, and of feeling, not *fear*, but certainly a wariness around him were swirling around and rising to the surface of Mimi's mind, like a creek, whose silent, muddy depths had at last been disturbed.

Mimi licked her dry lips and tried desperately to hold onto the only truth she had ever known. 'You and Mum always stuck together. You drove him away —'

'HE LEFT!' Sabrina screamed. 'He left because he couldn't give a shit about any of us! All he cared about was drinking. And Mum looked after us until she couldn't cope any more because he'd spent so many years making her feel worthless. And then I had to look after both of you when *she* just gave up. And I am sick of it – do you hear? I am sick to death of looking after you all. I couldn't have been happier when you left for overseas because finally – *finally* – I didn't have to look after you any more. Now, with Mum gone, I can live my own life. I wish —' Sabrina stopped, tried to regain control of herself.

When Mimi spoke, her voice was deathly quiet. 'Say it.'

'I wish that you'd never come back.'

There was a long silence. Sabrina finally looked up. She was shocked to see that Mimi was smiling at her; an odd, twisted sort of smile.

'Fuck you, Sabrina.' Consumed by hatred and the horror of her sister's revelations, Mimi picked up the framed wedding photograph of their young, smiling parents and hurled it at her sister's beautiful face.

Sabrina dodged but only just.

The photograph landed face down on the polished wooden floor and the glass smashed. The sisters stared at it in shock and then

Mimi broke into shattering sobs. She turned to face her sister, who was still standing, immobile.

'You've finally got what you've been wanting then. Mum and Dad are dead. And I don't want anything more to do with you. Enjoy your life, Sabrina. You're on your own.' Blinded by tears, Mimi ran out of the room, slamming the door behind her.

Sabrina knelt on the floor and carefully sifted through the fragments of glass. Gently, she tried to smooth the torn surface of the ruined photograph. When she realised that it was a futile task, she simply held it in her hands. Then, for a long time, she sat cross-legged on the floor. As darkness fell outside, Sabrina closed her eyes and continued to sit there, the back of her head resting against the smooth, cool wood of her mother's casket. Finally alone, she waited for a sense of peace that never came.

*

The following day Mimi sat at a bar. It was empty on this mid-week morning, save for a couple of elderly men, perched on their favourite stools, who watched the young woman drink herself into a stupor with a mixture of curiosity and admiration for her capacity. She drank steadily, with a determined precision, until she could no longer feel anything: not grief for her mother's passing or anger with Sabrina, or, most importantly, guilt and shame for not returning home before her mother died. She drank to block out the memory of Sabrina's voice screaming the hateful truth about their father. She drank until the room started to swing and nothing mattered. She drank until she couldn't speak or move properly, and when at last all of her money was spent and she was aware that she had achieved her goal, she stumbled out into the bright sunshine, making her way slowly across the road to Botany Bay.

Mimi staggered across the white sand, the brilliant sun causing pinpricks of light to dance before her unfocused eyes. Unwittingly, she paused in a spot quite close to where, decades earlier, her mother had played in the sand with her older sister and they had paused, laughing, while their photograph was taken. Now, almost fifty years later, her youngest daughter suddenly lost control of her legs and passed out on the sand.

For the rest of the afternoon, passers-by walked and ran past her inert body, not out of a lack of compassion, but because, lying there, face down in the sand, Mimi looked for all the world like just another sunbather.

*

So it was that as their mother's coffin was lowered into the grave, Sabrina stood alone: her back erect, her eyes dry and her face expressionless, her real self floating free and far away.

31

Mimi the Giant Chicken

While listening to the doctor's summation of Mimi's injuries from the accident, Sabrina, perversely, wanted to laugh. Slight concussion, superficial cuts and abrasions, mild shock. No broken bones and no internal injuries. Mimi, the perennial escape artist, had done it again.

'She was lucky not to be killed,' the doctor said severely. 'According to the driver, it was a blessing that the oncoming lane was unoccupied. He was able to swerve so that his car only struck her a glancing blow. At the speed he was travelling, if he'd hit her directly . . .' The doctor allowed her voice to trail off. She seemed to disapprove of Mimi's narrow escape, simply on principle. 'Anyway, she's awake. You can go in to see her now.'

Sabrina caught Bron's eye and then looked away. 'You go in,' she said uncomfortably. 'I'll wait out here.'

Bron glared at her niece. Sabrina had come straight to the hospital still dressed in the outfit that she had intended to wear to her station's Christmas party. She looked incongruously beautiful in the harsh fluorescent lighting of the hospital corridor.

'Coward,' Bron said crossly.

An unfathomable expression crossed Sabrina's face but she said nothing, simply picked up an outdated glossy magazine from a pile on a small table and then sat on one of the hard plastic chairs provided and began to leaf through the pages.

Bron knew that she was a hypocrite for telling Sabrina off for avoiding her sister, although she was also 100 per cent certain that Mimi and Sabrina had no idea what had led to the estrangement between their aunt and mother. So Sabrina couldn't possibly have known whether Bron was at fault. But as she made her way through the door, Bron couldn't shake the unsettling feeling that Sabrina had just passed judgement on her and that the verdict had been severe.

*

'As if it's not bad enough that I've been hit by a car, that doctor keeps telling me off,' Mimi announced crossly from her hospital bed, as soon as Bron entered the ward. 'Whatever happened to doctors having a comforting bedside manner? I can't help thinking she wishes my injuries had been *worse*.'

Bron leant over her and kissed her. Despite the bravado, Mimi was shockingly pale, and the deep cuts and bruises on her face and arms showed that, although she had been immensely lucky, she hadn't escaped entirely scot-free.

'From what I understand, *you* hit the car,' Bron said briskly, sitting down on the edge of Mimi's bed and taking her hand. 'How are you feeling?'

'A bit flat. Oh, don't look like that. It was a *joke*. And it's funny because I didn't actually get run over.' Mimi paused and then said in a chastened tone, 'I'm sorry to have given you such a fright. I just . . . didn't look.'

'Yes, so I gathered,' Bron said drily. 'I suppose it's too much to ask what you and Sabrina were fighting about that distressed you so much you stepped in front of a moving vehicle?'

'What has Sabrina said?'

'Not much. She's been too upset.'

Mimi immediately propped herself up on her elbows. 'Has she been *crying*?' she demanded, a note of hope in her voice. She had never seen her sister cry. Not when their dad left or when their mum died. Not once.

Bron didn't answer and Mimi slumped back against the pillow. 'Silly question. Forget I asked. Everyone knows that Sabrina never cries.'

'That doesn't mean she's not affected by things. Some people internalise everything and Sabrina is definitely one of those people. Now back to my original question.'

Mimi closed her eyes. 'If Sabrina hasn't told you, I'm not going to.'

Bron looked at her recalcitrant niece and gave a sigh of frustration. 'Do you know what you and Sabrina remind me of, Mimi?'

Mimi opened her eyes. 'What?'

'An old married couple. You love each other but you're so comfortable with each other that all you do is snap and argue and fight.'

'*Love* each other? Me and Sabrina? Are you out of your mind? On our good days we manage to tolerate each other. Right now we're back to hating each other's guts.'

'If Sabrina merely tolerated you, she wouldn't have made you her bridesmaid.'

''Course she would. She didn't have a choice. She doesn't have any ugly friends.'

'Miriam Falks, that's utter rubbish and you know it. Sabrina doesn't rely on many people but she relies on you.'

'That's only because she's paying me.'

'Ah yes. The subject of payment. From what I've managed to winkle out of Sabrina, which admittedly isn't much, you two had an argument about money.' Bron paused and looked at Mimi severely over the top of her glasses. 'I must say, I'm surprised that that's what you two are fighting about, of all things, considering your inheritances.'

Mimi shifted uncomfortably against her pillow. Her aunt had

never asked Mimi why she had chosen to stay with her, assuming perhaps that it was for familial reasons rather than from financial necessity.

'I really don't know what the matter is with the two of you. You used to get along so well when you were young.'

Mimi was about to make a smart remark when memories of those long-ago childhood days crept unbidden into her mind. To both her and Bron's surprise, she instead answered honestly, 'I know. We actually used to have fun.' She paused and then added, 'Did anyone ever tell you about our No Knickers standoff?'

Aunty Bron laughed. 'No. Do I want to know?'

'I was about five, I think, which would mean Sabrina was eight. I decided that I hated all underpants and utterly refused to wear them. It drove poor Mum mad. So of course Sabrina decided that if I wasn't wearing knickers, she wasn't going to wear any either.'

'How did your mum get you to start wearing undies again?'

'She just let us wear our swimming costumes underneath our clothes every day for about three weeks and then I got sick of it and the rebellion stopped as abruptly as it started. And, as usual, whatever I did, Sabrina did too.' The laughter left Mimi's face and her expression hardened. 'Anyway, that's all in the past. Things have obviously changed since then. We're not kids any more, Aunty Bron. We're completely different people now. Sabrina and I aren't going to be running around without knickers anytime soon and our relationship is never going to go back to the way it was.'

'I know that Sabrina has changed because of her career and Edward, but what I can't quite work out is what happened to you,' Aunty Bron said softly. 'What happened to all of that confidence and daring? All that I see now are the endless jokes – you use them defensively and to attack but the real Mimi never shines through any more.'

Mimi's face closed up. 'This is the real Mimi. It's my fate to be the human equivalent of the chicken crossing the road joke. It's a fowl job but someone has to do it.'

'Very well, have it your way,' Bron sighed. She stood up and her voice became stern. 'Sabrina's right outside. Shall I send her in?'

Mimi avoided her aunt's gaze. 'I'm feeling a bit tired right now. I think I'd rather just have a sleep.'

Bron looked at her youngest niece in frustration but decided it wasn't the right time to push her any further. She kissed Mimi good-bye and then left, pausing to draw the curtains around her bed. She stole one final glance at Mimi as she lay in her hospital bed, her eyes now shut. For perhaps the first time in her life, Mimi the Indomitable looked vulnerable and defeated.

Be careful, Mimi, Bron said silently. *You're not just in danger of losing your sister. Unless I'm very much mistaken, you're well on the way to losing yourself. The two go hand in hand, you see.*

And if anyone understands that, she thought, as she slipped quietly out of the ward, *it's me.*

32

Message in a Bottle

For weeks after their father left, it had come as a surprise to everyone that Sabrina was the one who had nightmares. Eight-year-old Mimi couldn't help feeling slightly aggrieved. Without a doubt, it was Mimi who had loved him the most. *She* was the dramatic one who ought to have been afflicted by a disturbed subconscious. Yet night after night, while Mimi slept soundly, it was Sabrina who woke, screaming and distressed, tangled in the bedclothes and pleading, *'Don't leave me. Come back, come back, come back.'*

*

The day after their father left was a day of eerie quiet. Mimi was used to a comfortingly noisy house: doors slamming, voices raised in argument, her father either shouting or singing and, lately, Sabrina's tape deck playing loudly. Mimi wasn't entirely sure why her father had left but she knew that it had something to do with Sabrina. For the first time in her young life she felt as though she was truly experiencing hatred. She hated her sister. The facts remained murky but she just knew that somehow it was all Sabrina's fault that Dad had left.

Missing him desperately, Mimi crawled into the wardrobe and settled herself amongst his remaining clothes and shoes. He hadn't taken everything then. Maybe that meant he would be coming back, if only to pack up the rest of his things. If she was here when he returned, maybe she could convince him to stay. She would never go to school again. She would just sit here and wait for him to come home.

Mimi shifted around to make herself more comfortable and in doing so she knocked against something hard, hidden amongst the shoes. Feeling around in the semi-darkness of the wardrobe, she wondered excitedly if maybe her father had left something behind for her to find on purpose; a secret message perhaps, that would tell her why he had gone, where he was and when he was coming back for her.

She pulled out the object and looked at it. It was a half-full bottle of scotch. Her dad's favourite. She examined the label carefully for hidden meanings. Mimi was very familiar with the label on this brand of scotch. Disappointingly, there was nothing different about this one.

Opening the bottle, she pressed her nose to the rim and inhaled deeply. The smell comforted her. It smelt like her dad. She was about to replace the lid when an idea occurred to her. No-one was allowed to touch their dad's drink. Not even Mum. He flew into a tearing rage if he so much as *thought* someone had been at his liquor cabinet, even though no-one would ever have dared.

So maybe, just maybe, if Mimi drank from this bottle (the idea was both exhilarating and terrifying), he would come back. If she did something that bad, surely he would have to come back, even if it was just to punish her.

She tipped the bottle up and took a tiny sip. It tasted horrible – her throat burned and it made her eyes water. She couldn't understand why her dad loved scotch so much. Lemonade was much nicer. Mimi took another cautious but larger sip. The taste made her gag and she spat it out. But even at eight years old, if Mimi put her mind to something, she had formidable powers of resolve. She fixed a picture of her dad firmly in her mind. He was smiling and she could hear his booming voice calling her name as he walked through the front door.

Concentrating on this image, she was able to force another swig of the horrible liquid down. And then another.

She was unconscious when Sabrina found her, sprawled half-in and half-out of the wardrobe. Mimi would never know that at first her eleven-year-old sister thought she was dead. She knew nothing of the terrible, overpowering panic that gripped Sabrina's heart when she thought that she had lost her only sister. She never knew that when Sabrina calmed down enough to realise that Mimi was breathing, that she then set about methodically sponging the vomit off Mimi's face and out of her hair and that she tucked her up in bed in her pyjamas, the way that she had seen Mum take care of Dad when he passed out. Mimi never saw or heard Sabrina's uncontrollable sobs as she savagely hurled the depleted bottle of scotch against the back wall of their brick veneer house, smashing it into oblivion.

Sabrina would not cry again like that for almost twenty years, not through the long nights beside their dying mother's bedside or after her death or even during her funeral. Sabrina would never again cry like that, until the moment that the doctor, avoiding her gaze, gave her the definitive test results; the ones that said there was no hope at all.

And Mimi would never know that in the first few minutes after Sabrina discovered her small, unconscious body, her sister had knelt beside her and shaken her wildly, made vicious with terror, as she begged hoarsely, over and over again, *'Don't leave me. Come back, come back, come back.'*

33

Edward & Nate's Plan

It was Christmas Eve and Edward and Nate were holding an emergency meeting in the pub. Nate put a couple of beers on the small table and then sat down.

'What are we going to do about them?' asked Ed, without preamble.

'What can we do? They're grown women.'

'Who are acting like children. Sabrina is miserable, I know it. Mimi is her only family apart from their aunt who, between you and me, is worse than useless. Never thinks of anyone but herself as far as I can tell. She hasn't shown any interest in the wedding at all.'

'Maybe we shouldn't interfere. Just because you're family doesn't mean you have to like each other.'

Ed digested this novel concept and then asked, 'How's Mimi?'

'Physically better. She was discharged from the hospital after twenty-four hours. They just kept her in overnight for observation because of the initial concussion. I went to see her at home. She kept making jokes, of course, but I could tell that she's completely eaten up with anger over her fight with Sabrina.'

'What's going on with you two? You seem to spend a lot of time together and I could tell that day we bought our suits that she's pretty keen on you.'

Nate shrugged. 'I'm not sure you're right about that. I think Mimi's great. There's nothing going on though.' Which was frustrating the hell out of Nate. Mimi had reacted so badly the one time he had dared to flirt with her that he had never attempted it again. So absolutely nothing intimate had happened between them and Mimi hadn't given Nate any indication that she would like it to. This made it even more pathetic that he had been so worried about her after visiting her at home that he had called Ed to set up this meeting. However, just because Nate had a reasonable idea why Mimi's welfare mattered so much to him didn't necessarily mean that he felt like examining it in detail with Ed right now.

Ed and Nate had been friends for long enough that Ed knew it was time to switch the subject back to its origin. 'The problem with those two is that they just let things go on and on, like that fight they had when Mimi came back for their mother's funeral.'

'Do you know what that one was about?'

'Only the bare outline. Sabrina can be impossible sometimes. Whenever something's wrong she just clams up and I can't get a word out of her. It's exactly the same this time. Don't you wish we could just lock the two of them in a room until they talk to each other?' he finished, in frustration.

He looked up to see a smile breaking out on Nate's face. 'Bloody good idea, mate. Let's do it. Your place or mine?'

'Don't be an idiot. They're adults. We can't lock them in a room until they sort things out. That's what you do to six-year-olds.'

'I don't see why not. They're acting like six-year-olds, only they don't have anyone except us to pull them into line. Do you want this to drag on like their last fight? Your wedding is less than two months away, remember?'

Ed's brow furrowed. 'Sabrina *is* miserable,' he conceded.

'Exactly. Can't have a miserable bride. It'll ruin the whole wedding.

So do you think you'll be able to get Sabrina over to her aunt's place tomorrow morning?'

'But tomorrow is Christmas Day!'

Nate grinned. 'Even better. We should have the spirit of the season on our side.'

*

Sabrina stopped dead as Edward led her into the living room of Bron's house. 'Edward told me you'd be staying in your room while we visited,' she said in as hard a tone as she could manage. The sight of Mimi's injuries and bandages was an unexpected shock. 'I'm just here to see Aunty Bron.'

Mimi looked up from her book. 'And Merry Christmas to you too, Sabrina,' she said, in a voice that dripped sarcasm. 'I hope my Christmas gift from you is a cheque. You know how much I love getting money out of you.'

Edward was there as a peacemaker but unfortunately he blew it with his choice of opening. 'Baby, stop it,' he began.

'Don't call her that! She is *not* a baby!' Sabrina said furiously. Edward looked at her in hurt surprise and Sabrina inhaled deeply. 'Can we *please* just see Aunty Bron and then leave?'

'She's not here,' Mimi said. 'Which I'm pretty sure you already knew, Teddy, considering that I heard Aunty Bron tell you on the phone last night that she would be having morning Christmas drinks with the neighbours.' She finished with an inquiring look at Edward who flushed as Sabrina turned on him.

'Whatever this is about we can discuss it in the car,' Sabrina said frostily. 'As Aunty Bron isn't here, there's absolutely no point staying.' Without another glance at Mimi, she made her way towards the door. She was halted by the entrance of Nate, who stood with his arms crossed, smiling cheerfully, but barring the threshold like a benevolent bouncer.

'Sorry, girls. We've decided to not let you out of this house until you sort things out.' He looked over to Mimi. 'Merry Christmas, by the way.'

Mimi looked at Nate in outrage while Sabrina directed a very similar look at Edward.

Edward looked shamefaced. 'Sorry, darling. But it really is for the best.'

'This is the stupidest thing that I've ever heard. You have no right —'

'I have every right. I have to live with you and you've been completely miserable since your fight with Bab— Mimi.'

Mimi looked curiously at Sabrina, who had pointedly turned her back towards Mimi. Sabrina had been miserable? Aunty Bron had said the same thing but how could anyone tell when Sabrina rarely showed emotion?

'And you're about to explode from anger,' Nate added, directing this comment at Mimi. 'The horrible truth is that you two need each other. Either you apologise now and start talking or we're going to lock you in here and leave until you sort things out. We have the full cooperation of Bron, by the way. She's promised not to come back until we ring her with the all-clear.'

'You can lock all the doors but we'll just climb out a window,' Mimi said defiantly.

'Go ahead,' Nate said kindly. 'But somehow I don't think you're in any condition to do that, and I'm pretty sure Sabrina won't do anything of the sort. Very conscientious people, paparazzi. It wouldn't surprise me if some of them were working, even on Christmas Day. So are you ready to start talking to one another?'

There was unyielding silence from both Mimi and Sabrina.

Nate heaved a sigh. 'This hurts us more than it hurts you, believe me. Ed, have you got Sabrina's handbag?'

'Got it.'

'Wait a minute —'

'Sorry, darling. Can't leave you with a telephone of any description. Don't want you calling for help. Nate, have you got Mimi's phone?'

'I – will – in – just – a – minute,' Nate panted, engaged in a spirited tussle with Mimi. 'Bloody hell, Mimi. Even after being hit by a car, I can tell how much your strength has improved.'

'It has?' Mimi asked, pleased with the compliment and momentarily relaxing her grip.

'Yep. Sadly it's still no match for mine.' Nate held the mobile aloft in triumph. 'Okay, Ed – let's go. Bron disconnected and hid the home phone for us, took Mimi's keys and locked the back door before she left so we're all set.'

Edward crossed the room and joined Nate in the doorway.

'Wait a minute, wait a minute!' Mimi called out in alarm. 'What if there's a fire?'

'Good point. Nate?'

'You can sit in the bath and turn the taps on. Or try to find a packet of marshmallows. Any other questions?'

'Oh for God's sake, this is ludicrous,' Mimi exploded. 'Fine. Have it your way.' Without looking at Sabrina she said, 'I'm sorry I threw my notebook at you, Sabrina.'

Sabrina kept her gaze fixed on Edward. 'Apology accepted. And I'm sorry I . . . offended you. Now can we *please* leave?'

Nate cocked his head at Ed. 'What do you reckon?'

'Dismal.'

'Agreed.' Nate checked his watch. 'The timing's perfect. It's half past nine now, and we're both having Christmas lunch with our families, so you can expect us back around five. Oh, and, Mimi, if you were counting on your friends Amisha and Raj to come over and save you, then you can think again. I called them last night so they're in on it too. The sooner you set things straight with Sabrina, the sooner you can see them. All right then, have fun.'

The two men turned to depart.

'Don't you dare —' Sabrina began, while at the same time Mimi said, 'If you even *think* about leaving us here —'

'Too bad. You had your chance. Bye, girls.'

'Come back right now!' Mimi yelled as the front door was firmly locked from the outside.

The sound of retreating footsteps penetrated through the door.

'I can't believe they would do this —' Sabrina began, and then shut her mouth as she realised that she was addressing her sister.

'Yes, do be quiet, Sabrina,' Mimi said sarcastically. 'I'm unworthy of your scintillating conversation, remember?'

*

Nate and Ed drove about fifty metres down the street and then parked. Ed looked anxiously at his best friend.

'Do you think this is going to work?'

'God knows. We'll give them an hour and then go back. But at least we can say we tried.' He turned on the radio, which was playing an endless stream of Christmas carols, and then grabbed a paper bag from the back seat and offered its contents to Ed. 'In the meantime, I brought supplies. Mini Christmas pud?'

*

Sabrina and Mimi sat in stony silence for twenty minutes before Sabrina finally broke the deadlock. It was the bandages and bruises on her sister's face, arms and legs that did it. Although she knew that Mimi was technically fine, it was the first time that she had seen her sister since the accident. The sight of Mimi's injuries recalled the terrifying dread that Sabrina had felt when she received the telephone call, asking her to come to the hospital. She had been horrified to belatedly realise that the ambulance sirens she had heard outside her apartment building had been for Mimi. As much as Sabrina tried to suppress the awful thought, she couldn't. She hadn't lost Mimi this time. But she had come unnervingly close.

Sabrina took a deep breath. 'I know I hurt your feelings.'

Mimi looked over at her but said nothing. She merely crossed her arms and waited.

'God, Mimi, what do you want me to say? I *am* paying you to be my bridesmaid. I just assumed that if I asked you to organise my hen's night, that you'd expect overtime. Is it really so bad that I'm a fair employer?'

'You're not just my employer, you're my sister!' Mimi instantly flared, never able to maintain an icy demeanour for very long. 'And I didn't ask you for more money – I didn't even mention money. You're the one who's obsessed with money. You always think the worst of me, you know that, Sabrina? When I told you I had to fly to Melbourne, you thought I was trying to get a free trip out of you. When I was surprised that you'd trust me with organising your hen's night, you thought I wanted more money. I don't care about money! I never have! That's why I went out and spent the money that Dad left me on having a good time, as soon as I could.'

'And I never understood how you could touch that money,' Sabrina said, her face white.

'Why shouldn't I? Do you think it was tainted just because it came from Dad?'

'Dad didn't leave us that money,' Sabrina snapped. 'He never had a cent. It was Granny's money.'

Mimi shrugged. 'I know that. But Dad would have inherited it if he'd been around.'

Sabrina laughed. 'Trust me, there was no way Dad would have ever got that money.'

'What are you talking about?'

'Gran changed her will just before she died,' Sabrina said, in a hard, flat voice. 'She wanted to leave the money to Dad but she put in a clause that he would only get it if he stayed sober for twelve months. If he couldn't do that – which obviously he couldn't; he couldn't stay sober for twelve *hours*,' Sabrina's voice dripped contempt, 'it was to be divided between us when you turned twenty-one.'

Mimi was sitting stone still. Sabrina pressed her lips together and continued, in the same monotone. 'Gran's plan backfired. Badly. She had hoped that the inheritance would be the incentive Dad needed to clean up and look after us. Instead, the knowledge that there was this great pile of drinking money sitting there that he couldn't access drove him completely wild and made him even worse. And then he left.'

When Mimi spoke her voice was little more than a croak. 'I didn't know. Why didn't you or Mum tell me?'

'I wanted to tell you when we received the money but Mum wouldn't let me,' Sabrina said bitterly. 'You were so excited, so over the moon about all that free money. You couldn't wait to go overseas and leave us. You didn't really care where it had come from or why. Mum didn't want to ruin it for you. She wanted you to enjoy yourself. And if we'd told you, you would have found out the truth about Dad. Mum knew that you loved him. She didn't want you to know what he was really like.'

'Well, you didn't wait long till after her death to fill me in, did you?' Mimi's anger was rising again, remembering the shock she had felt in the funeral parlour, upon hearing those horrifying stories about her beloved father. 'You were dying to tell me, weren't you? Which, when I think about it, is really fucking weird, Sabrina, considering that all these years you've been punishing me for being on Dad's side and for spending his money. And the only reason I didn't know the truth about any of it was because *you* chose not to tell me.' The injustice of the situation now made Mimi boil over. 'So that's why you turned so cold when I said that I was going to use the money to go overseas? Jesus, Sabrina! I didn't know! How could I have known?' Mimi yelled the last sentence in pure frustration.

Sabrina sat there silently, not looking at Mimi. How could she explain that she had been brought up to believe that Mimi was to be protected, indulged, spared the pain of harsh realities? More to the point, how could she make Mimi understand without letting the resentment she had always felt that no-one had ever tried to protect *her* erupt?

Sabrina's refusal to show any emotion only inflamed Mimi more. She looked at her sister in disgust. 'You are such a hypocrite,' she spat out in fury. 'If you're so noble and felt that strongly about the money, then why didn't you give your share away? It's not like you need it. Why did you put it in a bank account instead of giving it to some alcoholism charity?'

'Because I kept it for you.'

There was a stunned silence.

'You what?' Mimi asked weakly.

'You heard.'

When Mimi spoke, her voice was a whisper. 'Why?'

'Oh for God's sake, Mimi, it was only commonsense. I knew you'd waste your inheritance. And you've never stuck to anything or held down a job in your life. I wanted to make sure that you had something to fall back on in case anything ever happened to me or you got into trouble one day.'

'I . . . I don't know what to say.' Mimi realised that she wasn't feeling gratitude or relief that she once again had a nest egg. She was too busy drowning in humiliation.

'Don't say anything,' snapped Sabrina. 'It's no skin off my nose. I never wanted a cent of that money anyway. My main concern was for Aunty Bron. I didn't want you becoming a burden on her.'

'You thought I would ask Aunty Bron for money?' Mimi asked in disbelief. 'Why do you do that, Sabrina? Why do you always think the worst of me?'

'Have you ever done anything to disprove me? You've never had a proper job, you have absolutely no sense of responsibility —'

'It's different for me. You wouldn't understand. It's easy for you – things have always come easily to you. You're lucky —'

'Don't you dare. Don't you *fucking* dare.' Sabrina spoke very deliberately and Mimi almost cowered. Sabrina rarely swore. 'There are a million pretty, talented girls who want to be actors out there, and none of them have my job. I *earned* this job, Miriam. I wake up at five a.m. on weekdays, and working a sixteen-hour day isn't unusual. I've worked my guts out since I left school and I've never had any real friends because all I ever do is work. And that's fine – they're the choices that I've made and I stand by them. But I am sick to death of you throwing the excuse that I'm successful because I've had it easy in my face. *You're* the one who's had it easy. Every single time you've been faced with a choice, you've taken the easy option. You quit NIDA because it was too hard to stick with it. You took Dad's money. You didn't come home until after Mum died. You've always done exactly what you want whenever you want. But that's not enough for you. You have to constantly put me and my achievements down in order to make your own life acceptable.' Sabrina paused and then spoke very slowly so that every word was invested with meaning. 'I don't give a damn if you want to spend the rest of your life living in backpacker hostels and working as a waitress. The only responsibility I've ever wanted you to take is the responsibility for your own choices. But you can't even do that, can you?'

Mimi sat on the couch, the colour draining out of her face. She wanted to defend herself, to justify the choices that she had made. What Sabrina construed as irresponsibility, Mimi had always seen as a liberating lack of convention – an admirably bohemian attitude to life that saw glorious triumph in avoiding mundane realities like bills, a nine-to-five job and a bank account.

But for the first time in her life, she couldn't. Because the shameful truth was that she had ended up depending upon Aunty Bron, and Sabrina was financially supporting her, even if she was making Mimi earn it. Mimi therefore had only one line of defence to fall back on and she took it. She decided to attack.

'You just hate me because you hated Dad. Sometimes I think you have trouble telling us apart.'

'That's true. It's especially hard to tell the difference when you lose your temper and throw things at me.' Sabrina added caustically, 'Exactly like he used to.'

Mimi flinched. 'He didn't mean it. I know he didn't. Don't say that.'

'I'll say it as much as I want because it's true. Anyway, how exactly do you throw a broken beer bottle straight at your eleven-year-old daughter's face or hold a lit cigarette to her arm and *not mean it*?' Sabrina gave a harsh laugh. 'It's just like old times really, when you lose your temper and try to physically hurt me.'

Mimi looked away, biting down hard on her bottom lip. She was trying not to imagine the serious little girl that Sabrina had been (neatly bobbed hair, those ribbed denim jeans and the floral T-shirt that she had always worn) being seriously injured by their drunken, out-of-control father.

'We should have told you,' Sabrina said, suddenly sounding defeated. 'It's just that Mum and I always tried to keep you out of it, and funnily enough, so did Dad. The violence —' Mimi winced at Sabrina's matter-of-fact use of the word, 'usually happened after you were in bed. You were always his favourite and I really believe he didn't want you to think badly of him. And, stupidly, neither did Mum.' She paused and looked at Mimi, her face pallid. 'You probably should have known the truth all along. It's just, once he left, there didn't seem to be any point in telling you. We only did it to protect you.'

'Mum never protected me! She was always too busy taking your side,' Mimi said bitterly. In comparison with Sabrina's tales of drunken violence, her childhood grievances sounded like those of a petulant child and she knew it. But she couldn't stop herself. Throughout all the years after their father left, Mimi had felt isolated within her family. Her mother and Sabrina had shut her out – for the crime of taking her father's side – without ever giving her the other side of the story. If only she had known the truth, perhaps her constant defence of their father's memory might not have been so ardent, which, in turn, might have allowed her back into their closed circle. 'You and Mum never included me in anything. I always felt left out and alone!'

Sabrina stared at her and then, to Mimi's surprise, she laughed. But the laugh sounded high and unnatural, almost as though Sabrina had laughed so as to avoid crying. '*You* felt alone? What about me? *You* left *me* alone! All of you! I had to sit with Mum, day after day, in that hospital room. I had to organise her funeral and, Jesus Christ, I was the only one even *at* her funeral!' Sabrina took a deep, shattering breath. 'You know the funniest part? Everyone thinks that *I'm* the selfish one. The one with the glamorous life who's moved on and up and left you all behind. And it's so unfair because it was all of you who decided to do exactly what you wanted and left *me*. Dad left us. You didn't come back from overseas when Mum was sick. Aunty Bron didn't attend Mum's funeral because she would have found it too difficult. Did it ever occur to any of you that someone has to stay? That someone has to organise things, hold everything together and just be there? And that that someone is always *me*? None of you, not once, ever thought about *me*. That maybe *I* needed you there.'

Mimi looked at her sister, aghast. 'But . . . but . . . you never need anyone. You never *once* called to ask me to come home when Mum was sick.'

Mimi watched as conflicting emotions played themselves out over Sabrina's face. 'I should have rung you and told you how ill she was,' she finally admitted. 'That was wrong of me.'

'Why didn't you? You must have known that I would have come home straightaway.'

Sabrina knew that she could – and should – have rung Mimi to tell her to come home. She also knew that the reasons she hadn't were tangled and confused. Part of her had felt a martyr-like gratification at once again slipping into the role of 'the strong one'. As much as she sometimes hated the role, oddly, she also took a strange pride in it. Then, too, the worst, most selfish part of her had wanted to keep her mother to herself. Sabrina had known that as soon as Mimi walked through the door of their mother's hospital room, bringing with her that magical Mimi trinity of light, laughter and an irrepressible life-force, that her own qualities of duty and patience would seem very poor gifts by comparison. But Sabrina's greatest reason for not calling had been simple, straightforward pride. She had been too proud to call Mimi and ask, or, God forbid, beg, her to return. Sabrina had learnt over the years never to ask for help. She had not been about to start at the time of her greatest need.

Mimi, who was still waiting for an answer, decided to continue. 'How could I possibly *know* you needed me when you just shut me out?' Mimi demanded. 'And then when I did come back for Mum's funeral you were so distant and cold – like you *wanted* to be left alone. You *told* me in these exact words that you wished I'd never come back.'

'I shouldn't have said that,' Sabrina said wearily. 'I'd just . . . I'd learnt not to trust you. It's easier to rely on myself. You all just let me down. Over and over and over again.' Her head dropped as she looked down at her perfectly manicured hands that were clenched tightly in her lap.

For the first time in years, Mimi suddenly felt tremendously sorry for Sabrina. Her beautiful, perfect sister seemed like one of the saddest, loneliest people that she had ever seen.

'Well, you're trusting me now,' Mimi said tentatively. 'That is, if you want me back as your bridesmaid?'

Sabrina looked up. 'Yes,' she said simply. 'I do.'

Mimi gave her a small smile. 'Breens?'

'Yes?'

'Why did you *really* ask me to be your bridesmaid in the first place?'

Sabrina looked at her sister. 'Because I'm getting married and you and Aunty Bron are the only family I have. And, God help me, as much as I've tried to pretend that doesn't mean anything, it does. Exactly what, I still don't know. But something.'

'Maybe it just means that we're better than nothing?' Mimi suggested.

'Maybe.'

'It's not surprising that you wanted to disown me, given how perfect Teddy and his family are.'

'Edward? You think Edward is perfect?'

'Isn't he?'

Sabrina seemed to be on the verge of saying something but then she shut her lips and gave a forced smile. 'I suppose he is.'

'And his family are like something out of a Martha Stewart catalogue.'

Sabrina didn't know what to say. Based on appearances, Mimi was right; the Forsters were the perfect, happy family. That's why it made no sense whatsoever that whenever she was in their company for any length of time she was overcome with the desperate desire to run away.

'Then again, their perfection must make them annoying, so that means they're imperfect anyway,' Mimi said mischievously.

'You have no idea,' Sabrina said fervently, thinking about the annual ordeal of Christmas lunch that still awaited her. She realised what she

274

had said and placed a belated hand over her mouth, looking guilty. 'I did not say that.'

Mimi clapped her hands in glee. 'Of course you did. I don't know what you're looking so guilty for. They *are* annoying. All families are annoying or else they wouldn't actually be families. They'd be something else. Like the cast of *Friends* perhaps.'

'They could be kind of annoying too.'

'True. Maybe the annoying principle extends to all groups of human beings who spend lots of time together.'

There was another silence and then Mimi asked softly, 'Do you think Mum loved him?'

An expression of tremendous sadness crossed Sabrina's face. 'I'm sure she did. That's the saddest part. I don't think she ever stopped loving him, even when he was a complete brute. If he hadn't left, I know she would never have left him.' Sabrina paused and then added softly, 'The drinking and the violence were horrible but the absolute worst thing of all is the knowledge that when he left he still broke her heart. She ought to have been dancing with joy but instead she was so grief-struck that as soon as I was earning enough money to support us all, she just gave up on life. That whole time you were overseas, she barely left her flat.'

'How could I not have known about what went on? I wasn't that young.'

'I don't know. Mum and I tried to shelter you as much as we could. Maybe you did know but you've blocked it out.' Sabrina shrugged. 'Be grateful. They're not pleasant memories. I wish I didn't have to carry them around for the rest of my life.'

'I'm sorry, Breens.'

'Don't be. I don't need anyone to be sorry for me.'

'Well, I am,' Mimi said fiercely. 'I'm sorry for you and me and for Dad and Mum for the stupid, pointless waste of their lives.'

'I don't know. Maybe their lives weren't a total waste. We're here, aren't we?'

'Mmm. And look how emotionally healthy and functional we are,' Mimi said drily. They caught one another's gaze and suddenly dissolved into helpless giggles.

'I think I just heard a car.' Sabrina went over to the window and looked out. 'Yes – it's Nate and Edward. I guess they weren't feeling quite as brave about coercing us as they pretended.'

'Shall we hide?' Mimi asked mischievously, as Sabrina came away from the window. 'We could mess up the living room first – make it look as though we've had a terrible fight. I think there's some tomato juice in the fridge that we could splash around if we want to really panic them.'

Sabrina laughed. They could hear Edward and Nate walking up the driveway and the sound of keys being ostentatiously jangled. Obviously unable to bear the suspense a moment longer, Edward called out in a hearty tone that didn't quite mask his anxiety, 'Sabrina? All okay in there?'

'Breens?' Mimi said quickly, knowing that she only had a few moments to say in private what she suddenly desperately needed to say.

Sabrina looked at her. 'Yes?'

Mimi felt a wave of unaccustomed shyness swamp her. 'Just . . . Merry Christmas.'

Sabrina smiled. 'Merry Christmas, Mimi.'

And, for the briefest flicker of a moment, it actually felt like Christmas.

Six Weeks
Before the Wedding

- Consider a wedding announcement for family or friends who are not invited to the wedding

- Complete and lodge a Notice of Intended Marriage form

- Confirm honeymoon accommodation and flight bookings

34

New Year's Eve

CELEBRITY CONFIDENTIAL: THE PARTY ISSUE!

Party with Celebrity Confidential *as we take you behind the scenes to the best of the A-list New Year's Eve bashes! We're the only celebrity magazine with an exclusive Access All Areas pass, which means that you'll be able to see exactly what all of your favourite stars get up to on the biggest party night of the year! Well, make that all of your favourite stars except one . . . An inside source has told us that Sabrina Falks has given in to pressure from her unsociable fiancé (who has never accompanied her to a party or awards ceremony) so Edina will be spending New Year's Eve holed up by themselves. BORING! What's the matter with you, Sabrina? Surely a girl from the western suburbs hasn't got too good for the rest of us?*

To Mimi's great surprise, Sabrina had declined all invitations to the numerous glamorous New Year's Eve parties to which she had been invited, and had instead asked Mimi if she, Amisha and Raj would like to join Edward, Nate and herself for a small gathering.

'Edward has booked a suite at the Four Seasons. We'll have spectacular views of the fireworks from there so I thought your English friends might like to come. The only drawback for them is that it's not going to be a big, loud party with lots of people. I asked Aunty Bron to come but she said she can't bear to leave the house on New Year's Eve any more because of the crowds and road closures. And Edward's family all have their own plans so if you come it will just be the six of us.'

Mimi sighed. A suite at the Four Seasons on New Year's Eve. Oh, to be rich and famous. Then she cheered up. She might not have fame or fortune herself but having a sister who did was the next best thing. At least she got to enjoy some of the perks.

'That sounds great. I'll ask Amisha and get back to you.'

Neither Mimi nor Sabrina need have worried about Amisha and Raj's reaction to the invitation. 'I know it's probably a bit dull when you're here on holidays,' Mimi added hastily, after outlining the plan. But that was as far as she got.

'Spend New Year's Eve at a private party with *Sabrina Falks*!' Amisha whooped, while Raj tried, and failed, to look nonchalant. 'My mum will positively *die*!' She added, 'That's so nice of Sabrina to put on a party for you.'

'For me?' Mimi asked, bewildered.

'Well, that must be the reason she's not going to some amazing party, mustn't it? It's because you're not up to much more than sitting around,' Amisha said sternly, looking at the healing cuts on Mimi's face and limbs, which were visible now that the gauze bandages had been removed.

It was Mimi's firm opinion that Amisha's bedside manner left a bit to be desired. She and Raj had visited Mimi in the hospital. As soon as she had been assured by the nurse that her friend was essentially in one piece and suffering from nothing more than cuts and bruises, Amisha had vented her relief by giving Mimi the sort of scold that made both Mimi and Raj privately think that Amisha would one day make an excellent mother.

Trying to forestall another lecture, Mimi now hastily said, 'Don't worry about me, I'm fine. And I don't think I'm the reason Sabrina is having a quiet New Year's Eve. She and Teddy aren't what you would call party people.' This was a complete mystery to Mimi and one of the few drawbacks that she had uncovered about Teddy. What was the point of being famous and/or wealthy if you didn't accept invitations to all the fabulous parties?

'You just hate giving Sabrina the benefit of the doubt, don't you?' Amisha said with a grin. 'Oh well, whatever the reason behind the party, at least we'll get to meet your mystery man.'

'Who?' asked Mimi, startled, and wondering whether Amisha could possibly have guessed at her crush on Teddy.

Amisha shot her a strange look. 'Your personal trainer, of course.'

'Who, Nate? Oh. Yeah, he'll be there. He's great. You'll like him.'

Amisha cast her friend an exasperated glance. What was wrong with the girl? This Nate was apparently lovely, a personal trainer (read: gorgeous, fit body), and was choosing to spend New Year's Eve with two other couples, one of whom was unknown to him, when the only single female present would be Mimi. Was Mimi completely dense? Or, Amisha thought, with a sudden rush of compassion, was she just still not ready to consider a relationship after the catastrophe that had made her flee London?

*

It was a few minutes past eleven on New Year's Eve. A delicious meal had been consumed and champagne had been drunk, although the latter had been shared only by Mimi and Nate. For once Sabrina wasn't the only one practising abstinence. As Hindus, neither Amisha nor Raj drank alcohol, although they both admitted that they knew plenty of Hindus who weren't so strict. Presumably out of respect for his fiancée, Edward wasn't drinking either. So while it was by far the smallest and most sober New Year's Eve party that Mimi had ever attended, she had come to the happy conclusion that she really couldn't have given Amisha and Raj a better time. It was definitely much nicer than queuing for the public toilets amongst the crowds gathered on the harbour foreshore for the fireworks display.

Despite their initial nervousness at meeting Sabrina, Amisha and Raj had quickly overcome the oddness of meeting someone whom they were both used to constantly seeing on the television in their families' living rooms. Everyone was getting along well and Mimi couldn't help thinking that it was turning out to be one of the nicest New Year's Eves that she'd had in years.

She settled back on one of the luxurious sofas with a refilled flute of champagne and heaved a sigh of contentment. The suite was gorgeous and they would have an amazing view of the Harbour Bridge exploding with colour and light when the fireworks began. Then again, she thought longingly, watching Teddy laughing at something Nate had said, who needed fireworks when the best view was right in front of her? She tried not to think about how everyone would kiss one another at midnight. Which would mean that Teddy would have to kiss *her*. God, he was marrying her sister in six weeks. It was really time that she put a stop on her uncontrollable tendency to fantasise about Teddy. If only he wasn't *quite* so good-looking. Mimi heaved another sigh, a despondent one this time, and then sternly forced herself to tune back into the conversation.

'So how did you two meet?' Nate was asking Amisha.

Amisha turned to Raj and they shared a peculiar look and then laughed.

'Shall we tell them?' asked Amisha, with a twinkle in her eye.

'Why not?'

Amisha turned back towards the others. 'We met through our parents.'

Nate looked disappointed. 'What's the big deal about that? I was expecting an outrageous story from the way you two were carrying on.'

'In India our story is very common. But I'm pretty sure you'll find it peculiar. Our marriage was arranged.'

Mimi managed to simultaneously choke on her champagne and almost fall out of her chair. 'You're kidding,' she spluttered, when she had recovered. 'How could I not know that?'

'You never asked,' Amisha said kindly.

'Why would I? I can't believe that your *parents* arranged your marriage!' Mimi paused to gather her thoughts and then added, 'But you knew each other first, right? You were old family friends or something?'

'We met each other for the first time about a week before the wedding. We had both been studying in the UK and had to fly back for the wedding. So we met for the first time in India.'

'That's so *weird*,' Mimi said, in awe.

'Mimi! You're being rude,' Sabrina reprimanded her.

'Oh, Mish and Raj know what I mean. I didn't mean to be rude. It's just, you two seem so . . .'

'Normal?' asked Raj, with a smile. 'In India, we're very normal. Ninety-five per cent of Indian marriages are arranged.'

Reassured by their relaxed response to her irrepressible younger sister, Sabrina's natural curiosity took over. 'Were you worried that you wouldn't like each other? I mean, what if you weren't . . . physically attracted to one other?'

Amisha shrugged. 'There are more important things.'

'Hey!' Raj protested.

Amisha grinned but ignored him. 'He comes from a very good family and I knew that he was studying law, like me, so we would have common interests.' She smiled and then said, 'And as it turned out, I was lucky – I got a spank!'

'Spunk,' Mimi corrected her slang automatically. 'Was the wedding night *weird*?'

'*Mimi!*'

Amisha gave a wicked smirk and ignored Sabrina's scandalised interjection. 'He went off like a hog in a frock.'

'She means a frog in a sock,' Mimi interpreted for everyone's benefit. 'And eeew. That's disgusting. I don't want to know details.'

'You just asked!'

Raj leant over and patted his wife's knee approvingly. 'Much better. No more of this common interests rubbish, okay?'

Edward tried to steer the conversation into more genteel territory. 'So, do you think arranged marriages are a better system than our way? I mean, is it better than individuals choosing to marry for love?'

Raj shrugged. 'It's hard to say. The divorce rate in India is about four per cent.'

'Australia's divorce rate is about forty per cent,' said Edward.

Raj nodded. 'But that doesn't necessarily mean that arranged marriages are a better system. Some people argue that the low Indian divorce rate has as much to do with our culture and a lack of options for women as it does with successful marriages.'

Amisha nodded vigorously. 'What you have to understand is that Indian culture prizes the obedience of children, even when the children are grown up. To go against the wishes of your parents is a very serious thing. So it is likely that many people stay in unhappy marriages for the sake of their parents.'

There was silence for a moment and then, to everyone's surprise, Sabrina emitted a soft laugh.

Mimi looked at her. 'What's so funny?'

The image of their mother's unhappy face flashed through Sabrina's mind and she gave a twisted smile as she met Amisha's gaze. 'Nothing really. It's just that in Australia, unhappily married people are more likely to stay married for the sake of their children.'

Mimi looked down into her drink as Edward placed a comforting arm around Sabrina. She longed so intensely to have someone slip a consoling arm around *her* that it felt like actual physical pain.

Having a partial knowledge of the Falks' family history, Amisha tried to smooth over the awkward moment. 'There are other bad aspects to arranged marriages. It's very much about controlling society. Spouses are often chosen for their caste or social status so there is a snobbishness and almost apartheid mentality at work also. I really don't know whether one system is better than another; there are many arguments on both sides. All I can say is that for Raj and me it has worked out.' She reached over for her husband's hand and they smiled at one another. 'We fell in love as husband and wife. I know how strange that seems to you because my English friends reacted the same way. They found it hard to understand that I could live such a modern life and yet be so old-fashioned – as they saw it – in this way. They thought arranged marriages were for village girls, not a Cambridge-educated lawyer. But for me, it was the right decision.' She suddenly grinned and in a lighter tone added, 'If nothing else, it saved me from the endless search for The One. I saw the film *Sex and the City*, you know. Imagine being in your early forties like Carrie and still trying to work out if you're with the right man! And Samantha was *fifty* and still in and out of relationships. It made me tired just thinking about it.'

Nate laughed and the solemn mood that had descended lifted slightly.

'Anyway,' Amisha continued, popping an olive in her mouth, 'as far as I'm concerned, *we're* normal.' She nodded at Mimi. '*You're* the one who took the unconventional path.'

Sabrina looked puzzled. 'What are you talking about?'

It happened so fast that Mimi didn't have the chance to even think about stopping Amisha, let alone time to feel dismay.

Amisha looked around the room in surprise. 'Mimi, of course. Surely you all knew that she was married?'

35

The Adventures of Mimi

The first place Mimi went when she left Australia was Indonesia, which is where most Australians head on their first overseas jaunt. Specifically, she headed to the island of Bali. Nervous about travelling alone, and still overcome by the novelty of the amount of money she had at her disposal, she pre-booked accommodation at a rather swanky resort. After checking in, she settled down with a paperback in a deckchair overlooking the infinity pool and proceeded to have one of the most miserable times of her life.

The setting looked exactly like a travel brochure, with the turquoise waters of the swimming pool in the foreground and the white sands of the beach beyond. Smiling staff carried elaborate cocktails to holiday-makers reclining in swimsuits and sarongs. The only wrong note was Mimi. Because the travel brochures *never* showed anyone holidaying by themselves. Mimi was the only solo person requesting a table for one in a resort world populated by honeymooners, retired couples and the occasional well-heeled family.

Dutifully trotting off on tourist excursions organised by the resort (air-conditioned bus, an endless supply of cold, bottled water, personal tour guide, etc.), Mimi wandered miserably through the Monkey Forest in Ubud in the hand-holding wake of Jayne and Matt from

Melbourne (honeymooners) and shared lunch tables with Dot and Larry (retirees from regional New South Wales), all the while wishing desperately for someone of her own age to talk to who wasn't superglued at the hand, waist or lips to their freshly minted spouse.

And then, one day, while visiting the amazingly beautiful temple at Tanah Lot, which perched on a crag jutting into the sea, Mimi lagged slightly behind the rest of the group and somehow fell into conversation with two girls and a guy around her own age. The girls were German and were travelling together; the guy was Danish and had just met the girls the day before in the hostel where they were all staying. They were backpackers. After only ten minutes spent listening to their tales of spontaneous journeys to out-of-the-way destinations and a lifestyle committed to exploration and new experiences, Mimi was deeply ashamed of both her unadventurous spirit and her five-star hotel. She made plans to meet up with them that night for a drink and then sheepishly rejoined her tour group, who were patiently waiting for her at a reserved table in one of the air-conditioned, cliff-top tourist restaurants.

In retrospect, Mimi cringed with embarrassment. She was *Australian*, for God's sake. If Australians didn't precisely invent backpacker culture, it was fair to say that for a country with only 22-odd million people, it must certainly seem to the rest of the world that there are at least nineteen million Australians between the ages of eighteen and thirty-five currently eating two-minute noodles in hostels from Phuket to Rio de Janeiro, wearing hiking boots and Explorer socks in the Uffizi and on Fifth Avenue, and trying to scam free trips on their Eurail passes.

But while Mimi might have been a late bloomer, she was also a quick learner. Within a week she had checked out of her fancy resort hotel and into the hostel where her new friends were staying. From that moment on, she proceeded to live, sleep, sightsee, drink and party with people her own age from all around the world. And from pretty much that first day, Mimi was hooked on the backpacker lifestyle.

She *loved* it. She loved the noisy hostels, the shared kitchens, the constant ebb and flow of people in and out of her life. She loved the spontaneous day trips and cricket matches on the beach and renting clapped-out scooters to visit places which were never seen by that most despised breed: 'the tourists'. She loved the night-time drinking and dancing and the love affairs that were always too brief to break your heart. She loved the ephemeral nature of people and place. But, most of all, she loved the whole-hearted embrace of an ethos of irresponsibility.

Admittedly she didn't like the sometimes grotty showers and lack of privacy in the shared dormitories (someone was forever stumbling in loudly, drunk at three in the morning), and the endless conversations about how to make your funds stretch out, so that it was like some bizarre reversal of misfortune where privileged Westerners had to live on only a dollar a day. And the only two books anyone ever seemed to read were the Lonely Planet travel guide and *The Beach*. But the rest more than made up for it.

From Indonesia Mimi joined an unofficial backpackers' trail that wended its way through Thailand and India to Turkey, and then on to Greece and through Western Europe, until she finally found herself in London, where she decided to stay for a while.

Through Craig's List, Mimi found a room in a share house in Earls Court. (She later grew to suspect that her former colonial masters had had every Australian implanted with a microchip homing device that led them straight to Earls Court as soon as they reached the Mother Country.) She shared the house with a girl named Mattie (her real name was Madeleine but she hated it), who was an environmental activist and the only person Mimi had ever known who kept an assortment of boltcutters and tyre clamps in her bedroom. (She used them to disable logging trucks.) Her other flatmate was Jared, who supported himself financially by busking and sleeping with women.

Jared wasn't technically a gigolo – he didn't actually charge women for his sexual services – but he did manage to avoid incurring a lot of life's necessary expenses by picking up a new girl, staying at her house for a week or two, consuming all her food and alcohol and doing his laundry there. When the girl eventually got tired of his leech-like behaviour (the smarter ones figured it out within a week), he'd move on. Unbelievably, the adjective most people attached to Jared when describing him was 'cool'. It was as though the impression he first made outlasted every other outrageous and scuzzy action that he later performed. How he managed this Mimi didn't know but it had served him well in his twenty-eight years of life.

When it came to sorting out bills, Mattie and Mimi had actually had arguments with Jared where he'd refused to contribute to heating or water bills because he could prove that that month he had been living with Skye or Willow or the 'redhead' (it was common for him to forget their names). They usually gave in because he did pay his share of the rent on time, more or less, and it suited them both to have the room let but to have a frequently absent flatmate.

Mimi's flatmates assumed that she had a job with a telemarketing company, as this was what she had told them. She'd had to tell them something or they would have wondered how she supported herself financially. When Mimi realised that she was going to settle in London for longer than she had originally thought, she even went and worked at one of those places so that she could make her cover story seem more plausible. She had made phone calls for three days until she started to lose the will to live and left. But it had served its purpose. Mimi had her place of work, knew enough about it to fudge details when Mattie and Jared asked her how her day had been, and could even complain about how Sue in the cubicle next to her kept using her coffee mug. Without wanting to be too smug, Mimi honestly thought that she might have had a brilliant career with ASIO. Her cover was perfect.

What she actually did during the working week remained her glorious secret.

She went to the theatre.

Day after day, Mimi sat through performances of musicals, drama and comedy. She haunted the West End and the Open Air Theatre at Regent's Park and tiny venues located above pubs. She went to the Covent Garden Festival and saw the Royal Shakespeare Company more times than she could count. She watched Hollywood stars in vanity projects and soap stars in pantomimes. Occasionally, when she knew that she was reaching saturation point with the West End because she couldn't get a tune from *The Lion King* out of her head, or the woman at the *tkts* booth at Leicester Square had started to greet her by name, she'd buy a ticket to a graduate performance or catch the tube to some godforsaken draughty warehouse in an industrial estate and sacrifice three hours of her life to sitting through a piece of earnest performance art that was so bad it was good.

She would often have to call upon all her meagre drama training when she returned home after a day supposedly at 'work' to sound beaten down about the crowds on the tube or the irritating clients on the phone, when she had in fact spent the day enthralled by a spectacle of swirling colour and movement or a performance so moving that it had made her weep silently in the dark. Mimi would especially have liked to have told Mattie the truth and to have taken her to the theatre occasionally, but it simply wasn't possible. Theatre tickets were outrageously expensive in London and her flatmates would have wondered about the origin of all of her disposable income. Of course if they'd discovered that she was at the theatre during the day, that would also have comprehensively blown the cover on her 'job'. Which would have led to them wondering why Mimi was sharing such a dump with them when she clearly had a lot of money and no need to work. And then Mimi wouldn't be one of 'us' any more and she'd be back to being the only young, single person in the financially stable world of couples and families. So until Mimi met Amisha, who became her regular weekend theatre companion, she went by herself.

Mimi's life in London therefore became an endless fantasy fuelled by the theatre and her web of lies. Although she tried hard not to think about it, she knew all along that somehow, at some stage, it would all unravel. That was to be expected, really. But she just kept trying to put the moment off, by knotting herself up in more and more lies, in a desperate attempt to stave off the truth and the knowledge that she couldn't live this way indefinitely.

The irony was that when the unravelling finally came (in a rather more dramatic fashion than even such a theatrical devotee as Mimi would have wished), it was because her final knot was the most complicated and disastrous one of all.

It was the proverbial knot that you tie when you get married.

36

Mimi's Wedding

When Mimi looked back, she often thought that the weirdest part of this very strange time in her life was how she ever ended up in a relationship with Jared in the first place. When she met him at the interview for the room in the Earls Court house, she privately nicknamed him 'Dumb Jared'. It was mean but he did have an undeniably dim, caveman-like aura about him. His matted dreadlocks and bulky physique, combined with his habit of always leaving his mouth hanging slightly open, all contributed to the suggestion of a prehistoric being.

However, this was not to say that he was unattractive. Far from it. His big brown eyes, impressive muscles and habit of soulfully playing Devendra Banhart covers on his guitar on street corners ensured that there was an endless parade of hippy-ish looking girls in and out of his less-than-clean bedroom. But he didn't do it for Mimi. Which, because he had already slept with Mattie (an episode that she deeply regretted and attributed solely to the fact that she had been in an exceptionally good mood that night following the official announcement that the Trafalgar Square pigeons had been declared a protected species), naturally drove him mad.

At first he resorted to unsubtle and unwittingly hilarious techniques to win her over, such as engaging Mimi in long conversations when he had just emerged from the shower wearing nothing but a towel wrapped around his hips. When this strategy failed he started having very loud sex with other girls. His bedroom was adjacent to Mimi's and presumably his thinking was that Mimi would feel jealous of what she was missing out on. The only effect it had was to make Mimi bang on the wall, and when that didn't silence him, she sang the Celine Dion song from *Titanic* at the top of her voice. That usually worked.

Finally, Jared took the only sensible option open to him. They got drunk together. With beer goggles on, Mimi somehow forgot about his love of violent computer games and habit of eating cold spaghetti straight from the tin and instead realised that he had a lovely voice and an even nicer body. There was also the little matter that she hadn't slept with anyone since Paris (the city, not the heiress), which had been at least six months ago. At two in the morning, after seven beers, flouting the 'Don't Sleep with Your Flatmate' rule, just for once, hadn't seemed like such a bad thing.

To everyone's surprise, not least Mattie's, who was horrified and earnestly lectured Mimi every chance that she got about his unsuitability, Mimi and Jared somehow drifted beyond a one-night stand and became a sort-of couple. Like everything else in Mimi's London life, being with Jared was just easy. She no longer even had to leave the house to spend a night on the couch watching DVDs with her boyfriend. He was the quintessential slacker boyfriend for her lovely slacker life.

Everything changed with the rapid approach of the third of December. That date would mark the first anniversary of her mother's death and Mimi was dreading it. If anyone had told her that that date could get *worse* for her, she simply wouldn't have believed them. But they would have been right, because it was about to become a double anniversary for Mimi.

For the rest of Mimi's life, the third of December would forever be the day that her mother died – and her wedding day too.

*

Jared and Mimi got married because they were drunk. They hadn't meant to, of course. It wasn't as though they were in love. They were just drinking as usual, and on that fateful night they happened to be in Las Vegas.

Mimi told Jared that she had won a holiday to Las Vegas by entering a competition run by *The Sun*. He had looked at her blankly.

'You don't even read *The Sun*. You read *The Guardian*.'

'I know. But *you* read *The Sun* and I was flicking through it and they had this competition and I entered it and – I won.' She sounded unconvincing even to herself. Luckily, the idea of Mimi having the private means to fly them both to America was even more inconceivable to Jared, so he swallowed her story.

With hindsight, Mimi not only wanted to kick herself, she also wanted to slap, tea-towel flick and Chinese burn herself. But she had been dreading the first anniversary of her mother's death, which would be swiftly followed by the anniversary of her fight with Sabrina and the revelations about their father. Within one week she had effectively lost all of her immediate family, while even her treasured memories of her beloved father had been sullied. The guilt over not returning home to see her mother before she died still haunted Mimi, making her want to flee to a different place where she could forget for a while in new surroundings. She was restless and wanting to move on but she had also slipped into a comfortable sort of existence in London.

So she compromised. She bought both Jared and herself plane fares, organised accommodation and then told Jared that she had won a newspaper competition.

And of all the places in the world that they could have gone, she chose Las Vegas.

It had made sense at the time. She wanted to go to an unashamed party town, somewhere bright and loud and hedonistic, where she could lose herself in drinking and dancing and not have to think or remember. She had already been to Ibiza so Las Vegas seemed the next obvious choice.

Las Vegas, Mimi would later constantly berate herself. *I had to pick Las Vegas.*

The only place on the planet that offered legally binding, instantaneous weddings.

*

At midday on the fourth of December, Mimi woke up in her Las Vegas hotel room feeling like someone was drilling into her skull. Sitting upright in bed felt like a feat that ought to have won her an Olympic gold medal, but shortly thereafter she outdid even that achievement by sprinting to the bathroom in world-record time in order to throw up in the toilet.

She had never been so hungover in her life, which led Mimi to the logical conclusion that the previous night she must have been the drunkest she had ever been in her life, which was saying something.

Mimi staggered through the bedroom door and into the living area of their hotel room, where Jared was eating one of those disgustingly enormous American breakfasts that contain about ten slices of bacon, three eggs and an entire field of potatoes. The smell of fried food made Mimi want to vomit again.

She held onto the doorframe, waiting for the nausea to subside. Sensing her presence, Jared looked up. He gave her a wolfish grin but kept chewing, his mouth slightly open.

'Good morning, wife,' he greeted her.

Mimi looked at him with incomprehension. 'Huh?'

He took another bite of his breakfast and she watched, revolted, as egg yolk dribbled down his chin. 'You know, now that we're married, you really ought to be making my breakfast. I'll let you off this once, seeing as how we're on our honeymoon.'

She looked away from the egg yolk before she really did vomit again and tried to still the pounding in her head so that she could concentrate. He was obviously joking but she couldn't for the life of her see what was funny.

'Jared, what are you talking about?' At this point she was only paying him the barest of attention. The part of her brain that was still functioning was wondering how she was going to make it to the kitchen to get a glass of water.

He threw back his head and roared with laughter. 'I love it! We got married and you don't even remember!'

Mimi let go of the doorframe in shock and then grabbed it again for support as she lost her balance. Somewhere, in the far recesses of her mind, she remembered how she had always wanted to travel to the USA so that she could visit Broadway. Now she was here, but instead of being in the theatre district of New York, she was in the middle of a strange fantastical desert city, feeling like she was about to die from thirst, while a guy with egg on his face was telling her that they had just got married.

She made her way limply over to the couch and sat down as she tried to piece together the events of the night before. And then, horribly, it started to come back to her.

'*Oh my God*,' she wailed, horror-struck. 'We *did*, didn't we? We actually got married.'

He nodded and stuck another forkful of grease into his relentlessly chewing mouth. At that precise moment, he was the most repulsive thing Mimi had ever seen. 'What do you think Mattie will say? Ten quid says she'll be jealous. She's always had a bit of a thing for me.'

Mimi ignored this bit of self-delusion and concentrated on recalling the actual ceremony. She couldn't quite remember it. Her memories of the night before were just a blurred kaleidoscope of lights and loud music and strange faces, none of which made sense.

'Did Elvis marry us?' she asked, taking a stab. They were in Las Vegas, after all. Weren't all Vegas shotgun marriages conducted by Elvis?

Jared shook his head and his dreadlocks jiggled. 'Nup. You were too out of it so I got to choose the celebrant. Here.' He ferreted around in a pile on the messy table and then threw a photograph over to her.

It was a large, cheap, laminated photograph that had been taken in a brightly lit, tawdry-looking wedding chapel. Jared and Mimi were standing (strictly speaking, Mimi was leaning), clearly drunk out of their minds, on either side of the wedding celebrant.

Mimi wanted to die from shame. Their marriage ceremony had been officiated by an Anna Nicole Smith doppelganger. She had been married by the look-alike of a drug-addicted ex-Playboy bunny who was *dead*. Appalling didn't even begin to describe it. And what on earth had she been *wearing*? She appeared to have some sort of veil sideways on her head and was holding a bouquet of plastic peach-coloured roses, complete with artificial raindrops. In her teeth.

'Hey, we should ring the newspaper. They love this sort of stuff. They'll probably put us up in a honeymoon suite somewhere posh and put our wedding picture on the front page.'

'What on earth are you talking about?' Mimi snapped. 'What newspaper?'

He looked at her strangely. '*The Sun*. The whole reason we're here. The competition you won, remember?'

'Oh. Of course.' Mimi wanted to throw up again. She couldn't keep track of all the lies and disasters. She just wanted to crawl into bed and make it all go away: Jared and the pounding in her head and the sick feeling in her stomach and the horrible nightmare of being married to someone who she was beginning to realise she didn't even really like.

*

By mid-afternoon Mimi was feeling much better, both physically and mentally. She had vomited again, crawled back into bed and slept for another three hours and then had a shower. After that she had had an excruciatingly embarrassing conversation with the lovely, understanding hotel concierge. He had displayed such a lack of surprise at her predicament that she was left with the comforting impression that her horrendous drunken marriage was an essential part of the Las Vegas tourist experience that it would almost have been a shame to miss out on.

'We can get an annulment,' she informed Jared triumphantly, when he returned from the gaming tables where he had spent the afternoon. 'It costs almost a thousand dollars but then it will be as though it never happened.' *Thank God*, she added mentally.

'Well, I don't have a thousand dollars,' he drawled. Mimi briefly wondered how Jared could have spent the afternoon placing bets in the casino when he rarely had any money, but his next comment completely put that thought out of her mind. 'So too bad. We're stuck with each other.'

'I have money,' Mimi said, before realising her mistake.

He shot her a calculating look that she didn't like at all. 'A holiday to Vegas and now money stashed in the bank? Are you holding out on me, Mimi? Maybe I've just gone and married a rich bird.'

'I told you that I won the holiday,' Mimi scrambled hastily. 'And although I do have a job, I don't have a bank account, remember?' Mimi had an oft-expressed horror of banks and despite her large inheritance she had discovered that they weren't too keen on her either. Her lack of a fixed address or permanent phone number and her string of discarded email addresses and mobile phone numbers (she simply set up a new email or mobile account every time she forgot her password or changed countries) caused them to regard her with deepest suspicion. For all of these reasons, Mimi no longer had a bank account or credit card, preferring instead to use traveller's cheques.

Jared still looked suspicious but she quickly set about being sweet to him so that he'd agree to the annulment. Mercifully, Jared's fear of commitment far outweighed what had seemed a hilarious joke to him that morning, so he didn't take much convincing. Mimi needed to keep him happy until the papers were signed, however, so just to be on the safe side, when she realised that a substantial amount of money was missing from her purse she didn't mention it, although that did explain how Jared had been able to finance his day's entertainment.

In any event, escaping from the entanglement turned out to be easy. Too easy. Because it was an uncontested annulment, all they had to do was sign some papers, pay the fee and then the clerk promised to mail the formal notification of the dissolution of their marriage within two weeks. Almost beside herself with relief, Mimi cashed several traveller's cheques and treated Jared to round after round of celebratory drinks that night. She was so drunk on vodka and a sense of liberation that, towards the end of the night, she recklessly instructed the bartender to shout the whole bar. She was so drunk that she paid no attention to the fact that for once Jared's drinking wasn't keeping pace with hers. And she was so drunk that she interpreted a sudden shrewd, calculating expression on his face as he watched her as caring attentiveness.

It was all so obvious in retrospect that Mimi still found it hard to believe that at first she was surprised, even anxious, when she woke up after midday the following day and discovered that Jared had vanished. All of his belongings had gone too. She soon discovered that he had also taken with him the thick wallet containing her traveller's cheques. He had generously left her two cheques with a combined value of a thousand dollars, which was decent of him, considering that she still had to pay the hotel bill. Apart from that, all she had was her plane ticket back to London, her passport and her purse.

Arriving back in London, Mimi tried to book a flight home to Australia, intending to pay her fare with what was left of her money and with funds she had raised through an appeal to the nice lady who worked in the *tkts* booth in Leicester Square, who agreed to give her a refund on several expensive theatre tickets. But Mimi soon discovered that a last-minute purchase of an international plane ticket during the peak holiday season was virtually impossible, unless she flew first class, which Mimi most emphatically could no longer afford. The first available economy seat was therefore on a flight that was booked to leave London in January. Unable to afford even her rent, Mimi made up a story for Mattie and then turned to the only people in London that she trusted to help her.

Amisha and Raj had listened to her story in horrified silence. At the end of it they had begged her to call the police, to no avail. When they realised that she would not be moved on this point, they had offered her the only assistance that remained in their power to give by insisting that she sleep on their sofa for the remainder of her time in London.

During the long flight home, as movies that she couldn't concentrate on unfolded in front of her and the plane flew ever southwards, Mimi was unable to stop her mind from returning to the unpleasant truth that, as it turned out, Dumb Jared wasn't so dumb after all. Not only had he successfully graduated from a lifestyle of sponging off women to full-blown larceny, if he'd stayed married to his 'rich bird' and they'd ultimately got a divorce, he would have been entitled to half of Mimi's inheritance at most.

This way, he got it all.

37

Fireworks

'*You're married?*'

Mimi wasn't sure who said it first. She thought it might have been all three of them simultaneously. Even Teddy lost his composure. She was dismayed to discover that when Teddy was surprised, his eyebrows shot up into his hairline. For the first time ever, he didn't look particularly attractive. Sabrina actually jumped to her feet, which Mimi supposed she couldn't help given that years on *Sunshine Cove* had ingrained dramatic responses to these sorts of disclosures. As for Nate, well, Mimi wasn't entirely certain what his initial reaction was as she hadn't been looking at him. By the time she did, he was sitting back quietly, just looking sort of watchful. Not shocked or outraged. He was simply waiting to hear what she had to say. It calmed her down.

'Was,' Mimi muttered. 'Not any more.'

'You've been married and divorced and I didn't even know about it?' Sabrina's voice had gone shrill.

'I'm not divorced. I'm . . . annulled.' God, she hadn't even bothered to find out the correct term for her state. She wasn't a wife and she wasn't a divorcée. She was some sort of weird creature from the bog – an anullite, perhaps. It sounded like a category of fossil.

'Who did you marry?' Sabrina demanded.

Why she was getting so antsy Mimi had no idea. Sabrina had gone off and got engaged to Teddy and hadn't told *her* a thing about it.

'His name is Jared,' Mimi said shortly. 'He was my flatmate back in London.'

She felt a hand on her arm and she looked into Amisha's remorseful gaze. 'Mimi, I'm so sorry,' Amisha said pleadingly. 'I just assumed that you would have told them about Jared and what he did to you.'

'What are you talking about? What did he do to her?' Now Sabrina wasn't even looking at Mimi. She was focused on Amisha as though only she could be trusted to disclose the truth.

Amisha looked at Mimi with mute contrition.

'Nothing,' Mimi said firmly. 'He just married me and then ran off. Before you all start feeling sorry for me, you may as well save your energy. I wasn't in love with him and he didn't break my heart.'

Teddy spoke up, sounding bewildered. 'But if you weren't in love with him, why did you marry him?'

Mimi looked at him helplessly and wondered how she could explain to Teddy a drunken night out in Las Vegas that had turned into an impromptu marriage. It was utterly impossible. Teddy would never understand. It was too far out of his range of experience. The most shocking, irresponsible thing Teddy had ever done probably involved a prank with a whoopee cushion when he was eight.

Sabrina had switched her gaze back to her sister and Mimi could have sworn that gaze was cutting through to her bones. 'What happened to your inheritance, Mimi?' she asked suddenly.

'None of your business.'

'Did you have to pay him off for some reason?' Mimi could see Sabrina's mind working rapidly, probably going through every plot from the last five seasons of *Sunshine Cove*: blackmail, extortion, kidnapping, gambling debts.

'No, I did not!' *Bloody hell*, thought Mimi. It was probably easier to tell them all the truth and to have them know that she was just stupid rather than a traumatised victim. 'Look, we got married in Las Vegas. We were drunk. We got an annulment the next day and to celebrate we got drunk again. When I woke up the next morning he'd stolen all of my traveller's cheques and done a runner. End of story.'

'You had all that money in traveller's cheques?' Sabrina gasped. 'Why didn't you have a bank account?'

'Oh for God's sake, Sabrina, if you bring up high-interest accounts now, I'm going to pour champagne over your head. Yes, I had it all in traveller's cheques. It was easier than having a bank account. I was never in a fixed address long enough to receive mail from a bank, and with traveller's cheques I didn't even have to remember an access code.' Mimi hated passwords and personal identification numbers as she could never be bothered taking the time to commit them to memory.

'But he would have had to show identification to cash them and they were in your name.'

'He just had to forge my signature – which wouldn't be hard – and they were printed with only my first initial. M Falks could just as well be a man. As for showing ID, there are plenty of dodgy money exchanges around that don't ask for it. Half the time when I changed cheques into cash they didn't even look at my passport.'

'What did the police say?' asked Teddy sombrely.

'Nothing. I didn't call them.'

As Teddy and Sabrina digested this further folly, Amisha spoke up in a small voice. 'Raj and I tried to make her report it but she refused. Nothing we said could make her change her mind.'

'He robbed you of – what? Two hundred thousand dollars? More? How much did you have left?' Sabrina didn't wait for an answer. 'And you didn't go to the police? What is *wrong* with you?'

Mimi was silent. This bit she knew she definitely couldn't explain

303

to their satisfaction. She actually had made a half-hearted attempt to get her money back, although she hadn't gone to the police. Instead, she had made up a vague tale for the sympathetic hotel concierge, implying that she had lost a substantial amount of traveller's cheques. (He had been very concerned at the terrible time she was having in Las Vegas.) He had immediately told her that all she needed to do was supply her traveller's cheque agency with the serial numbers of the missing cheques and they would immediately put a stop on them. She would also need to know who had supplied the cheques. Were they American Express? Thomas Cook? Bank of America? Mimi had no idea. Remembering the source of cheques and writing down serial numbers as a safeguard was the sort of thing people like Sabrina did. It didn't fit Mimi's beloved ethos of irresponsibility. So she had thanked the concierge and hung up, abandoning any faint hope she'd held of getting her money back.

However, it wasn't solely the practicalities of retrieving her money that held Mimi back from calling the police. The main reason she had decided not to report Jared was the realisation that the money was the only thing keeping her overseas. She was homesick and desperate to escape the tangled web of lies that had become her life in London, but it had seemed stupid to go back to Australia while she still had the means to live it up in a foreign country. And she had no other real reason to go home. Becoming penniless was Mimi's excuse to herself that she needed to return. If the police had found Jared and she'd got the money back, that excuse would have evaporated and she would have been forced to drift once more.

Mimi looked around the room, feeling hunted and wanting desperately to escape from further questions. And then, for the first time since Amisha's revelation, Nate spoke up.

'Mimi, you look like you could use some fresh air. Why don't we go for a quick walk?'

She looked at him gratefully. 'Sounds perfect. Amisha, Raj, you don't mind if I leave you for a few minutes, do you?'

'Of course not,' Amisha said quickly. Sabrina's face told a different story, but before she could object and question Mimi further, Edward laid a restraining hand upon her arm. Sabrina subsided and Mimi avoided her gaze as she and Nate quickly slipped out of the suite and made their way to the elevator.

'Thank you,' Mimi said gratefully, as soon as the elevator doors had closed.

'No problem,' he said easily. 'You looked as if you thought you were about to be burned at the stake or something.'

They made their way through the lobby and out onto George Street. They were given no choice as to the direction they went, as there were still throngs of people making their way towards Circular Quay for a view of the midnight fireworks. So they simply joined them and let the crowd carry them along.

'Nate, about what you just heard —' Mimi began.

'You don't owe me an explanation, Mimi,' he said firmly. 'It's none of my business.'

'I know. I want to tell you though,' Mimi said, surprising herself. It was true. She hadn't talked about any of this since she left London. It was almost a relief to have it out in the open. 'I know that whole story you just heard makes me seem like a complete flake but it all made sense to me at the time. The thing is Jared kind of reminded me of Dad. Wait – that sounds creepy.' She stopped and then started again. 'I mean, not in looks, but in the way he lived his life. I always thought that it was admirable to go through life laughing at responsibilities. Mortgages and bills and settling down were for boring people who liked living in the suburbs.' She paused and swallowed painfully. 'Of course, when I found out about Dad a couple of years ago – do you know about our dad?' She paused and Nate nodded. 'Well, I realised

305

that Dad's attitude must have been a cover for his drinking. He couldn't hold down a job because he was never sober so that's how he justified it to himself. But I never knew that. So I always thought that financial responsibility and having a stable job were the prime indicators of someone who didn't understand what life was really about – excitement and adventure. I still believed that up until about a week ago when I found out that Sabrina had put money aside for me so that I wouldn't ever be a burden to Aunty Bron . . .' her voice trailed off.

'But didn't the money come from your dad? How was he able to leave you money if he never had a job?' Nate asked. He had taken Mimi's hand, which seemed like an entirely natural thing to do given that they were in a crowd of about a hundred thousand people. But it was also very comforting.

'He came from a wealthy family. There was a trust fund. Sabrina told me that Granny – that was Dad's mum – changed her will just before she died. Dad had to stay sober for twelve months to get the money. He never managed it. So the money was divided between Sabrina and me when I turned twenty-one. I took off overseas a month later.'

They came to a stop as the crowd was now too dense to go any further and, disappointingly, Nate let go of her hand. It was strange. All around them were people in high spirits, yet they were having a serious heart-to-heart. It felt all wrong. Nate and Mimi weren't meant to be the serious types.

Mimi thought for a moment and then took a deep breath. 'Sabrina always says that I'm exactly like Dad – and she's right. He used to throw things when he lost his temper and that's exactly what I do. The night before Mum's funeral I threw a framed photograph at Sabrina's face. And when we had our fight over her hen's night I threw a heavy notebook at her. I only just missed.'

Back in London, whenever Mimi had lost her temper and thrown things, Jared had semi-encouraged her. He had laughingly called her 'crazy' and had once likened her to the fiery, unstable artist character played by Penelope Cruz in Mimi's favourite Woody Allen film *Vicky Cristina Barcelona*. She had been secretly thrilled with this comparison. Now it made her feel sick. She waited for Nate's response, hoping with all her heart that he would condemn her behaviour, not excuse it, like Jared had.

He did neither.

'Well, that's something that's within your control,' Nate said. 'You can make sure that it doesn't happen again. It's up to you.'

She looked at him, surprised by this novel response, but before she could answer, the countdown began around them. Nate grabbed her hand again and as he yelled out the numbers from ten to one, Mimi joined in, shouting at the top of her voice. Then the sky and the Harbour Bridge exploded with fireworks and all around them everyone cheered and started to kiss one another as they welcomed in the New Year.

Even though there were fireworks exploding in the sky behind Mimi and Nate, when the inevitable happened it didn't feel dramatic or spectacular. It just felt right.

Nate bent his head and kissed her gently on the lips.

'Don't look so sad, Mimi. It's a new year. The perfect time for a fresh beginning.'

Two Weeks
Before the Wedding

- Hold bachelor party – DO NOT schedule it for the night before the wedding!

- Choose ceremony readings

- Write speech for reception

38

Cold Feet

CELEBRITY CONFIDENTIAL RUMOUR ALERT!
One soon-to-be-wed star, who has always been less than sociable, seems to have changed her tune right before her wedding. Well-placed sources say that for the past few months, Sabrina Falks has been spotted at several discreet locations around town, enjoying intimate dinners in the company of former on-screen love-interest (and Sydney's Most Eligible Bachelor) Ethan Carter, who has recently returned from the City of Angels . . . Stay tuned for breaking wedding day drama!

In the same way that Sabrina was the 'pretty one', it was an incontrovertible family truth that Mimi was the actor of the family. Only Sabrina, watching from the sidelines, forming part of Mimi's appreciative audience, knew otherwise.

Mimi was the clown. It was she, Sabrina, who had always been the serious actor. She was the one who always hid what she was thinking and feeling, who played the role of dutiful daughter to her mother and supportive older sister to Mimi. Inside, she was really someone else.

And the roles kept accreting. Glamorous soapie star. Edward's beautiful wife-to-be. Soon she would become a daughter-in-law, a sister-in-law, an aunt. Of course, everyone played roles in other people's lives, but it had always seemed to Sabrina that other people managed to remain the protagonist in their own lives, whereas she often felt as though her primary purpose was to be a supporting character in the stories of others. Sometimes she felt that there was no 'real' Sabrina. There was only that beautiful golden girl, whom everyone felt that they knew and owned a part of, with the sole exception of Sabrina herself.

When people spoke of a private life, they were referring to a hidden self. So it made complete sense that the majority of Sabrina's private life was on display for all to see. For she was nothing but shiny surfaces, reflecting back at everyone whatever it was that they wanted to project onto her, while inside there was just barren nothingness; no life or hope at all.

*

'I have a going-away gift for you,' said Edward, two weeks before the wedding. He had just arrived home from work, bearing a gift-wrapped box under one arm.

Sabrina, who was making a rice noodle salad for their dinner, looked at him uncertainly. There had been a stiltedness between them of late, a sense that something already had or was about to go terribly wrong. She knew that Edward didn't read the tabloids or gossip columns but she had made no secret of the fact that, on several occasions when he'd had to work late, she had had dinner with Ethan. She knew that he trusted her, as she did him. Nevertheless, it had been impossible for Edward, like Mimi, not to notice her increasing withdrawal and seeming lack of interest in the wedding. He had tried on several occasions to gently get to the bottom of what was bothering her, to no avail. As many journalists knew to their chagrin, probing Sabrina on personal matters simply had the effect of making her retreat further. So Edward had eventually given up, trusting in the hope that she would tell him in her own time. Besides which, he knew better than most people how counter-productive it could be to have loving concern foisted on you when you were in no mood to accept it. Instead of forcing her into a conversation that she quite clearly wasn't ready to have, Edward had decided to try breaking down her barriers indirectly. He had come bearing a gift.

Sabrina tried to make her tone sound light. 'But you're the one going away!'

'Even more reason. I feel bad going to Hong Kong for an entire week and leaving you with all the wedding hassles.'

'You're going to Hong Kong for your bachelor party! And I know it had to be in Hong Kong if you want your brother to be there so stop feeling guilty and just enjoy it. Anyway, you know that the wedding planner and Mimi are handling everything so stop worrying about me.' The last sentence, which Sabrina had meant to come out in a reassuring tone, instead sounded, even to her own ears, snappish and on edge. Lately, everything that she'd said had come out sounding like that. She couldn't seem to help it.

In silence Edward watched Sabrina tear the paper off the gift-wrapped box. She opened it and lifted out a pair of raspberry-pink Ugg boots. They were lined with sheepskin and looked gloriously comfortable and warm.

Sabrina looked at him in confusion. 'They're lovely Edward. It's just —' she hesitated. She didn't want to seem ungrateful. 'It's summer. It's thirty-five degrees outside! And I don't even know what I've done to deserve a present.'

'They're a good-luck charm.' He swallowed hard. 'To stop you getting cold feet.'

She was immediately overwhelmed with compassion for him. She had been so immersed in her own private world that it hadn't occurred to her that Edward, who had been jilted once before, obviously feared it happening again. For a moment, as her heart filled with love and sympathy, she almost thought she might confide in him. But then fear rose up, fear such as she hadn't felt since she was a child. She loved Edward but he meant so much more to her than just romantic love. Their life together was a sanctuary for Sabrina. Losing him – and she had no doubt that if she told him the truth about what was worrying her she would lose him – would also mean losing her safe haven, her emotional security, that had taken her so long to find. The very thought of it made Sabrina sick with fear. She knew that she was no different from most people in wanting to feel safe and loved. But she had often suspected that other people didn't crave the element of safety in quite the same way that she did.

Edward had been watching her intently. 'Not ready to tell me?' he asked quietly.

Sabrina found herself thinking about Mimi's eighth birthday party. Of how, even though she had been terrified and had wanted to scream, she had stayed quiet and kept her expression carefully neutral. She felt like that again now. On the outside she appeared serene. Inside she was dying.

She looked down at the slippers that she was still holding. It was only then she realised her hands were shaking.

Edward took her in his arms. 'I promise you, whatever it is that's bothering you, we can find a solution together.'

Sabrina returned his kiss mechanically. When he went into the bedroom to change out of his suit she clenched her fists over and over again, trying to stop her hands from trembling.

She was living on borrowed time. Some day soon the truth had to come out and, when it did, all of those shiny, shiny surfaces that she had worked so hard to flawlessly maintain, would shatter into a million pieces and everyone would see her for what she really was.

She had to tell him.

But, oh God, she thought, her fists still clenched, *please, not yet, not yet, not yet.*

*

It was unsurprising that Edward had put a lot of thought into how he would propose, and the final result was very Edward: a lavish setting, a stylish set-up and a heartfelt pièce de résistance. When he whisked Sabrina away for a romantic week on the Hawaiian island of Kauai, she'd had an inkling that he was intending to propose, although when he first produced the black silk blindfold, the thought that they were about to embark on some unusual sex game briefly crossed her mind too. She immediately dismissed the idea given that it was the middle of the day, they were on Kalapaki Beach in full view of dozens of people, and unusual sex games weren't exactly either Edward's or her own style.

Blindfolded, she let him lead her by the hand to a shaded spot. He helped her to sit down and then placed a gift-wrapped parcel in her hands. Only then did he remove the black silk covering her eyes.

She was sitting on a traditional woven mat in a quiet spot on the beach, with an uninterrupted view of the ultramarine water and the sparkling white sand. Sabrina looked at Edward inquiringly. The gift-wrapped box that she was holding in her hands was not the shape of a ring-box. To begin with, it was too big and it was also quite long and cylindrical.

He smiled at her. 'Open it.'

Sabrina tore off the paper and, opening one end, tipped out the contents. It was a scroll. She untied the velvet ribbon that was holding it closed. Smoothing it out, she realised that the scroll depicted two family trees side by side: Edward's and hers.

Edward, who was sitting beside her, gently put his fingertip to the paper and began to trace the names. 'See, now here, that's my great-uncle Victor. Lived a perfectly respectable and uneventful life and then went as mad as a cut snake when he turned eighty-two. Used to wander around in his old army cap and nothing else, humming show tunes. And here – that's my great-grandmother, Norah. She had a brilliant mind but wasn't permitted to go to university. She had five children and somehow still managed to read three books a week right up until she died.' His finger moved lightly over to the side where her family tree was illustrated. 'Your turn. Tell me about your great-great aunt Nancy. She never married or had children, which was unusual for that time. Do you know much about her?'

Sabrina ignored the question and instead looked at him with wonder. 'Edward, how did you do this?'

'It's quite easy these days, actually. There are all sorts of websites and computer programs to help. Then I simply took it to a calligrapher to have it transcribed.' He waited a moment and then said quietly, 'You asked the wrong question, though.'

She looked at him in confusion. 'What should I have asked?'

He smiled. '*Why* did I do this?' He took her hand and she felt her heart begin to beat faster. 'This is where we've both come from, my Sabrina.' He knelt on one knee before her. *Now,* she thought. *It's happening right now.*

'I love you and I want you to marry me. I want our names, joined together, to link both of these family trees.'

Sabrina looked at him. She did not feel a great rush of emotion or sentimentality. Instead she felt a simple joy, as she imagined coming home must feel like for people who had come from happy homes.

'Yes,' she whispered. 'Yes, Edward, I will marry you.'

Many minutes later, he gave her a teasing grin. 'In that case, would you like to see your ring?'

*

Now, as she waited at the restaurant table for Ethan to arrive, with Edward thousands of miles away in Hong Kong, she fidgeted with

316

her diamond engagement ring, turning it around and around on her slim finger.

For Sabrina couldn't stop thinking about that blindfold and how it was the perfect metaphor for their forthcoming marriage. The only flaw she could think of was that it ought to have been Edward who was wearing the blindfold, not her.

39

The Reading

Two nights later, Sabrina was sitting with Mimi in the living room of her apartment, as they attempted to finalise the readings for the wedding ceremony. It was the start of February and over the past few weeks Mimi had had a lovely time showing Amisha and Raj around Sydney, which had culminated in a farewell dinner at Aunty Bron's house the night before. Neither Nate nor Edward had been present as they were in Hong Kong for Edward's bachelor party. Mimi had been both thankful that Nate wasn't there (as she was still not sure what she felt about their unexpected New Year's kiss), and oddly put out by his absence. Mercifully, however, the topic of her shotgun wedding hadn't arisen again. For weeks Mimi had steeled herself to fend off an interrogation from Sabrina, but her sister had been oddly preoccupied. As Mimi knew nothing of the snippet of snide innuendo about Sabrina and Ethan that had run in *Celebrity Confidential*, she was at a loss to explain Sabrina's lack of probing. However, she was far too relieved to have escaped further questioning to spend more than a few minutes pondering the cause.

Mimi had dropped Amisha and Raj off at Sydney Airport (with Amisha still apologising for letting the cat out of the bag right up until she disappeared through the departure gates), and then, on a whim, had driven to Sabrina's apartment. Knowing that Sabrina was alone, she had thought they could use the time to choose the ceremony readings. Already, however, Mimi was regretting her spur-of-the-moment decision. Sabrina hadn't looked particularly happy to see her, nor did she seem terribly interested in the task of selecting the readings. She had already flatly rejected the perennial favourite from Corinthians (*Love is patient, love is kind . . .*), Sonnet 116 by Shakespeare (*Let me not to the marriage of true minds admit impediments . . .*), anything by Pablo Neruda or Khalil Gibran, and had actually snorted when, in desperation, Mimi suggested 'The Magic of Love' by Helen Steiner Rice.

'All right then, what about this one?' asked Mimi, wondering, not for the first time, why she was bothering when Sabrina clearly couldn't be bothered herself. 'It's called "The Art of Marriage" by someone called Wilfred A. Peterson.' Mimi read aloud:

'*In the art of marriage the little things are the big things . . .*
It is remembering to say "I love you" at least once each day.
It is never going to sleep angry . . .
It is forming a circle of love that gathers in the whole family —'

'No,' Sabrina said sharply.

Mimi looked up in surprise. 'I haven't finished yet. I know it's a bit twee but, quite honestly, most of the readings chosen for weddings are.'

'I don't like that one at all.'

'Why not? Do you object to saying "I love you" to Teddy once a day?' asked Mimi, sounding harsher than she had intended.

Instead of answering, Sabrina began to flick restlessly through one of the books of inspirational readings and quotations that Mimi had brought with her. She paused at a page with a quote by Scottish writer George MacDonald. *'To be trusted is a greater compliment than to be loved.'* Sabrina stared at the sentence for a long moment and then closed the book and pushed it away.

Mimi looked closely at her sister and noticed for the first time how pale and unwell Sabrina was looking.

'Breens? Are you all right? Is anything the matter?'

For the briefest of moments, Sabrina was tempted to tell Mimi what was wrong. Then she dismissed the thought. The relief of unburdening herself would be far outweighed by the repercussions of telling Mimi. Mimi would never be able to keep it to herself. The only way to keep a secret was to do exactly that – keep it.

'I'm fine.'

'Fine' in the Falks family had long been code for 'there is something wrong but I have absolutely no intention of discussing it with you'. Still, Mimi persisted.

'It's just – for a bride-to-be you don't seem very happy.'

The familiar weariness crept over Sabrina once again. She didn't want to talk, she didn't want to sit here and go through wedding arrangements. She could feel that strange sense of detachment that she had first experienced after their mother died, descending upon her once again. She knew that she ought to resist it but she was too tired. Anyway, she liked the way that it made her feel, as though nothing was really that important. It meant that she didn't have to make the effort to care.

Mimi was waiting for her to say something and the words just popped into her head. 'The last time I had to choose a ceremony reading was for Mum's funeral.'

Mimi's expression immediately changed. 'Sabrina, I'm sorry. I didn't think of that.'

For a moment Sabrina felt ashamed of herself for making Mimi feel bad, when she hadn't been thinking of their mum's funeral at all, but then she mentally shrugged. There was no other explanation that she could give Mimi right now as to why she didn't want to do any of this. Anyway, it *had* been horrible choosing readings for their mother's funeral. Another thing that she'd had to do alone.

Not from a desire to punish Mimi, but out of genuine curiosity, Sabrina now asked, 'I've always wanted to know – what did you do the day of Mum's funeral?'

Mimi swallowed. 'I went to a bar and got drunk. And then I passed out on the beach at Botany Bay. I was unconscious for hours. I don't even remember getting home. Aunty Bron told me that the police brought me back to her house that night.' She paused and added, 'I don't remember anything from that day apart from drinking at the bar. Not a thing.'

The memory of their mother's coffin being lowered into its grave flashed into Sabrina's mind. She suddenly wished with all her heart that she had got drunk on the day of the funeral; that for her, too, that day was nothing but a refreshing pool of oblivion.

'That sounds nice,' she said unthinkingly.

Mimi looked at her, startled. 'You think being drunk and unconscious in public sounds *nice*?'

'No, I meant —' Sabrina stumbled, all of her natural poise deserting her. 'The bit about escaping to Botany Bay. Do you remember how Mum used to take us there and remind us of its history? She used to say that you could feel the weight of history in the sand. I love it there.' Sabrina knew that she had to keep talking, preferably about Mimi. As long as they did that, then they wouldn't be able to talk about her.

'Are you . . . like Dad?'

'Aren't you always telling me that I'm *exactly* like Dad?' Mimi asked, puzzled.

'That's not what I meant. I mean —' Sabrina faltered over the phrasing. 'I asked the wrong question before you started work for me, didn't I? I asked if you were a drug user, but you're not. You're an alcoholic.'

Mimi sighed. 'I know you like to think the worst of me, Sabrina, but, believe it or not, I really don't drink very often at all.'

'But I bet when you do drink, you don't stop,' Sabrina said, without malice, but as though she were simply stating a fact.

Mimi looked at her, taken aback. 'That's not true. We spent New Year's Eve together. You've seen that I'm perfectly capable of having a few drinks and stopping. Sabrina, what is this all *about*? Are you worried that I'm going to get plastered and embarrass you at your wedding or something?'

Fatigue overwhelmed Sabrina once more. All she wanted was to curl up in bed and go to sleep. And really, who cared if Mimi was an alcoholic? People had to make their own choices and live their own lives. Everyone, that is, except for her, who seemingly had to live her life for other people.

'Forget it. Look, just leave the books with me and I'll choose something within the next few days.' She glanced at the clock. 'Do you mind if I ask you to leave now? I'm very tired for some reason. I think I might go to bed.'

Although they still had a terrifying number of wedding details to finalise and the time frame would soon be measured in days rather than weeks, Mimi had no choice but to comply.

As she exited the lift on the ground floor, an incredibly handsome man, who looked vaguely familiar, entered. On a sudden hunch, Mimi jumped back into the lift, mumbling about having forgotten something, and randomly pressed the button for level two. The stranger pressed the button for the penthouse.

He smiled at her as she got out but Mimi didn't smile in return. Instead, she exited the lift and then took the stairs back down, all the while wondering who exactly that man was, why he was visiting Sabrina at this time of night, when Edward wasn't home, and whether he had anything to do with Sabrina's strange antipathy towards her forthcoming wedding.

40

Mimi's List

Mimi was most definitely *not* an alcoholic. She had given a lot of thought to this matter ever since Sabrina's revelations about their father, and she was extremely confident that she was in no danger of meeting the same fate as him. She could go for days, for *weeks* without a drink, and not give alcohol so much as a fleeting thought. She couldn't count the number of occasions she had met up with friends at the pub and drunk nothing but lemon squash all night, while still remaining the life and soul of the party. She didn't need alcohol to relax, to be sociable or on a daily basis.

Mimi's only vice (if you could even call it that) was that she liked to occasionally go out and 'get smashed', as she put it. And there was certainly no harm in that. It was practically un-Australian *not* to get drunk every weekend during your twenties. It was Mimi's firm belief that if she had abstained from benders and been non-sporty, she would have had to apply for citizenship of another country. Like New Zealand perhaps.

All of which meant that Sabrina's accusations were utterly groundless. She was not an alcoholic. Never had been and never would be. Mimi hated what she had belatedly realised alcohol had done to her family and it would have been the height of stupidity to have replicated her father's fatal flaw. And, whatever her faults, Mimi was very far from being stupid.

Nevertheless, an uncomfortable feeling dogged her every waking moment over the next few days. It was there when she went for her morning run. It followed her to dress fittings at Corinna's salon and was present throughout telephone conversations with Claudia. It sat uncomfortably close to her on the sofa at Aunty Bron's, sticking its persistent and pointy elbows into her ribs, preventing her from relaxing and concentrating on her book. And it was all to do with that one phrase that Sabrina had used: *'But I bet when you do drink, you don't stop.'*

Regardless, it was really more from a sense of exasperation, rather than a belief that Sabrina could be right, that Mimi eventually sat down and tapped a few words into Google on Aunty Bron's computer.

A myriad links to webpages sprang up and she looked at them aghast, before eventually clicking on a page whose information she assumed she could trust, given that it was provided by the Australian Government.

Scrolling down the page of information, she felt reassured. She was not an alcoholic. Just as she'd known, none of the key indicators applied to her.

She was about to exit the website when a link to another page caught her eye. She clicked on it and the heading 'Binge Drinking' came up.

As she started to read, a feeling of uneasiness crept over Mimi, but the more she read, the more she rebelled against the idea that this could in any way apply to her. Of course she'd gone on massive benders in the past – hadn't every 25-year-old? And she would undoubtedly do so again. It was called having a social life.

'If you're unsure whether any of this applies to you, write a list of the last five to ten occasions on which you consumed alcohol to excess,

noting the date, how far apart they occurred, what precipitated them and any consequences.'

Mimi rummaged in the drawer of the desk for a pen and paper and then sat there, chewing the pen as she thought. Some of her really big nights out had been ages ago. Oddly enough, however, while it was almost impossible to remember what had actually happened during those lost days and nights, she could easily remember the exact circumstances that had led to the last five really big binges that she'd had.

Before NIDA exams
The day of Mum's funeral
Christmas in England
Wedding to Jared
Annulment of marriage to Jared

Looking at the list, Mimi felt pleased. She wasn't an alcoholic and it seemed that she didn't even have a binge-drinking problem. Her list only comprised five incidents and they were spaced over a period of almost six years.

She looked at the list again and then, despite the warmth of the afternoon, suddenly felt cold. Every one of her major drinking sessions coincided with a significant life event or decision. In the case of her disastrous marriage to Jared, the binge had been the sole reason she had got married. And now that they were written down in front of her, she could see that all of the worst moments of her life didn't exist in isolation; every bad choice had spiralled into the next one.

It was while she was studying at NIDA that it had first occurred. She had been one of the star students, nevertheless, as the exams approached, she had started to feel a sense of overwhelming panic. She was terrified of failing, of being exposed as a fraud or – even worse – as just average. Her father had drummed it into her that she was special. The night before her first-year exams began, she had tried to stay in her room and rehearse her part in *The Cherry Orchard*. It had been impossible to concentrate, so she had ducked out for a quick drink to settle her nerves. Which had somehow turned into an all-night drinking session.

Mimi had woken up the following evening. The three days that immediately followed had been so consumed with the effort of recovering physically from her massive drinking session that she barely remembered her interview with the Head of Acting when she had quit her course. The only thing she remembered with clarity was that she hadn't had to face the ignominy of failing her exams and of being kicked out of NIDA. Her departure had been on her terms. When she had broken the news, everyone had shrugged and smiled and said that it was typical Mimi – a true free spirit, hating to be pinned down to anything, even the chance of a lifetime. Only Sabrina had told her, unsmilingly, that she thought it was the worst decision of her life and one that she would come to regret.

Mimi had loved her time at NIDA, she now remembered with a jolt. She had loved acting; she had always been passionate about it and had dreamed of a career on the stage. She had never wanted to be famous like Sabrina. She hadn't cared about the trappings – she had only ever wanted to act.

And she had thrown her chance away because of one drunken night.

The next item on the list was even worse. *She had missed her mother's funeral.* What kind of person missed their own mother's funeral to get drunk instead? It hadn't seemed so bad until now, partly because even though the police had brought her home that night, Aunty Bron had never uttered a single word of reproach. They had been complicit in their cowardice, in their inability to deal with their emotions, Mimi realised. Neither of them had given a moment's thought to Sabrina or to how she must have felt that day.

For the first time ever, Mimi tried to imagine what Sabrina must have gone through at the funeral and through the long, torturous hours of the wake: having to talk to people and accept their condolences, surrounded by everyone but the people who should have been there – her family.

The English Christmas binge most certainly wasn't the worst episode on the list but still Mimi flushed with mortification at the memory. She had been twenty-three years old, staggering around a toy shop and stinking of booze in front of small children who were innocently waiting to see Santa. Oh God, what must people have thought of her? And why had she done it? Fear and cowardice, once again. It had been preferable to get drunk rather than telephone Sabrina or Aunty Bron and admit that she was lonely and homesick. Travelling the world solo, she had prided herself on being Dora the Explorer to Sabrina's stay-at-home Malibu Barbie. But when it came to displaying true courage, fearless, adventurous Mimi was the biggest lie of all.

And then, of course, there was Jared. Jared, whom she had never loved. Never really liked that much, in all honesty. But whom she had ended up in a relationship with simply because he showed interest in her. She shuddered at the realisation of how pathetic and insecure she must have been. Then she had married him because she was drunk, and as soon as she'd extricated herself from that nightmare, she'd gone and got drunk all over again, which had enabled him to rob her blind. And she had never even tried to find him, to track him down or to hold him accountable. Because deep down she felt as though it was justice because she was weak and undeserving and a failure. Knowing that she was Jared's victim had felt good in a bizarre way. It meant that she was, at least, better than him. Being one step up from a thief and the victim of abandonment once again had, perversely, given her a sense of self-esteem.

Mimi switched off the computer and went and lay down on her

bed. She curled up into a tight ball and remained there for a very long time. As the afternoon sunshine faded into evening she didn't switch on a light or pull the covers over her.

Mimi wasn't an alcoholic. Of that, she was still certain. But for the first time ever, she felt that perhaps the most important choices of her life hadn't really been choices at all.

41

The Boxing Match

'Is anything wrong, Mimi?' Nate looked at her closely as she greeted him with an abrupt hello. They had both just got out of their respective cars parked on the road overlooking Tamarama Beach. It was half past seven in the morning and they were going for a run.

It was the first time that Mimi had seen Nate since their chaste New Year's kiss and she was extremely nervous about meeting up with him again. She had managed to avoid him for weeks, claiming to be too busy with the wedding and Amish and Raj to attend her regular exercise sessions. However, while Nate had been in Hong Kong with Teddy, Mimi had come to the conclusion that the New Year's Eve kiss must have been an act of convention, nothing more. Furthermore, she was going to have to face him at the wedding. She had therefore emailed him to arrange this workout for the day after he returned from Hong Kong. Meanwhile, Nate had mulled over Mimi's history with Jared and decided that she couldn't possibly be ready to think romantically about anyone. For the time being at least, he would have to settle for friendship.

'Yes. No. Not really.'

'Well, that's all cleared up then.' He waited. He was getting to know Mimi very well and he was fairly certain that in another minute she would probably tell him exactly what was on her mind.

She jiggled her car keys restlessly in one hand. 'It's just . . . Have you written your speech for the wedding?'

'I haven't written anything down yet. But I've worked out in my head the main points that I'm going to make.'

'Like what?'

'Nice try. I'm not going to give you my best material when you'll be making your speech first.'

'Nate, honestly, I need help. I don't know what to say.'

'You're naturally funny, Mimi. Make a few jokes and then just be honest about how you feel.'

But I don't know how I feel about Sabrina, thought Mimi. It depended on the day. Sometimes, like immediately after their enforced conversation on Christmas Day, she felt almost close to Sabrina. Other days she was back to being irritated by her, especially as lately Sabrina had been increasingly withdrawn, moody and even more difficult to deal with than usual. Mimi couldn't shake the preposterous thought that Sabrina didn't *want* to marry Teddy. It was the only explanation that made sense of Sabrina's seeming lack of interest in the accumulating tide of wedding arrangements and details. The only other possible explanation was the one that Mimi had just discovered was being gleefully touted by the blogs and the tabloids. They were hinting that Sabrina was having an affair with the man in the lift, whom Mimi had discovered was an actor named Ethan Carter. Even though she had seen him going to visit Sabrina late at night, Mimi still couldn't bring herself to believe it. But the suspicion lingered. Just thinking about it now made her slam the door of Aunty Bron's car with more force than was strictly necessary.

Nate regarded her thoughtfully as she aimed the remote locking device at the car as though she was firing a gun.

'You seem . . . angry.'

'Don't be silly. Why would I be angry?' She almost smiled as soon as she'd responded because naturally even her denial sounded angry. She almost smiled, but not quite.

The truth was that ever since she'd made that *stupid* list, Mimi had been a simmering cauldron of fury. She was livid and fed up with just about everyone and everything. She was angry that she had somehow ended up spending *her* life focussing on Sabrina's life. She was furious that she was orchestrating a wedding for a bride who seemed completely uninterested in a groom who was unutterably perfect. She was filled with rage at the fact that her life seemed to be nothing but a string of failures and that it was undeniably all her own fault. And she was incensed by the idea that Sabrina, who was lucky enough to be with Teddy, might be so unbelievably stupid as to throw it all away for some beefcake actor.

'I've got an idea.' Nate opened the boot of his car and rummaged around in his bag of sports equipment. Triumphantly he pulled out a pair of boxing gloves and pads. 'Change of plan. We're not going for a run today. We're going to box instead.'

'Why?'

'Therapy. Just trust me.' He locked his car and then led her over the road. They made their way towards an open patch of grass, near the beach. He held up the pads as Mimi pulled on the gloves. 'Okay, ready? Ten uppercuts followed by — ow!'

'Sorry. You asked if I was ready and I was.'

'Fine. Forget the uppercuts. Do whatever you feel like. Just throw punches. Go.'

Mimi took a deep breath and then started to throw hook punches.

'Good. Don't forget to swing your hips. Excellent power. Right. Steady on a bit. That's really quite strong. Watch where you're hitting! You almost got me in the face. Jesus, Miriam —'

'WHY DOES EVERYONE ALWAYS CALL ME THAT WHEN

THEY'RE ANNOYED WITH ME? MY – NAME – IS – MIMI!'

She punctuated the last four words with savage punches that almost knocked Nate off balance.

He fell back and then held up the pads, not as an invitation for her to start punching again but as a sign of submission. 'No, you're not angry at all,' he muttered. 'All right. Start again,' he said quietly. 'And this time I want you to take your time. If you want, you can preface every punch by telling me something that makes you angry.'

Mimi nodded and held up her fists.

'I hate my beautiful tasteful bridesmaid's dress!' POW!

'Good. Keep going.'

'I hate my job!' BAM!

'Perfect. Remember to keep your elbows in.'

'I HATE Jared!' THWACK!

'I hate —' She paused and took a deep breath. 'I hate my sister.' And then Mimi burst into tears and collapsed onto the ground. Nate immediately came to sit beside her. He put an arm around her and let her sob onto his shoulder. 'Why did she have to get *everything*? She has everything, Nate – she got the acting career and the looks and the fame, and now she has Teddy too. It's not fair. She has everything, *everything* that I want.'

Mimi suddenly felt Nate go very still and she froze as she realised what she'd said.

'Oh no. Not you,' he said softly. 'Not you too, Mimi.'

She looked up, her breath still heaving, and tried desperately to think of a quip to alleviate her blunder but nothing came to mind.

Nate gave a sudden laugh as he withdrew the comfort of his strong, warm arm that had been wrapped around her. 'I'm such an idiot. You'd think after all these years it wouldn't surprise me. I guess I assumed because he's engaged to your sister . . .'

'Nate, listen to me,' Mimi said desperately. 'It's not what you think.'

'It's exactly what I think, Mimi,' he said flatly. 'You're either in love with Ed or at the very least have a crush on him. Like every other woman on this planet.'

'I . . .' There was nothing that she could say. There were absolutely no words to make this humiliating moment go away.

Nate waited a moment and then said, almost as though he was thinking aloud, 'Do you know I think in a weird way that your relationship with Sabrina might have been what initially attracted me to you. You were always in Sabrina's shadow, exactly like I'm in Ed's. I felt like you understood.'

'Great. So you thought that together we could be Losers Anonymous?' She regretted the sarcastic comment as soon as it rolled off her tongue.

He looked at her in a very measured way. 'I don't think I'm a loser and I don't think you're one either. I know this might surprise you, given how successful and rich and handsome Ed is, but I wouldn't want to change places with him for one minute.' He then added, with disarming honesty, 'Don't get me wrong – I've spent quite a bit of time in the past wishing that I could swap lives with Ed but then . . .' He shrugged. 'I don't know. I just gradually realised that I'm happy with who I am. I love my work. I'd hate Ed's job – wearing a suit and tie every day and the hours that he has to do. Sabrina told me that when they went on holiday to Hawaii he was constantly on his BlackBerry, checking his emails, or else he was taking work calls for hours each day.' He smiled. 'If I went to Hawaii, I'd rather be scuba diving.' He was quiet for a moment and then he asked, in a gentler tone, 'Do you mind me asking what exactly it is that you like about Ed?'

Mimi looked at him in confusion. 'What do you mean?' she asked, stalling for time, wondering how she could answer 'Well, he's perfect', without hurting Nate's feelings even more.

'I mean, can you name the qualities or characteristics that attracted you to him?'

Mimi's mind went completely blank. 'I don't know,' she finally answered. 'He's just —'

'Perfect?' Nate suggested. She jumped, as though he'd read her thoughts. But he didn't wait for her to respond. 'I thought you might be thinking that. I've been friends with Ed for a long time now and I've noticed something about him. People – men and women – project what they want to see onto him. Even his name gets changed to fit the different ideas of him. Sabrina likes the conventionality of his family and upbringing so she calls him by his full, formal name. I call him Ed, which is more like the bloke I know. You call him Teddy, which is warmer and more intimate.' Mimi's cheeks grew hot. 'Claudia used to call him Ned, which I have to say I never thought suited him. She had her own reasons for wanting to change him.'

'What are you trying to say?'

'I'm trying to say that for some reason everyone has their own idealised version of Ed, a bit like how Sabrina's fans idealise her. I've always wondered whether that similarity is what initially attracted Sabrina to him. Because she knew the truth, right from the start, that Ed is very far from being perfect.'

'I don't understand. Why would you say that?' Mimi felt as though she had fallen through Alice's rabbit hole into a topsy-turvy world, where nothing made any sense, least of all the fact that she was discussing her crush on Teddy with *Nate*.

'Do you know how – or should I say where – Sabrina and Ed met?'

Mimi shook her head. 'No idea.' Various glamorous scenarios ran through her mind. On board a yacht in Sydney Harbour? At the after-party of a film premiere?

'They met at an Alcoholics Anonymous meeting.'

Mimi started to laugh. 'An AA meeting? You have got to be kidding. Sabrina has never touched alcohol *in her life*.'

Nate didn't smile. 'No, she hasn't,' he agreed. 'We all know how much she hates it after what your father put her through.'

'So what was she doing there?'

'Her psychologist suggested she attend a meeting to gain some insight and empathy into alcoholism. Sabrina had difficulty seeing it as a genuine disease, rather than a personal weakness.'

'Sabrina has a psychologist?' The idea of her intensely private sister opening up to a stranger was utterly unbelievable.

'Not any more. She saw him pretty regularly for a few months and he helped her a lot, but then she just stopped going. Ed thinks there might have been reporters sniffing around and she was frightened that anything she said in confidence might end up as magazine fodder.'

'When was all this?' Mimi felt dazed.

'Just after you left for overseas for the first time, I think. Ed told me that she was very angry all the time back then – a bit like you are now.'

Mimi thought this through and then realised that something else still didn't make sense. 'But that doesn't explain what Teddy was doing there.'

Nate simply waited as comprehension slowly dawned.

'Teddy?' Mimi gasped. 'Teddy is an *alcoholic*?'

'He's a reformed alcoholic,' Nate corrected her. 'He's been sober for over three years now. Mainly thanks to Sabrina's influence I should say.'

'But . . . but . . .' Mimi's mind felt like scrambled eggs.

'It's not possible because he's perfect?' Nate asked ruefully. 'It's true, Mimi. That's why he never goes to parties and he's often in meetings that he can't miss. They're AA meetings. He goes less frequently than he did in the beginning but he still needs them. He was at an AA meeting the time I first met you at the funeral parlour, and that's where he was when we all met to discuss the wedding at his family's house.' Nate allowed this to sink in and then continued, 'He'd always been a heavy drinker but people tended not to notice because he drank good wine. Connoisseurs can get away with drinking a bottle a night and everyone just thinks they're incredibly sophisticated. But after Claudia jilted him his drinking spiralled out of control. His mother and I were the ones who finally got him to go to AA. And that's where he met Sabrina.'

Mimi sat there, trying to make sense of it all. Sabrina, the Ice Princess, had anger-management issues and had let down her guard to a complete stranger. And Teddy, her perfect Teddy, was an alcoholic. She suddenly looked up, aghast.

'Oh God. Sabrina didn't fall for him because she was trying to – I don't know – fix him or make up for Dad or something?'

Nate shook his head. 'I think they fell in love because they're incredibly similar. Perfect on the outside but damaged within.' He paused and then said softly, 'Like you.'

In any other circumstances, Mimi would have felt compelled to make a comment which demonstrated that she didn't take seriously the suggestion that her appearance was perfect. But right now she couldn't manage it.

'I thought you were using me to get to Sabrina,' she whispered.

'I'm used to women using me to get to Ed,' he countered, with a wry smile. Mimi wanted to die of shame. For the first five minutes after meeting him she had been one of those women. But it had only been five minutes, she consoled herself. Right from the start she had liked Nate for himself.

'I'm not used to getting male attention when Sabrina is around. Every guy in the world wants to be with a girl like her.'

'Did you grow up feeling that you were in Sabrina's shadow?'

She looked at him in confusion. 'No. No, it wasn't like that when we were kids.' Mimi didn't know how to explain that it had been the complete reverse. The idea of Sabrina ever having been in her shadow seemed ludicrous now. Yet that was how it had been throughout their childhood and most of their adolescence. For the first time ever, Mimi wondered if Sabrina had felt like Mimi herself so often did these days. Over-looked. Jealous. Angry.

'Well, for the record, I think your sister is very beautiful and I happen to think she's also very sweet.' Mimi was about to suggest that she prostrate herself, so that Nate could just kick her while she was down and be done with it, when he added, 'But – and don't you dare ever repeat this – she's not very funny.'

'Oh please. I hate that old saying that what people most want in a partner is a sense of humour. It's such a cliché.'

'So you'd be happy to spend the rest of your life with a male model who never made you laugh?'

'Depends on which male model. Are we talking about the guy on the gigantic underwear billboard near the Darlinghurst overpass?' Nate gave a faint smile but looked disappointed, and Mimi cursed herself for being flippant. She just couldn't help herself. It was her automatic response in situations where she felt exposed. Serious made Mimi uncomfortable.

'Nate, I'm sorry. I know that you're trying to be nice and it's not that I don't appreciate it. It's just . . .' Mimi struggled to find the right words. 'I'm a lost cause. I'm the human equivalent of the chicken crossing the road joke.'

Whatever Nate had been expecting her to say, it certainly wasn't that. 'You're what?'

Mimi gave him a small, unhappy smile. 'I make jokes all the time so that I don't have to think about anything serious. Like the fact that my mother and father are dead and my sister barely tolerates me and I have an aimless life with a bizarre, temporary job, no boyfriend and virtually no family. And the best punch line of all —' Mimi took a deep breath and then finished resolutely, 'is that I have a crush on a man who would probably never even have spoken to me if he hadn't happened to be engaged to my sister.'

Nate was quiet for a moment. 'Do you want to know the strange thing about the chicken crossing the road joke? The thing about that joke is that it's not really funny. The humour comes from the expectation that the answer will be funny but it's not. At heart it's serious.'

'That sounded profound but I have no idea what you're getting at.'

'I just mean that I don't think you're a complete joke, Mimi. Maybe, like me, you just need to start appreciating what you have instead of focussing on what you don't have.' He let her think about this for a moment and then leapt to his feet. He reached out a hand to haul her up. 'I have an idea that might help you.' Nate hesitated and then took a deep breath. 'After this wedding is over, I think you should go on a date with me.'

Mimi looked at him in confusion. 'You mean a date date?'

'Yep. A proper date. You and me. No sneakers or boxing gloves allowed.'

'But, Nate, you know . . .'

'That you have a crush on my best friend who also happens to be your sister's fiancé? I know.' He looked at her with a crooked smile. 'It's all right, Mimi. I've had more than a decade of competing with Ed. I'm used to it. But the thing is, I like you very much and I love a challenge. I was going to take it slow with you because I thought maybe you needed time to get over your shotgun wedding. But if you're capable of having feelings for Ed, I think it would be much better if you channelled those emotions in my direction.' He paused and then laughed. 'That makes me sound sad, doesn't it?' He thought for a moment and then said carefully, 'The thing is, Mimi, I know what it's like to have feelings for someone who is in love with someone else close to you. So I also know that it's possible to get over it.'

Mimi didn't dare to look directly at him. 'Claudia?' she said softly.

'Claude told me you knew all about it,' he said ruefully. 'Yes, Claudia. I knew her first. I had a crush on her when I was a kid and I never really grew out of it. But she never felt the same way about me. I introduced her to Ed and from then on, not only did I become the third wheel but I had to sit back and watch them fall in love. The whole time that she was engaged to Ed I had to bite my tongue and be happy for them. It was torture.'

Mimi digested this and then said tentatively, 'Are you sure you really do like me? Maybe what you feel for me is just sympathy because you've been through it.'

He shook his head. 'Nope. I really want to kiss you again.'

As Mimi's cheeks flushed scarlet, he hastily added, 'Look, forget I said that. Just think about my offer of a date. You don't have to answer now. Take your time and then let me know.'

'Okay,' said Mimi slowly. She lifted her head and met his gaze. 'I mean, okay. I think I'd like to go out with you. After the wedding. Although it seems crazy and I think you might be a masochist.'

'I was happy with okay. You didn't need to say anything else.' He pulled on the boxing pads again, gestured for her to pull on the gloves and then threw her a cheeky look. 'That's sorted then. Now let's just hope that other old saying holds true.'

'What old saying?'

He grinned. 'May the best man win.'

One Week
Before the Wedding

- Have final dress fitting
- Avoid stressful situations & try to relax!
- Hold hen's party

42

The Final Fitting

CELEBRITY CONFIDENTIAL ONLINE POLL! YOU BE THE JUDGE!

They've been together for years, and we've all seen Sabrina's ring bling, but will it last? Because, as everyone knows, nothing ruins a good relationship like the stress of tying the knot! With the wedding of the year only one week away and Sydney abuzz with rumours about Sabrina and the dreamy Ethan Carter, we're running an online poll that asks you whether Edina will live happily ever after or if their marriage is going to end in tears before it's even begun . . . Vote in our online poll and you could win a sexy dress just like the one worn by Britney Spears when she wed K-Fed! Oops – guess that marriage didn't last either . . .

Corinna stepped back from the podium and surveyed the completed effect of her efforts. Although Mimi knew that it was ridiculous to care what the designer thought of her, she found that she was holding her breath. As a pleased expression broke across Corinna's face, to Mimi's annoyance, she found herself smiling.

'Good girl, Mimi!' Corinna said, in a delighted tone. 'Not only have you lost weight but those arms and calves of yours are looking marvellously toned. You suit the dress beautifully.'

Instead of this comment infuriating her, as it would have done previously, Mimi was amused. *Shouldn't that be the other way around?* she wondered silently. Surely the dress was meant to suit *her*? But despite her natural instincts, she couldn't get cross. She was too pleased with the way she looked. Even though it wasn't her idea of a bridesmaid's dress, it *was* a beautiful dress. It made her want to hold the skirt out and twirl around like a six- year-old.

Mimi and Sabrina were attending the final fitting for their respective dresses for the wedding. Even though Sabrina was the main event and Mimi's dress fitting was just the warm-up act, Mimi knew that everyone in the salon had been apprehensive about how she would look in her dress. Now that she had passed the test, and given that Sabrina always looked perfect in everything, the anxiety lifted and a palpable sense of relief and good humour filled the salon. Even Flora, Fauna and Merryweather, who had perpetually nervous expressions on their faces, looked almost happy.

'Sabrina? We just need to know that you're satisfied with Mimi's dress and then she can go and change and we can do your final fitting,' Corinna said, in the habitually syrupy tone that she used whenever she addressed Sabrina.

At the sound of her name, Sabrina tilted her head to one side and narrowed her eyes as she walked around the podium, inspecting Mimi's dress for imperfections. It was such an obviously studied performance that, for a moment, Mimi thought she might laugh out loud.

She tried to catch her sister's eye but Sabrina refused to look her in the face, concentrating instead on the dress. And that was when Mimi realised that Sabrina wasn't putting on a performance to slyly poke fun at Corinna's obsessive attention to detail. Sabrina was acting like this to convince everyone that she was actually concentrating on what was happening in the room. *Am I the only one who sees that she's not really here?* thought Mimi in frustration. She glanced at

Corinna and the assistants. None of them seemed to have noticed anything amiss.

'It's fine,' Sabrina finally said. She seemed to pull herself together enough to realise that this was an inadequate response. 'I mean, it's lovely.'

'Are you sure? Because if you'd like anything changed – the lace on the straps for example . . .'

'I knew we should have done it in Porcelain, not Alabaster,' Fauna muttered.

'No.' There it was again. The unintentionally sharp tone. Sabrina couldn't help it. Everything was such an *effort* these days. Other people were an unbearable burden. Above anything else, she just wanted to be left alone, preferably so that she could curl up and go to sleep, but that was impossible. Not only was she Sabrina Falks, she was a bride at the centre of a wedding maelstrom. Solitude was for other, normal people.

Conscious of Mimi's gaze upon her, Sabrina made another Herculean effort. 'No, I wouldn't change a thing. It's perfect, Corinna.' This time she got her tone exactly right. Warm, with a hint of excitement. The perfect pitch for the bride-to-be. As Corinna visibly relaxed, Sabrina knew that she had fooled everyone, with the exception of Mimi.

Mimi headed to the opulent dressing-room to change back into her jeans and T-shirt. When she emerged, Sabrina was already standing on the dais, being helped into her wedding dress by the flock of assistants, all of whom were wearing white cotton gloves, while Corinna directed proceedings with the sort of authoritarian manner that was more commonly displayed by field marshals general during wartime.

Watching her sister being *arranged* (there was no other word to accurately describe it) into the dress, Mimi was forcibly reminded of a doll. A beautiful doll with whom everyone loved playing dress-ups.

Inanimate – that was the word for Sabrina these days. Did she come alive at night, when she was alone? Or did she just lie there limply until morning, waiting for other people to move her, to dress her, to put her into situations of pretend?

Ever since their argument over Sabrina wanting to wear their mother's wedding dress, the sisters had studiously avoided the subject. Until today, Sabrina had attended all of her dress fittings alone. So now, for the first time, Mimi saw the dress that Sabrina was to wear in place of their mother's wedding gown.

It was the most extraordinary, beautiful dress that Mimi had ever seen in her life. *Dress* didn't seem an adequate term to describe it. It was a fairytale confection of satin, crystal beading and lace. Three strands of dainty crystals looped over Sabrina's right shoulder. Her other shoulder was bare. The bodice was hand-beaded with more crystals and then gently ruched to gather at Sabrina's left hip. The material of the gown, which was a champagne colour with only the slightest hint of dusky pink, then fell softly to her knees where a layer of delicate French lace appeared. Another layer of satin emerged beneath the lace, blossoming out over an underlying hoop to skim the floor at the front. But it was the back of the gown that took Mimi's breath away, as the satin skirt unfurled into an eight-foot-long train of billowing softness.

'You look like Cinderella,' Mimi breathed, all of a sudden wondering why she, Claudia and Sabrina had all been so scathing in their refusal to even consider such elements as a horsedrawn carriage, a tiara or a full cathedral wedding. Looking at Sabrina in that dress, those things now seemed not only right but *essential*.

No-one replied. Flora, Fauna and Merryweather were watching Corinna's every move for their next instruction. Corinna, pins pressed between her lips, was working feverishly on ensuring that the fit was perfect.

Her sister really was Cinderella, Mimi decided. Even the knowledge of Edward's alcoholism and that Sabrina the Ice Princess had once needed a psychologist failed to tarnish the golden lustre of perfection that surrounded her. She'd had a horrible childhood but now Sabrina was beautiful, adored and about to marry Prince Charming. Maybe that was why people loved reading about the lives of celebrities so much. It allowed grown-ups to keep believing in fairytales.

After a few more minutes, it became apparent that something was not going to plan. A barely perceptible crease, which had had to fight for its life against layers of Botox, had appeared between Corinna's eyes, signalling that something was very wrong indeed. The assistants appeared agitated and the sense of tension that had been present during Mimi's fitting was undeniably back in the room. After another few minutes, during which Sabrina wriggled, clearly uncomfortable, it was obvious that there was a problem. So when Sabrina confronted Corinna with a direct question, the designer was left with no choice but to tell the truth.

'Corinna, what's going on? It feels like the dress is cutting into me.'

There was a silence and then Corinna spoke, in a voice that was so low Mimi had to strain to catch what she said.

'Sabrina darling, don't take this the wrong way but it seems that . . . you've put on some weight.'

Mimi burst out laughing while Sabrina looked impatient.

'That's not possible. Your measurements must have been wrong.'

'No,' Corinna said quietly. '*That's* not possible. We triple-checked them and then you signed for them.' Corinna was silently thanking her stars that she had made Sabrina sign the standard policy for couture gowns. She had learnt from experience that it protected her business against accusations of poor fitting from disgruntled clients who weren't as disciplined with their diets and exercise as Sabrina and never quite seemed to grasp the concept of made-to-measure.

She had almost waived the policy for Sabrina, before remembering the debacle over the rejected Logies gown. Sabrina's wedding dress was far too expensive and important for Corinna to risk anything going wrong. So Sabrina, like every other client, had had to sign a contract, binding her to the purchase of the gown. A contract that had explicitly listed the measurements, fabric, lace and beading to be used, along with every other minute detail that had been agreed upon.

'Yes, but I didn't check what I was signing, did I? One of your assistants must have written them down wrongly.'

Mimi watched as Flora, Fauna and Merryweather immediately looked horrified. To everyone's considerable surprise, Corinna came to their defence.

'There's not the slightest chance that any of my girls would have made a mistake of this magnitude. But let's not worry too much. Obviously you won't be able to take the dress away with you today, but providing you watch what you eat during the week and don't put on any more weight, it can certainly be fixed. I just need to let the side seams out a fraction.'

'*I haven't put on any bloody weight,*' Sabrina said through gritted teeth. 'I haven't put on weight since puberty.'

Mimi tried to think of something funny to say that would relieve the tension, but for once nothing came to mind. She felt surprisingly sorry for Corinna who was obviously in an awkward position: knowing that she was right, but unable to argue further with her star client.

There really wasn't much more to be said, so, at a gesture from Corinna, the assistants sprang forward to help Sabrina out of the wedding dress. As soon as she had stepped out of the enormous froth of satin and lace, Sabrina headed towards the dressing-room. A delicate cough from Corinna stopped her and made her swing around.

'What is it?' she demanded ungraciously.

'I'm afraid you can't get dressed quite yet. I need to take your measurements again.'

Without a word, Sabrina ascended the podium once more. She stood there in only her knickers, her arms stretched out as Corinna personally measured her once again, barking out the numbers and then ordering Flora and Fauna to repeat them back to her.

Mimi tried not to stare at Sabrina but it was impossible. She immediately noticed two things. The first was that Sabrina looked clammy and pale. The second was that Corinna was right. There was a slight roundness to Sabrina's flesh that hadn't been there for years. A suggestion, not of plumpness – Sabrina was still far too thin for such a thing to even be contemplated – but of the merest hint of a softer curve emerging from her bony frame.

'Sabrina? Would you like me to get you a glass of water?' Mimi asked tentatively.

Sabrina didn't answer but, instead, continued to stare straight ahead. Although Sabrina was facing the bank of mirrors, Mimi knew that her sister was avoiding the sight of her own reflection.

Several minutes later, when Sabrina emerged from the dressing-room wearing the casual, figure-hugging cotton-jersey dress that she had arrived in, no-one said anything but everyone cast discreet, speculative glances at her.

'When will it be ready?' Sabrina asked, not even attempting to mask her bad mood.

'I personally won't be seeing any other clients until your gown is finished,' Corinna promised her. 'I intend to do it all myself.'

This was obviously a concession of some magnitude but Sabrina didn't seem conscious of the favour being bestowed upon her.

'You'll have to deliver it to the apartment. I don't have the time to waste in coming here again.'

'Sabrina!' The admonishment escaped from Mimi's lips before she could stop herself. She had never before heard Sabrina speak in such a nasty tone to anyone apart from herself.

Sabrina didn't even glance at her sister. She merely swung her bag onto her shoulder. 'Are you coming?'

'I'll be a minute. Can you wait for me in the car?' Mimi had intended to give Corinna a cheque to cover the final instalments of their dresses, but now that they weren't taking Sabrina's dress away with them, she was awkwardly unsure as to whether she ought to finalise the account. Regardless what arrangement she came to with Corinna, with Sabrina in this mood, it was a conversation that she preferred to have without her sister there.

'No, I can't wait. You'll have to catch a taxi,' Sabrina snapped. With that she exited the salon, without another word or as much as a backwards glance, leaving Mimi utterly thunderstruck by this display of most un-Sabrina-like behaviour.

After the door had crashed to a close behind Sabrina, Merryweather sidled up to Mimi. 'I know that she's your sister but does she ever make you want to use the B word?' she whispered.

'Bitch?'

'Bridezilla.'

*

Sabrina stormed out of Corinna's salon and into the quiet street in a filthy mood. She was brought up short by the familiar sounds of a camera taking pictures and the oily voice of Lewis Reynolds.

'Sabrina baby! How's the wedding dress looking? You don't feel like giving your old mate Lewis a sneak preview now, do you?' He winked at her and she felt physically repulsed. 'Save me trying to bribe those assistants in there. Don't like to mention it but it wasn't very sporting of you to make them close all the blinds and lock the doors while you tried it on.'

God, she hated him. She was tempted to give him the same

treatment that she'd just meted out to Corinna, but she retained just enough self-control to know that that would be professional suicide. Instead, she forced a smile to her face and stood there stiffly as she let Lewis take what he needed from her.

How many images of her existed, she wondered. Thousands? Hundreds of thousands? Why did they need new ones? Surely everyone knew what she looked like by now. She thought about how some primitive tribes refused permission for their photograph to be taken, believing that the camera could steal their soul. If such a thing was possible, given the multitude of images of her that existed, it was no wonder she felt so dead and empty inside.

Lewis flashed her what he thought was his most persuasive smile. It gave Sabrina the creeps.

'Now just turn sideways for me, Sabrina,' he coaxed. 'That's it. A profile shot.'

She did as he bid. She could feel the strain showing on her face and a warning presentiment of danger raced down her spine as she noted the intensity with which Lewis was taking careful aim with his camera. She was about to say, for the first time ever, that she had had enough.

But it was too late. The shutter snapped cruelly closed and Sabrina didn't have to wait to see the sly expression of triumph on Lewis's face as he straightened up to know that she had just made a fatal mistake.

'Well, well,' Lewis whistled through his teeth. 'Who's looking a bit porky, then?' He continued in a tone of malicious insinuation. 'I wouldn't have thought it was like that stuck-up fiancé of yours to put the cart before the horse, eh?'

Sabrina looked at Lewis, hatred coursing through her body, making her feel physically ill. She wanted to call him every swear word she had ever heard; she wanted to hit him and kick him until he bled.

He saw the emotion on her face and instantly recognised it for what it was. It was the sign of someone about to lose control. An almost sexual thrill shot through his body. *Finally*. After years of waiting, he was about to get the picture that he so desperately wanted to take of Sabrina Falks.

'That's it, darlin',' he said softly. 'Let it go. Show me how much you hate me. Do you know how much a picture of Australia's sweetheart swinging a right hook is worth?'

Nausea, mixed with hot hatred, filled Sabrina's throat and surged up. Lewis prepared himself for the assault, knowing exactly how to position himself to get the photos and yet still protect his precious Magnum. But the attack never came. Instead, Sabrina sank dizzily to her knees and then threw up, over and over again. Dimly she was aware of her mane of hair hanging in front of her face, of the famous, silken strands getting caught in the stinking liquid rush.

Memories from long ago, from her childhood, came back. Time and again, her mother was holding their father as he knelt on the tiled floor of their small, suburban bathroom and vomited into the toilet bowl. In the intervals between retches was an incoherent ramble of whining self-pity mixed with pleas for forgiveness. 'It's all right, darling,' her mother would say soothingly, as she rubbed her husband's back. 'Bring it all up. You'll feel much better. This will be the last time, I know. It's okay. I'm here.'

Sabrina blinked and her mother disappeared. She wasn't ten years old, catching a glimpse into the mysterious, private world of her parents. She was alone, on her hands and knees on the pavement, in the glaring mid-afternoon sunshine of Double Bay, and the only sound was of Lewis's camera taking photo after photo after photo.

She was still retching when he started to check the images.

'How am I ever going to thank you? Unless I'm very much mistaken, you just paid for my new car.'

Feeling faint, she managed to lift her head and he looked at her in disgust. 'Fuck me, you look revolting. Clean yourself up.' He paused and then added venomously, 'You media whores are all the same. Do us all a favour and top yourself, you silly bitch. Take it from me, it's the best career move you'll ever make, Princess.'

She watched him stroll off, as her whole body continued to shake. She tried to mentally connect with Mimi, who was only a short distance away inside the salon, but the door and the blinds remained closed and no-one came to help her. It didn't occur to Sabrina to call out for help.

Groping in her bag, she found a packet of tissues and wiped off the worst of the vomit from her face and hair. Unsteadily, she stood up, made her way to her car and drove home. Once inside, Sabrina locked the door and then stood under a hot shower for almost an hour. After that she went to bed, where she lay and stared at the ceiling, knowing that tomorrow the storm would break.

43

The Baby Bump

'I want to know what the fuck this is!'

Nigel Thompson, the CEO of Australia's most commercially successful television network, threw the special issue of *Celebrity Confidential* magazine onto his impressively large desk and glared at the network's number-one star, who sat composedly in the leather armchair opposite him.

Sabrina was tempted to answer that it was a magazine but she thought she'd better not push her luck. So, instead, she sat there silently, knowing that Nigel would be unable to keep quiet for more than another five seconds. She counted. He lasted three.

'Leaving aside the major issue for the time being, how would you say you looked?'

Sabrina didn't even glance at the magazine. She had already viewed the incriminating cover image, and the other ones inside the three-page spread, at about six that morning, which was when her publicist, Laura, had rung in hysterics, demanding that she check her emails that instant. Laura had insisted that she would hold while Sabrina did so, as she needed her immediate response for an already baying media pack. Sabrina had listened to her unemotionally and had then hung up on her. She then switched off her mobile phone, ignored the home phone, which immediately began to ring, and read the article that had run with the pictures Lewis had taken.

Ignoring Laura was one thing, but when Nigel had sent a car to her apartment, with an unfolded handwritten note that had been delivered by an embarrassed chauffeur, Sabrina knew she had no choice but to face the music. The note, in typical Nigel style, had been explicit.

Get the fuck in the car. Now.

Sabrina now forced herself to answer Nigel. 'I would say that I look tired. And ill.'

'Really?' Nigel exploded. 'That's interesting. I'd use the words "shithouse". And "ugly". Now why would you be looking like this right now? What's going on in Danielle's life, hmm?'

This was the tricky part about having conversations with Nigel. Given his propensity to call all of the *Sunshine Cove* actors by their characters' names, one never knew whether he was referring to the script or to Sabrina's real life. She took a punt.

'Well, in the episode we're shooting when I return from my honeymoon leave, Danielle comes face to face with her stalker for the first time and —'

'Stuff the script!' Nigel roared. 'The script doesn't matter right now. I'm talking about *you*! You're about to marry some rich-as-shit banker. *You're* the hottest story in Australia. So what I want to know is what the *fuck* are you doing letting yourself be photographed spewing your guts out and looking like *shit* when you've just been trying on your wedding dress? You should be glowing like Charlize fucking Theron and smiling and flashing that bloody great rock on your finger. Do you have any fucking idea how much money we spend on making you the top face of this channel? Any idea? Ballpark? No? The answer, Danielle, is FUCKING SHITLOADS. And we don't pour money into dressing you up in designer gowns and draping you in diamond necklaces for expensive channel promos to see you piss it all away by letting some pap take your picture so you can end up on a magazine cover looking like THIS!' Nigel stabbed her image on the front cover of the magazine so hard Sabrina was sure she could feel the shock of it on her own throat.

Let them? she thought, too tired to even conjure up indignation. *Does he really believe that I let them take photos of me? That I have any choice in the matter at all?*

'What about the story inside?' His eyes narrowed as he finally got to the crux of the matter. 'They're saying that you're pregnant. To Ricky – I mean Ethan.'

She stared him down. 'I know what the rumours are saying.' She waited a beat. 'I should know. I started them.'

Whatever he had been expecting, it clearly wasn't this. 'What the fuck are you saying, Danielle? That you're the one behind all this?'

She nodded.

'That's bullshit. Why would you trash your own reputation?'

'Drama,' she said coolly. She steadfastly ignored what might happen if her gamble didn't pay off. She intended to use Nigel, and for it to work, he had to believe that she had control over the situation, that she knew the best thing to do.

He paused, still breathing heavily from his tirade, a fleck of spittle in one corner of his fleshy lips. 'What the fuck are you talking about?'

'Oh come on, Nige,' she mustered a smile. 'You know as well as I do that no celebrity wedding ever goes smoothly. The audience needs to think something's going to go wrong. That's what I'm giving them. And the more coverage *I* get in the press, the higher our ratings go. And if *I'm* the story, the more valuable I become and the more you have to pay me.' She finished with a light, girlish laugh.

He looked at her disbelievingly for a long moment and then suddenly his face broke into a leering grin. Sabrina thought longingly of how good it would feel to throw something at that smug and sweaty face.

'Jesus Christ,' he said in admiration. 'I should sack the whole PR department and get you to run it. That's genius. Not just a pretty face, are you?' Before she could reply, he answered his own question. ''Course you're not. You also have an excellent pair of tits.' He sniggered and she felt a deep disgust well within her.

'What about this then?' Nigel pointed to the headline on the cover that screamed in large lettering and bold red font, 'SABRINA'S BABY BUMP! EXCLUSIVE PICTURES INSIDE!'

'A bad angle and probably some photoshopping,' Sabrina said flatly. 'And the throwing up wasn't due to morning sickness. It was because I ate some bad sushi.' She stood up. She was wearing figure-hugging jeans and a cotton singlet. She spun around. 'Do I look pregnant to you, Nigel?' As his gaze lingered on her breasts, she immediately felt the need for another long, hot shower.

'No, I can't say that you do,' he growled appreciatively. He drummed his fingers against the desktop. 'Right, which way does it go from here then?'

'Whichever way we want to spin it. That's the important thing. *We* have to spin it, not them,' Sabrina said, nodding towards the magazine on Nigel's desk. 'So I need you, as the CEO of the network, to deny the rumours.'

He immediately looked suspicious, as she had known he would. Having worked his way up in the cutthroat world of commercial television, Nigel's primal instinct was to mistrust the motives of anyone who approached him with even the mildest of requests. He was also extraordinarily sensitive about his authority and deeply resented demands being made of him. Despite these obstacles, Sabrina knew that the denial of the rumours had to come from the top. The media pack would expect denials from her and her publicist. But Nigel wading into matters like this was rare and the media knew it. His word was the only one that could quash the rumours, and although the damage to her reputation and possibly her relationship was already done, this was her sole chance to kill the story.

'Why?'

'Because a denial, especially from you, will mean the story continues to run,' she lied. 'You never comment on stories like this. If you deny it, it's a bigger story than if Laura or I give a standard refutation. Couple that with the special edition that they're running on my wedding and for the next week we'll have saturation coverage across the weekly mags and the news and current-affair programs too.' Sabrina mentally crossed her fingers and waited. She was banking on the fact that Nigel would believe she had been in control of the situation all along and that he would therefore trust her judgement. She needed him to get on the phone and make a statement to the media while she was in the room. If he ran it past Laura or any of the other media advisors, she was sunk. She knew they would immediately tell him that a denial from him would extinguish the story, not inflame it.

She could see him weighing things up. 'Come on, Nige,' she said flirtatiously. 'When have I ever let you down?' She pulled her iPhone out of her Gucci bag. 'I have the number for Rachel Jones, the entertainment reporter from the *Sydney Morning Herald* right here. I can call her now.'

Sabrina had deliberately chosen pretty, buxom young Rachel Jones, who was utterly shameless about doing anything necessary to get a story. Rachel knew Nigel well and could be relied upon to win him over.

Nigel said nothing. Watching him carefully, Sabrina pressed the call button.

'Rachel? It's Sabrina Falks – of course it's absolute rubbish. The source is *Celebrity Confidential*, what do you expect? No, that wasn't on the record. But I have Nigel Thompson here and he'd like to make a public comment on my behalf. Yes, really – wait a moment, I'll put him on.'

Holding her breath, Sabrina handed him the phone. After a brief hesitation he took it, and she exhaled as she saw him visibly relax under Rachel's expert manipulation. Within a few minutes it was done. Nigel Thompson, CEO, had given a brief statement, utterly refuting all suggestions of an affair between two of his network's biggest stars, Sabrina Falks and Ethan Carter. Rachel and her editor would later regretfully decide to paraphrase Nigel's 'All that shit about Danielle being knocked up is complete bullshit too' into the more tactful 'The station's CEO also made it emphatically clear that the pregnancy rumours surrounding Sabrina Falks are completely without foundation.'

Nigel hung up on the effusively grateful Rachel and slid Sabrina's phone back across the desk. 'Right. I've handled that one then. Now make sure you stay away from dodgy sushi, because if I see one more photo of my prime-time princess looking like some shitty, knocked-up suburbanite, I'll cut your pay in half.' He gave a throaty chuckle. 'One more thing, Danielle. You owe me. So make sure you sit me next to a bridesmaid at your wedding. Bridesmaids are usually gagging for it, I've found.'

He dismissed her and Sabrina left his office with her customary graceful movements. It was only when she was halfway down the next corridor that she sagged against the wall.

She had killed the rumours, although she knew that there would always be a certain proportion of the general public who would believe that she had had an affair and fallen pregnant. She wasn't too concerned about Nigel belatedly discovering that her advice had had the opposite effect on the story that he had wanted. She was certain that when he realised, it would just confirm his opinion that, as a female soap star, she didn't know her arse from her elbow. She would rather he thought her stupid than know that she had skilfully used and manipulated him.

Now that she had dealt with the public face of her scandal, she faced the much harder task of dealing with the fallout on her private life. Only the fact that Edward was still overseas was saving him from having to face this humiliation. He had stayed on in Hong Kong to spend a few days with his brother after his other friends had flown back to Australia. She wondered how long it would be until his mother or someone else called him to tell him. She wondered if Mimi knew.

It was now Tuesday and she was meant to marry Edward on Saturday. She had wanted so desperately to try to make everything right before the wedding but it wasn't going to work out that way. She had run out of time and now the truth had to come out.

*

That evening, Sabrina sat on the cold, hard edge of the bathtub. Edward was due home tomorrow. This was her final chance. She had to do it now.

She didn't bother to read the instructions on the box. She knew exactly what she had to do. After she had finished, she laid the plastic stick on the bathroom vanity and then forced herself to count to 100, very slowly. Then she found herself incoherently muttering the speech that she had given at the Logie Awards.

I am overjoyed and delighted, she said, over and over again, barely aware of what she was saying. *Delighted and overjoyed.*

Finally, she stood up and walked over to where the innocuous plastic stick lay, like a ticking bomb. Knowing in advance what it would say but still praying for a miracle with the last tiny shred of blind, foolish hope that remained to her, Sabrina picked it up with a shaking hand and gazed at the indicator window.

With a broken sob, she hurled it against the mirror. She slid down the wall, with her back against the cool tiles and then, for only the second time in her adult life, knowing that she was alone and couldn't possibly be spied upon by any long lenses, Sabrina finally allowed herself to cry.

44

Comparisons

'Have you spoken to Sabrina today?' Aunty Bron came to meet Mimi as soon as she opened the front door on Tuesday night, an anxious expression on her face.

'And hello to you too,' Mimi said grumpily. She had spent the entire day running around the city, checking off tasks on her to-do list for the wedding. It didn't seem to matter that she hadn't stopped for lunch and had juggled phone calls to suppliers, while picking up the wedding rings and Sabrina's engagement ring, which had been left for engraving and cleaning with the jeweller. No matter how much energy she threw into her job, the list just never seemed to get shorter. How Claudia could *want* to do this every day for a living was utterly beyond Mimi.

'I said —'

'I heard what you said, and no, I haven't spoken to her since I saw her at the dress fitting yesterday.' This was quite odd now that Mimi thought about it. Sabrina usually called or texted her with a wedding-related query at least twice a day.

'Have you called her?'

'No,' Mimi answered shortly, going through into the living room. She had been so frantically busy, and she was still so cross with Sabrina after her appalling turn at Corinna's salon that Mimi hadn't particularly wanted to talk to her. Right now Mimi was very tired and all that she wanted was to flop on the sofa and not have to think about Sabrina or the wedding until at least tomorrow morning.

'I thought you would have rung her immediately,' said Aunty Bron, in a surprised tone. Mimi finally looked at her aunt properly and realised that something was going on. She threw her bag and accordion file onto the sofa.

'Aunty Bron? What's the matter?'

'What do you mean, what's the matter? Haven't you seen the papers? Haven't you seen *this*?' Bron snatched up the offensive copy of *Celebrity Confidential* from the coffee table. 'Irena Markov from next door came around with it this morning. She bought it at the supermarket. It's all lies and it's *everywhere*!'

Mimi took the magazine from her aunt. As she scanned the cover, a horrible feeling crept over her. She turned the pages to the full story inside and read it swiftly.

Aunty Bron was still brimming with indignation. 'They're lies,' she said furiously. 'It's just a pack of vicious lies.'

'Of course it is,' Mimi said soothingly, ignoring the voice in her head that was whispering: *It could all be true*.

'How could you not know about this?' Aunty Bron demanded.

'Quite easily. I've spent the entire day running around and I haven't spoken to Sabrina. Reading trashy mags wasn't high on my to-do list.'

'Well, you'd better call her now. Edward is still in Hong Kong so she's all alone.'

'Okay, okay. I'll call her right this second.' Mimi found her Black-Berry in her bag and rang Sabrina's number. A few minutes later, she shook her head. 'Her mobile's switched off and her home phone is engaged.'

'Well, you'll have to go around there.'

'Me? Why me?'

'She's your sister!'

'And she's your niece!'

'Yes, but I won't know what to say to her. All this stuff – pregnancy and affairs – what do I know about any of that? You're Sabrina's age. You'll know what to say. It's better that I don't get involved.'

Mimi looked at her aunt and suddenly realised that what she was feeling was a crushing sense of disenchantment. She was fond of Aunty Bron and she was sincerely grateful to her for letting her stay since her return from overseas. But for the first time ever, she looked at her normally cheerful, busy aunt and wondered about her life. Bron lived in a small, cosy cocoon of her own making, content to stick with regular routines and outings. She was only fifty-nine but seemed decades older – not in looks, but in the solitary, self-contained way that she lived her life. She loved her nieces but rarely interfered with their lives. Up until now Mimi had been grateful for this lack of interference but now she couldn't help questioning whether there was something more to it. Was it normal for their sole living relative to have remained completely detached from all of her niece's wedding preparations? And why hadn't *she* called Sabrina as soon as she read the story? Bron had never asked Mimi any questions about why she had returned to Australia either. Mimi suddenly realised that she didn't know if Bron knew about her catastrophic marriage to Jared or how he had run off with her inheritance.

'Aunty Bron?'

'Yes?'

Just looking at her kind, worn face, Mimi felt terrible to be thinking about her aunt with such suspicion. Yet she persisted. 'I just – I wondered whether Sabrina had told you about what happened to me. About Jared and . . . my inheritance.'

Bron looked surprised. 'Of course she did.'

Mimi looked at her, flabbergasted. 'But you've never mentioned it.'

'Neither have you. I naturally assumed that you didn't wish to discuss it.'

'Yes, but . . .' Mimi floundered. She wasn't sure why Aunty Bron's approach seemed so unnatural but she just felt that an older relative sweeping things under the carpet like this seemed manifestly wrong. 'You didn't want to ask me about it?'

'Miriam, you're an adult. If you want to tell me something, I'm sure you will. I've never interfered in the lives of you girls and I don't intend to start now. I can't imagine that you'd thank me for it anyway.'

'No. Of course we wouldn't.' Mimi hesitated, not knowing what to say, but her mind was racing. For the first time she was recognising a remote quality to Bron that was exactly like Sabrina. The only difference was that Sabrina's aloofness was noticeable because it fit her all-round Ice Princess demeanour. Bron's was masked by a cheery exterior that somehow made everyone oblivious to the fact that she remained utterly uninvolved with everyone around her.

Out of the blue, Mimi wondered why her mother and aunt had never been close. She didn't even know whether Aunty Bron had known about those terrible, violent years when their father was still around.

'Aunty Bron? Did you know about Dad? I mean, not now, but at the time. When he was drinking and . . . doing those awful things.'

A guarded expression came over Bron's face. She sat down heavily on the couch and then looked up at Mimi. 'No,' she said quietly. 'I didn't know. Your mother and I rarely spoke and we never visited one another. I only saw you girls when you visited your grandparents. I had no idea. Sabrina only told me after your mum died.'

The uncharitable thought crossed Mimi's mind that even if Aunty Bron had been around and had known what was going on, she probably wouldn't have made any difference. She might have just sat and watched from a discreet distance and said nothing at all. Mimi abruptly felt the urge to shock her aunt out of her cocoon; to see what she would do if someone did lay a problem in her lap and looked to her for advice.

'Aunty Bron? The thing is, I'm not sure that I'm the best person to go and speak to Sabrina about her relationship with Teddy.'

'Why not?' Bron asked impatiently.

'Because . . .' Mimi faltered, then took a deep breath. What the hell. Nate knew, Claudia had guessed and even Sabrina had an inkling. 'Because I . . . I like Teddy.'

'What do you mean, you *like* Teddy?' Aunty Bron's tone was sharp.

'I mean I like him. Like I shouldn't like him when he's about to become my brother-in-law.' Mimi dropped her head, her cheeks aflame. This was mortifying. This must have been how fourteen-year-old Sabrina had felt when she found out that Mimi had been reading her diary.

There was a dead silence and then Mimi heard a strange, muffled sound. She lifted her head and looked at her aunt. To her bewilderment, she saw that Bron was laughing. She was laughing so hard that tears had already started to roll down her cheeks.

'It's not funny!' Mimi said, scarlet with shame.

'Oh, but it is, Mimsy,' said Bron, trying to choke back her laughter. 'Oh, darling, don't look like that. I'm sorry. Truly I am.' She patted the cushion next to her. 'Come and sit down and I promise I won't laugh any more.'

Still humiliated, Mimi begrudgingly sat down next to her.

'All right.' Aunty Bron took a deep breath. 'Let me make sure I've got this straight. You and Sabrina have been arguing more or less since you arrived back from overseas but *not* over Edward, even though both of you are in love with him.'

'That's right. I think Sabrina suspected it but I said something to throw her off and she hasn't brought it up since.'

'Does Edward know?'

Mimi shook her head as she felt her face grow warm again. 'No. I don't think so.'

Bron looked at her niece thoughtfully. 'I can see the attraction, of course – Edward is *very* good-looking – but have you ever asked yourself whether you're *really* in love with Edward or whether he's just another example of you coveting everything Sabrina has?' She paused to allow this to sink in and then continued. 'The problem with you, Mimi, is that you don't value your own judgement. And while I think Edward and Sabrina are a very good match, I can't help thinking that lovely boy Nate is probably much better for you,' she finished slyly.

'Nate asked me out,' Mimi revealed.

'Are you going to go out with him?'

'I think so. I do like him. He doesn't look like Daniel Craig like Teddy does but —'

'Daniel Craig?' Aunty Bron snorted. 'Edward doesn't look like Daniel Craig. He's not sexy for starters.'

Mimi looked at her aunt, scandalised. 'Aunty Bron!'

'Oh what? You think just because I'm almost sixty I can't judge a young man's sex appeal? Let me tell you, that Nate has more sex appeal in his little finger than Edward has in his whole body. Edward is remarkably good-looking but that's not the same as being sexy. He's far too stiff and proper for my taste, although that formality of his makes him a perfect match for Sabrina.'

Mimi turned this surprising revelation over in her mind. The mere fact that Nate was interested in her had made her suspect that there must be something intrinsically wrong with him. Which said far more about her poor self-esteem than it did about Nate.

'The thing is, I thought maybe Nate just felt sorry for me because he understood how I felt. You see, he used to be in love with Claudia.'

'Claudia?'

'You remember – she's the girl who was engaged to Teddy before Sabrina. She's also Sabrina's wedding planner.'

Aunty Bron boggled. 'And I always thought *Sunshine Cove* was far-fetched,' she finally managed. 'You do realise this is verging on the completely absurd?'

'I know it must appear that way from the outside,' Mimi said apologetically. 'But from my point of view it's a drama, not a comedy. Don't tell Sabrina or Teddy about Claudia, by the way. They don't know who their wedding planner is.'

'I'm not sure that I completely understand what's going on, so consider it a secret kept.' Aunty Bron thought hard. 'Okay, first things first. Do you love her?'

'You mean him. Are you talking about Teddy or Nate?'

'I meant *her*. As in your sister, Sabrina. Do you love her?'

Mimi squirmed uncomfortably. 'God, Aunty Bron. I don't know. Can you still love someone if you've spent the past few years not really liking them?'

'I'm asking the questions,' she replied inflexibly. 'And I'm still waiting for an answer.'

Mimi heaved a sigh. 'She is my sister. Fine. Yes, I suppose I do.'

'Good. Then start acting like it. She's getting married on Saturday and right now, her life is a complete mess.'

'*She's* a complete mess? What about *me*? I just asked you for advice about my crush on Teddy. Why does everything always have to come back to Sabrina?'

'The problem with you and your sister,' Bron said reflectively, 'is that you've always been eaten up by jealousy for one another.'

'Sabrina? Jealous of me? Did I miss the social revolution where the beautiful, famous, skinny girl with the glamorous life and the perfect fiancé suddenly wants to be unemployable, fat and single?'

'You weren't fat, you were out of shape. And you're not even that any more. Anyway, I can't believe you don't know this, Mimi, but it always surprised me that it was Sabrina who became the actress, not you. You have a way of commanding attention whenever you walk into a room. You're bright and funny and people love being around you. At that engagement party, you made two smart remarks and had Edward eating out of your hand after three minutes. Sabrina looked like she wanted to bite your head off.'

'You're making that up.'

'I am not. And you know you do it, too. Furthermore, you can be very cruel to Sabrina. I've seen you use that wit of yours to put her and her achievements down.'

'That's crap,' said Mimi bluntly.

'Is it? How many jokes do you make about *her* weight? Because I've heard more than I can count. They're not very funny either. Jokes about Sabrina starving herself and not having eaten for years. If she had made the reverse comments about you overeating, you would have been up in arms. But because she's skinny you feel you can say what you like.'

'God, if the worst thing that people could make fun of me for was being skinny, I'd be happy,' Mimi mumbled, but she didn't sound convincing.

'I'm only going to say this once, Miriam, so listen carefully. Don't use Sabrina as an excuse and make her responsible for all of your poor choices and failures. You're not Sabrina but you are twenty-five years old. It's time that you stopped being jealous of her and started to live your own life. Because the reality is that there are millions of Sabrinas in the world. There's always someone prettier or more successful or seemingly happier than you. You may as well compare yourself with Jerry Hall or Christie Brinkley.'

'They're kind of old, aren't they?'

'They weren't in my day,' snapped Bron. 'Fine. Whoever your

generation's equivalents are. Kylie Minogue or that Angelina Jolie. The only difference with Sabrina is one of proximity. She happens to be right in front of you so that's why you always compare yourself to her. Believe me Mimi, jealousy is a complete waste of time.' Aunty Bron fell silent for a moment. 'So you have a choice. Either spend your entire life wishing you were Sabrina or start working with what you've got.'

'That's it? Those are your words of wisdom? A variation on "have confidence and believe in yourself"?'

'Not entirely. There's one thing more.' Bron paused and grinned. 'You might have to work hard.' She added, 'All of which leaves us back where we started. Sabrina has been the victim of a vicious attack only days before her wedding. She's all alone and, unless I'm very much mistaken, you're the only person she'll talk to, given that Edward is away. So the question is: are you going to do anything about it?'

Two minutes later Mimi left for Sabrina's apartment, still thinking over everything that Aunty Bron had said, but with an underlying feeling of reassurance. Her fleeting suspicions about her aunt had been complete nonsense. Her aunt wasn't aloof or uncaring or hiding her real self at all. Mimi felt quite ashamed of herself for even thinking such things and was only glad that she hadn't voiced them aloud.

As the sound of Mimi driving away receded into the distance, Bron sat rigidly on the sofa, the habitually cheerful appearance that she had fixed onto her face for Mimi's sake gradually fading. It was replaced by a strange expression that not once in thirty-nine years had she allowed either her nieces or anyone else to see.

It was a look of bitterness, mingled with long-held grief.

45

Bronwyn

She was twenty years old when she saw him first.

In Bron's mind, that was where the fundamental injustice of the whole situation lay. From the very beginning, her and Margaret's unwritten but sacred code had always meant that the sister who saw something first laid an inalienable claim to it. When they were young this applied to toys and books and dolls. Throughout their teenage years it was transferred to clothing, and it became an oft-cited principle, given their similarity of taste. Bron could still remember a purple miniskirt that she longed for with all her heart. She wasn't allowed it, though, because Meg had already seen it in the window of David Jones and had started to save up for it. Every time her sister wore it Bron felt a streak of jealousy shoot through her like poison. Meg did let her borrow it though. Twice.

He was the very first time that their rule was broken.

He only took Bron out a couple of times but it still felt like Meg stole him. Bron knew she'd never had a chance; not really, not once he saw Meg. It was obvious to everyone, and their mum had said as much straight out. 'He prefers Meg, Bronnie. Count your lucky stars. You're well out of it.' But it didn't feel like luck to her. Their mum was the only person who didn't like him. She was never taken in by those deep-blue eyes of his, or his family's money.

This was when Bron first learned to act: to seem happy when she wanted to cry, to pretend that she still loved her sister when she hated, she hated, she hated her.

Bron was the bridesmaid at their wedding. She cried that day. She was always thankful that no-one ever questioned the reasons behind her tears. They would have been quite shocked if she'd answered truthfully.

She cut off contact with her sister after the wedding. Meg tried for months to make her talk. Eventually she gave up. She had more pressing troubles of her own by then.

Like everyone else, Bron knew that he drank a lot, but no-one thought anything of it. So many men were heavy drinkers back then. It wasn't like now, Bron often thought, with all of these new-age husbands who change nappies and drink light beer. She hadn't known about the rest of it. Like Mimi, when Sabrina had finally told her about the years of drunken violence, she hadn't wanted to believe. She still didn't want to believe it, although she knew it must be true.

When she heard that he'd left, she thought about telephoning or visiting her sister. But somehow it never happened. The years passed and both Bron and Meg became recluses in their own way. One evening Sabrina telephoned to say that Meg had died and Bron realised that the chance to say or do anything was gone.

Bron didn't go to Meg's funeral. She couldn't explain to the girls that it was because it would only have reminded her that Meg and her husband were together again once more. She knew how unnatural this would sound. To make sense of it all, you had to understand family. Or, at the very least, their family.

Bron never saw the drunken, monstrous side of Meg's husband, so she was free to cling to memories of those startlingly blue eyes, that smile and easy charm, his movie-star looks. She remembered how proud she had felt when they had gone to the pictures together and all the other girls had watched them enviously, wishing that *they* could be the lucky girl on his arm.

So perhaps fifty-nine-year-old Bron could be forgiven her final error of judgement.

She still missed him.

46

The Hen's Party

Mimi pressed the button on the intercom in the lobby.

'Breens? It's me. Let me in.'

There was a pause and then the static crackled as Sabrina's voice came through the speaker. 'I don't want to see you or anyone else, Miriam. Leave me alone.'

'Can't,' Mimi said cheerfully. 'I'm here for your hen's party.'

'My *what*?'

'Your hen's party. It was meant to be a surprise but all the media waiting out the front saw me arrive and one of them asked what I was doing here and it just slipped out. Sorry. Guess I need more practice dealing with journalists.'

There was a pause as Sabrina weighed this up. Mimi crossed her fingers. She was banking on the fact that the mention of the media pack camped out in front of Sabrina's building would get her past Sabrina's defences. If she believed that Mimi really had told them that she was arriving for her hen's party, then she couldn't let them see her leave again straightaway. That would only add fuel to the rumours that her wedding was in trouble.

The static crackled once more and Sabrina spoke curtly. 'Come up.'

The security door buzzed and Mimi quickly opened it and made her way to the elevator. Sabrina was holding the door to the apartment ajar when she arrived.

'Were you serious about the hen's party?' Sabrina demanded, closing the door behind her sister and securely locking it.

'Nope. But I had to say something so that you'd let me up.' Mimi took a good look at her sister. Anyone else in Sabrina's situation (okay, maybe just Mimi) would have been wearing pyjamas or tracksuit pants and would have had unwashed hair and red eyes. Sabrina was wearing a loose, flowing top and a pair of shorts. Her glossy hair was tied back in a neat ponytail and she looked showered and moisturised. The only hint that something was amiss came from the tight expression on her face and the merest suggestion of bags under her eyes.

Sabrina looked at her sister as though she was about to snap out a retort and then all of the fight just seemed to drain out of her. 'You may as well come and sit down. If you leave straightaway, the next story will be that we're feuding. That's how these things run. They need constant twists and turns to keep the story alive, and if they don't get it they just make it up.'

'I'd hate to see a story about us fighting in one of those trashy mags,' Mimi remarked demurely. 'It would spoil their record of only publishing pure fiction.'

To Mimi's relief, Sabrina's lips gave a brief twitch of amusement, although she didn't go so far as to actually smile.

'Would you like something to drink?'

'Cup of tea would be nice.'

Mimi followed Sabrina into the gleaming kitchen and perched on one of the Philippe Starck stools, as her sister busied herself with putting on the kettle and taking the cups from the cupboard. For once in her life, instead of just leaping in, Mimi was actually trying to think of the most tactful way to broach the subject.

The problem was that Sabrina was unused to sharing confidences.

There was a social aspect missing from Sabrina that Mimi couldn't help but think came back to the fact that she had never had close girlfriends. Sabrina had missed out on the classroom laughter, the shared after-school gossip and the hour-long teenage telephone calls about nothing in particular. Then again, Mimi couldn't really hold it against Sabrina for not being willing to impart secrets. Mimi hadn't exactly been forthcoming about her own aborted marriage.

Mimi finally decided that it was best to go with the familiar route. She took a deep breath and waded straight in.

'Breens? About that stupid magazine article . . .' Her voice trailed off as Sabrina looked up and coolly met her stare.

'Yes?'

'I . . .' Mimi floundered, caught off guard. She had expected Sabrina to interrupt her with protestations of innocence or a curt snub that she didn't wish to discuss it. She blundered on with the first thing that came to mind. 'It's not true, is it?' Instantly Mimi cursed herself for allowing the final words to slip out.

Sabrina turned her attention once more to the tea cups. 'No, Miriam, it's not true,' she said, with not a hint of emotion in her voice. 'I'm neither pregnant nor having an affair with Ethan.'

'I saw him,' Mimi said quickly. 'When I left your apartment the other night. I saw Ethan arriving.'

Sabrina pushed Mimi's cup of tea across the bench top towards her. 'So?'

'So . . . Edward was in Hong Kong and you were alone and —'

'From that you deduced that I was sleeping with him?' The contempt in Sabrina's voice made Mimi blush. Sabrina's tone sharpened. 'You wouldn't happen to be the "unnamed source" that that rag based their story on, would you?'

'*No*,' gasped Mimi, horrified. 'Sabrina, how could you even think that I would do something like that?'

Sabrina looked at her steadily. 'I suppose the same way that you could think I'm capable of cheating on Edward right before our wedding.'

Shame washed over Mimi. 'I'm sorry,' she finally managed. There was nothing else to say.

Sabrina sighed. 'Apology accepted. Oh forget it, Mimi. You're no worse than every other person who reads that crap and takes it all as gospel. There have been rumours about Ethan and me for months now. For the record, we're not romantically interested in one another. Never have been.' Sabrina didn't add that Ethan was the only person that she really counted as a friend.

'Have you spoken to Teddy yet?'

'No.' Sabrina had ignored all telephone calls and had seen no-one since the story had broken, apart from Nigel and now Mimi.

'He gets back tomorrow, doesn't he? I'm sure he won't believe a word of it, Breens. He's too smart for that. Anyway, I have a great idea. You should do a pregnancy test and when it comes up negative you'll have proof that the story is complete rubbish. If you made the result public, you could probably even sue the magazine for libel.'

Sabrina didn't reply.

'Do you want me to leave?' asked Mimi, after an awkward silence. 'I think I'm making things worse.'

Sabrina gave her a tired smile. 'Weirdly enough, I don't. I've been locked up in the apartment all day by myself. I just don't want to talk about this any more, okay?'

'Okay. We could go over wedding stuff instead if you like?'

Sabrina shook her head. 'I don't want to do that either.'

'Well, why don't we just veg out in front of the telly? Do you have any DVDs we could watch?'

'Some.' Sabrina picked up her cup of tea and led the way into the enormous living room. 'They're over on that shelf. Pick anything.'

Mimi ran her finger along the spines. 'I never would have picked Teddy for an action-flick fan,' she remarked.

Sabrina looked guilty. 'They're mine.'

'Really? God, you even have the collector's edition of *Rambo*. That's commitment.' Mimi paused at a row of DVDs in matching white jackets. 'What are all these?'

Sabrina looked defensive. 'They're old episodes of *Sunshine Cove*.'

'Can we watch one?'

Sabrina looked at her suspiciously. 'Why? You think it's complete rubbish and you've always been so proud of the fact that you've never watched a single episode.'

'Well that just makes me look like an idiot. I can't know it's rubbish unless I've actually seen it, now, can I?'

*

An hour and a half later, Mimi finally spoke, in a deeply confused tone. 'But *why* is Danielle wearing a red wig to the dinner with her biological parents?'

'Because she doesn't want them to know that she's their real daughter,' explained Sabrina, re-crossing her feet that were comfortably resting on the coffee table.

Mimi took another chocolate biscuit from the plate that lay between them on the sofa. 'I thought she had a birthmark on her right arm that matches her natural mother's,' she said, between bites.

'She does.'

'So then why is she wearing a sleeveless dress?'

'Just wait. Her mother has to see the mark or she won't realise she's not just their next-door neighbour; she's really the daughter who was abducted at birth.'

'Danielle was abducted at birth?' Mimi gasped. 'I thought they gave her up for adoption!'

'That's what Danielle thinks too,' Sabrina said mysteriously.

'I still don't see why she needs the wig,' Mimi muttered.

'Shut up or I'll —'

'Set fire to me?' Mimi suggested.

Sabrina shook her head. 'Don't be silly.' She paused. 'You're my sister. I could never fire my sister.'

Mimi looked across at Sabrina but Sabrina was staring straight ahead at the screen.

'Breens?'

'Mmm?'

'You're a really good actor. I mean it.'

Mimi watched as a ghost of a smile flickered across Sabrina's face. Without another word, they both settled back comfortably to watch as Danielle reconnected with her true family.

47

Father of the Bride

'Why are you looking so cheerful at five-thirty in the morning?' grumbled Claudia to Olivia as she poured herself a cup of coffee. They were once more ensconced in the hotel suite that served as their Sydney base. It was Wednesday, only three days before the Falks–Forster wedding, which meant that the clock had started to run down on the enormous checklist that had to be finalised. Claudia's job was further complicated by the fact that she was over-seeing the finer details from arm's length and through a proxy, so as not to risk letting Sabrina or Ned stumble upon her true identity. The one bright spot was that Mimi had turned out to be almost as competent and trustworthy as Olivia, if not quite as efficient in her use of time. This was a godsend, as normally Claudia would have been giving a wedding of such scale her sole attention, but because of the clash with Priscilla's fifth wedding, she was doing two wed-dings at once. Hence the early starts and late finishes. Olivia was well and truly earning the generous pay rise that Claudia had given her three months ago.

'Because I have good news,' Olivia answered, as she switched on her laptop. 'I think I might have solved our second-last major problem with Prissy's wedding.' She paused for dramatic tension and then announced, 'I finally found a suitable actor to play Prissy's father-of-the-bride!'

Claudia stopped dead. 'You're kidding.'

'I'm not. I think he's perfect actually.'

'Will he require a ventilator or the assistance of a palliative-care nurse during the ceremony?' demanded Claudia.

Olivia shook her head. 'Nope.'

'Book him. Actually, wait a second,' Claudia looked at her assistant suspiciously. 'How old is he?'

Olivia hesitated and Claudia pounced. 'Aha! I knew there had to be a catch. Come on – out with it.'

'He's sixty-one,' Olivia disclosed reluctantly.

'*Sixty-one?* Olivia, he could be Prissy's son!'

'I know but, Claudia, you have to see him. He's brilliant. He came in wearing make-up and a wig and walking with a cane and I *swear* I thought he was ninety at least. He even *sounded* old. And he really needs the job.'

Claudia looked at her assistant doubtfully and then sighed. Olivia had never let her down before. She may as well trust her judgement this time.

'All right then, book him. I don't have time to vet him myself. Now, as soon as the clock ticks over to six, give Mimi her wake-up call. We have masses to get through today and I need her at the car-hire company's head office no later than eight a.m. Not on the phone to them, but physically there, talking to the manager, so that she can explain that a Bentley Mark VI might be a lovely wedding car but it is not acceptable when we have a legally binding contract for a Jaguar Mark 1 convertible. Make sure she says the words "legally binding contract", okay?'

'Will do. Ah – Claudia?'

'Yes?'

'Are we quite sure that Sabrina's wedding is going ahead?' The impeccably discreet Olivia looked embarrassed to have brought the topic up at all but Claudia couldn't blame her. Ever since the gossip about Sabrina's baby bump had become the biggest entertainment story in the country, most of the population of Australia had been wondering the same thing. Claudia had been trying not to think about it. The thought of Ned having to endure another abandoned wedding was unbearable.

'We've received no instructions to the contrary from any of the parties involved so we'll carry on as planned,' Claudia said, managing to keep her tone brisk and businesslike.

Olivia nodded. Claudia was about to go through to the room that served as her office when she suddenly stopped. 'What did you mean when you said you'd solved "the second-last major problem with Prissy's wedding"? What's the other problem?'

'She left a message overnight. She's worried there won't be enough guests at her wedding. Apparently a number of their friends have either died or had to go into nursing homes lately so there'll be a lot of empty places at the tables. She was hoping that we could invite some extras to make up numbers.'

Claudia groaned. 'I will say this for Prissy – she somehow still manages to dream up new challenges just when I really thought I'd seen everything that a bride could possibly throw at me.' She took a deep breath. 'Okay. Get the exact number of guest cancellations from her and we'll find a rent-a-crowd somehow.'

'Won't Prissy and Alexander find it odd to be getting married in front of a whole lot of strangers?' Olivia wondered aloud.

Claudia cast her a withering look. 'We're talking about *Prissy*. The 78-year-old bride with the 61-year-old pretend father. And at least substituting a rent-a-crowd means we won't have to reconfigure the entire seating plan. Anything else?'

Olivia shook her head and Claudia proceeded into the next room. Half a minute later she popped her head back out again. 'What's that actor's name by the way?'

'Jonathon. Jonathon Francis.'

'Well, Mr Jonathon Francis had better be as good as you say he is or else I'm putting you in charge the next time Prissy walks down the aisle.' With this threat, she closed the door of her office behind her. Olivia permitted herself a brief grin and then settled down to work.

The Night
Before the Big Day

- Set up ceremony & reception venue

- Try to spend some quality time on your own

48

Sabrina's Secret

At seven p.m. on the night before her wedding, Sabrina parked her car in the driveway of Edward's parents' house. She switched off the engine and then sat there, terrified to go in.

Edward had arrived home from Hong Kong two days ago. She was yet to see or speak to him. He hadn't returned to their apartment. He hadn't answered her calls.

When she finally gathered up the courage to press the doorbell, it was almost a relief to see Blanche open the door. The relief was to prove only momentary.

'Sabrina.' Edward's mother's normally welcoming smile was absent. Blanche had left several messages on Sabrina's phone, none of which Sabrina had listened to or answered. Sabrina had dialled the number for Edward's parents' house but had hung up when his father answered. The only person she felt able to speak to right now was Edward. From everyone else she just wanted to hide.

'Is he here?' Sabrina's voice was little more than a croak. She had been so consumed with thoughts of Edward, she hadn't thought about what facing his family would feel like. Now she knew that it felt like condemnation.

In answer, Blanche opened the door wider and gestured for Sabrina to enter. She led Sabrina towards the closed door of the formal drawing room where, all those months ago, the planning meeting for their wedding had taken place. Blanche seemed to be on the verge of telling Sabrina something but then she pressed her lips together and opened the door.

Edward was seated in an armchair, a depleted bottle of red wine on the glass-topped table in front of him. He was holding a wine glass by its stem, twirling its contents around and around as though hypnotised. Sabrina recoiled violently when she saw the alcohol, as though someone had hit her. *No*, she thought, *please make this not true*. Edward hadn't touched alcohol in over three years.

He looked terrible – unshaven and gaunt. The meticulous care that Sabrina had taken with her appearance before venturing out (knowing that there would be paparazzi waiting to take more photographs of her) now seemed like a calculated insult. She ought to be visibly altered by what was taking place between them, if only as a mark of respect.

Blanche closed the door behind her and the sound made Edward look up.

There was silence between them for a long moment until finally Edward broke it.

'I was wondering when – or if – you were going to show up.'

'You didn't return my calls. I've been worried about you.'

'I got back from Hong Kong two days ago, Sabrina. Surely it didn't take you two days to work out that I was staying with my parents?' His tone was uncharacteristically belligerent and Sabrina's heart sank. She had known, coming over here, that what she had to tell him would end things between them. But still, stupidly, she had held out hope for a miracle of forgiveness.

'We live together, Edward. Why didn't you come home?'

'I was curious to see how long it would take you to swallow your pride and come to me.'

An unexpected spark of anger flared up in Sabrina. 'So this was some kind of *test*? What would have happened if I hadn't come around? We're supposed to be getting married tomorrow, for God's sake!'

Edward twirled his wine glass again and looked faintly amused. 'Why should I be the one chasing after you? I know that you prefer it when I'm forced to prise things out of you, but I think in this situation the least that I deserve is an explanation without having to fall at your feet and beg for it.'

'Beg for it? You usually do everything you can to pretend there's never anything wrong with me. You don't really want to know when there is.' Dread, fatigue and now desolation caused by the sight of Edward drinking made Sabrina slip into bitterness. 'You're like everybody else. You just want me to be perfect.'

He raised one eyebrow, mocking her. 'But you're not, are you? Perfect, I mean. If one was to believe everything one reads, you're quite the little slut, my Sabrina fair.'

Sabrina stared at him in shock. And that's when she realised that, despite his seeming composure, Edward's speech was slightly slurred. He wasn't just drinking. He was drunk. Her heart sank.

'Do you know what everyone's thinking and saying?' Edward continued, in an almost conversational tone, as though they were discussing the weather.

'Of course I know! They're saying those things about *me*!'

'Is it true that you're having an affair with Ethan Carter?'

Sabrina stood very still. 'Are you really asking me whether I'm cheating on you?'

'Yes! Yes, I bloody well am! I don't know what to think or whether I can even trust you any more.'

There was a long pause and then Sabrina sighed inwardly. There was no other way out. *I'm sorry, Ethan*, she thought. She looked Edward in the eyes.

'Ethan's gay.'

Edward laughed. 'Like hell he is. He's been voted Sydney's most eligible bachelor by about a hundred different magazines. When he's not with you, the guy is out with a different girl every night.'

'Of course he is,' Sabrina said scornfully. 'If he stayed with one girl for any length of time she might start to wonder why he never had sex with her.'

'I don't believe it.'

Sabrina shrugged. 'So don't. For the record, the reason that I'm not having an affair with Ethan is not because he's gay but because I'm in love with you and we're engaged to be married. But somehow I didn't think that would be enough to convince you.'

Edward frowned. 'How can he have kept it a secret all this time?'

'He's discreet. Very. He has to be or he'll have no career. Do you think Nigel would have even hired him if he'd known? Nigel wouldn't be caught dead in the same *room* as a "bloody poofter",' she finished bitterly.

Edward looked at her and the distrust in his gaze broke her heart.

'What about the baby? Is it mine?'

'There is no bloody baby.' The cruel irony of it made her want to weep. 'Edward, please, I know you're furious with me but I need you to listen to me, okay? And please, just let me finish before you say anything else.' She started to will herself into the state of detachment that had served her so well on other difficult occasions. It would make what was to come easier. This room wasn't real, Edward wasn't real, even she wasn't real. She could float away when all of this was over. None of it really mattered. Nothing mattered.

The walls of the room melted away and the glorious, safe feeling of unreality started to descend. Sabrina felt an eerie calm come over her as she began to speak.

'This all started years ago, just after Dad left. I was only eleven but I stopped eating proper meals.'

Startled, Edward looked up. But Sabrina was looking beyond him.

'Starving myself made me feel strong. It was something I could control – it proved how self-disciplined I could be. How much control I had. It was bad, really bad, when I was about sixteen but then I got better. That's what I thought. Except then I got the job on *Sunshine Cove* and in every second scene I had to wear a bloody bikini. You should have seen the way people looked at me in the studio cafeteria if I ordered a sandwich for lunch – a sandwich! I never stopped to consider how strange it was to be in a world where snorting cocaine on a daily basis was considered normal but eating bread was a criminal offence. Anyway I . . . just sort of stopped eating again. I didn't think I was anorexic – I didn't think I was truly starving myself; I just thought that I ate in moderation. I even thought I was eating healthily. It's normal for me to have a glass of juice for breakfast, a small tin of tuna for lunch and a salad for dinner. But . . .' Sabrina faltered as her private grief momentarily broke through her carefully assembled armour of detachment. 'It wasn't enough. It wasn't anywhere near enough. I'm a grown woman and I've been starving myself for years and now my body – this supposedly perfect body – won't do what it ought to do.'

She lifted her head and looked at him, her eyes huge in her white, drained face. 'I've had test after test after test. I can't marry you, Edward, because I could never give you a family. I'm infertile.'

*

Now that it was finally out in the open, Sabrina simply felt tired. She had anticipated all the questions that he would inevitably fire at her after the first shock had worn off and she was doing her best to remain patient and answer them. But it was an effort. He didn't want to believe it was true. She could sympathise; she had reacted exactly the same way when her suspicions had first been confirmed. But the sooner he realised that it was an incontrovertible truth, the better for both of them.

Edward's face had turned an ashen grey. Her heart ached to see his alcohol-addled mind searching desperately for a way out of this nightmare, to make it not true.

'What about the weight you've put on? And the throwing up?'

'I've been trying to eat properly lately to help me fall pregnant. I thought maybe if I could get pregnant, then I could go through with the wedding, without ever having to tell you. But my body went into shock. I couldn't keep the food down. It made me sick. Then I discovered that the one thing that I could keep down was a revolting diet drink – a sort of protein shake – that I found in Aunty Bron's pantry. So I bought some more and tried to drink it as often as I could. I thought that maybe if my stomach could grow a bit bigger, then I could start eating things like meat and pasta again. But it didn't work. Every time I tried to eat carbohydrates I threw up. So somehow I've managed to put on weight with no nutritional benefit whatsoever.'

'But surely – I mean, you've only been trying for a few months. If you keep trying and have vitamin injections or something – God, I don't know. There has to be *something* —'

Sabrina shook her head. 'It's too late. Believe me – I've consulted every specialist available bar African witch-doctors. It's really very simple. I starved myself for a very long time. It doesn't matter how much I try to play catch-up now; my body simply can't regain its normal functions. I have amenorrhea.' She saw the look of incomprehension on Edward's face. 'It means that I don't menstruate. I haven't for years. My body has been in starvation mode for so long that it shut down all non-essential functions in order to survive.' Sabrina tried to banish the memory of the futile pregnancy test that she had taken a few days ago. She had known that there was absolutely no way she could be pregnant. But she hadn't been able to stop herself from foolishly hoping for a last-minute miracle.

'What about IVF?'

'We could use your sperm but the eggs would have to be donated. My periods might come back if I somehow manage to learn how to keep food down, but my ovaries are severely damaged. The REI specialist —' She checked herself, realising that the all-too-familiar, cold, clinical terms that fell so easily from her lips were all new to Edward. 'Reproductive endocrinology and infertility specialist,' she elucidated, 'was quite clear. I'll never be able to have a child of my own.' Inexplicably, Sabrina wanted to weep and laugh at the same time. It was all just too, *too* glamorous, darling. She had an eating disorder which meant that she would never be able to have a child, while poor Ethan couldn't even fall in love in case it became public and ruined his career. She wondered what currency the price of modern fame was measured in. Pounds of flesh and vales of tears, perhaps.

'Who knows? Have you told anyone? Mimi? Or your aunt?'

Sabrina shook her head and then spoke in a small voice. 'The only person who knows is Ethan.'

'*Ethan knows?* Some bloody actor that you work with knows but you couldn't tell *me*?'

Sabrina tried to steady her voice. 'I didn't mean to. I was upset one day when he rang me from L.A. I'd just come out of the specialist's office. And . . . I told him. That's when I found out he was gay.'

'How sweet. The two of you sharing secrets while keeping everyone else in the dark. Perhaps you should marry Ethan instead of me tomorrow. He's obviously the only person that you trust.'

'Edward, please, it's not like that. Somehow it was possible to tell Ethan because it was over the phone and he was so far away; it was more distant. I wasn't frightened of telling Ethan the way I was scared of telling you. I didn't want to lose you. I kept trying and trying to fall pregnant so it would make all of this go away and you'd never have to know. I even did one stupid, final pregnancy test the other night just hoping that somehow we could have a happy ending . . .'

He looked at her and laughed. 'Didn't you win an award for that episode of *Sunshine Cove* where you gave birth to your daughter? You should have been given an Academy Award, shouldn't you, Sabrina?'

'*Edward*,' she whispered. Of all the responses she had imagined from him, she'd never envisaged drunken cruelty. It was the one thing against which she had never been able to fight back.

Edward's disbelief was slowly turning to anger. She could see it stirring in him. It had happened to her too, although it had taken a little longer. The seven stages of grief.

'So what am I in all of this? Am I just some sort of minor detail? You tell me you've been starving yourself and throwing up and trying to fall pregnant and going to see doctors, and all of this was going on behind my back? You didn't even *think* of telling me? What the hell kind of marriage were we getting into?'

'How was I meant to bring the subject up? I mean, Christ, Edward, look at how you proposed to me! You had our family trees drawn up! Telling you that I could never give you a family was —' Sabrina broke off and with a bitter laugh she concluded, 'inconceivable.'

He stood up for the first time, swaying slightly on his feet. 'What exactly do you think marriage is, Sabrina? You've been carrying on a little secret society for one and making major decisions that we should have been making *together*. As a result, the rumour mill is now running riot, you've humiliated both me and my family, and then you – *you* not *us* – make the decision that our wedding isn't going ahead because of something you've chosen to tell me the night before our wedding. What *the fuck* is wrong with you?'

Sabrina could feel his virulent words piercing her heart. As always happened when she was attacked, she turned to ice. 'I'm not sure that I did make the wrong decision in not telling you,' she said coolly. 'Has it not occurred to you *why* I kept it from you for so long?'

He looked at her, taken aback.

'I wasn't sure how you would handle it. *If* you could handle it.' She paused and then said, very slowly, 'I was frightened that you might feel locked in to our marriage. Obligated to marry me even though I couldn't give you a family. I was terrified that if you felt trapped or depressed or had a . . . significant emotional shock of any kind, that you might start drinking again.' She paused and then said softly, 'And I was right.'

He gave an unpleasant laugh. 'I was wondering when you were going to mention that. Save the best till last, did you? It must feel good to know how marvellous you are compared with everyone else. Little Miss Perfect, who has never known what it feels like to be weak or a failure.' Very deliberately, he refilled his wine glass and then tipped his head back and drank the entire contents in one go. With an unsteady hand, he filled the glass once more, slopping some on the table.

Sabrina felt her heart break as she watched him. *I did this to you*, she thought. *Edward, I'm sorry. I'm so, so sorry.* She gave it one final try. 'I know what failure feels like,' she said quietly. 'And I wish that I'd told you sooner. The only thing that I can ask is for you to understand how difficult this was for me. I don't —' Sabrina stumbled and choked. 'It makes me feel like I'm not . . . a real woman.'

Edward looked at her and then, to her horror, he laughed. 'That's the very least of your problems, darling. You're so cold that most of the time I'm not even sure you're a real human being.' With a slow but sure movement he lifted his arm and for a moment she thought he might strike her. She cowered and then flinched as Edward hurled his glass of red wine with deliberate aim at the wall behind her.

It smashed. Moments later there was the sound of two doors slamming in quick succession. Sabrina lifted her head, her face white with shock.

Edward had gone.

She felt a wetness on her face and dazedly, she lifted her hand to her head. At first she couldn't think what had happened, but then she realised that some of the red wine must have splashed on her when Edward had thrown the glass. She looked at herself in the ornate, gilt-framed mirror above the mantelpiece. From this distance it looked like the old scar on her head had reopened and that blood had started to drip down her face once more.

49

Mimi's Other List

It was the night before the wedding and Mimi had forty-five minutes to herself before she had to meet Claudia at Strickland House. Thanks to a highly infectious bout of summer flu that had ripped a swathe through the staff of the event stylist, Claudia and Mimi would be spending at least two, possibly three, hours tonight creating origami swans or performing some other vital decorating task that was apparently crucial to the success of the wedding reception.

Mimi had decided that it was high time she laid her crush on Teddy to rest. Given the success of her last list, she had therefore decided to write another one. She drew a wavy line down the middle of a sheet of paper and then another horizontal one halfway down. On one side she wrote 'Teddy' and on the other side she wrote 'Nate'. She then headed her four boxes 'Pros' and 'Cons'.

In Teddy's 'Pros' box, she started to write a list of everything that she adored about him: his looks, his charm, the air of success and assurance that hung about him.

If she was being honest, she didn't *love* his choice of career. All those long hours and the pressure that came with a corporate environment. Wearing a suit every day and only getting a few weeks of holidays every year. There didn't seem to be much freedom.

Another drawback was that Teddy wasn't very funny. He understood jokes and always laughed at Mimi's but he rarely made any of his own.

Nate's side of the list now had: good job (more freedom, no suits) and funny. Because Nate *was* funny and he made Mimi laugh, which was a nice change. She was always the one who was expected to make everyone laugh. Having someone else in charge of the humour was quite a relief.

Under Nate's 'Cons' heading Mimi wrote: *Sporty and has made me sporty*. She thought for a moment and then added: *Owns lots of track-suits* and then followed that up with *Used to be in love with Claudia*. Although that wasn't really a con now that she thought about it. Mimi liked Claudia and, if anything, having a crush on her showed that Nate had excellent taste in women. Also, his crush had apparently lasted a very long time. He was capable of commitment. Mimi scribbled it out.

She chewed her pen and realised that she had forgotten one of Teddy's biggest negatives entirely. She added it to Teddy's side of the list: *Loves Sabrina. Is marrying my sister tomorrow*. Then in Nate's 'Pros' box she wrote: *Prefers me*. She briefly thought about writing *Loves me*, but that seemed a bit presumptuous.

Reading back over the lists Mimi felt indescribably foolish. It really was a no-brainer. She and Nate were far more compatible. Nate was available and, for some unfathomable reason, he liked her. In all honesty, if he hadn't been standing in Teddy's shadow, she probably would have been far more receptive to him earlier. More importantly, however, Teddy wasn't available, and even if he had been, he'd never shown the slightest bit of interest in Mimi beyond the fraternal.

Only then, all of a sudden, he did.

50

The Way Back

Mimi walked through the colonnaded entrance of Strickland House and gasped. Although there were still mysterious bubble-wrapped items and taped-up cardboard boxes waiting to be unpacked, as well as at least a dozen young people dressed in a kind of casual uniform of black T-shirts and jeans running around doing obscure things with swathes of fabric and staple guns, the transformation of the early Victorian, heritage-listed mansion into a glamorous wonderland, replete with flowers, mirrors, candles and soft silks, was already well and truly under way. It was startlingly beautiful.

She made her way into the ballroom where she spotted Claudia, deep in conversation with a woman who looked like a retired ballerina. The woman had high cheekbones, dark hair pulled back into a tight bun and the most fabulous posture Mimi had ever seen. Like her staff, she was also wearing a black T-shirt but had teamed it with a pair of black pants, a headset and a tense expression.

'Ah, Mimi. Thanks for coming in at the last moment,' Claudia greeted her. 'Mimi Falks, this is Trish Dobson, the wonderful stylist who is bringing the theme of Modern Glamour to life for us.'

Trish's head whipped around and all the colour drained out of her face. 'Falks? *Falks?* You're not —'

'Sabrina's sister,' Mimi said cheerfully, holding out her hand. 'Yes, I am. How do you do?'

'The *bridesmaid* shouldn't be here the night before the wedding!' Trish hissed to Claudia. 'She should be at home, in bed!' She stared hard at Mimi. 'Preferably with a moisturising face mask on.'

Mimi's hand went self-consciously up to pat one cheek as Claudia looked amused. 'Normally I'd agree with you, Trish, but Mimi's position is somewhat unique. She's been working side by side with me on this wedding from the start. Now stop worrying and tell us what you need us to do. The sooner we start, the sooner Mimi can go home.'

With a disapproving sigh, Trish led them over to a trestle table that was piled high with boxes of small frangipani-scented candles, delicate cylindrical glass vases, stacks of pre-cut, shimmering gold Florence Broadhurst fabric, and more cardboard boxes filled with beaded tassels.

'These vases need to be covered with the fabric like this,' Trish said. She quickly drew a line of fabric glue down one side of a piece of material and then expertly rolled one of the vases up. She ran her thumb down the seam, tied a tassel exactly midway down the vase and then gently pushed one of the candles into place on the metal spike that protruded from the inside base of the vase. In less than ten seconds, it seemed to Mimi, she was showing them the finished object. 'It's really very simple, and I feel terrible getting you to do this low-level work, Claudia, but this damn flu has knocked out at least eight of my staff and finding people that I can trust to do the simplest things is just about imposs—' She stopped mid-sentence as a voice came over her headset, and then, without another word, dashed away to deal with whatever new crisis had presented itself.

'I'm *terrible* at art and craft,' Mimi said mournfully, taking a seat at the trestle table.

'So am I,' Claudia said cheerfully, sitting down next to her. 'Don't worry, we'll probably botch a few up at the start but we'll be old pros by the time we finish, given how many we have to do.'

'How many do we have to do?' asked Mimi fearfully.

Claudia consulted a list. 'Five hundred.'

Mimi groaned. 'I should have brought my sleeping bag.'

'You won't be here that late,' Claudia said immediately. 'Trish was right – you really ought to be at home getting your beauty sleep and I'm not going to keep you a second longer than I have to.'

'Don't you start,' Mimi protested. 'What with Trish commenting on my dried-up complexion and now you insisting that I need ten hours' beauty sleep minimum, I feel as though I should wear a paper bag over my head to the wedding. A designer, vintage-patterned paper bag, tastefully tied around the neck with a beaded tassel, of course,' she added, sounding quite shocked that she had almost left this out.

Claudia grinned. 'Naturally. I am sorry about this though, Mimi. You wouldn't have to be here at all if only Olivia could be here.'

'Where is Olivia?' asked Mimi, carefully concentrating as she squeezed out thick, unevenly spaced gobs of glue that bore no resemblance whatsoever to the neat line of adhesive that Trish had created.

'Remember Prissy and her father-of-the-bride request? Olivia is currently overseeing the actor's suit fitting. I'm double-booked, remember? I'm doing Prissy's wedding tomorrow while Olivia will be overseeing Sabrina's wedding.'

'Sabrina *and* Teddy's wedding,' Mimi rebuked her. 'Everyone always forgets the groom.'

'I did no such thing. He got his own Post-It note, remember?'

'I don't think we ever actually wrote anything on it.'

'Oh. Well, if you remind me later I'll draw a smiley face or something on it. What *are* you doing to that tassel?'

Before Mimi could respond, Trish made a sudden dramatic entrance at the top of the staircase.

'CHANDELIER EMERGENCY! I need EVERYBODY in the drawing room NOW!' she bellowed. She pointed to Claudia and Mimi. 'Not you two! Permanent staff who are covered by my insurance policy ONLY! Now MOVE!' She disappeared and a dozen black T-shirts immediately bolted up the stairs in her wake.

'Shouldn't you go and check what's going on?' Mimi asked doubtfully, once the stampede was over.

'I'll go in a minute. Trish and I must have done over twenty weddings together. I'd say she averages about three of these sort of emergencies for every wedding we do. My guess is the specialist lighting company has delivered one branch-style chandelier rather than the dozen teardrop-style ones that she ordered. I'm sure that whatever it is will be easily fixed.'

'Do you ever get stressed out?' Mimi asked admiringly, looking over at Claudia who was still working neatly and unhurriedly away.

'Very rarely. I've been doing this for a long time, remember? At the start I had to learn how to keep my nerves under control, but I've seen and dealt with most things now so I know that solutions can usually be found.' They worked in silence for a few minutes and then Claudia continued reflectively, 'I worked on a wedding once where the video cameraman somehow missed the bride walking down the aisle. I wanted to kill him. It was right at the start of my career and it could have ruined both his professional reputation and mine. I saw only one way out of it. So, after the ceremony concluded, I took the bride aside as soon as I decently could and confessed. She was semi-hysterical until I suggested that we re-enact it.'

'What? The whole ceremony?'

'Of course not. Just the walk up the aisle. So while the groom was outside accepting congratulations from family and friends, we hastily pulled the bride and her father back into the church and filmed her walking up the aisle on his arm, nodding and smiling away to the empty pews, while the organist played the bridal march all over again.'

'Was she furious?'

'That's the odd part. She couldn't have been happier because she said she was so nervous when she was doing it for real that she wasn't smiling. Although I was relieved, of course, I couldn't help wondering what on earth would be going through her mind when she watched the video in the future. Because it didn't capture a real moment or a real emotion. It was just an artificial and edited part of what had become a convoluted wedding production.' Claudia sighed. 'I love this industry but I'll admit that, like you, there are times when I question its values.'

Claudia looked so pensive that Mimi felt compelled to reassure her. 'You're amazing at what you do. You've even brought me around to your way of thinking. I kind of like it now that people put so much thought and effort into their weddings. If we must create a big fuss over something, why not make it over love?'

Claudia raised an eyebrow. 'Don't tell me that Mimi the Eternal Cynic has succumbed to the siren song of Weddings Inc?'

Mimi stuck her tongue out at Claudia as she anchored a candle into its holder. 'I'm just saying there are worse ways to embark on a marriage than holding a beautiful ceremony and party.'

'Such as?'

'Such as getting drunk in Las Vegas and having a wayside-chapel wedding conducted by an Anna Nicole Smith look-alike,' Mimi said dolefully, without stopping to think.

Claudia laughed. 'With the exception of Britney Spears, I don't think anyone really does that, Mimi. It would be so unbelievably *tacky*.'

Mimi looked at her and then suddenly started to laugh. She laughed so hard that the tears streamed down her face. 'Sorry,' she gasped, as Claudia looked at her in astonishment. 'It's just – *you're right*. It's not tragic at all. It's just —' she hiccupped. 'It's just the most hilariously *tacky* thing in the world.'

'Are you quite all right, Mimi? Shall I get you some water?'

Mimi shook her head, unable to respond as she tried to get herself under control. She failed and another gale of laughter pealed forth. Claudia shook her head as she stood up.

'I haven't the faintest idea what's so funny but I'll wait until you can speak again to find out. In the meantime, I'm going to check on Trish and the chandelier. Back in a moment.'

Mimi nodded helplessly and waved her away. Moments later she was still giggling under her breath when a shadow fell across the table. Expecting to see Claudia, Mimi jumped in fright when she realised that a large male figure was looming over her.

'Teddy!' she exclaimed in relief. 'You almost gave me heart failure. What on earth are you doing here?'

'Hello, Baby,' he slurred.

Mimi's eyes narrowed. Something wasn't right. And then she realised that Teddy was drunk. Extremely drunk. The full implications of Teddy being drunk hit home and she felt dismay wash over her. She sat, paralysed for a moment, wondering what to do. At any moment, everyone could return from upstairs and see the groom drunk and then Claudia – *oh God*, thought Mimi. *Claudia*. Teddy's ex-fiancée. This was turning into a complete nightmare. She suddenly desperately wished that Nate was by her side. He would know what to do.

Mimi bit her lip and then quickly made up her mind. The best thing to do would be to pretend that she had no idea about Teddy's past as an alcoholic. She would treat his drunkenness as though it wasn't a big deal. She just needed to get him away from here and then she could call Nate for help.

'The whole point of having your buck's night in Hong Kong was to get this kind of thing out of the way well before the wedding,' she scolded him lightly, putting aside the vase that she was working on. 'You're not meant to get drunk the night before the wedding too. Sabrina won't be happy if you're hungover tomorrow.' She looked around as she stood up and moved around the table. 'Are you here alone?' With increasing consternation, she added, 'Don't tell me you *drove*?' Sabrina would kill him if she found out. Sabrina was very judgemental when it came to anyone behaving irresponsibly while under the influence of alcohol.

'Don't worry about Sabrina.' Teddy swayed, and now seriously alarmed, Mimi jumped forward to help steady him. She put her arm around his waist, reeling as the stench of alcohol hit her. He was incredibly heavy and she wasn't sure how long she could support his weight.

'Come and sit down over here, Teddy,' she said, starting to tug him in the direction of the staircase. He resisted the momentum and instead tightened his grip on her ribcage. His left hand was disturbingly near her breast. Feeling uncomfortable, she tried to wriggle away but then he deliberately moved his hand up.

For a moment she was so shocked she couldn't move. Then she started to struggle. He instantly removed his hand but only so that he could hold her tighter against him.

'*What are you doing?*' Mimi gasped, horrified. At this close range, he looked a little mad.

'Oh come on, Mimi. You're always making puppy-dog eyes at me.' In a high-pitched tone he mimicked her voice, '*Teddy* this and *Teddy* that. Maybe I just picked the wrong sister.'

She tried to fight him off, but even in his inebriated state he was still too strong for her. 'Ted – Edward, stop this. Leave me alone and I'll drive you home. You can go to bed and sleep it off.'

He ignored her and instead bent his head. It happened so fast that Mimi didn't even realise what was coming.

For almost a year now, Mimi had dreamed about being kissed by Teddy. But when it finally happened it was nothing like her romantic daydreams. It was brutal and horrible and he tasted unpleasantly like alcohol. Moreover, the feeling of powerlessness that accompanied the kiss made her so simultaneously furious and distraught that the urge to physically hurt him, like she had never hurt anyone before, rose up like a torrent within her.

He finally lifted his head and Mimi pulled back one leg as far as she could and then kicked him with all her force. He instantly let go of her as he staggered in pain.

'I said *leave me alone!*' Mimi's eyes spat fire as she backed away from him.

He straightened up and Mimi feared that he was about to grab her again. Her hands instinctively curled into fists, ready to punch, the way that Nate had taught her. And then, from the top of the staircase, a harsh voice cut across the room. 'Leave her alone, Ned!'

Edward looked up in shock – straight into Claudia's clear brown eyes.

'Jesus Christ,' he said, in a wobbly tone. 'What the —'

Claudia ignored him. She rapidly descended the staircase and placed a comforting arm around Mimi, who had begun to sob tears of anger and humiliation. The sound and sight of Mimi crying seemed to jolt Edward back to his senses.

He abruptly sat down heavily on one of the unopened cardboard boxes and looked at her, still glassy-eyed. 'Mimi, I'm sorry,' he said, in the self-pitying tones of a drunk. 'Sabrina and I had a fight —'

Mimi looked at him with revulsion. 'So you thought you'd take it out on me?'

Claudia forced Mimi to look at her. 'Why don't you go home, Mimi?' she suggested gently. 'Will you be all right to drive yourself?'

Mimi nodded, still trying to quell her tears.

'Text me when you get there so that I know you're home safely, okay?'

Uncharacteristically, without another word, Mimi picked up her bag and left the mansion almost at a run, giving Edward a wide berth. As she left, he called out after her but she ignored him.

'Let her go,' Claudia said, severely. 'You're in no state to fix this now.'

Edward ran a shaking hand through his hair as he sat, still slumped on the box. 'Am I dreaming? Or are you going to curse me every time I try to get married? What the hell are *you* doing here?'

'I'm your wedding planner,' Claudia said tautly, still trying to control her shock at seeing him. 'Mimi hired me on instruction from Sabrina. Before you ask, Sabrina has no idea who I am. We've never met or even spoken. All of my contact has been through Mimi.'

Edward shook his head as though trying to clear it. '*You're* our wedding planner?'

Claudia judged that the best thing to do would be to simply wait for comprehension to sink in. Edward shook his head again and then looked at her with his dazed expression. 'I spent so long thinking about what I would say to you if I ever saw you again. And now – I just feel nothing.'

She bit her lip. 'Did you get the letter I sent?'

He laughed. 'Yes. It was very considerate of you to offer a written explanation three days after you humiliated me in front of everyone we knew.' He stumbled slightly over the longer words, his thoughts and speech still blurred by alcohol. But his anger with her, even after all these years, was palpable.

Claudia flinched. 'I know it was cowardly of me. If it's any consolation, I paid a heavy price for what I did and I'm still paying it.'

He glanced at the fraudulent wedding ring on her fourth finger. 'Not so heavy that you didn't move on. Was he the real reason you left me?'

Not for the first time, Claudia cursed the professional necessity of wearing that stupid ring. But it was too complicated and Ned was too drunk to give a full explanation now. 'No,' she said shortly. 'He wasn't.'

'Well, I'm glad you were able to go through with it with someone, even though the thought of marriage to me was so fucking terrible you had to run away.'

'Ned, listen to me. What happened between us was years ago and it wasn't your fault; it was all mine. We probably should have met to talk about it but once I ran away I just . . .' Claudia faltered. 'I couldn't find my way back,' she finished softly. 'But that's why I'm here now. I was trying to make it up to you by giving you your perfect wedding day.'

He didn't respond, simply sat there, with his head in his hands.

'Ned, please, what's going on with you and Sabrina? Why did you treat Mimi like that?'

He finally looked up and the helplessness and anguish on his face tore through the old wounds of her heart. This must have been how he had looked on their wedding day.

'Sabrina —' he began and then stopped. He shook his head and she knew instinctively that whatever had happened between him and Sabrina, he would never tell her.

'You look terrible, Ned,' she said, altering her tactics. 'Let me drive you home so you can sober up.'

He shook his head. 'Not home. Don't want to see anyone.'

'I'll take you to a hotel then. Come on. I'll help you up.' She picked up her bag and then, as Mimi had done, slipped her arm around his waist to help him stand.

They stood for a moment, their arms around one another, and he looked at her, as though still disbelieving that she was real. She gave him a tremulous smile.

'Ready?'

'I used to love you,' he said, in a wondering tone. 'I really did. But I don't any more.'

Her heart gave one quick contraction – of regret, shame, hurt pride; she wasn't entirely sure what caused it. And then she was able to look him straight in the eyes.

'I used to love you too,' she answered. 'But I don't any more either.'

He gave a sudden, wry smile. 'Good thing we didn't get married, huh? There are already too many divorces in the world.'

'And unhappy marriages,' she agreed.

There was a pause.

'I love Sabrina. More than anything in the world.' His words carried a sudden conviction, that seemed as much about revealing the truth to himself, as it did about declaring his stance towards her.

'I'm glad,' she said simply. Her heart lifted as she realised that she was speaking the truth. She smiled at him. 'Come on. We need to sober you up so that you have a clear head for your wedding tomorrow.' She waited a beat as she started to lead him out towards the car. 'You do still want to get married, don't you?'

Edward didn't immediately answer. She was brought to a stop as he suddenly grasped her hand and looked at her with the intensity of a man begging for salvation. 'Claude?' he whispered hoarsely. 'Have I ruined everything?'

She looked back at him for a long moment. 'I don't know,' she answered softly. 'But I do know this; whatever you decide to do, the most important thing is not to run away.'

The Wedding Day

- Enjoy one of the most perfect days of your life . . .

51

The Idea Of Perfection

'I've come to apologise.'

It was half past seven in the morning, on the day of the wedding, and Edward was standing on the doorstep of Aunty Bron's house. Oddly, Mimi was more taken aback by his rumpled appearance than she was by the fact that he was there at all. Edward's customary debonair style was entirely absent. He was wearing the same suit and shirt that he had been dressed in the previous evening and an expression that wasn't so much contrite as fearful. With good reason. Not only was Mimi still blazingly angry, her entire face was slathered with some sort of moisturising concoction. Apologising to a woman whom he had treated appallingly was a novel experience for Edward, let alone one whose face was bright green.

Mimi crossed her arms in front of her chest and said nothing, choosing instead to glare at him aggressively. Edward was forcibly reminded of a Papua New Guinean Highlands warrior.

'Mimi, please just hear me out. Last night I . . . I think I went a bit mad. I haven't had a drink for years and . . . I didn't handle it very well.'

'No,' Mimi said thoughtfully. 'No, I don't think you handled it very well.' The sarcasm was practically visible, dripping from each measured word.

Edward started to sweat but knew that he had to persist. 'You have to understand, I've spent the past few days wondering whether Sabrina was having an affair behind my back. I know those bloody magazines and blogs are just vicious rubbish, but when it's your life they're discussing it's impossible to completely ignore them. And there was something wrong with Sabrina lately but she wouldn't discuss it and —' he flushed in shame, 'I never pushed her to tell me what was wrong. She's always private and the strong one —' Mimi jumped at his use of the familial term, 'so I just left her alone. I shouldn't have done that.'

He paused, looking so woebegone that Mimi had to conjure up the indefensible scene from the night before to ensure that her heart remained sufficiently hardened against him.

'I got back from Hong Kong, dying to see her, only to be confronted by that damn article saying that she was pregnant with Ethan's child. There were the photos of her throwing up and of that imaginary baby bump . . . I was surrounded by family and friends who kept asking after Sabrina and assuring me that they knew it was all lies, but the whole time I could see it in their eyes – they were wondering whether it could possibly be true.'

A sliver of guilt crept up Mimi's spine. She knew Sabrina better than anyone and even she had been unable to banish all doubt.

'Sabrina called me, of course, but I was so angry and proud I wouldn't return her calls. She knew where to find me and I felt that she owed it to me to come and explain herself. God, I sound like a complete arsehole, don't I? I never once put her feelings first. I was so busy feeling humiliated and suspicious that I never stopped to remember that the article was about *her*.'

'It's not true,' said Mimi defiantly. 'Not a word of it.'

'I know it's not,' Edward said gently. 'Because I know now that the truth just makes those lies even more despicable.' He drew a deep breath. 'Last night Sabrina told me that she can never fall pregnant.'

'*What?*'

'She said you didn't know,' Edward said wearily. 'I wasn't sure.'

Mimi shook her head. 'No, I — why? Why can't she?' she demanded.

'Can I come in? Please?'

Mutely, Mimi nodded. He followed her into the living room and she gestured for him to sit down. She remained standing.

'She's infertile,' he said, saying it aloud for the first time, 'thanks to years of starving herself so that she could fit into a size-six bikini for that damn show,' he finished bitterly.

Mimi was silent for a long moment as a wave of grief for Sabrina welled up inside her. 'You had no idea?' she finally asked softly.

He shook his head. 'None. And I . . . didn't take it well. I was so angry with her for waiting until the night before our wedding to tell me something so important. I was already drunk when she came over, feeling sorry for myself, imagining another abandoned wedding and wondering what I had done to deserve this treatment. When she finally told me, something inside me just exploded. I yelled at her – I hardly even remember what I said, but I know that I threw a glass over her head and smashed it against the wall.'

'Oh no,' Mimi breathed, still remorseful over her own violent outbursts. 'Not you too. You know that Dad —'

'I know what he did!' Edward snapped. He pressed one hand to his forehead. For the first time Mimi noticed that his hands were shaking uncontrollably. 'I'm not like him, Mimi, you know that I'm not. I would never harm a hair on Sabrina's head.'

Mimi said nothing. She simply let the truth of his actions hang between them, damning him. She knew that Edward felt the weight of the unspoken accusation.

He swallowed hard, wanting now just to finish his story. 'So I left and got into the car and somehow I ended up at Strickland House. I saw the lights on inside and then . . .' He looked up at her. 'I'm sorry,

Mimi. I don't know what else to say except that I swear I've never behaved like that before in my life.'

Mimi thought for a moment as she pulled her dressing-gown tighter around her. 'Do you have a thing for me?'

'God, no! I mean, no,' Edward hastily altered his emphatic tone as he took in Mimi's expression. 'No offence – I think you're great fun – but no, I've never felt like that towards you. I was just drunk and livid with Sabrina and . . . and I knew that hurting you was the best way to hurt her.' Edward buried his face in his hands. 'I know how this is making me sound. But I'm not a bastard, Mimi. I swear I'm not. I just . . . lost control.'

Mimi tried to quell the waves of sympathy – *no, make that empathy*, she thought – that she was feeling. If anyone knew what it was like to do stupid, out-of-control things while you were drunk that you would later deeply regret, it was her. And in the same way that she wasn't the foolish victim that Jared probably remembered, she knew in her heart that Edward wasn't really an untrustworthy sleaze. Nevertheless, the memory of that assault of a kiss remained. She could understand how it had happened but that didn't mean she was ready to forgive him.

'Have you spoken to Sabrina since your fight last night?' she demanded, in as cold a tone as she could muster.

Edward shook his head. 'No. Claudia drove me to a hotel and booked me a room so that I could sleep it off. I wanted to see you first to apologise and —'

'To find out whether I'd told Sabrina?' Mimi guessed astutely.

He looked at her with a hangdog expression.

She relented. 'I haven't told her. Yet,' she added warningly, as his expression lightened. 'I still might though.' She paused and then added with difficulty, 'I think I might be able to forgive you for what you did last night. One day. Not today and probably not soon. Maybe in five years' time when you've stored up some good behaviour credit to prove that what happened really was a once-off.'

'Isn't there anything I can do to make it up to you or to show you that I'm not really like that?' he asked bleakly.

She looked at him appraisingly and then suddenly clicked her fingers. 'There is one thing that might help actually. It's kind of a split-personality test to expose people who appear too good to be true but are really something else altogether underneath.' She paused and then said firmly, 'Take your tie off.'

Edward looked at her in confusion. 'Why?'

'You're in enough trouble as it is. Just do what I say.'

He complied, still looking bemused.

'Good. Now roll your head around. From side to side. That's it. Does your head feel quite secure?'

'I haven't the faintest idea why you're making me do this,' said Edward, still obediently rolling his head around.

Mimi smiled. 'You can stop now.'

Edward regarded her anxiously. 'Did I pass the test?'

'With flying colours. Aunty Bron always thought that if you undid your tie, your head would fall off. But it didn't.'

'And that means . . . ?'

'That you're a real human being. You're not a freaky perfect android.'

'Of course I'm not perfect. No-one is.'

'I'm beginning to understand that. It's taken me a while to figure it out but I think I've finally realised that a real relationship is about loving someone for their imperfections as much as for their desirable traits.' She smiled to herself. 'Which makes a Pros and Cons list redundant really. If they're the right person, everything is a Pro in an odd way.'

Edward, who clearly had no idea what she was talking about, simply

415

looked at her in confusion. Mimi relented and sat down next to him on the sofa. For a moment there was silence.

'Mimi?'

'Yes?'

'Why is your face green?'

'It's avocado,' Mimi said crossly. 'It's meant to be very good for a dry complexion.'

'Oh.'

There was a further silence.

'Ted— Edward? You know that thing that I just said about loving someone for their imperfections? You know now about Sabrina's – well, flaw I guess, although I hate to call it that. You won't be able to have children together.' Mimi paused and then said what everyone confronted with this revelation inevitably said. 'She's positive that there's no hope at all?'

'Apparently she's had every single test available.'

'And she went through all that alone?' Mimi suddenly felt as though she was about to burst into tears. 'Without having anyone beside her?'

Edward was silent but Mimi saw the muscles in his jaw work as he fought back his emotions.

'It must have been killing her, knowing that she could never give you something that you wanted so much. She loves you. And,' Mimi gulped and continued, 'Sabrina will do anything for the people that she loves. She tends to do it in secret, mind you, like the way she kept money aside for me, but she never asks for anything or for help for herself. Never. She always tries to handle everything by herself.'

'She should have told me!' Edward said, unable to keep the frustration out of his tone.

'Of course she should have told you but it's not her fault. It's the way our family made her.' Mimi was quiet for a moment. 'Do you love my sister?'

'Yes. Of course I do.'

'Do you still want to marry her?'

There was a long silence during which Mimi held her breath. Then Edward looked up. Despite the tiredness and strain etched into his face, she could see something else that she instantly recognised. It was a silent, anguished plea for a happy ending.

'Yes. If she'll still have me.'

'Do you faithfully swear that you will never again act like a drunken, lecherous creep?'

A faint spark lit up Edward's eyes as he heard her stronger, more teasing tone. 'I do.'

'If you're lying and I ever catch you acting like that again, I won't tell Sabrina. I'll just kill you myself. And not in a nice way. Understood?'

Edward nodded meekly. 'What are we going to do?' he asked anxiously, as Mimi bounded up, suddenly full of plans and energy.

'*You* are going to go home and get ready for your wedding. And *I'm* going to do what all good bridesmaids ought to do.' A brilliant smile lit up Mimi's green face. Edward thought that she had never looked as beautiful to him as she did at that moment. 'I'm going to ward off all the evil spirits and make sure that this wedding comes to pass.'

52

The Bride's Side

Mimi had had the forethought to borrow Edward's security pass and key, so she was able to dodge the paparazzi and let herself into Sabrina and Teddy's apartment, after repeated pressing of the buzzer yielded no answer.

'Sabrina?' she called out, as she opened the door. 'Sabrina, it's me.'

There was nothing but silence. Mimi walked through the empty apartment, pausing only to gaze at the immense bulk of Sabrina's wedding dress, which hung in the spare bedroom, sheathed in a protective layer of white gauze. Mimi shivered and retreated, closing the door behind her. It was stupidly morbid but she couldn't help thinking that the dress looked like the ghost of a woman who'd been lynched.

*

For several minutes, Mimi stood in the apartment and chewed her lip, wondering what to do next. There was no point calling Sabrina's mobile, because it was lying on the dining table, switched off. Mimi tried to quell her anxiety. Maybe Sabrina had simply gone for a run. She tried to hold on to this reassuring thought but then she realised how idiotic she was being. It was Sabrina's wedding day and she'd had an enormous fight with her fiancé the night before. It was unlikely that she was out making exercise her top priority.

The intercom buzzer suddenly sounded and Mimi ran to answer it. On the video screen, the faces of Delta and Eamon, Sabrina's hairdresser and make-up artist, came into view.

'Sabrina, it's us. We're here to get started on your wedding-day transformation!'

Their voices were pitched with such exhilaration that, for a brief moment, Mimi recalled that this was how a wedding day was supposed to be. Filled with bustle and excitement and nervous tension, rather than the aching anxiety that she was currently experiencing.

'Oh! Hi there. It's Mimi.' She thought quickly, wondering what on earth she was going to say. 'Um, listen, there's been a change of plan because of the paparazzi. They're everywhere and Sabrina and Teddy have an exclusive deal with one photographer. So we won't be getting ready here.' Her brain worked feverishly. She had always been good at improvisation at NIDA. She could do this. She concentrated on making her voice sound light and convincing. 'We need you to go to the Four Seasons Hotel in the city. Explain the situation to the concierge and book a suite under Sabrina's name. You shouldn't have any problems – he knows us. Just ask if the suite we hired on New Year's Eve is available. We'll meet you there but in the meantime order room service – have whatever you want to eat or drink.' She added the last sentence to ease her conscience about sending them off on a wild-goose chase. If you were going to be lied to and have your time wasted, there were worse places to be sent than a suite at the Four Seasons, she reasoned. She was sure that Teddy would pick up the bill.

Delta's voice came back over the intercom and Mimi could see by the expressions on both of their faces that they were thrilled with the intrigue.

'Okay then, we'll see you there. Don't be long though – we really need to get to work if we're to have you both ready by half past three.'

They disappeared from the video screen but Mimi was no longer paying attention. Her uneasy suspicion had been confirmed by Delta and Eamon's scheduled rendezvous with Sabrina. Her sister had definitely run away.

Mimi stood very still, thinking furiously, as she tried to work out where Sabrina would have gone. Her gaze wandered around the beautiful apartment, searching for clues. Everything was so stylish, so modern. Only one, very familiar object seemed out of place. Mimi walked over to the shelf where it sat, right at the back, and picked it up.

It was a black-and-white wedding photograph, housed in a simple wooden frame, of a style that had been popular over three decades ago. Although Sabrina must have taken the photograph to an expert conservator, Mimi could still make out the faint traces of damage that the smashed glass had wrought upon the photograph's delicate surface, the day that she had hurled it in anger at her sister.

Mimi thought back to that terrible day, as her smiling parents, so young and beautiful and seemingly happy, gazed unseeingly into their shared future.

And, all of a sudden, she knew exactly where to find her sister.

*

For several terrifying minutes, Mimi thought that she had got it completely wrong. She had parked the car and run out onto the soft sand at Botany Bay, quickly scanning every female figure on the beach or swimming in the sea to try to identify Sabrina.

Later, she realised that, stupidly, she had been looking at all of the women who were with someone, because she was so unused to seeing Sabrina unaccompanied. Whenever she was in public, Sabrina was always surrounded by a small knot of onlookers, pestering her for an autograph or a photograph.

When Mimi finally spotted her, Sabrina was entirely alone. As she got closer, Mimi realised that her failure to recognise Sabrina was partly due to the fact that at some stage during the previous night,

Sabrina had hacked off all of her famously beautiful hair. The thin, white-faced girl with the unevenly shorn head, sitting hunched on the beach with her skinny arms wrapped tightly around her knees, looked nothing like the radiant, glamorous Sabrina Falks.

As Mimi approached, Sabrina lifted her head. Mimi stared, shocked by the sight of her sister without her mane of glossy hair. The ugly scar that their father had given her all those years ago was now clearly visible. Underneath Sabrina's eyes were purplish stains that looked almost like bruises.

'How did you know where to find me?' As soon as Mimi heard Sabrina's voice she recognised the tone. It had the same strange, detached quality that had been present the day of their fight in the funeral parlour.

Mimi sat down next to her sister on the sand and hugged her own knees close. She looked straight ahead, preferring to gaze out across the water, instead of at the disturbing sight of this cadaverous Sabrina.

'I remembered you asking me what I did the day of Mum's funeral and of how you said that you wished you could have escaped to Botany Bay like I did that day. It made sense that you'd feel like escaping today.'

'Edward told you,' Sabrina said, in her curiously flat voice.

'Yes. He did.' She knew better than to say aloud anything like 'I'm sorry' or 'It's terribly sad.' Nothing she could say would comfort Sabrina. The truth would simply continue to exist, cruel and unalterable.

At that moment Mimi knew that she would never tell Sabrina what had taken place between herself and Edward the night before. For the first time ever, she recognised Sabrina's apparent coldness for what it truly was: an excess of emotion, which, if it were allowed to spill forth, would drown her sister in unimaginable grief. Mimi suddenly felt a fierce protectiveness towards Sabrina. *I'm here, Breens*, she thought. *I won't leave you alone this time, I promise.*

'I always wanted to have a child,' Sabrina said, still in that same hard tone. She laughed unpleasantly. 'You'd think with our family tree that the last thing either of us would want is to pass on our useless genes. But I did want it.' She ended on a strangled sob and Mimi fought back a lump in her throat. 'It's strange, isn't it?' Sabrina continued, still staring straight ahead. 'This longing for family, even though our family was such a fucking disaster.' For the first time there was a tremor in her voice. 'I think maybe that's why I wanted my own family so badly – to make a fresh beginning and get it right this time.'

'I think you got it right the first time,' Mimi said softly. She finally dared to place an arm around her sister's shoulders. Sabrina felt so bony and fragile. 'You were a caring daughter to Mum right to the end. And we used to be good at being sisters. It's only lately we've both been getting it all wrong.' She paused and then added softly, 'I know it's not much consolation but you mustn't forget that you do have a family of your own. You have me.'

'It's not the same.'

'I know.'

There was another silence but, with her arm around her sister, Mimi could feel that some of the rigidity was draining out of Sabrina's body. She decided to take a risk and bring up the subject of Edward.

'What I don't understand is why you jumped to the conclusion that Teddy wouldn't marry you because of . . . it.'

Sabrina didn't turn to look at her, but when she answered, Mimi was relieved to discover that she no longer appeared to be in that other place.

'I think I just assumed that he was like everyone else. That he wouldn't want me if I wasn't perfect.'

'How could you ever think that? He loves you – the real you. He's not one of your fans, in love with you just because you're famous.'

Sabrina acknowledged the justice of this comment with a little dip of her head but her jaw jutted obstinately. 'That wasn't the whole reason. You don't know Edward. Family means everything to him. His family isn't like ours. They're like the goddamn Waltons. An infertile wife doesn't fit the perfect picture.'

Emboldened by Sabrina's clearer tone, Mimi opted for firmness. 'You can't have known that because you never even gave him a chance to tell you otherwise. You just made assumptions and left him with no choice.' Mimi waited a moment and then added, 'As it turns out it was especially unfair because I talked to him this morning and your condition makes no difference to him. He still loves you and wants to marry you.'

Sabrina's head snapped around and for the first time she looked directly at her sister. 'He does?'

'I'm absolutely certain that he won't change his mind, even when he sees that weird haircut.' Sabrina ran a self-conscious hand over her head and Mimi laughed. 'I bet you fifty dollars that every teenage girl in Sydney will have cut her hair off with a pair of shears by the end of the week,' she said mischievously. 'Now forget about your hair. You love Edward and he loves you. And everything is out in the open now. The other good news is that we have a very lavish and lovely wedding all planned for this afternoon. So what do you want to do?'

For a long minute there was silence, apart from the sound of the seagulls and the tide gently slopping against the sand.

Sabrina's face suddenly contorted and she buried her head in her hands. 'I want to marry him, Mimi. I do. More than anything. But I can't get up in front of all of those people and go through with the wedding today. Not any more. Not . . . like this.'

This reminded Mimi of something that she had been wanting to ask Sabrina for a very long time. 'Why *did* you invite all those people you hate to your wedding?'

Sabrina lifted her head from her hands. 'Because I needed to have someone on my side. Even if it was people who hated me.'

'What are you talking about?'

'During a wedding ceremony the room is always partitioned into the groom's side and the bride's side. As soon as Edward insisted on a big, traditional wedding I knew that I was in trouble. Can you imagine what it would have looked like if Edward had had 150 people on his side and on my side there was you, Aunty Bron and about fifteen cast and crew members from *Sunshine Cove*? We don't have family and I've never had any friends, apart from Ethan. So I just compiled a list of everyone that I could think of.' Sabrina smiled wanly. 'God, hearing myself say it out loud makes me realise how pathetic I am. I can't believe I let things go this far. I've hated the idea of this wedding from the start and it's been almost unbearable for the last few months.'

'Okay, but you definitely still want to marry Teddy, don't you?'

Sabrina nodded.

Mimi smiled. 'Don't worry. I know just the person who can fix this for you.'

She jumped to her feet and then took her sister's hands and pulled her up. Still holding one of Sabrina's hands, she gently led her back across the sand.

Mimi and Sabrina could never know it but the fleeting impressions that their feet left in the sand traced the same path as those of a laughing Bron and Meg, who, fifty years earlier, had also held hands as they raced up the beach, their sand- and salt-encrusted buckets and spades swinging merrily by their sides.

The tide continued to flow in and out, the land and sea silent witnesses to the weight of history.

53

The Wedding

'Claudia? It's Mimi. Now listen, promise me you won't freak out. Okay, here goes . . .'

*

'Hello? It's Claudia speaking. Yes, I know the wedding is in four hours. I just need to put something to you . . .'

*

'Olivia? It's Claudia. Take down exactly what I'm about to say. We're going to need more chairs and I need you to hit the phones and call everyone on the guest list . . .'

*

Jodi Liakos, nee Morrison, who had tormented Sabrina mercilessly throughout high school, twisted her body and craned her neck inelegantly as she sat in her organza-beribboned chair, waiting for the ceremony to begin. She couldn't quite believe that she was here as she still hadn't worked out why she had been invited. The best guess she had been able to make was that Sabrina was trying to make herself look good; as though she hadn't lost touch with the humble suburb from which she'd come. This suited Jodi perfectly, as she had been able to tell everyone that she was being shamelessly used, while condescendingly adding that it would be bad manners not to attend, given that she had been Sabrina's best friend in high school.

She had nagged her husband into arriving forty-five minutes early, so as not to miss anything, and had come armed with her digital camera, even though the elegant invitation had politely requested that no cameras be brought into the wedding venue. Rude, that's what it was, telling people what they could or couldn't bring, like they were better than everyone else. Well, she wasn't about to let anyone dictate to *her*.

She was disappointed that she hadn't yet glimpsed any celebrities, but it was only a matter of time. She tried to still the excitement in her stomach. She had read in a magazine that Chad McGyver was definitely invited. Jodi *loved* Chad and the thought of seeing him in real life was a heady one. She'd been on a diet ever since the invitation arrived and had managed to lose five kilos. She looked good. Of course she didn't look anything like Sabrina but it was a well-known fact that men didn't really like skeletons like her. They liked *real* women. It was a shame she hadn't been able to lose a couple more kilos though.

She glanced across at her husband George and then shifted slightly away from him. She could hardly bear to be seen with him. He was so *meek*, such a wimp. Nothing like Chad, who was always throwing Sabrina's character, Danielle, down on the bed and kissing her tenderly but in a real *manly* way. Jodi would have given anything to be kissed like that by Chad. Mind you, she wouldn't kick that Ethan Carter out of bed either. She didn't lust after him as much as she did Chad (there was something a bit *too* scarily good-looking about Ethan), but she intended to introduce herself to both of them at the reception tonight, and if either of them got drunk enough and she saw a chance, she was going to take it. She shivered, just thinking about it. If she had an affair with one of them, maybe *Celebrity*

Confidential would pay her for the story. They might even give her a makeover and do one of those glossy photo shoots. That would show everyone back in Grovedale that bloody Sabrina Falks wasn't the only one who was famous!

As Jodi continued to sit there and dream of a life of celebrity, her husband ran a finger around the inside of his sweaty shirt collar. He was wondering how early he would be able to sneak off from the reception and away from his overbearing bully of a wife. George had plans to see his mistress. They had booked a fancy hotel room in the city. He couldn't wait to throw her down on the bed and kiss her all over.

*

Lewis Reynolds lined up another shot. He still couldn't believe that his invitation and exclusive contract to shoot the Falks–Forster wedding hadn't been revoked after the baby bump scoop. His antenna was up, sensing something amiss, but whatever it was he was yet to put his finger on it. There was a crowd of at least 200 guests already assembled, although no-one he recognised had yet arrived. The celebrant was waiting on the floral bedecked dais with an elderly man, whom Lewis presumed was Edward's father.

He mentally shrugged off his sense of unease. He had made it past security and there wasn't a single other photographer present. Sabrina's wedding was all his and that was all that mattered. In Lewis's world, exclusivity translated to a premium price and it was his intention to extract every last cent from what was turning out to be the opportunity of a lifetime.

His mobile phone vibrated and he checked the caller ID. His editor, Dana. He was tempted to ignore it but then he changed his mind. She had been crawling up his arse with praise ever since he'd delivered that scandal-making set of photographs of Sabrina, but the instant the baby bump edition of *Celebrity Confidential* had hit the news-stands, she had started to get jittery over the viability of their wedding scoop. She too had been unable to believe that he would be allowed past security. Lewis had sneered at her concerns and had impressed upon her the weight of his fearsome reputation and far-reaching influence. Dana hadn't bought it hook, line and sinker, but she had backed down and shut up with her whining, which was all that he cared about.

'What do you want?' he now demanded unpleasantly. He had never treated Dana with respect but he no longer felt the need to project even a veneer of professionalism.

'Are you in?'

'Of course I'm in. Is there any other reason that you're wasting my time?'

'Jesus Christ,' she breathed. 'I can't believe they're actually sticking to our contract.' The wedding was going to make a *sensational* cover story to follow up on the baby bump exclusive. Sales would go through the roof.

'My contract,' he corrected her. His lip curled in pleasurable antici-pation. She had absolutely no idea what was coming.

'What?'

'I said, my contract. The contract to shoot this wedding lists only my name.'

She still didn't get it. 'Yes, but you work for *Celebrity Confidential*.'

'Not any more.'

'What in the hell are you talking about?'

He sighed. She was so stupid. It was almost boring having to explain things step by step. 'I'm talking about the fact that I've decided to turn freelance. As of today. I quit. I'll be offering the pictures of Sabrina's wedding to the highest bidder, which I am legally allowed to do, considering that the contract makes no mention of the magazine whatsoever. You really shouldn't have treated me like a fucking courier, Dana, asking me to drop the signed contracts back to Sabrina's lawyers.

It was very easy to have my own lawyer make a simple amendment to the parties involved.'

'You . . . you . . . you can't do this!' The panic in Dana's voice was palpable.

'I can and I will. But because I like you, Dana, I'll give you a heads up. The price for today's photographs is going to begin at approximately twice the amount that you negotiated with Sabrina's lawyers in *my* contract.' He paused to let this sink in. 'See you at the auction then, Dana.'

Chuckling, Lewis hung up and switched off his phone. Dumb bitch. It served her right for trusting him to finalise those contracts. He practically rubbed his hands as he thought about the gleaming new monster 4WD that he had taken possession of the day before. With the bonus cheque that he'd received for the photos of Sabrina's baby bump and vomiting episode, and now with the money that he would earn for today's shoot, he would have that frighteningly expensive car paid off in full by the end of next week.

Lewis was recalled to the present by a flurry of activity near the entrance. The bridal march started up, played by a string quartet, and all of the guests rose in their seats. Caught off guard, Lewis scrambled for position and finally decided to quickly clamber up the perimeter wall.

He was about to swing his camera in the direction of the bride when he noticed a clutch of paparazzi on the other side of the wall, jostling for higher ground to try to see into the wedding. Incensed, he realised that five of them – five heavy men, loaded with photographic equipment – were standing on the hood and roof of his beautiful, brand-new monster jeep. They must have seen him arrive and deliberately chosen his car to stand on. One of them saw him and cheerfully stuck up his middle finger at Lewis as he performed a little jump.

Impotent with fury, Lewis was recalled to the job at hand by a sudden gasp from the assembled crowd, as the bride began her time-honoured walk up the aisle. Cursing under his breath he turned away from his competitors and expertly adjusted his focus.

The beautifully made-up face of the bride jumped into startlingly close view through his lens. There was a roaring in his ears as the blood rushed to his head. In complete shock, he toppled off the wall, falling outside the mansion's grounds and losing his grip on his beloved Magnum. It fell to the stone path and all of his considerable bulk landed on top of it. He knew immediately by the sickening, splintering noise beneath him that the lens had cracked beyond repair, mirroring the fracturing of his world.

Dazedly, Lewis pulled himself up onto his hands and knees, still staring at the remains of his camera. It took only a few seconds for him to realise that he had somehow gone from enjoying a lucrative, powerful vocation to now facing unemployment and debt. His camera was ruined, his brand-new car was almost certainly damaged, he had quit his job and he had no exclusive.

Lewis was royally screwed, Sabrina had triumphed and it was all being captured for eternity, for the five paparazzi, hysterical with laughter, had swung their cameras in his direction and were taking photo after photo after photo.

*

Blissfully unaware of her role in the much-deserved downfall of Lewis Reynolds, Priscilla Tennyson-Banks-Worthington-Fitzroy, soon to become Mrs Sheridan, radiated with joy as she walked up the white carpet, through a scattering of red cymbidium orchids, towards her beloved Alexander. She was escorted up the aisle by her dog, Periwin-kle, and her elderly, although surprisingly spritely, father.

Watching from nearby to ensure that all went perfectly, Claudia had to hand it to Olivia, who was standing next to her. Her trustworthy assistant had skilfully diverted all of Priscilla and Alexander's guests from nearby Vaucluse House to Strickland House, she had conjured more chairs out of thin air and she had even cheerfully volunteered to answer the post-ceremony questions of the hundred or so guests from Sabrina's wedding, who, on Mimi's strict instructions, had *not* been informed of the change of wedding party. Furthermore, the actor that Olivia had hired to play Prissy's father was turning in an utterly pitch-perfect performance and it was impossible to tell his real age underneath the expertly applied make-up and wig.

As the bride and supposed father of the bride neared the dais, he caught sight of Olivia and gave her a fleeting wink.

And that's when Claudia recognised him. When she thought about it later, if he hadn't winked she would never have guessed, not in a million years. It was only that brief combination of the cheekiness of the wink with the exceptional deep blue of his eyes that gave him away – because she had seen both of those things before.

He had the roguish manner of Mimi but the unmistakable genes that he had passed onto Sabrina.

Jonathon Francis was their father.

*

The last-minute relocation of Priscilla's fifth wedding to Strickland House was undoubtedly one of the professional highlights of Claudia's career, but the minute that the ceremony was concluded, she wasted no time in self-congratulation. Making her way through the crowd, she found Jonathon Francis standing at the centre of a group of puzzled guests, holding forth with completely imaginary recollections from Priscilla's childhood.

Claudia managed to discreetly detach him from his audience and then led him into a small antechamber off the main ballroom, which they were using as a storeroom for extra glasses and other supplies. She politely asked the young waiter who was polishing wine glasses to leave and waited until he had closed the door firmly behind him.

There was no electric light in the musty room, so the only illumination came from the last rays of the afternoon sun that filtered through the small, heavy glass window.

Jonathon looked at her and raised one of his fake, bushy, old-man eyebrows. 'This is all very cloak-and-dagger.'

'I need to talk to you.' Suddenly Claudia felt foolish. But then she looked into his eyes once more – Sabrina's eyes – and the suspicion hardened into conviction. 'I want to know your name. Your *real* name.'

His air of easy charm evaporated and he went very still.

'Is your first name really Jonathon?' Claudia persisted. 'Because I'm reasonably certain your true surname is Falks.'

There was a silence and then he suddenly laughed and peeled off his wig. He grabbed a nearby napkin and started to scrub at his make-up. Before her very eyes, the old man was disappearing and in his place was a man who looked so much like both Mimi and Sabrina, she couldn't believe that Olivia hadn't recognised him.

'Have we – er – *met* before?' he asked, with a strange inflection on the word 'met'. His next sentence revealed his meaning. 'I have a terrible memory, I'm afraid, but I would have thought you were too young even for my taste.'

'We've never met,' she said tartly. She was unsurprised that he had considered the possibility that they might have slept together. His handsome face bore the hallmarks of time and other ravages, but she had no difficulty in believing that over the years many women would have been charmed and seduced by him.

'How did you know?' he asked, not seeming in the slightest bit put out by the revelation of his true identity.

'I know your daughters. I recognised you from a photograph that Mimi once showed me. There's also a strong family resemblance. They look a lot like you.'

'That's kind of you. Sabrina is very beautiful.'

'So is Mimi,' she said shortly. 'They think you're dead.'

'Yes, I know. I believe "death in absentia" is the correct legal term. One is declared legally dead after seven years, which seems a reasonable time frame.'

Claudia felt a sense of bewilderment. He didn't seem the least bit discomposed at being found out. 'Have you been living in Sydney the entire time?'

'Good God, of course not. No, I've lived in a number of different places over the last – let me think, it must be seventeen or eighteen years. Some more salubrious than others. One of the inconveniences of being presumed dead, you see. One is unable to apply for government benefits of any kind. Hence my theatrical work.' He finished scrubbing off his make-up, threw aside the greasy napkin and gave a flourishing bow.

'So you really are an actor?'

He shook his head, looking wistful. 'I wouldn't presume to give myself such a grand title. I consider myself a mere player. Are you familiar with the term? It's what actors were called in Shakespeare's time. They tended to be itinerant, like your humble servant, and not particularly well paid or respected. The roles were either tragic or those of a fool or clown, which seems particularly apt, don't you think?' He finished with an engaging smile that did nothing to win Claudia over. All of her thoughts were with Mimi and Sabrina.

'Did you apply for the job with Priscilla's wedding because you knew Sabrina and Mimi would be close by? Were you going to try to see them?'

He looked amused. 'I haven't seen my daughters in almost two decades. Why do you imagine I would have a burning desire to do so now?'

'But then – what are you doing here?'

'I needed this job. Or rather, I needed the cash payment from this job. I had read about Sabrina's wedding, of course, but I've been in close proximity to my daughters before this without any touching reunions occurring. Besides, I only got the job a few days ago and from all that I'd been reading in the papers, it seemed that my eldest daughter's wedding was unlikely to go ahead at all. When Olivia called me with the change of venue, I knew that Sabrina's wedding must have been called off and the remote possibility that I would run into my daughters was now an improbability.'

Claudia was silent for a moment. 'What are we going to do?'

'About what?'

'About telling your daughters that you're alive!'

'My dear girl, what on earth would be the point?'

'You're their *father*!'

'You seem to be labouring under the delusion that this binds me to some sort of duty or obligation. As I just told you, I've neither seen nor spoken to my daughters in close to twenty years. Surely that gives you some sense of my attitude towards fatherhood?'

Claudia looked at him, shocked. His charismatic quality had slipped, just briefly, and she was certain that the final sentence had been loaded with vicious sarcasm.

As though sensing her misgivings, he switched back to his prior, smooth tone. 'What would be the point? My daughters would have inherited some money when I was declared dead. They might be accused of committing fraud . . .' He sounded distressed but she couldn't be sure that the emotion was genuine. She already knew that he was a talented actor.

'That wouldn't happen if you swore that they had no idea you were alive,' Claudia said stubbornly. 'They're your daughters. They deserve to know the truth.'

He suddenly hissed in exasperation, and when he looked at her again, the cajoling expression had entirely disappeared. 'The truth? The truth, my little detective, is that I'm a drunk. Have been for most of my adult life. And I'm not the nice kind of drunk, do you understand? My one good deed in life was to leave those children and my darling doormat of a wife and even that was out of a sense of self-preservation. My idiot wife called the police and I couldn't risk going to jail. Other prisoners are not – kind – to those who hurt children.' He saw the horrified, disbelieving expression on Claudia's face. 'You don't believe me? Ask Sabrina what I did to her in my last drunken rage before I left for good. Actually, do ask her because I have only the faintest recollection. I'm reasonably certain, however, that she probably still bears the scars today. I have vague memories of a broken bottle and of being unable to find my ashtray. I believe I used whatever came to hand. Do you understand what I'm saying?'

Claudia felt a shiver go through her as she caught a glimpse of genuine menace. This feeling was made worse when the sight of her fear seemed to have a calming effect upon him.

'I never could understand the emphasis people place on family,' he continued, in a quieter tone. 'As though it was something sacred. It's just a collection of people that you're forced into a relationship with. Like all relationships they can grow irritating and stale and noxious. And, on the whole, disappointing. I was a tremendous disappointment to my mother and father. I proved a disappointment to my wife and daughters.' He gave a sudden chuckle. 'For a drunk, I've managed to remain surprisingly consistent.'

Claudia stood there, frozen, as the sounds of the wedding reception filtered through the heavy door. She remembered an article that she had once read in a magazine about a sick old man in his eighties, who was being deported back to Poland to stand trial. He had been accused of being a Nazi and committing atrocities more than six decades ago. She had stared at the picture of the kindly looking, snowy-haired man with the twinkling eyes, who had been surrounded by children and grandchildren. It had been impossible to believe that he could have committed the crimes of which he was accused. The flow of history and the dignity of age seemingly expunged the brutality of the past.

Now she looked at the man before her, who was watching her carefully. She did a quick calculation. Sabrina must have been – what? – ten or eleven when he left? And her own father had — Claudia didn't even want to think about what he'd done. She suddenly wanted to be sick.

He looked at her as though he could read what was going through her mind. 'You need to understand that I had very good reasons for disappearing the way I did. Although many were undoubtedly selfish, the outcome for Miriam and Sabrina was, I believe, for the best. I've spent years erasing my past. I have no wish to be found.' He paused and then added softly, 'I couldn't possibly explain to you what it's like to leave everything behind and start again.'

Claudia felt an unwelcome jolt of empathy shoot through her. She cleared her throat. 'You don't need to try to explain. I do understand.'

He held her gaze for a long moment and then the smile crept back onto his face. 'I believe you actually might.' He hesitated and then asked, haltingly, 'I read about Sabrina all the time but my Miriam . . . How is she?'

'She's . . . cheeky.' She watched as his expression softened. 'Mimi's great. She's smart and funny. I like her very much.'

The information seemed to please him. 'She was always like that as a child. I'm glad that she didn't lose her spirit. Parents aren't meant to have favourites, I know, but, then again, I was never exactly a model parent, was I?' He laughed. 'Miriam was always my favourite. Purely from a narcissistic point of view, some would say. She was a lot like me in many ways.' He looked pointedly at Claudia. 'You see, she's a case in point that the intrinsic nature of some people never changes. It sounds as though Miriam hasn't changed. And I certainly won't. I would just disappoint them again. You might think it's cruel to allow them to remain in ignorance but it's really by far the kindest thing I could do.' He waited for her response but when she remained silent, he made his way towards the door.

He grasped the handle and then turned back. 'I'll understand if you tell them. I'd rather you didn't.'

She didn't look up as she replied. 'I won't.'

He opened the door and for a brief moment the light and hubbub from the party erupted into the small dark room of secrets. Then the door closed behind him and he was gone.

For a long time, Claudia stood there as the afternoon sun finally faded, leaving her alone in the darkness. Gradually she realised that he had slipped away without even revealing his real name. He was a ghost, nothing more.

Claudia found that she was shivering, not from cold, but from a sudden awareness that she had been drifting rudderless through her life. For the last eight years all that she had thought about was escaping from her past. She had never stopped to consider her future.

She imagined herself in thirty years' time, exactly like Jonathon. Still cut off from her family, hiding in shadows and alone.

Claudia opened the door and made her way through the party and out of the mansion, pausing only to collect her bag. It was dark now and the summer night was sweet with the smell of jacaranda. There was a stony outcrop on the edge of the manicured lawn, which overlooked the crashing waves beneath. She sat down on one of the rocks and, with a trembling hand, took out the mobile phone that was reserved for personal use and dialled the number that she still remembered so well.

When the familiar, beloved voice answered, she found that she couldn't speak. Then, terrified that they would hang up, she managed to find her voice, through an unstoppable flood of tears.

'Mama?' she choked, slipping back into the childhood term of endearment. 'Mama, it's me, Claudia.'

54

The Other Wedding

On the day of the wedding, ten minutes before the ceremony was scheduled to begin, Mimi stood in the centre of the spacious hotel room, a shaft of sunlight striking her white gown.

Sabrina paused in the doorway for a moment as she looked at her younger sister. 'You look beautiful,' she said softly.

'I know,' Mimi answered morosely. 'It's horrible. Just look at me – all toned and made up and clad in my made-to-measure dress – sorry, I mean, designer-work-of-art gown. I feel like an imposter.'

Sabrina smiled. 'That's why I bought you this.' She handed her sister a small, gift-wrapped parcel.

'A present? For me?'

'Open it. It might make you feel more like yourself.'

Mimi tore the ribbon and wrapping off. Laughing, she held up a pair of bright purple knickers which had the words 'Your Honour' written across the bottom.

'Try them on.'

'But my dress is white! They might show through.'

'What do you care?' Sabrina looked at her sister and a smile played around her lips. 'I dare you.'

Mimi's eyes twinkled with mischief. 'I love them but I have an even better idea. We'll both do it. It'll be just like the old days.'

Sabrina watched her sister and then grinned as she realised what she was up to. A moment later she was enthusiastically following suit.

All a flutter, Aunty Bron bustled into the room, dressed to the nines. 'Girls, it's time!' She was brought up short by the sight of her nieces.

'You look gorgeous,' she said, overcome with emotion. 'Both of you. But, Sabrina, you look . . .'

'Like Mum,' Mimi finished softly. 'You look exactly like Mum. Especially with your hair like that.'

Sabrina put one hand up self-consciously to the stylish waif-like haircut that a horrified Delta had somehow conjured from the ruined tresses of Sabrina's act of self-mutilation. As Mimi had predicted, the haircut had instantly become all the rage, with the result that a personal cut by Delta was so sought after that Delta's mobile phone number had entered the hallowed little black book of the concierge, James, right beneath Claudia's entry.

As Bron looked at Sabrina she saw, not her beautiful niece, but the tangible ghost of her dead sister. Her throat closed up and she stepped forward and held Sabrina tightly for a moment. Bron whispered one sentence into Sabrina's ear – a sentence that was simultaneously a plea for forgiveness, a magic charm and a belated, regretful truth. Overcome with emotion, she pressed her lips to Sabrina's cheek. Then, dabbing her eyes with a hanky, she stepped back.

Sabrina smiled at her aunt and decided not to mention that although Bron had whispered into her ear that she loved her, she had accidentally called her niece Meg.

Trying to lighten the emotion in the room, Mimi now said honestly, 'I'm so glad that you're wearing Mum's wedding dress. It's perfect.'

This had the opposite effect that Mimi had intended, for now tears welled up in Sabrina's eyes.

'Don't you dare start crying,' Mimi said fiercely, her gentle tone instantly dissipating. 'There's no personal make-up artist on standby here and I won't be held responsible for the bride having raccoon eyes.'

'Mimi!' Aunty Bron expostulated, laughing. 'You can't mention "raccoon eyes" and the bride in the same sentence on her wedding day!'

'Why not? Is that some ancient wedding tradition that I don't know about? I thought I knew them all by now. Speaking of which, we should do a final check. You have your something old – that's Mum's dress. Something new could be the earrings that I gave you; sadly not Bulgari diamonds but I still think they're pretty —'

'They're beautiful,' Sabrina said firmly. 'And my something borrowed is the clutch that Aunty Bron has lent me.'

'It was your grandmother's,' Aunty Bron said, smiling mistily at her niece.

'What about the something blue? Oh my God, I can't believe we forgot to get you something blue!' Mimi said, panic-struck.

'Mimi, it's just a superstition. Don't worry about it.'

'Don't *worry* about it? Of course I'm going to worry about it! I want this wedding to be *perfect*!'

'It's the marriage that's important, not the wedding,' Sabrina said sternly.

Mimi gave her a withering look. 'Yeah, right. If you really believe that, then take that dress off and get on a plane to Las Vegas. I can probably get you a family discount with an Anna Nicole Smith-lookalike celebrant that I know. Now, don't move.'

Mimi vanished through the open door and Aunty Bron wailed after her. 'Mimi! Where are you going? We're going to be late!'

'Oh well,' Sabrina said placidly. 'That's another tradition – that the bride is always late. And it's not as though we have far to go.'

To Bron's immense relief, Mimi reappeared in under a minute.

'Unzip your dress,' she ordered Sabrina.

Shaking her head and looking completely mystified, Sabrina

nevertheless complied. Mimi pulled down the bodice and then, using the blue ballpoint pen that she had grabbed from the hotel's front desk, Mimi carefully wrote the name 'Edward' just above Sabrina's heart.

She stepped back and surveyed her handiwork with satisfaction. 'What do you think of your temporary tattoo?'

Sabrina smiled. 'It's the perfect solution. You should think seriously about becoming a full-time wedding planner, Mims.'

'I have other plans for my future,' Mimi said mysteriously. 'Okay, I think we can go now. Turn around and I'll zip you up again.'

'What's that over there? Is that something you've dropped?' Aunty Bron asked, as she spied a small heap of crumpled linen on the floor.

Mimi grinned wickedly. 'Don't worry, Aunty Bron. It's nothing that we need. Ready, Breens?'

'I'm ready.'

Aunty Bron watched them walk through the door, but some impulse made her hesitate and then go over to the corner to investigate the curious items. She bent down and then, in puzzlement, straightened up again.

In either hand she was holding a pair of discarded, frilly knickers.

*

The Falks sisters paused for a moment in the bright Hawaiian sunshine. Only a hundred or so metres away they could see Edward standing on the beach, not far from where the froth of the waves lapped at the white sand. Edward was wearing a lightweight cream-coloured suit, a sky-blue shirt and (Mimi grinned to herself) no tie. He was standing beneath a simple white fabric canopy, the only decoration being the strands of freshly picked frangipani blossoms that were wreathed around the canopy's posts. There were two rows of unadorned white wooden lawn chairs, which was ample for the dozen guests who had assembled, laughing and talking softly, with the exception of Edward's niece and nephew who were running gleefully towards and then away from the incoming tide. There was no white carpet, no expensive layer of imported flowers underfoot. To reach her groom, Sabrina would walk barefoot across the sand.

As Aunty Bron hurried past them to take her place, Sabrina put her hand on Mimi's arm. 'Does it bother you that despite all that work you put in, you don't actually get to be my bridesmaid?'

'Don't be silly. I get the honour of walking you down the aisle instead. I'm about to finally get my wish. I've been dying to give you away for years.' Mimi's attempted joking tone didn't fool Sabrina for a second. There were tears in her younger sister's eyes.

Sabrina suddenly grabbed Mimi in a fierce hug. 'Promise me we'll always be there for each other, Mims?' she whispered.

Mimi held her sister close, kissed her on the cheek, and then carefully wiped away the tears from her own cheeks that she had forbidden Sabrina to shed. 'Hard to say. We are family, after all.'

With that Mimi led her sister to the same spot on the beach where Edward had proposed. In a simple ceremony lasting no more than fifteen minutes, Sabrina and Edward were married. There was no fanfare, no paparazzi and no fuss.

As Sabrina kissed her husband, she felt her spirit soaring up into the brilliant blue sky. But this was not her habitual trick of detachment, propelled by a desolate need to escape or to maintain a tight control over her feelings. This glorious sensation was a joyous abandon, as Sabrina finally experienced something that felt very much like hope and happiness and coming home.

*

The small reception was in full swing as the famous Hawaiian sunset started to take place. Mimi, who was taking a breather after an energetic burst of dancing with Edward's niece, stepped out onto the balcony and gasped as she was confronted with the brilliant technicolour sky.

'It's amazing, isn't it?'

Mimi turned around, hoping that it was Nate, and was disappointed to see Edward behind her, a drink in his hand. He looked more handsome than ever but she felt not a thing. Not the merest twinge of attraction. Who knew that one horrible kiss from the man of your dreams could so comprehensively quash all feelings for him? She should have done it sooner, she thought impishly.

'Don't worry,' he said, before she could say anything. He nodded at his drink. 'It's mineral water.'

'Glad to hear it, brother-in-law,' she said, mock sternly. 'I'd hate to have to tell on you at our next meeting.' For a fleeting moment they shared a resigned but rueful look. Attending AA meetings together was a form of family togetherness that both Mimi and Edward would have preferred to live without. As Edward started to talk about something else, she tried to focus on him, although she was utterly distracted by the sight of Nate, who was talking to Edward's brother-in-law Giles/Miles at the bar. She really must learn his correct name before this trip was over.

Edward looked over his shoulder and seemed pleased when he found the object of her gaze.

'Has Nate ever told you how he got that scar on his leg?' he asked, apparently apropos of nothing. 'He was rockclimbing and he fell twenty feet down a cliff face. He had to spend the night on a precipice. It was freezing and he almost died. When I saw him in hospital he was already cracking jokes about what a great story he had to use on girls he wanted to impress.' Edward stopped, arrested by the outraged expression on Mimi's face.

'Is that the truth?'

'Of course it is.'

'Will you excuse me?'

Puzzled, Edward watched as Mimi stalked over to Nate and unceremoniously interrupted his conversation.

'How did you get that scar on your leg?' she demanded. Sensing some sort of showdown looming, Giles/Miles made a swift exit.

'I was attacked by a rabid hamster when I was eight.'

'You told me you got it skateboarding when you were thirteen.'

He sighed. 'I was thirteen. The *hamster* was skateboarding. He was doing a figure eight.'

'Nate. Look at me.'

He looked slightly nervous as he met her unflinching gaze. 'Good. Now tell me how you got that scar. No more jokes.'

Something about her manner compelled him to answer truthfully. 'I was rockclimbing. I lost my grip, fell down and nearly froze to death. I actually did tell you the truth the first time but then I felt silly. Are you happy now?'

'Almost. How did you feel?'

'Terrified. Petrified. I was in agony and I thought I was going to die.' He was silent for a moment and then gave himself a small, rousing shake. 'I have no idea what this is all about but fair's fair. What's your deep, dark secret?' The habitually teasing note of playfulness was back in his voice.

Mimi took a deep breath. 'I have a problem with alcohol. I don't drink all the time. Just —' she stumbled. 'Just at really important times. When I feel that I can't cope. Or when I'm scared. I'm basically a coward who always takes the easy way out. And I've made a mess of my life because of it.'

Nate looked at her, stunned.

'I wanted you to know,' Mimi said in a rush. 'It seemed . . . important.'

She looked up at him with an expression on her face that made Nate catch his breath. He tried to dispel the tension with a small laugh. 'Hey – are we actually being serious with each other?'

Mimi felt as though she knew how Nate must have felt right before he fell over that cliff. What the heck. She may as well jump. She took his face in her hands. 'I couldn't be more serious about you if I tried.'

They looked into each other's eyes for a long moment.

'Are there any other secrets I should know?' he finally asked, with a small grin.

'Isn't that enough for you? I've been married, I've lost a fortune, I'm a binge drinker . . .'

'That's just all the bad news. There's good news too, you know. I've been waiting for the right moment to tell you,' Nate said softly.

'What is it?'

'I know why the chicken crossed the road.' He took her in his arms. 'To get to the other side.'

Mimi smiled. At the same time tears began to slide down her face but it didn't seem to matter. Without further ado, she kissed him.

*

'This wedding cake is delicious,' Edward's mother Blanche said approvingly. It was half past ten. The children had gone to bed but the rest of the wedding party were seated around a big outdoor table, which was lit by flickering candles and the moon. 'We never had chocolate wedding cakes in our day. It was always fruit cake.'

'It's not just a chocolate cake,' said Mimi self-importantly. 'It's a bittersweet chocolate ganache torte. It's one of the few elements we kept from the original wedding.' The last sentence was whispered only to Nate, who was sitting next to her and trying, not very successfully, to keep his hands off her.

'Bittersweet is a funny concept, isn't it?' remarked Edward's father, Harold. 'I mean – it's a combination of two things that are precisely the opposite.'

'It's a good word for you two girls,' remarked Aunty Bron. 'Given your names.'

'What do you mean?' asked Edward's brother, Harry.

Mimi pulled a face. 'She means that my name, Miriam, means "bitter". Sabrina's been rubbing it in for years. Sabrina is probably Latin for "as sweet as a rose in full bloom" or something sickening like that.'

'Sabrina means "princess",' said Edward cheerfully.

Mimi made a gagging noise.

'I think both of your names must have several meanings,' said Aunty Bron thoughtfully. 'Because your grandmother was there when your parents chose your names, and she told me that Sabrina is actually from the Hebrew word "sabra". It's a type of cactus.'

'A *cactus*?' Mimi gasped in glee. 'Princess over there is actually named after a cactus?'

'It has a very beautiful flower,' Bron protested. 'And it's sweet inside.'

'Yes, but it's still a cactus, which means that it's all prickly on the outside, right?' Mimi clapped her hands as Sabrina pulled a face in her direction. 'What about my name?' Mimi continued, all agog. 'Does it really mean "bitter" or did Sabrina make that up?'

'I did not make it up,' Sabrina said indignantly. 'I know that it's true.'

'Miriam might have that meaning but it also quite suitably means "rebellious",' said Aunty Bron. 'But I'm certain your mum chose it because of its other meaning. It can mean "to be light" or "to shine".'

'All those years,' Mimi said, shaking her head at Sabrina. 'All those years, you teased me about my name meaning bitter and you were nothing but a cactus, while I was really a star-like creature.'

'I'm very happy for you, Star-Girl, but I want to return to the original topic,' Nate interjected. 'Because knowing how affiliated you feel with chickens, I have a chicken-and-egg-style conundrum for you. Which comes first?' He tasted his cake experimentally. 'The bitter or the sweet?'

'I'm fairly certain that it's meant to be sweet with a bitter aftertaste,' said Blanche, after quickly racking her brain to remember what Jamie, Nigella and Gordon might have said on the matter.

'I don't see how you can separate it. It tastes like both at once to me,' remarked Edward.

'I disagree. I don't see how it's possible to experience two opposing sensations at exactly the same time,' chimed in Edward's sister, Phoebe, cradling her newborn baby.

'Why not? If you can cry with happiness . . .' said Mimi, looking at Nate.

Or be deliriously happy even though there's a part of you that will always grieve, thought Sabrina, taking Edward's hand and casting a fleeting glance at the sleeping baby. Edward looked at his wife and held her hand tighter.

'Then I don't see why something can't be bitter and sweet at exactly the same moment,' Mimi finished. She took another bite of her cake and chewed it thoughtfully, as though she was a wine connoisseur, rolling a unique vintage around in her mouth. The taste of the bittersweet cake was bringing back a distant memory from her childhood but annoyingly, she couldn't pin the feeling of déjà-vu down to its original experience. For a brief moment the recollection tried to force its way to the surface but then Mimi pushed it away. It wasn't important. Besides, the present was far too delicious, with the beautiful island setting, Nate's lovely, warm hand on her thigh and Sabrina and Edward's quiet joy, to waste any more time in the past.

'Anyway, it tastes the other way round to me,' she announced firmly. 'Bitter first, then sweet.'

Sabrina took a bite of her cake. 'Me too.'

'Aren't you a couple of optimists,' said Giles/Miles, beaming.

Everyone gathered around the table looked at the Falks sisters, as they shared a conspiratorial look and then began to laugh.

'What's so funny?' demanded Aunty Bron.

'Nothing. Not really,' said Mimi.

Sabrina smiled. 'Maybe it just means that we prefer happy endings.'

Epilogue

'Who the hell is Candace Spencer?' Sabrina demanded, turning around to confront Mimi, as her apartment's intercom buzzed and an excited voice came through the speakers.

'Who? Oh, Candace. Is she here already? Buzz her in.'

'Yes, she's here and she's demanding to see me and saying that *you* promised her a one-on-one lunch with me and a signed photograph,' said Sabrina indignantly, nevertheless allowing Candace entry.

'She's the receptionist for Nicole Kidman's Australian PR company. I forgot to mention it before but I organised for you to take her out to lunch at Aria today. You'll probably have to pay,' Mimi added airily. 'But it's important that you get to know one another if she's going to be your personal assistant.'

'My what?'

'Well, she can't be your bridesmaid because you don't have a wedding to plan any more. But I do think you still need a good personal assistant. Especially now that I'm quitting. Sorry to get in first and not let you set fire to me but I have my reasons.' Mimi paused and added shyly, 'I've been accepted into NIDA. Again.'

'You have?'

There was a knock on the door and, unable to wait another

moment, Candace poked her head around.

Mimi got up from her sprawled position on the couch and slung her bag over her shoulder. 'Sabrina, say hello to Candace. Candace, this is *Sabrina*. Not Danielle. Danielle is a fictional character on a television soap opera. Sabrina is the real person you'll be working for. Got it? Good. Then I'll leave you both to it.'

She strode towards the door, then stopped and rummaged in her bag. She pulled out a piece of paper and ceremoniously handed it to Sabrina.

'What's this?' asked Sabrina curiously.

'My bank account details. It would be great if you could deposit my final pay straight in via the internet, if that's okay by you. It's a high-interest account so the sooner you do it, the more money I can extract from the bank.'

The corners of Sabrina's lips twitched. Mimi turned once more to leave but this time it was the sound of Sabrina's voice that stopped her.

'Miriam?'

Mimi swung around.

'Go set the world on fire.'

Mimi grinned. 'Thanks, Breens.'

*

CELEBRITY CONFIDENTIAL EXCLUSIVE!

Ex-soapie star and has-been actor Sabrina Falks (whose Sunshine Cove *character, Danielle, plunged to her death from a clifftop several seasons ago) and her banker husband, Edward Forster, have recently adopted a six-month-old boy who will become a brother to their four-year-old daughter, Posy. Both children were adopted from the orphanage run by the foundation set up by well-known Sydney socialite Mrs Priscilla Tennyson-Banks-Worthington-Fitzroy, now known as Mrs Sheridan. It's all a bit too Brangelina/Madonna circa 2006 for us, but, then again, some people will do anything to stay in the limelight.*

In other news, Sabrina's baby sister, Mimi, has been attracting attention for all the right reasons. Currently appearing as Cordelia in the Sydney Theatre Company's acclaimed production of King Lear, *the NIDA-trained actor, who has been accumulating accolades since her graduation, is attracting rave reviews for a performance that critics have described as 'honest', 'compelling' and 'deserving of serious attention'. Golden girl Mimi is also basking in the glow of true love, having recently become engaged to long-term boyfriend Nate Jamieson.*

Given that the two sisters have reportedly never got along, big sister Sabrina's eyes must have turned from that famous blue to gorgeous green. We can't wait for the wedding melodrama to begin . . .

Acknowledgements

The first thank you must go to my readers. Without you I would not be able to have this career that I love, so thank you one and all, you lovely, discerning bunch.

I need to thank my publisher, Julie Gibbs, for daring me to show a more serious side in my novels, and my wonderful agent, Tara Wynne, for telling me that I could do it when I promptly freaked out.

Thank you to my lovely editor, Anne (Pam) Rogan, for your endless patience, brilliant suggestions, supportive comments and for liking all the really mean nasty fight bits, which is hilariously at odds with your warm, kind disposition! I'll also be eternally grateful to you for introducing me to the term 'double qualifying preposition', which I am still waiting for an opportunity to drop into casual conversation.

A very warm thank you to Dr Peter Rankin and the world's most delightful maternal health nurse Felicity Dawson. They very kindly assisted me with medical information about eating disorders and infertility. However, any distortion or skewing of the facts for the sake of fiction is solely my responsibility.

I long ago ran out of new ways to say thank you to my amazing and generous mum, Marie La'Brooy, for her constant help with my boys, which enables me to write. Mum (a former bank manager) also provided me with invaluable advice in devising the best way to commit (fictional) grand larceny. Mum, I think I'll quote my eldest son and simply say, 'Sank you, bank you', which is Dashie-speak for thank you. We would be lost without you.

Thank you to my dad, Keith La'Brooy, my sister, Nene, and my parents-in-law, Liz & Frank Daalder, all of whom babysat the boys at various times, usually when a terrifying deadline was fast approaching.

Love and gratitude to my other family: the opposite-of-evil twins Diana Hodgson and Danielle Calder, Sarah Rogers, Jaynie Tuttle, Lara Merrett and Estelle Andrewartha, as well as my cousin Joanna Woutersz. You all always stick by me, even though I'm such an absent friend these days as I learn how to juggle the demands of work and family.

My beloved husband, Charlie, is the only person who really knows exactly how much work went into the writing of this book – and most of it was done by him. My love, thank you for all those weekends that you looked after the boys by yourself while I wrote, for putting up with my tears of tiredness, and for every beautiful, supportive word and deed that showed me how much you love me. Mi bilong yu.

And finally to my boys. Sank you, bank you, my Dashie for being so very good at being three and making me laugh and for being the only person in the world who loves to hear me sing. And to my Raleigh, my beautiful, happy baby – welcome to the world and to your mad, noisy, adoring family, my darling boy. Our family, like every other family, will undoubtedly be an odd, perplexing, troublesome thing to you at times but we will always love you and we will always be ever so glad that you chose us.